TO RAISE A KING

Book One of the Broken Crown

JUSTIN
ORTON

To Raise a King
Book One of the Broken Crown

Justin Orton

Editor: Shadowcat Editing

Cover: Infernixx

First edition published December 2016

Copyright © 2013 Justin Orton

Publisher's Note: This novel is a work of fiction. Any references to real events, businesses, organizations, and locales are intended only to give the fiction a sense of reality and authenticity. Any resemblance to actual persons, living or dead, is entirely coincidental.

Dedicated to my wife, Lisa, without whose support, understanding and love this project would never have come to completion

And

To the memory of my father, who spent countless miles listening to a would-be-author's tales and never stopped believing in me

ACKNOWLEDGMENTS

Left to my own devices I would still be re-writing Chapter 1! Many people have provided support and encouragement on the long road to completing this novel and I cannot possibly list them all here-you know who you are-and I am grateful to each and every one of you.

I would like to offer special thanks to the following:

- Editor-Robin J. Samuels of ShadowCatEditing.

- Tristan Orton (my son) who has provided encouragement and advice while waiting patiently for each chapter to be completed.

- Kyle Kurth for his insight into the characters and the story.

- My wonderful Beta Readers who found the holes and provided encouragement and advice.

- And Lisa Orton, who somehow remains sane despite reading the same story over and over and providing ideas, criticism and an endless supply of support and encouragement. You can take a break now darling, until the next one -

To you all-thank you.

PART ONE

MATT

Chapter 1
Runaway

Inverdeer, Scotland
Wednesday

A fierce autumn storm had battered the east coast of Scotland for most of the afternoon. Its tattered remnants now scurried inland, dirty streamers of charcoal-colored cloud that raced before a bitter wind. It had been too much for the stately beech trees that lined the broad length of Albert Avenue, stripping their leaves into a crisp gold carpet that crackled beneath Matt's pounding feet and swirled in flurries around the dog that loped beside him.

From a nearby bus shelter an elderly couple watched the young man pass. They sat huddled together with coats pulled tight against the cold, but Matt barely felt the evening chill.

He slowed his pace as he approached the intersection of Albert Avenue, Main Street and Forest Drive. Cars idled at the stop light and clouds of blue-gray exhaust rose around the kilted figure of the World War II memorial like gun smoke from a long-forgotten battlefield.

Matt glanced at the traffic light and with a burst of speed cut across Main Street onto Forest Drive. His heart was racing and he paused a moment to catch his breath. One by one the street lamps flickered on and pools of orange light spilled across the sidewalk. Shadows of trees and parked cars seemed to lean drunkenly against the old granite walls.

I'm out! I'm actually out!

Matt trembled with excitement, though his stomach churned with a sickening fear.

How much time—?

He looked at his watch, a treasured Christmas gift from the townsfolk who donated to Inverdeer Home for Boys. Only ten minutes had passed since his escape.

"They've probably called the cops by now, lass..." He bent forward, resting his hands on his knees, and took several deep breaths. "'bout another ten and they'll be looking for us."

As if on cue, blue light bathed the walls around him.

"Shit!" Matt pressed into the shadows, ignoring the gritty discomfort of the coarse stonework against his cheek, and waited as the police car sped by, lights flashing but siren silent.

Matt looked around furtively, afraid his suspicious behavior had been noticed, but the street remained quiet. The traffic light changed to green and disinterested drivers continued their journey home. He patted the husky.

"Okay Mia— time to go!"

Ten minutes more and the pair reached the familiar iron railings of Forest Park. It was getting darker now. Bats flitted among the trees and a hedgehog, startled by the squeal of the heavy gate, scurried through the leaves that had collected beneath the railings. With an excited bark Mia raced into the open grassland beyond.

"Hey! Get back here!"

Obediently the husky bounded back, blue eyes wide with adoration, and Matt ruffled her ears.

"Not today, lass." He tilted his head toward the line of trees beyond the swings, where Inverdeer Forest stood black and silent guard over the northern edge of town. It was a forbidden border to the boys of Inverdeer House.

Crap. It don't look that menacing at daytime!

Mia scampered around him, still hoping for a thrown stick, but Matt resumed his jog across the park and the dog trotted obediently beside him, passing the slides, swings, and climbing frames that stood stark and cold against the darkening sky.

Matt slowed to a walk as they approached the tangle of nettles and briars that seemed to spill from the trees in a constant effort to devour the park.

"We'll be okay, girl. It's not full dark yet." He spoke more to comfort himself than Mia, for while the sky remained a leaden gray it was almost black as night beneath the slowly swaying canopy of the forest. Mia sniffed the dank air beneath the trees, and Matt squatted beside her.

What the hell am I thinking? Three meals a day and a warm bed...

He had contemplated leaving Inverdeer House for months. The lack of an alternative place to go had become his excuse for staying, but deep down he wondered if he really stayed out of fear. Was he scared to leave behind the security of routine, and the guarantee of shelter? He pulled Mia close.

I should have waited. Left in the morning. Damn it's dark in there...

All it had taken was a brief look at his juvenile record, found exactly where Deglin the gardener had said it would be.

Deglin. Now there was a strange man. He had arrived at the Home the previous year, replacing the former groundsman who had died under what everyone agreed were somewhat strange circumstances. A quiet loner of a man, Deglin kept himself apart from the boys. It had not taken long for a plethora of wild and menacing stories about the lonely figure to permeate the Home, yet Matt had always felt a strange empathy with the solitary figure who tended the lawns, vegetable plot, and few remaining flower beds of Inverdeer House.

Outcast by the other kids, Matt often took walks around the grounds or would find a secluded spot beneath the old pines to read. It had been on one such occasion that he had discovered the husky stray. Much to his amazement, the thin bedraggled animal had been allowed to stay and had become the ward of the gardener and pet to all the boys.

It was Matt's attachment to the dog that had finally brought him into more frequent contact with Deglin, and over the fading weeks of summer the man had befriended the boy. Matt had found himself confiding more and more in the odd character and inevitably the conversation had turned to Matt's unknown history. How had he ended up in a children's home? What had happened to his parents? Part of him still felt the basic human need to love and be loved, and in quiet moments of reflection Matt would find himself daydreaming about the mother and father he had never known, fantasizing about the anguish they had felt as they were forced by some twist of fate to abandon their only son. But as the years had passed, so he had felt himself drawn more into a world of anger and betrayal, tempered only by those moments when he found himself helplessly adrift in a sea of morbid self-pity. At such times he would wonder if his parents had died, almost hoping they had, for the fear they had simply rejected him, casting him aside as an unwanted burden, was too painful to consider.

It had been Deglin's suggestion to look at his file, and so Matt had approached Matron, asking for permission. She had refused. "Not until the day you leave this establishment, young man. On your eighteenth birthday you will be given your file. I and a member of Social Services will be present to answer any questions you may have." Eighteen! Another year. It seemed an eternity. He had shared his disappointment with Deglin and the man had hinted at another way. So three nights ago Matt had broken into the office and found his file, and there on the top had been a handwritten note; Matt's parents had been located, living in Inverness, little more than a hundred miles away. Since then Matt had thought of little else but escape.

An owl swooped from the trees somewhere to his left and he jumped; the ghostly screech had snapped him from his reverie and his heart hammered loudly in his ears.

I should go back...

A sickening feeling of doubt gnawed at him as he realized just how unprepared he was for the journey ahead, but a surge of teenage bravado overcame the fear of the unknown. He gave an involuntary shudder and looked back at the twinkling lights across the park. Lights in homes where kids had families, where there was laughter, warmth and love.

Would he ever know that life?

In the distance the owl screeched again, though this time it did not scare him.

"Fuckin' bird," he mumbled, and with quiet determination turned his back on the town and plunged into the gathering gloom of the forest, Mia at his side.

Inverdeer House, Scotland
Wednesday

Inverdeer House had seen better days. Built in the early nineteenth century, its weathered sandstone walls clearly showed the ravages of time. Drab cream-colored paint, chipped and faded, gave the once-grand windows the appearance of scars, while rot slowly ate away the high-pointed gables. A daisy-riddled lawn at the front of the home was surrounded by large rhododendrons that led back to both sides of the house. To the rear a terraced lawn and playground had replaced the ornate gardens that had once graced the property.

The entire scene was one of sad neglect. The old house could easily have passed for abandoned if not for the carriage lights that burned on either side of the door, and the distinct blue and white of the Inverdeer Police car that sat on the gravel drive before the timeworn steps of the main entrance.

Inside, the excited residents had been ushered to their dormitory, a series of interconnected former bedrooms. Mrs. Greyson, the thin-lipped Matron, now stood stony-faced as the police officer reviewed his notes.

"So you have no idea where the boy may have gone?"

"Oh, please! If that was the case I wouldn't be wasting my time with you, now would I?" The officer looked up from his notes, eyebrows raised. Matron looked away. "I'm sorry. No. I have no idea."

"So all you can tell us, Madam, is a boy in your care has gone missing, has taken the dog with him and..."—he looked at his notes—"stolen supplies from the kitchen pantry? You can't tell us what he was wearing, perhaps?"

"Jeans, a sweater. I don't know, maybe his black rain jacket? That's all I can think of."

"Okay. And the sweater? A color...?"

Before Matron could answer, another voice cut in from the stairs behind them.

"Blue, navy blue."

Greyson and the police officer turned to see a middle-aged man reach the bottom of the stairs. Dressed in faded jeans, a brown checked shirt, and a well-worn, almost threadbare corduroy jacket, he strode purposely across the hall to the officer.

"I found this under his bed." He held out a piece of paper.

The officer carefully unfolded a simple hand-drawn map. He thought for a moment, then reached for the radio at his lapel.

"DC185 to Control."

"Go ahead 185."

"Can you get a patrol car to Albert Street and send another along to the intersection between the A-950 and the A-98? We have a young man on the run from the local boys' home and he'll probably be thumbing a ride. He's about five-ten, brown hair, average build; blue jeans, blue sweater, black jacket and carrying a red backpack. Tell the patrols to keep an eye out for benevolent truck drivers."

"Roger that 185, two units will be dispatched."

The officer snapped off the radio and looked at the stern-faced Matron. "I'll need to keep this and make some additional calls. I have an idea where your young man is going, and I think I know how he plans to get there." He looked to the man who had found the note. "Thanks for your help Mr.— ?"

"Carter. Trevor Carter. Glad I could help."

"Yes, thank you Trevor," Matron said. "Go and settle the boys for the night, will you? I'll see the officer out."

"Sure."

From the landing above Trevor caught a glimpse of light blond hair as a head jerked back from the stair rail. Feet pounded along the upstairs hallway and he sighed, wondering who the eavesdropper had been. He made his way up the stairs and reflected on the missing boy. Matt was a good kid. To be sure he had been a little withdrawn of late, but he was polite, an almost non-existent trait in the rest of the Home's occupants. Sadly the attributes that endeared Matt to the staff made him a natural target to the more troublesome boys. Trevor had often been forced to intervene to prevent things from getting out of hand. *Why did teenage boys always need a victim?*

He reached the corner landing and headed up the last flight of stairs. A babble of voices from the dormitory spilled into the hall then faded as the door closed again. Whoever had been listening had evidently slipped back into their room. Pushing aside the thoughts of Matt alone in the night, Trevor paused outside the dormitory. He took a deep breath and then entered a sea of excited voices.

"All right you miserable lot, settle down!" He walked into the room with his best parade ground swagger, ignoring the empty bed before him. "It's late. Lights out!"

As he spoke, he noted the boys around the room. There were eleven of them, the majority with light blond hair. He looked across at the most likely suspect, an overly large boy who everyone called Brick. Unlike the others who were sitting on their beds talking animatedly about Matt's disappearance, Brick was under his blankets trying unsuccessfully to look innocent. His face was flushed.

"You know the rules about leaving the dormitory at night, Brick." It was a statement not a question, and delivered with a penetrating stare.

Brick had arrived at the Home a few months after Deglin. Homeless, living on the streets, he had been caught by the police throwing bricks through factory windows. The name had stuck.

"Aw c'mon Mr. C. Cut me some slack!" he replied, "I've been here all the frickin' time." He looked across at the opposite bed, adding, "Ain't that right, Grant?" He grinned mischievously, looked back at Trevor and pointed to the empty bed. "You got the wrong kid Mr. C. It's Matt that fucked off—not me!"

Trevor crossed the room in two quick strides and leaned over Brick's bed. "Don't screw with me, son. I don't care for your language and I sure as hell can't abide liars." He pointed to the bottom of the bed where Brick's foot was clearly visible hanging out of the covers. "You might think I'm stupid but I can assure you, boy, I'm not so far gone *I* sleep with my slippers on!"

A chorus of laughs caused the already-flushed Brick to color up further and he jerked the offending slipper under the covers, glowering around the room with a look that silenced many of the younger boys.

Trevor returned to the door and flipped the light switch. "'Night boys. See you in the morning."

Brick waited for the door to close before kicking off his slippers. "Asshole," he muttered, then climbed once more into bed.

As the upper floor windows went dark, Deglin continued to crouch beneath the thick beech hedge that ringed the old building. He shifted his weight, taking pressure from his aching heels, and cursed the police officer who seemed to be lingering unnecessarily in the nearby squad car. Finally, the engine coughed to life and the crunch of fine gravel beneath tires marked the officer's departure. He watched the flare of brake lights as the car paused at the old iron gates, and then it was gone.

Deglin slipped into the shadows of the kitchen yard. He moved carefully by the kitchen windows and reached the lawn at the rear of the home. Heavy clouds gathered across the night sky and he smiled as the moon was obscured from view. He took advantage of the darkness and strode more confidently to the tool shed and quickly opened the door. He fumbled briefly with a shielded lantern and then with one last look back at the former manor house, he stepped into the shed and pulled the door closed behind him.

Inverdeer Forest, Scotland
Wednesday

More than an hour had passed since Matt had entered the forest.

Cold and scared, he dropped to the ground and fell back against a large oak. He was lost and completely despondent. Mia sat quietly at his feet, a puzzled look of expectation on her face.

"You hungry too?"

The dog tipped her head to one side and stared at his bag. "Ok, lass." He set the backpack between his feet and with a cigarette lighter he had lifted from Matron's desk he peered into the bag. A pack of crackers, a can opener, two small cans of beans, a lump of cheese and three cans of dog food made up the contents of the bag, along with a small stub of candle he had found at the back of a cupboard.

Matt carefully scooped a small hollow in the ground and set the candle in it. Once confident it would not fall, he lit it and took some instant comfort from the dancing flame. It provided little in the way of heat, but gave enough light to see by, and he dropped the lighter onto his bag and pulled out a can of dog food. "You want this?" he asked the waiting dog.

Mia's answer came in the form of a rhythmic swishing as her bushy tail swept back and forth through the debris of the forest floor.

Matt emptied the can on the ground, "Sorry, girl—I should've snagged a bowl, huh?"

Evidently she did not care, gulping down the food and an occasional leaf while Matt finished a hasty meal of crackers and cheese.

"God, it's cold!" Matt drew his legs up and hugged his knees. Shadows seemed to grow and shrink in the flickering light of the candle, and Mia turned her head away, a wary eye on the wavering flame. Matt gave her a wan smile.

"You think Mum and Dad will be pleased to see us?" His voice seemed loud in the silence of the trees, and he hugged himself tighter. He imagined himself cold, wet and hungry knocking on their door the next day. He suppressed the fear they would call the police, disown him, turn him away—and imagined instead them welcoming him in with tears of joy on their faces, his mother clasping him to her and telling him she loved him.

Matt felt the familiar knotting of his stomach and the dry lump in his throat. At almost seventeen years old he couldn't remember ever hearing anyone say they loved him. He swallowed and blinked back the tears.

Geez get a grip!

He wiped a sleeve across his nose, pushed away the childish feelings, and instead focused on his immediate dilemma.

Can't sit here all night. Think, dammit...

Beyond the radius of the candle the looming shapes of trees and bushes were darker patches in the night. Mia's breath puffed in little clouds that quickly dissipated into the darkness. It was growing colder and there was a chill dampness to the ground and air. Matt reached in his pocket for the map he had drawn and an icy chill gripped him when he felt nothing but an empty pocket. "What the...?" He stood up quickly and cried out as he slammed the back of his head on a stumpy branch.

Grasping the back of his head he lurched away from the tree, catching the candle with his foot as he staggered to regain his balance.

"Shit!"

Darkness engulfed him as the candle spluttered and died and he dropped to his knees groping blindly for the discarded lighter. His questing fingers found nothing at first, then they brushed across the bag and he swore again as he heard the lighter fall into the leaves. Ignoring the throbbing pain in his head he scrabbled amongst the leaves, desperate for the one source of light he had. It was no use. Disoriented, he felt for Mia and clung to her, cursing the fact the only flashlight at the Home had contained dead batteries.

There was no wind, not even a breeze. Matt's voice trembled. Fear was starting to give way to panic. "Which way, Mia?"

The dark outline of the dog remained still and Matt strained his ears listening for traffic or any sounds of civilization to guide him from the trees. He had never experienced such total blackness, and robbed of vision, his ears became more attuned to the night. He became aware of the scratching and scurrying of unseen creatures. The sound of a falling leaf seemed ridiculously loud and the night became full of unseen things slowly closing in around him. Each sound filled him with exaggerated terror.

Something ran multi-legged across his hand and he slapped at it, dancing to his feet, and frantically brushing his clothes.

"Fuck this...!" he fought the urge to run blindly into the trees. Then, in the distance, faint despite the silence of the night, came the wail of a siren.

Mia barked and Matt turned to face the sound trying to pinpoint its location before it faded away. "C'mon girl!" Matt pulled his bag from the ground, shook it furiously then slung it across his back as he headed toward the distant sound.

Low-hanging branches whipped at his face and brambles snagged and clutched at his jeans, threatening to trip him as he blundered through the forest. If it wasn't for Mia he would have become hopelessly entangled in the dense undergrowth, but she seemed to find the clearest path with ease. Twice he had to call for her to wait while he clambered over fallen trees that she had easily wormed her way under, but now she led him past the last spindly saplings and through the bracken and nettles that marked the forest edge.

"Hell yeah! We made it, Mia!"

Already the loss of the route seemed less of a problem. Free from the oppressive atmosphere of the trees, he breathed the fresher air of the open hillside and felt his spirits lift. The orange glow in the sky to the northeast marked the port town of Peterhead—of that he was certain. There was sure to be someone traveling from there to Inverness.

He watched the faint lights of a distant car and prepared to head off down the grassy slope when something flickered at the edge of his vision. Something felt wrong. His skin prickled.

Relax...it's nothing...

Matt took a hesitant step backward.

Someone's watching me...

Beside him Mia tensed and he heard a low growl as she bared her teeth.

Oh crap. She feels it too!

Matt raised his fists and stared intently back toward the tree line.

There! Oh my God—

A shadow, darker than all the others, drifted off to his right, vanishing behind a bush.

"Who's out there?"

Too afraid to move he continued to wait, and then a soft silver light bathed the scene before him as the moon shone through a break in the clouds. What he had taken in the darkness to be a bush was not a bush—it was a stone, a standing stone. There were several of them, each taller than he, and they formed a rough circle, their tops seeming to lean in toward him, their moon-cast shadows reaching out toward him.

"Mia! Let's go!"

He turned to run but a faceless figure loomed before him. Matt caught the silver flicker of moonlight on the blade of a knife and screamed.

Chapter 2
Myrthinus

Near Inverdeer, Scotland

Gradually the twin stars that danced before Matt's eyes like out-of-focus fairies merged into a solitary candle flame that flickered in the draft of a shuttered window.

His neck was stiff and his head ached. He stifled a groan, and fearing to move glanced around the room. Where the hell was he? There was no ceiling, just large wooden beams that stretched from wall to wall supporting a steeply pitched roof. It took Matt a few moments of puzzled concentration to determine the textured pattern above was thatching; *thatching*? He shuddered at the sight of cobwebs high above, so thick and heavy with dust they resembled dirty lace curtains tacked across the corners and angles of the room. *What was this place?* The room smelled musty, old, a subtle blend of wood smoke, dust, and age.

Moving his head, he looked to the side and felt his pulse quicken. A figure sat across the room. The head was bowed in apparent sleep, and a mane of silver hair completely obscured the face. Matt's heart beat wildly as he recalled the knife and the circle of standing stones. This figure wore a chillingly familiar dress or robe.

Matt scanned the room. A single door was directly in front of him.

Taking care not to disturb the sleeping figure, he slid his legs toward the edge of the sleeping pallet on which he lay, his eyes darting nervously between door and chair. The figure shifted slightly and Matt froze. He waited, holding his breath, willing his captor to stay asleep. Slowly Matt let out his breath and rolled himself to the floor. Carefully he stood, the coarse wooden planks rough beneath the skin of his feet. His head swam and his vision blurred. He blinked his eyes to clear the wash of tears and almost groaned aloud from the hammering in his head. He steadied himself against the cold stone of the wall and waited for his eyes to clear. Still the sleeping figure did not move. Matt edged along the pallet, ignoring the pain in his head, each step bringing him closer to escape.

Almost there...

The chair behind him creaked.

"No!"

Matt leaped at the door and snatched the wooden latch. The room beyond was mostly lost in darkness, the only light coming from a feeble fire that crackled in a stone fireplace to his right. The lazy flames sent eerie shadows wavering across a sparsely furnished space. To his left he could make out a heavy-looking door framed by two small windows through which the velvet blackness of night presented an invitation to escape, to hide. Matt moved toward the door.

The chair scraped loudly across the floor and Matt risked a glance behind. A towering figure stooped through the doorway, then Matt found himself lurching across the room as he snagged his foot on an unseen rug. Off balance, Matt slammed into a large wooden chest and pain exploded in his shin. Somehow he hauled himself up and limped desperately toward the door.

Just a few more steps.

Heavy footsteps sounded behind him now and Matt could almost feel the long bony hands reaching out to grab him. He reached the door. The iron latch was dead cold in his sweating hand. He pulled but the latch would not move. Panting, he groped desperately for the key that protruded from the lock. His frantic fingers found it but then it was gone! Matt spun in disbelief as the key flew across the room into the outstretched hand of his captor. The tall figure grinned and closed gnarled and wrinkled fingers around the key.

"'Tis far too soon for you to be up and about, boy."

Matt felt like a cornered animal; fear and pain kept him pressed against the door while his numbed mind tried to rationalize what he had just seen. "What…?"

"I am a friend…" The man's voice was deep, yet gentle. He held out a reassuring hand, and Matt noted the bones and veins stood out tight against skin that was blotched with age. *Jeez he's old!* For a split second Matt thought about charging him down and making another break for freedom, but something held him back. He waited, breathing fast. The fear had subsided a little and he took in more details of the man before him.

The man was definitely old, yet stood very tall and straight, devoid of the typical stoop one would expect in a man of such advanced years. His dress was like something from a fantasy movie, a long robe, not black as Matt had first thought, but of the deepest green, cinched at the waist with a thick length of rope, the ends heavily knotted and sealed with what looked like pitch or tar.

Hair, more silver than white, and a somewhat unkempt beard framed an elongated face. High cheekbones and a proud forehead overshadowed a nose that appeared much too small for the face, and green eyes were set beneath thin and wispy brows. Matt found himself caught by a gaze that held a universe of knowledge.

For the briefest moment there was a sense of recognition, then a sickening rush of vertigo and he closed his eyes. A vision flashed before him.

He was an infant and an old man held him high against a shoulder. They moved quickly, and as they passed beneath a stone arch he saw a winding stone stair descending into shadow. He glanced behind into the darkness of the room they had just left. A small crib was set against a wall and candles illuminated a bed where a woman lay, her hair as black as night and her face pale as death. The rest of the room was dark, but Matt could feel its vastness. Thunder rolled outside and with a crushing detonation lightning tore apart the sky. In the brief burst of light that blazed through a tiny window Matt was startled to see the outline of another man standing deep in a recess, a hood pulled tight about a face lost in shadow.

Matt's vision swam back into focus.

"Who...are you?" Matt asked.

"As I said, lad, I'm a friend."

The voice was soothing, somehow melodious. The lines on his face deepened like cracks in well-worn leather as he smiled.

"I brought you here for your safety after the attack at the stones. You can trust me, laddie."

The old man gestured toward a low doorway to what was clearly a kitchen.

"Fear not, laddie. Come. Seein's you're up, let us sup and talk a wee while. You need to rest but a full belly will do you no harm. See there, your pup dines already."

"Mia?" Matt tentatively took a step forward.

"Aye. Mia. Now, if she trusts me" —the man winked—"kenna you not do the same?"

With that he rose and walked to the kitchen, ducking beneath the dark oak lintel above the door.

Matt was shaken. His head ached, his shin throbbed from his collision with the trunk and he realized he was ravenously hungry. Confused by the strange events, anxious to be reunited with his dog, and confident he could best his mysterious rescuer if it came to a fight, he limped toward the kitchen, taking extra care as he crossed the rug.

The kitchen was very small. Cracks scarred the whitewashed walls and brown stains betrayed dampness around the door and little round window. An assortment of herbs and dried plants hung from large black nails driven into oak beams that supported the low reed ceiling. Their subtle fragrance permeated the air with traces of thyme, rosemary and scents unfamiliar to Matt. He felt his stomach rumble at the stronger aroma of rich gravy and freshly baked bread. He made his way over the uneven stone slabs strewn with cut straw, and there beneath a deeply scarred table lay Mia, paws clasped protectively about a large knuckle bone. Her tail wagged as he bent to stroke her.

"Well, sit yourself down, lad."

The man indicated a somewhat imposing high-backed chair wedged between the wall of the little room and the table. Not totally at ease, Matt perched instead on a nearby wooden stool, its round top almost cracked in two but still serviceable. He waited quietly and watched as his host busied himself cutting large slabs of warm bread before ladling generous portions of venison stew into a wooden bowl.

Matt's mouth watered.

"You have many a question I no doubt?" the man passed the boy a steaming bowl.

Matt sampled the stew and broke off a piece of bread. Between mouthfuls he asked the question that was foremost in his mind.

"What happened to me? All I remember was some guy lunging at me with a knife!"

"Aye, indeed! You had come to the standing stones of Aikey Brae. You were attacked by one of the Cùra dubh."

"Cùra what?"

"Cùra dubh. The dark guardians. They are the loyal servants of your enemy, her personal bodyguard in fact. Very dangerous, laddie and"—he faced Matt, waving the ladle for emphasis—"to be greatly feared."

Matt scoffed, "Guardians?" He took another mouthful of stew. "You mean I stumbled over some drunk who thought he'd scare the shit out of me! Look"—he realized he didn't know the man's name—"whoever you are—"

"Myrthinus."

"Myrthinus?" *What the hell kind of name was that?*

"Aye, and this"—the man spread his arms—"is one of many temporary homes. It's in the same woods you traveled through this evening, save maybe a league further north."

"League? Did you just say league? Who the hell are you?" Matt looked at the robe, rope belt and long hair. "Gandalf?"

Myrthinus smiled. "Forgive me lad. I forget. You no longer gauge distances in leagues. Miles then? Let's say maybe three or four miles further north." He pointed to the empty bowl before Matt. "Would you like some more, or shall we adjourn to the fire?"

Matt almost asked for more—the stew had been good—but he was comfortably full and his hunger for information overcame his greed. "No, I'm fine. Thanks," he added as an afterthought.

They returned to the main room, leaving Mia with her bone, and Myrthinus poked the fire back to life. He threw a fresh log on the rising flames and sat back in a nearby rocking chair.

The fire crackled and popped and Matt felt very tired as he made himself comfortable among the cushions on the floor. His pounding headache had retreated to a dull throb and his shin had ceased to hurt. He fought the urge to relax and rallied himself.

"Look, I really appreciate the food, but I can't stay here. They'll have people looking for me and I need to be a long way from here by morning. If you can point me in the right direction—"

"Nay, laddie! You have far too many enemies to be wandering off on your own just now."

"Enemies? Get real! I may get picked on at school, but with all due respect, I don't need *your* help, okay? Besides, like I said, I've got somewhere—"

Myrthinus raised a hand, interrupting Matt's pronouncements. "Listen to me, Matt."

A sense of unease caused Matt to catch his breath.

"When did I tell you my name?" The boy spoke with a sudden caution.

Myrthinus ignored him, clearly choosing his next words carefully. "You're important, lad. Descended from a line far older, far greater than you could possibly imagine. There are those who would protect you..." He touched his own chest, then continued with eyes that burned with a deep intensity. "...and those who would bring you harm."

Matt's face registered his surprise and confusion. Unsure of which absurd statement to tackle first, he instead pressed again, "I asked you how you know my name?"

"Cos I've known you since birth, Matt. Back when you were a wee lad an' tragedy befell your folk. Your mother was taken captive by the Cùra dubh, the very forces that hunt you now. You came into my care and I did th' best I could for you, but with a small boy to care for I couldna help your mother nor find your father. 'Twas I that took you to the children's home. I put you there for your safety before I went in search of your father." Myrthinus paused, reading the stunned disbelief on Matt's face. "The past ten years have seen nothing but war and famine rage across this land, lad, but in my searching I learned others have discovered your existence. I was coming tonight to take you away. It would appear I was barely in time."

War and famine? The old fool had to be crazy but... "You really know my parents?" The old man's words reverberated in his head. "What others are looking for me?"

"Not now, Matt. You need rest, but first I need to know why you were in the woods alone?"

"Like hell!" Matt scrambled to his knees. "You say I was attacked by some guardian weirdos, you claim to know my parents, then make some wild statement about them being lost, and you want to question *me* on what I was doing in the woods? Fuck no! You answer my questions, dammit! How do you know my parents, huh? For all I know you could be the same crazy bastard that attacked me!"

Matt's face became flushed as the terror of earlier that evening flared again, this time manifesting itself in anger. Why was he even listening to this old fool? Matt stood up looking toward the kitchen. "Look, I'm sorry but I've got to be going..."

"Wait!"

But Matt's face had gone pale. There on a small table beside the chimney was a knife. The flickering fire light reflected like blood on the blade and Matt recognized it as the weapon he had seen earlier that night.

He looked back, panic in his eyes.

"It *was* you!"

Myrthinus looked over his shoulder to where Matt had been looking moments before, and Matt took his chance. Leaping forward he pushed Myrthinus hard, sending him reeling across the room. Off balance, Myrthinus grabbed at the kitchen door frame but missed and fell to the floor with a muffled grunt.

Matt ran quickly to the nearest window. "Mia!" he yelled as he twisted the latch. The heavy window swung outward and a blast of chill night air swept into the cottage. Struggling, Matt pulled himself onto the sill and prepared to duck through the window when he heard footsteps behind.

"Mia! C'mon!"

Matt had one leg through the window when powerful hands grabbed his shoulders. He struggled but the grip was too strong. He slipped and fell, and the crash as he hit the floor jarred his teeth together and reawakened the pounding headache. Sliding across the floor on the seat of his jeans he pushed himself away from the looming figure.

"Leave me alone!" he yelled. "Just let me go!"

"Matt! Relax! Listen to me..."

Matt felt the heat of the fire behind him, and glanced across to the table and the knife that lay there. He dove for it, sending a small wicker stool crashing into the wall.

Again he slipped and fell, but made it to the table, one questing hand slapping across it groping for the knife. His searching fingers found the hilt, but before he could tighten his grip it was wrenched from his grasp and sent spinning across the table.

Like the key earlier that evening, Matt watched in stunned disbelief as the knife now flew across the room to land in the man's outstretched hand. Myrthinus stood tall, his thin eyebrows bunched tightly over eyes that burned with emerald fire.

"Enough of this foolishness, boy!"

Matt cowered back against the wall and stared at the knife. "How did you do that?"

The boy looked around, desperate for somewhere to run or something to throw. Tears of frustration and fear stung his eyes. All courage had gone now, "Look, just let me go. Okay?" He hated the pleading desperation in his voice. "Let me go."

Myrthinus made a subtle gesture and Matt felt a sense of overwhelming calm and relaxation descend on him like a heavy blanket. He felt numb, somehow detached from his body.

Benefactor or captor Matt did not know, but he watched as the man knelt before him and laid the knife back on the table. He took Matt's face in his hands and wiped the tears away with his thumbs and looked deep into the boy's eyes.

"I took the knife from your attacker in the stones. Be assured, Matt, I am your friend." The sternness was gone, replaced by a lilting, soothing voice, full of compassion and care.

Despite the calming influence of the man's words Matt clung to the last shreds of his earlier anger. "So how do you know my parents?"

"Knew, Matt. I knew them. I havnae seen your folks for many years. Now please, you are in grave danger, lad. It was fear for your safety that made me come to find you." Heavy hands slipped to Matt's shoulders and held him firmly. "Now something caused you to leave the home afore I could get there, and I need to know what."

Matt reached inside his pocket for the crumpled piece of paper he had found in his file. With shaking hands he passed it to Myrthinus.

Myrthinus took the paper carefully and read it.

"How did you come by this?" he asked, his voice strained, almost harsh.

"Deglin."

"Deglin?"

"The gardener." Matt's voice shook. "I was asking about my parents and he told me how to get in the office and find my file. That was on the top."

"'Tis a lie, laddie!" Myrthinus stood up and crossed to the fire. "You must believe me, boy, this is a lie. You have no parents there, not in that time. This was nothing but a ploy to lure you from the home and into the hands of the Cùra dubh!"

As he spoke he crumpled the paper into a ball and flung it into the fire.

"No!" Matt crawled across the floor. "No!" He watched in horror as the first and only tenuous link with his parents blackened and curled before him, crumbling to ashes in the heat of the fire. The man turned to hold him, but Matt pushed him away and struggled to his feet. "You bastard! That was mine!" His punches failed to make contact and Myrthinus quickly waved a hand. Matt lurched, suddenly overcome with tiredness and his legs gave out beneath him. With surprising strength Myrthinus caught Matt before he hit the floor and carried him to the bed from which he had earlier escaped.

"I promise I will speak less in riddles and provide some answers in the morn'," the old man said as he folded a coarse woolen blanket over the half-sleeping young man. "For now you must sleep."

Waving a hand he murmured soft words in a strange language and Matt fell into a deep and healing sleep. Myrthinus watched Matt for a while, then turned and exited the room. The open window swung in the breeze and he pulled it closed.

Outside the trees swayed and creaked in the gathering wind. Above them, the moon and stars played hide and seek behind clouds that fled the coming storm.

It was the birds that woke Matt the following morning. A bright chorus of trills, whistles and warbles that spilled into the room carried on the widening beams of sunlight that shone through the knot holes and cracks in the shutters.

Mia lay curled across the bottom of the sleeping pallet oblivious to the world around her, sleeping soundly, and dreaming whatever it is dogs dream.

Careful not to disturb his companion, Matt rolled to one side and tested his ability to stand. His body should have ached, but it did not. A bruise on his shin like an overripe plum reminded him of the terror of the previous evening, but he marveled at the lack of pain. He opened the door. A few embers remained in the grate but there was no sign of Myrthinus. He felt a momentary pang of sadness as he remembered the burning paper that would have led him to his parents, but it just as quickly passed. A slow clicking of nails on the wooden floor announced Mia's departure from the bed and he ruffled her head as she sat beside him yawning and lazily sweeping her tail back and forth.

"C'mon girl—let's explore a bit." Mia hesitated as she gazed toward the kitchen where the bone or what remained of it still lay but she dutifully followed Matt toward the main door.

The key was back in the lock and Matt spent a few moments checking all around for any signs of twine or thin thread that could have been used to pull it from the lock. He found nothing. Of course the old man could have removed any such evidence while Matt slept; after all, the only other option was unthinkable. He looked across the room to the table but the knife was no longer there. He suppressed a shudder.

About to turn back to the door Matt checked himself as he noticed something on the floor. Dropping to his knees he reached beneath the crudely shaped table and withdrew what appeared to be a metal medallion. In the dim light he was unable to see any detail beyond the fact it was a rough metal circle embossed with some form of intricate design, surrounding a stone. He quickly slipped it into his pocket and returned once more to the door. He would examine it better by daylight.

It was a bright fresh morning and the sun streamed through the trees. The sweet scent of pine and the clean smell of recent rain lifted Matt's spirits, and stepping outside he took his first look at the exterior of the cottage. Like a picture from medieval times it was of plain stone construction with a thatched roof, complete with a wooden lean-to on one side which housed straw, firewood and spare thatching. The sunlight sparkled on something toward the rear of the shed and Matt moved closer to investigate.

Hanging in a corner was a sword. The hilt showed signs of significant wear. The reddish leather was cracked and dry, and the blade covered in dust and grime. Matt stepped closer and noticed two stones on the cross guard. They sparkled as they caught and reflected the morning sun. Hands trembling with excitement, he lifted down the weapon. It was heavier than he expected but he held it and took a hesitant step into the clearing, the medallion in his pocket now forgotten. Matt gave the blade a few experimental swings, then advanced across the clearing, battling imaginary foes as deeds of valor swept through his head.

Matt's early years had been tough. He had struggled to make friends, always preferring his own company. His peers thought him odd and either ignored or bullied him. As his schooling began he developed a love of books and sought constant escape from his own miserable existence into the lives of the heroes who lived among the pages of his favorite stories. Now, at the age of seventeen, it seemed he was caught up in some crazy adventure of his own.

As he whirled the sword, blocking imaginary blows, his head buzzed with questions. What had really happened last night? In the fresh light of day it all seemed somehow too incredible to believe. Flying keys and knives; the calming and relaxing that had fallen on him like a spell with the wave of a hand. *Crap like that only happened in fantasy novels or to Jedi knights!*

With aching arms he parried an imaginary blow and dealt a swift attack against a nearby tree. The blade cut cleanly through the branch and he dropped the weapon in surprise.

"Wow!" He looked in awe at the severed limb. It was small, no more than an inch thick, but he hadn't expected the sword to cut through it that easily. He retrieved the weapon from the grass and inspected the blade. Where it had passed through the wood it shone, all traces of dirt and grime gone. He rubbed a finger along its length and more of the dust fell away revealing gleaming steel beneath.

Tired from his exertions, he took the weapon to a nearby boulder and sat down in the shade. With the bottom of his shirt he began to carefully clean the sword. Absorbed with his task, he did not hear the footsteps behind him and jumped, startled, when a gnarled and bony hand appeared on his shoulder.

"I see you've found your sword." Myrthinus smiled warmly. "So how are you feeling this bright morning?"

Matt stood and looked at Myrthinus, his eyes narrowed. "My sword?"

"Aye. It belonged to a great warrior, one of the brotherhood. It came into my keeping several years ago and I've kept it ever since. Now it belongs to you."

At these words Matt felt himself become lightheaded and dizzy. He closed his eyes in an effort to blink away the unfamiliar vertigo. A memory, or fragment of some half-forgotten dream flickered at the edge of his consciousness. He fought the nauseous sensation but suddenly found himself falling...

A large hall formed before him and as the vision shimmered into focus he saw a man standing at a table, his back to Matt. A sword lay upon the table and Matt watched as the man removed a chain from around his neck and with obvious reluctance dropped it beside the blade. Matt staggered as he felt drawn into the vision and found himself standing at the table. The sword that lay there was the one Matt had recently been cleaning, but his eyes were drawn to a medallion that hung from the discarded chain. Almost circular, the medallion resembled a dragon crouched upon a blood-red stone. Matt knew he had seen it before but could not recall when or where. He struggled to face the man, a rising sense of tension and excitement building inside but the image revolved, the stone walls of the hall spinning before his eyes. His stomach churned at the strange motion but eased as his eyes locked upon a small boy rolling on the floor with two large wolfhounds. They played on soft animal skins before a roaring fire. Behind them strange shields and tapestries hung from the walls and the vaulted ceiling was supported on giant beams of smoke-blackened oak. With sudden clarity he recognized the boy as himself. He tried to pull his gaze back to the man, but the image was beyond his control. Again the room revolved and he saw a woman enter from a nearby archway. She was barefoot, and seemed to almost glide across the room, her simple white gown flowing from her shoulders, its length trailing on the floor behind her. She reached out for the man her beautiful face full of concern. Through lips he could barely feel Matt breathed *Mother?*

She turned to look at him but he swooned and the vision faded.

Myrthinus caught the boy and gently lowered him to the springy turf. "'tis okay, lad. I've got you."

An unfamiliar sensation of love, warmth and happiness lingered in Matt's mind and he closed his eyes trying desperately to resume the dream, but it had gone, and he lay back on the cool grass feeling lost, alone, and utterly drained.

"She loved you greatly."

Matt looked up at Myrthinus and saw the man's eyes were filled with compassion. There was an ancient wisdom in that face. A depth of understanding and knowledge that seemed to stretch back over thousands of years, and despite the fears of the previous night, the burning of the letter and the attack in the stone circle, Matt felt a sudden and overwhelming feeling of trust for this mysterious figure. He took the proffered hand and got unsteadily to his feet.

"You know what I just saw?"

"Aye, in part. There is much to tell but too little time for the telling. For your protection and the protection of others, your memories were locked away but if you're to believe and understand what I have to teach, you will need them back."

"How?"

"They are returning to you now. Triggered by events or scenes around you. Will not be easy, but there is strength in you, laddie. Come, 'tis time we talked."

Just then the forest filled with noise. Mia sat up, ears pricked and nose twitching. Matt held his breath as a deer, a large buck, bounded into the clearing. It stopped, not more than ten feet away, its hide glistening with sweat, its chest heaving. It regarded them through moist brown eyes.

To Matt the look was one of a sad acceptance, as if the proud beast was resigned to its fate. Behind it the sounds of the hunt grew louder and the buck trembled. On quivering legs it took a step toward them and Matt held his breath as it pressed a shiny wet nose against Myrthinus.

Something passed between them and the man placed a hand on Matt's shoulder.

"I need you to stand still, Matt. Do not move."

Matt nodded. Myrthinus closed his eyes for a few moments, then said quietly, "And now we wait."

They did not wait for long. Five large hunting dogs bounded into the clearing closely followed by three men on horseback.

The hounds made straight for the deer but it remained perfectly still, unmoving, and Matt realized Mia was likewise frozen, resembling a statue more than a living creature. The hounds circled the ground several feet from them while the horsemen waited.

Matt's skin prickled. What was happening? He looked directly at the men. They were dressed strangely, in tunics, leggings, and dark woolen cloaks. Each wore a sword and sat atop his steaming mount while the hounds scanned for a scent to follow. Matt looked directly at the nearest man but the figure seemed to look right through him.

"C'mon! Which way? Fin' the trail yer fuckers!" The leader of the men spoke with a strong accent.

Suddenly one of the animals barked excitedly and ran to the tree line.

"There," another rider cried. "They have the scent!"

The riders wheeled their mounts and plunged into the trees in pursuit of their baying hounds.

The air before Matt seemed to shimmer as if a sudden wave of heat had passed across the clearing. Mia roved back and forth, sniffing at the ground where the dogs had been. Myrthinus stroked the buck's nose and the animal bowed its head and stepped up to Matt. Hesitantly the boy reached out a hand and stroked the silky smooth neck. It was warm, and he could feel the quivering pulse beneath the skin. A lump came to his throat as the animal regarded him for a moment then backed away before turning and trotting back across the clearing and into the trees from whence it came.

Matt looked up amazed, his face full of wonder.

"How?"

Myrthinus winked, his piercing green eyes alight with some deeper, hidden power, but he remained silent and returned to the cottage.

The boy stood alone for several minutes and shook his head. What was happening to him? He knew what he had seen. The horsemen had passed the clearing as if he and the deer were not even there. But that was not possible. Slowly Matt made his way to the edge of the clearing where the brambles and ferns of the forest edge had been trampled by the passing horseman. He looked back at the cottage, a faint curl of blue smoke rising from the chimney. A gentle breeze carried it away and leaves danced crisply across the clearing, a swirl of red, brown and orange.

"I need some answers!" Matt muttered. "Now!" and he raced for the cottage door.

"So what just happened out there?" Matt demanded, marching into the kitchen and dropping the sword on the table with a clatter.

"An act of kindness," the old man answered, turning to regard the boy with a look of amusement on his face.

Matt began to feel a little foolish but pressed on.

"It's like you're a magician or something. I mean how did you do that with the key and the knife last night? And just now, the hunters...?"

Myrthinus sighed, "So many questions, and so ill mannered." Taking a thick cloth he lifted a heavy iron kettle from the fire where it had begun to steam.

"Wine?" he asked, as he poured the boiling water into an earthenware pot in which he had already placed a small cloth bag of herbs and a generous serving of a pungent berry-colored wine.

"Wine? Urrr...no," Matt responded, but eying a nearby loaf hungrily he added, "but I'll take some bread."

Myrthinus gave him a sidelong look, eyebrows raised.

"Please," Matt added.

Rich creamy butter was spread across the soft bread, which was then placed on a wooden platter. Matt watched as Myrthinus removed the lid from the pot, stirred the contents and then carried it to the table along with the bread.

"So," Myrthinus spoke slowly. "I'm a magician?"

It sounded ridiculous and Matt blushed, focusing his attention on the bread.

Myrthinus pulled a stained scrap of cloth from the dresser and used it to strain the rich aromatic wine into a wooden cup. He sat there for a while regarding the boy.

"I have a gift," he began. "Certain abilities that you may call magic or wizardry." Myrthinus chuckled. "It's somewhat more complex than that but for now such an explanation ken suffice." The wizard sampled his mulled wine and continued. "Last night I warned that you are in danger. Do you remember?"

Matt nodded.

"Good. Now 'tis time I explain. You are caught up in something far greater than you can possibly imagine, Matt, and to understand it fully I need to start at the very beginning. You remember the stone circle?"

"Yeah. Too well!"

"Well, the stones, or any ancient structure, can be used as a portal—a gateway if you will—that bridges two realities. Those with certain skills can open these portals, providing a pathway between one reality and another. You do not belong in the world you have come to know as home, lad. 'Twas I that took you there for your own protection, but now our enemy has learned of you and your life is in grave danger. The Cùra dubh have skills somewhat akin to mine. They are weaker, for they have limited understanding of how our 'magic' truly works. They rely more on devices fashioned by their late master for their power than their own strength of will, but to an ordinary man they are a formidable foe. The one they serve is an evil beyond anything you could imagine, and she is hunting you—hunting us."

Matt scoffed. "Awww, c'mon! You can't expect me to believe this crap. You're speaking of fantasy as if it were real. I mean, alternate realities?" He thought of the TV shows he had enjoyed on the subject. "Get real!"

"You are no longer in the world you know, Matt. Last night you were taken through one such portal." The magician suddenly grinned, "'Tis quite the welcome you've had to the sixth century!"

Matt's mouth fell open and he just stared.

"You yourself saw the hunters this morning. Do men like that roam the streets of your world?"

Myrthinus leaned across the table, his voice becoming more urgent.

"You were lured away from the Home by Deglin, to capture or kill you, which one I do not know. I had hoped to question him last night but he escaped. I had no choice but to let him go and bring you here. Your injury was far more severe than you realize and I dared not move you far. These are momentous times, young man. The world hangs on the brink of destruction and I will be needing your help to save it."

Myrthinus took another sip of his wine and indicated the last slice of bread on the platter. Matt shook his head, all sense of appetite long gone as the enormity of the wizard's words struggled to sink into his overburdened brain.

"So you healed me?"

"I employed my arts to aid your recovery, aye."

Matt let out a low whistle. "How does it work? The magic I mean. Is it something I could..." He waved his hand rather vaguely. "Something I could learn? Are you going to teach me?" A note of renewed excitement crept into his voice.

Myrthinus smiled. "It is a craft that takes years to understand, decades to perfect and centuries to master. Whilst it may be possible for you to learn something of the art, you're too old, I fear, to perfect much if any of it."

"Old? I'm seventeen!"

"But you've been conditioned to not believe in such things, and the very basis of magic is belief."

"But I believe what I've seen!"

Myrthinus reached across the table, patting the boy's hand.

"It is not quite that simple, laddie. The people of my race spent their entire lives devoted to it. Of course to us it was not magic. It was more an understanding of the order of things, our place within the very fabric of nature."

Matt said nothing but his look was one of rapt fascination so Myrthinus continued.

"We were a people that lived in total harmony with our environment. We had no gods or deities on which to base beliefs, or from which to draw reason for the unknown.

"We had over eons become masters of a higher awareness or energy that you would call magic, but to us it was just another science. Sadly the people of your world no longer believe in such things. Technology, machines and religions have taken away the need for magic, leaving it a memory or myth of the past."

"What do you mean?"

"Well...consider travel. For you 'tis not possible to believe you could travel across the sea without the use of a boat or a flying machine. But for my people there was no need for such machines—we could simply will ourselves from place to place."

"That's impossible!"

"And so you have been conditioned to think! Everyone has this power to some degree. It's all a question of belief—belief and strength of mind.

"Humankind has become too dependent on machines to perform its work and on gods to provide answers to the great mysteries. Your brains are shrinking, but they still carry a formidable power; a power that is wasted. Mankind talks so much of faith—but it's faith in themselves they are lacking."

"You sound like the Sunday school teacher that comes to the home every month. What has faith got to do with magic?"

"Well, what you call magic is really very simple. You will a thing to happen, and if you believe it enough, it happens. Take if you will miracles. Many cults and gods have been created throughout history to provide a focus for belief and thus the magic done in their name has worked. But these are not acts of some divine influence, Matt, but simply the power of collective belief. The performer of the miracle believes so intently that they are able to make possible what we would otherwise believe impossible. Whether they believe in themselves or some divine power is immaterial. It's the actual belief—the utter conviction that something can be done, that makes the act possible. That is the secret of magic—that is the power of the mind."

"So I could do this? If I believe…"

Myrthinus smiled. "There's a little more to it than that. For my people it took years of dedication, training and commitment. For you it will be harder still to actually believe that something is possible when you've spent your whole life believing it's not."

"So how—why—did we lose this ability?"

"Mankind is by nature inquisitive yet at the same time impatient. As a race you hunger for answers, always seeking to know the 'why' in everything, but seldom giving the time necessary to fully understand the question, let alone the answer. In their rush to discover information mankind has often created their own answers to these fundamental questions, and therefore fallen far short of the truth."

"I don't understand…"

"Take fire as an example. To primitive man fire was something to fear, something they could not make. They came to cherish it for it brought light to darkness, warmth to the cold, protection from beasts. When found, fire would be nurtured, kindled, and fed much like an infant. When lost it brought despair, darkness and cold. Early people had no understanding of fire. To them it came from the sky in the form of lightning. Rather than study, seek and learn its nature, this miracle from the heavens became a gift of the gods. Thus early man created their answer to the unknown. Cultures the world over revered their god of fire. Does that help?"

"A little, but last time I checked we weren't sacrificing animals to gods and goddesses. We know what fire actually is."

"Aye, that is true. You have learned, and over the centuries many of the old gods have been cast aside, no longer needed, yet still some linger on to explain those last few inexplicable mysteries science has yet to unlock."

"Maybe…"

"Well, my people were very different."

"So what happened to them? If they were so powerful, where are they now?"

The old man's face became grave and an age-old pain was reflected in his eyes.

"Our world was destroyed."

"Your world?"

"Aye. We were not of your—"

Myrthinus suddenly cocked his head to one side as if listening. Mia ceased her steady rhythmic gnawing on her bone and sprang to her feet facing the kitchen door. She growled menacingly.

"They come! We must flee!"

Matt stood up, a look of total bewilderment on his face as Myrthinus grabbed the heavy chair and wedged it against the kitchen door. A sudden crash came from the living room and the front door burst open revealing a tall figure wielding a sword.

"Matt, run!"

Myrthinus grabbed the sword off the table and pointed across the room, "The window—go!" As he spoke he raised his hand and the window exploded.

A series of solid thumps shook the kitchen door and the little window shattered. Myrthinus was shouting, his voice deep and powerful and his eyes ablaze with energy. A strange gray mist appeared beyond the gaping hole where the window had been, and taking a deep breath Matt sprinted across the room and leaped head first. He felt his jeans snag on something, then there was a sudden feeling of breathlessness and he crashed headlong into a thick tangle of wet undergrowth and brambles.

The temperature change and sudden wetness of the rain caused him to gasp in surprise. A mass of tangled undergrowth and trees lay before him, glistening from the steady rain that fell from gray and murky skies above.

Where was the cottage?

Matt spun around. All about him the forest stretched on—just the same expanse of pines, and leafless trees, miserable in their nakedness. There was no clearing, no cottage, no Myrthinus and no Mia. Fear clutched at Matt once more and he took a hesitant step forward.

His foot struck something hard and he crouched down, parting the ferns to reveal ancient and weathered stones. Thick green moss covered them, and he realized with sudden dread that all across the forest floor was a jumble of stones where hundreds of years ago a cottage had once stood.

There was a sudden crackle in the air, a burst of heat and a brilliant flash of light. Matt's bag tumbled from the air and the long shoulder straps snagged on a tree. The branch jerked from the sudden weight and Matt was showered with rain drops.

He stood for several minutes afraid to move, hoping that somehow the clearing would reappear, or Mia would suddenly burst into view, but the forest remained wet and silent.

Too many strange things were happening and fear threatened to crush the boy as he realized he was lost in the middle of the woods, with nothing but the food in his bag. He turned slowly, seeking a path or a trail to follow, and finding none he chose a direction where the trees at least seemed less dense.

After an hour of wandering aimlessly he finally forced his way, miserable and soaking wet, through a dense patch of fern and bracken to a small dirt trail that wound past a stand of berry-laden holly trees.

He stood for a while contemplating which direction to take next but his mind kept returning to the events at the cottage. Had Mia survived the attack? Was she now lost and alone like him, but hundreds of years in the past? Feeling overwhelmed, he sat on the edge of a crumbling tree stump and tried to think rationally about his situation.

He picked at a piece of bark, flicking the fragments into the ferns as he wrestled with his darkest fear. What if Myrthinus was the bad guy in all of this, trying to stop him from getting to his father? It was totally possible that the men who had burst into the cottage had been sent by his father to rescue him. Matt wrestled with his thoughts and fought to stop the rising sense of frustration. The more he thought about the situation the more he realized there was only one thing he could do, only one place left for him to go. Both Myrthinus and the mysterious Cùra dubh knew they could find him at Inverdeer House. He just hoped he would know who to trust if and when the time came. He stood up and brushed wet moss and pieces of bark from his jeans, then reluctantly followed the path downhill.

As he walked, the pines that had surrounded him began to thin out, giving way to birch, alder, and the occasional broad-limbed oak. The fine misty rain eased into a steady drizzle and the dark gray sky threatened worse to follow. To each side of the trail rocks and roots nestled in a spongy blanket of vibrant green moss, cut through here and there with rills and streams that gurgled and bubbled alongside the path.

Matt picked up the pace as a breeze caused the trees to sway and creak, but then he stopped. A sudden snapping sound had come from his left. Something black passed behind a tree, pushing through the undergrowth, and Matt took a hesitant step back. Another cracking came this time from his right. Visions of dark assassins with fearsome swords filled his mind and in blind panic he left the trail and plunged into the trees.

The springy moss made his footing treacherous and twice he almost fell. Jumping from rock to rock, he made his way uphill to dryer, firmer ground and reached a dense tangle of ferns. Matt started to run, crashing through the undergrowth. Wet branches slapped painfully across his cheeks and his jeans were soon soaked from the rain-drenched ferns. Brambles snagged at him, slowing his escape. His foot rolled then slipped on the uneven surface and with a frustrated cry he lost his footing and fell. Pine needles and wet leaves stuck to his clothing as he rolled and tumbled back down the slope. He heard a shout from behind and scrambled once more to his feet, bramble-thorns plucking painfully at his hands. He glanced over his shoulder and turned to run, letting out a muffled cry as he crashed headlong into a black-clothed figure. He tried to struggle and lash out but his captor held him close.

"Hey, steady on lad, you're safe, it's the police."

Matt looked up into the face of the man who held him.

"C'mon, sonny, quit your struggles. Your name Matt by any chance?"

Matt had little choice but to nod. Tears prickled at the corners of his eyes as the officer pulled out a radio and announced, "Control, this is PC241—I've found the boy." The police officer grinned at Matt. "He's alive and fighting fit." Matt sniffed but could not hold back the tears. He cursed himself for crying, trying to blink the tears away. Although it had been his intention to return to the home, being taken there by the police would make his humiliation unbearable.

They would watch him now. Not let him out of their sight and the other kids would pick on him all the more. His thoughts turned to Mia and his anguish gave way to despair.

He could not stop the tears, and walked on beside the policeman who had caught him, wishing he could die.

Chapter 3
Keeper of Excalibur

Passage from the Book of Myrthinus
- Beginnings

*H*ome. After so many lifetimes on this world one would expect me to see it as such yet on evenings like these, when I allow my mind to wander, I see my lost world so clearly and the yearning to return can be overpowering. I feel then some empathy with Dardanos, but it is short-lived. Unchecked, his insanity would have doomed Earth and all that dwell here to the same terrible fate that destroyed our home.

Nothing good comes from dwelling on sad and bitter thoughts, yet as our numbers dwindle, I live in growing fear of finding myself unable to recall the simplest detail of my former home. It was a thriving planet before the impact. Oceans, rivers and lakes teemed with fish. Snowcapped peaks towered above the plains, and giant birds akin to eagles soared for miles across the ranges. Leagues of forest gave home to a myriad of creatures, and insects buzzed across meadows lush with herbs and flowers of vibrant color. It was a beautiful world, and we lived in complete harmony with it. No heavy industry choked the air with fumes. Our land was not plundered for its resources. One could not imagine a more wondrous place, but surpassing all was the might and majesty of those creatures that shared our home. Dragons! Oh how my heart would soar with the sight of them! Brilliant Red and mighty Gold they would shine in the morning sun, yet in the evening their scales would reflect the muted light of our twin moons in hues of purple, amber and silver.

Dragons! I could fill page after page with tales and descriptions of these strange and powerful beings, but I digress, for that is not my purpose here. Perhaps if time allows then that tale can be told with the detail and richness it deserves, but this history serves a more desperate need. These pages are to explain the course I've charted through Earth's turbulent past, and to serve as a warning to those who will follow me should I fail, for I am old now. Old beyond measure, and the weight of the centuries, and the burdens I've carried lay heavy upon me, yet while the threat of Dardanos's legacy remains, I must strive to stand against it and recruit others to the cause.

So——Dardanos? Who is he, you may wonder? Well, once I counted him closer than any brother.

It was he who had first alerted the elders to the new star that had appeared in our sky. We were an inward-looking people and the path of the stars and planets, while well known, held little interest to us. His discovery was met with little more than mild amusement.

As the years passed, so this "star" grew in brightness, then gradually size. Then, for the first time, our society began to know fear. People talked of an impact that would destroy us all, and the elders became divided. Could we perhaps change the path of this thing we now understood to be a comet? Did we perhaps have nothing to fear and this visitor from the depths of space would pass us by? Or should we, as some demanded, seek a means to flee our doomed world? The latter suggestion was met with complete derision but time would not wait, and the comet grew larger as each month passed, seeming to hang threateningly over us each night, a constant reminder of our impending fate.

Dardanos and I, in secret, fashioned lenses to study in more detail our new star and our neighboring planets, and in Earth we found a possible escape, but how could it be reached? How does one travel such vast and empty distances? The comet was now visible in the daylight sky, and chaos gripped our people. Society inevitably succumbed to the basest human level, and our ordered culture began to tear itself apart. People blamed the elders, violence erupted in the streets; it was a time of darkness and decay.

The art of translocation was well practiced, but never had any of us attempted to move across the void of space. Could it be done? Ancient legends of our people spoke of the founders of our race traveling between worlds at will, but this had become a thing of myth. In desperation, we turned to anything that offered hope for our salvation. Dardanos and I pored over the old texts and crumbling tablets seeking a way to achieve what even to us seemed impossible.

To travel to earth we needed a location that could be visualized. Some would call it a pattern. If we could fashion that location on earth then we could travel between worlds at will. We first determined the spin and rotation of the earth in relation to our planet and the stars. We then looked for a reference point in space common to both worlds, and we chose the constellation Orion. During the spring season the three stars of the belt were bright and easy to spot, and we used these as alignment guides. Our telescopes, while crude, had shown us little more than a blue and white ball. But we worked hard perfecting the art of lens and mirror making, and as the months passed so our view of Earth improved dramatically until before us appeared a world of clouds, of oceans and land.

We made many assumptions. We assumed the oceans of earth would be akin to those of our home, and therefore targeted an area of coastline much like our own, a giant delta where a large river emptied into the sea.

Justin Orton

To will ourselves such a large distance would not be possible. No individual would be strong enough, so we built a gate that would open a channel between both worlds. Many great minds bent their wills to holding the gateway open, which was a considerable feat given we had no known target upon which to anchor the other end.

Many brave people died making the first attempts to cross the void of space and we had no way of knowing what had killed them. Had they arrived in a poisonous inhospitable atmosphere and choked to death? Was our portal misaligned and we had sent people to drown in the seas? Had we failed to create a bridge at all and sent our travelers not to Earth but blinking into nothingness, lost in the endless void of space?

There were so many failed attempts, but it took only one success to establish a bridge. It was slow and dangerous, but one at a time we made the journey. The energy expended to hold the portal open, even for a few minutes, was immense. If we were to save our people we had to find another way.

Earth was lush with vegetation and wildlife, and the different life forms we encountered were a constant surprise to us, but not all life was different! Who would have thought that two worlds harboring such diverse plant and animal life would have also produced creatures that were the same? Crocodiles we had never seen and they filled us with terror, but the hippos were identical to the kuowli of our home—river cows, we called them.

We spent many weeks traveling upstream along the river now known as the Nile, and here we encountered our first humankind. Primitive people yet proud. They looked on us with fear and called us gods, the shining ones, those who bridged the stars, and they gathered in awe as we began construction of the pattern that would act as an anchor between our worlds.

Our alien structures took shape over the coming months, reaching up in perfect alignment to Orion's belt, with the Nile a mirror of the Milky Way. When complete they were a poor comparison to the structures of home, but *given we spent less than a year in their construction, the three great pyramids would serve as a recognizable pattern to begin a mass translocation from our home—the planet Mars...*

Eilean Tioram, Scotland
597AD

The painting hung in the darkest recess of Aldivon's chamber. The details were lost in gloom but Aldivon knew each brush stroke intimately. Atop a grassy mound, rendered in a green so dark it was almost black, stood a man dressed in leather kilt and chain mail vest. His scarlet cloak was a vivid splash of color amid the somber tones of earth and sky. Long brown hair held back by a silver circlet revealed a face that was proud and strong. Arrayed about him, on a level slightly lower, stood twelve men similarly clad, each with sword raised in salute.

The painting was a beautiful work of art. A depiction of Arturius, as he was known then. Dux Bellorum—War Leader of the North—the man future history would come to know as the legendary Arthur of Camelot. It had hung in Arthur's keep until the battle of Camlann saw his fall and now it hung here in the bedchamber of Aldivon.

"Did you really know him?" a woman's voice asked. She lay upon the bed amid a tangle of woolen blankets and animal furs.

Aldivon looked to the woman and nodded. His steel blue eyes, set deep beneath a prominent brow, seemed fixed on a place she could not see. He blinked. Long, almost feminine lashes lent a false sense of innocence to his otherwise rugged and beardless countenance.

"I'm sure he was not half the man you are, my lord." The woman propped herself up on one elbow and pulled a blanket to her throat, more to ward off the constant chill of the castle than to hide her nakedness. Auburn hair fell across her face and she brushed it away, watching Aldivon as he dressed. He was an imposing figure, powerfully built, and he stood a little over six feet tall. Coal-black hair, shot with silver at the temples, fell just below broad and muscled shoulders.

"Arturius was a fool." Aldivon's voice was coarse and seemed to rattle somehow within his throat. He pulled a heavy fur cloak off the bed, exposing a pair of long shapely legs and the woman squealed playfully, drawing her legs up and clasping her hands about her knees. "My lord! Again?"

"Nay lass. 'Tis time you left."

He furled the cloak about his bare shoulders and lit a taper from a nearby candle. A wisp of black smoke and the sudden tang of sulfur followed him as he returned to the painting to light a nearby candle.

The soft patter of bare feet on the stone floor followed him, and he felt the woman press against his back. "My lord. Did I fail to please thee?" Her voice was a cajoling purr, and Aldivon turned in the circle of her slender arms. She looked up at his face and her pulse quickened as he pulled her to him and wrapped the cloak about them both. She, like many before her, was mesmerized by the commanding presence of the man. While no longer the handsome soldier of his youth he carried about him an intoxicating air that instilled an exciting blend of fear and desire. She trembled in his arms, and not just from the chill. His once-proud nose was bent to one side, his top lip pulled tight by a hard white scar; but the most prominent feature was a thick ridge of scar tissue that crossed his throat from one side to the other. She ran a delicate fingertip across it. "Should I return tonight sir?" Her voice was all but a whisper in his ear.

"If it please you, aye." He released the woman from the cloak and pushed her toward the crumpled pile of linen that lay beside the bed. "But now I am expecting someone."

He paused to admire the dimpled buttocks as she bent to retrieve the discarded dress, then returned his attention to the painting.

A golden glow from the freshly lit candle filled the recess and the shadowed face of Arturius suddenly came alive in the warmth of the light. His features had been captured in loving detail by the artist, but Aldivon's attention was not on the painting but the thirteen iron nails driven into the darkwood frame. There was one for each of the figures in the picture. Medallions hung from eleven of them, pewter dragons crouched atop an orb of blood red stone. He placed a fingertip on each of the empty nails and frowned. "Where are you two hiding?" he whispered. "Where—"

The sudden clatter of hoofbeats and raised voices echoed from outside and Aldivon took two quick strides to the narrow window of his bedchamber. A dappled horse flecked with mud and foam entered the cobbled courtyard. The rider slid from his mount and shouted to a nearby stable hand who rushed to take the weary animal. Aldivon moved quickly to the bed and pulled on a crumpled linen shirt followed by his customary black doublet. The candles in the room danced excitedly in the sudden draft as the woman opened the door and paused to look back at him. Her thick hair was now bunched up high on her head and the plain homespun gray dress completely hid what Aldivon had to admit was a most pleasing body. He buckled on his sword belt, then pulled two silver coins from a leather pouch at his waist and tossed them one after the other to the woman. She caught the coins and her eyes sparkled with delight. "Two!"

"Aye, lass." Aldivon growled. "Ye ken return tonight to earn the second."

Bowing her thanks, the woman left the room, returning to the lower levels of the keep and the kitchens in which she worked.

With the woman gone the room seemed lacking somehow, and a sudden emptiness fell over Aldivon. With a gentle reverence he drew his sword.

"Excalibur." His voice was a whisper as he traced his fingers along the highly polished steel. Not a mark—not a notch or nick marred its perfect edge. He let the cold blade rest against his forehead and closed his eyes. Sometimes when he stood like this he could almost see the history of the weapon unfold in his mind, or hear voices whispering like ghosts in his thoughts, but this time there was nothing. He sighed and angled the sword before him watching the light dance along its glittering length until he saw his own reflection. As always his eyes were drawn to the hated scar across his neck.

Anger welled inside and in a swift motion he sheathed the sword. For a moment he felt again the tugging of the blade that had swung in desperation at his head, the point catching his skin, biting into his vocal chords and forever leaving him disfigured with a voice that rattled deep in his throat, more a growl than voice.

He faced the door as hurried footsteps rang in the passage outside.

"Enter!"

"My lord."

The man who entered was as travel-stained as his horse had been but he still managed a formal, albeit stiff, bow.

"Deren." Aldivon acknowledged, "What news?"

"We almost had him, my lord."

Aldivon's face showed his disdain. "Not of him. He's her concern. What of it? Did you find it?" He grabbed a wooden goblet from a nearby table and took a mouthful of the mulled wine as he waited for the man to answer.

"Well?"

Deren lowered his eyes and took a hesitant step back. "No, we did not. We searched the entire cottage but found nothing. Not a trace."

"Damn that meddling fool!" Aldivon hurled the goblet into the nearby fire and flames flared for an instant, the pungent aroma of spiced wine filling the room.

"My lord, there was a boy with him."

Aldivon spun about, eyebrows raised. "A boy?"

"Aye. A boy, eighteen I would guess, maybe a little older. The wizard helped him escape. I lost two good men before the wizard himself fled."

Deren paused as if weighing his next words carefully. "Before he fled, the old man threw something to the boy." He licked his lips nervously, "It may have been that which you seek."

Aldivon stood before the slit that served as a window and gazed across the castle battlements to the windswept moor beyond. The weak light of evening was fading fast, the color seeming to leach out of the landscape beyond the castle walls. Tall grass rippled in the wind, and the last smudges of snow could be seen lurking in the shadows and dips of the distant mountains. The tangy salt taste of the sea blended with the reek of manure as a young lad below struggled with a heavy barrow of muck from the nearby stables. Deren waited patiently, careful not to fuel his commander's anger.

"You believe this boy to be from the other side?"

There were very few who knew of the existence of the other world, the place they called the other side, but Deren was one of them. Both Deren and his brother had been sent through a portal on more than one occasion, and Deren's brother served there still.

"I believe so, my lord. The boy was...strangely clothed?"

Aldivon's mind raced. Had the boy been Matthew? If so, why had the wizard chosen now to make a move on him? Aldivon was unable to mask the concern in his voice and he gestured to the door, "Very well, Deren. You may go."

Deren mumbled his thanks and moved to exit the room, then paused and looked back at Aldivon.

"What is it?"

"If this boy is the one you suspect, then what of my brother?"

"Your brother was under strict instructions to avoid confrontation. He was to have informed me if and when the wizard made a move on the boy."

"And yet you've heard nothing?"

"Nothing."

Deren paused, "Perhaps this boy is not the one then?"

"I think that somewhat unlikely. I must consult with the queen. Go eat and rest; I will send tidings of your brother when I have them."

Deren bowed, leaving his commander in quiet contemplation.

Aldivon glanced once more at the picture and the hanging medallions, his focus drawn to the two empty nails at the top of the frame. It was time to consult with the queen.

Aldivon paused before the door to the queen's chambers; a soldier barred his way, a heavy spear held across his chest.

"Stand aside!" Aldivon ordered.

The man maintained his position, "Her Majesty requested she not be disturbed."

"And I requested you stand aside!" Aldivon spoke quietly but his voice was edged with steel.

The guard eyed Aldivon nervously and noted the strong fingers tighten on the hilt of the ever-present sword.

"As you command, my lord," and fumbling nervously he slowly opened the door. Aldivon brushed him to one side and strode into the room, swinging the door closed behind him.

Most of the room was lost in darkness. The only light came from a pair of red wax candles that stood upon a heavy oak dresser, and a brazier of burning coals that sat in the center of the room. The candles illuminated a section of rich tapestry that hung upon the wall, and the dancing flames made the dimly lit scene of hounds and horses seem to move with a life of their own. A heavy scent filled the air, sweet yet musky, and it caught at the back of his throat causing him to cough weakly. He'd always hated the cloying fumes from the powders and herbs she burned.

Aldivon stopped and allowed his eyes to adjust to the gloom. From the shadows a woman stepped forward, her jet-black hair almost lost in the darkness. The candles cast a subtle luster on her otherwise pale skin, belying its natural whiteness.

She raised a well-manicured hand and pointed around the room. Candles set on tables, recessed in wall niches or suspended on ornate iron brackets suddenly flared into life, bathing the room in a brighter, warmer light.

Aldivon watched her step toward him. She was beautiful, moving with a poise and grace that was elegant yet somehow seductive. The rich velvet gown hugged her figure without being tight, and the deep midnight blue material accented the almost violet of her eyes. Thin, yet strangely sensuous lips parted in a subtle smile.

"Lord Aldivon, such a surprise."

The voice was soft and warm, the accent lilting.

He looked around the room, his eyes resting on a heavy oak table beneath the tapestry-covered window. Two crystal pyramids floated above it, one inverted below the other to create a diamond. Within them a blue-white fire slowly faded.

"We didn't get it." He ignored any formality of address. His relationship with the queen stretched back many years, before the death of her first husband and the coming of the Great One. He looked at her, his eyes lingering on the low-cut dress and the swell of her breasts before lifting to meet hers.

"Yes. I am aware of that." She stepped to a side table and took a wine skin from its stand. She poured the rich dark wine and raised a goblet in his direction. "Wine?" she offered.

He nodded and joined her at the table. Taking the proffered goblet he breathed the rich, subtly spiced aroma of the wine, then glanced through an archway to an adjacent chamber and suddenly caught his breath.

"Guenevere?" He entered the chamber and looked down at the frail form of the woman who lay on a divan. Her skin was a sickly white, the pallor of death, and if not for the slow rise and fall of her breast he would have believed her dead. Long blond hair framed a face that was gaunt and drawn, the flesh sunken around the bone structure of her cheeks and eyes.

She wore a short linen shift that had ridden up above the knee and his eyes traced the once shapely calves, now pitifully reduced to skin and bone, to the cruel scars at her ankles; the unmistakable marks of manacles. He looked again to the woman's face, but his eyes were drawn instead to her shoulder and the puckered scar of a whip lash that marred the otherwise perfect skin.

"You told me she was dead!" Aldivon spun and confronted the queen. "You told me she died months ago!"

He fixed the queen with a malevolent stare, and then looked back at the broken woman on the divan. "What by all the gods have you done to her?"

The queen's eyes suddenly flashed anger and she pressed a single finger firmly against his cheek, the long black-painted nail puckering the soft skin beneath his eye.

"Remember your place, Aldivon. I am your queen. I may allow certain leniencies due to former pleasures..." She leaned forward and brushed his dry lips with hers. "...but I will *not* have my actions questioned by you!" She held his gaze and twisted her finger cruelly, raking the nail along his cheek and drawing a bloody scratch from the corner of his eye to the edge of his mouth, "Do you understand?"

Anger flared in his eyes for a moment but quickly faded. He touched a finger to the scratch and looked at the beads of blood on his fingertip.

"I get the *point,* Your Majesty." He drained his goblet and turned once more to look at the woman on the divan.

"Where is the girl?"

"Naveena? She is on an errand and should return in due course. But come now, Aldivon—I'm sure you had some reason for disturbing me other than your pathetic infatuation with Naveena."

"Aye." Aldivon looked back at the queen. "Although naturally I wished to convey my respects to your *daughter.*"

He emphasized the last word and smiled at the reaction.

The queen's violet eyes flashed dangerously. "Step-daughter, Aldivon. Nothing more, and well you know it!"

He smiled mockingly. "Forgive me, my lady, but she is of such exquisite perfection it is easy to forget she is not from your own flesh and blood!" His expression remained serious but he relished the momentary look of pain in her eyes.

"Do not mock me!" she warned.

He again fingered the fresh cut to his cheek. "Mock you, my Queen?" he bowed, hiding his eyes. "I am ever your trusted servant."

"You serve no one but yourself!" she retorted. "Now enough of this—what did you come to say?"

He walked to the wine skin and refilled his goblet before moving to a nearby chair. The queen indicated he could sit.

"A messenger returned." His raspy voice became serious. "We were this close..." He leaned forward extending a hand with thumb and forefinger almost touching. "...to catching the old man." He paused, eying the queen carefully. "There was another with him but he fled."

"Through a portal, I believe."

Aldivon failed to mask his surprise. *How much did she know?* Had a report already been made or had she seen this through those damn crystals she prized so much?

"That has not been confirmed. No trace or trail was found when the area was searched. A gray mist was seen near the building so a portal may have been used. We do know the wizard sent something after him. It may be that which we seek."

"This other..." The queen's icy stare sent chills through Aldivon's heart. "...was not by chance a boy?"

Fear gripped him. She could not know of the boy. If she did, then the boy's life was in grave danger. He opened his mouth to reply, but had already been too slow in responding. He cringed under the weight of her questioning gaze.

"Yes it was a boy." Aldivon tried to pull her attention back to the item for which they had been searching. "Your Majesty—time grows short. If you are to open the gateway this year you must recover the rod of Dardanos soon."

The queen took several sauntering steps to where the crystal pyramids still hovered. She reached out a shapely hand and plucked them from the air. They sparkled like diamonds, yet had the clarity of highly polished glass. The blue-white light that had burned within had gone now, and she turned one of them in her hand, caressing it. A hole about an inch across was bored into the base. "Time does indeed grow short. But I am patient." She laughed, the sound almost girlish, and she ran a finger around the hole in the pyramid's base. "After all, have I not given us an eternity in which to wait?"

She returned the pyramids to the table and faced Aldivon. He saw her expression harden and her eyes burn with a sudden intensity. Through bloodless lips she said, "I have recently learned you have an interest in this boy, Lord Aldivon. You have had him under your eye for years, yet you have chosen to say nothing to me." Her voice dripped venom and Aldivon's mind raced for an answer as she leaned close to him and whispered, "What say you?"

"I felt it safer to keep him from you. Your lust for revenge would see him dead, and he may be useful to us. I did what I felt was right." Aldivon lowered his head in mock supplication, hoping to mask his eyes lest she see the lie. "May I ask how you discovered this?"

The queen threw a gaze over her shoulder at the recumbent figure of Guenevere. "She proved most useful."

She fixed Aldivon with the look a mother gives a scolded child. "You were wrong to hide her identity from me."

Aldivon said nothing but raised his head and somehow held her gaze.

The opening door distracted them both and together they turned to see a lovely young woman no older than nineteen enter the room. She curtsied to the queen but threw a reproachful look at Aldivon. She was slender and of average height, with thick red hair that spilled in loose waves across the soft white wool shawl hung from the shoulders of her dress. Her black-laced bodice was tight-fitting and the rich green fabric accented her curves and complemented the emerald eyes that sparkled in the candlelight.

Aldivon smiled and rose toward her. "Naveena. A joy to see you again."

She took a step back. "My lord."

The queen positioned herself between them and pointed through to the adjacent chamber. "Take Guenevere to her room and summon the apothecary. We have no further use for her now."

"Mother, NO!"

The queen's hand was a blur and the slap to the cheek caused the girl to stagger back. "Naveena, do not challenge me! I care not if she dies from poison or the headsman's block! She is the former consort to our enemy and must die. Now remove her from this room at once!"

"But—"

"Now, Naveena!"

The girl paused, biting back a response, then raised her skirts and ran to the adjoining room.

Aldivon watched her leave, his eyes following the dainty feet, swaying hips, and bouncing hair, until she pulled a heavy curtain from its bracket on the wall and shut herself from his gaze. His ragged voice betrayed his desire. "She grows more beautiful each time I see her."

"Aldivon!" The queen's voice cracked like a whip. "I may pander to your twisted desires and turn a blind eye to your darker perversions but you will cease this infatuation with Naveena." Her voice softened to a conspiratorial whisper. "I may resent the fact she's the offspring of my lord's mistress, I may even despise the little bitch for resembling her mother so closely, but I have worked hard these past seventeen years to train her and make her into something useful. I will not allow you to destroy that!"

Aldivon shrugged, cast one more look at the closed curtain, then returned to his chair.

"You were telling me how you found the boy."

The queen took a seat on a thickly padded bench before the window and indicated the curtained alcove.

"You knew who she was all those years, didn't you?"

"What of it? She served you well."

"What of it? 'Tis bad enough Naveena is not of my body—worse yet to know she was nursed and tended by Arthur's whore! But you knew of this! You knew and said nothing!"

"She was actually my trophy, as I recall," Aldivon said. "You took her as your servant when you sent me campaigning. Who am I to deny my queen?"

Anger flared in the queen's eyes but she held her temper. "Six months ago I found her weeping, but she would not divulge the source of her grief. I probed her mind, something I should have done years before, and I learned she had given birth to a child seventeen years past. A child you failed to take from her even though you knew how I hungered for his death!"

Aldivon's hands clenched at his sides, the knuckles whitening.

"How can you be sure the child my men saw and the one of which you speak are the same? You speak of events years past—the boy could have been anyone!"

"Don't toy with me, Aldivon. Your servant watches him daily. I would know the reason for your interest in Arthur's brat! His very existence is a threat I cannot ignore."

Aldivon gasped and the queen smiled. "Aye! I have spoken with your puppet Deglin. He serves me now and has shared everything. You were right about my lust for revenge. The boy must die and to that end he was to be brought here two evenings past. I wonder now if your men were intentionally lax?"

"I had the boy watched, yes. But I had nothing, nothing, to do with his capture or his escape!" Aldivon stood quickly and wine slopped from the goblet, trickling across his fingers like blood. "Frankly, I resent the accusation!"

"Sit down!" The queen's face flushed with anger. She paced for a moment and Aldivon dropped heavily into the chair and watched her, only too aware of the danger he was in. She stopped her pacing and faced him once more. "So you believe this boy has the rod of Dardanos?"

Aldivon carefully deposited the goblet on a nearby table and wiped his fingers on his doublet.

"It is possible, aye."

"Then find him. If it transpires you are correct then I will owe you my thanks. If not then no matter, for he will tell all before he dies."

"I will find him, Your Majesty. I will not fail."

She looked across at him lips pursed in a bitter smile. "It will be well for you that you do not."

Aldivon nodded, and without waiting for her permission he rose and strode from the chamber.

Chapter 4
The Book of Myrthinus

Passage from the Book of Myrthinus
- *Destruction and Rebirth*

It was the first day of winter when the comet struck. In the blink of an eye everything we knew, loved and cherished was gone. Our observations showed the comet actually missed Mars but as it passed through the gravitational influence of the planet it was quite literally torn apart. Two of the largest chunks continued on through space, bound together by their own gravity, but millions of tons of ore-laden rock, frozen water and gas showered down upon our home in a cataclysmic rain that destroyed everything.

For days a sustained bombardment of smaller fragments caused death and destruction. Those that impacted the oceans sent tidal waves racing ashore, sweeping man, beast, plant and tree before it. Then the main impacts occurred. Huge rocks, some miles across, slammed into the planet and the impact literally blew off part of the planet's crust. The atmosphere was torn apart and the very air sucked into space. In an instant our planet died. Water boiled and evaporated, plant life was vaporized, dust filled the sky and the sun's warmth was blocked. What little plant life may have survived quickly froze in the rapidly dropping temperatures. Starved of light, even those plants and microorganisms that could have endured such extremes died.

Earthquakes shook the planet for months, until eventually the shock waves subsided. When the dust settled a new Mars was revealed. Nothing remained but a dead and lifeless ball of red rock, frozen gas and swirling dust.

Fewer than two thousand people made the exodus to Earth before the impact.

Dazed and grief stricken, nearly six hundred more of us were claimed in the following months. We were so weak in the stronger gravity of Earth that any exertion tired us rapidly. To make matters worse, our bodies were assaulted by an abundance of viral infections and diseases that we had never encountered and knew not how to treat.

Many of our strongest, most powerful people had perished, preferring to put their trust and faith in the ruling elders and take shelter in the mountains and valleys of Mars. Some of us talked of going back, a few even tried. We never saw them again.

As the years passed, a small town grew around our pyramids. We took a greater interest in the stars and began recording the motions of the planets, comets and moons. As our first decade of life on Earth came to a close we were greeted with the most incredible sight; on the horizon, bright against the velvet black sky, was a lion—our nation's emblem. The lions of Mars were similar to those of Earth, perhaps slightly smaller, but no less majestic. We had not seen such a beast since arriving on Earth, but the constellation Leo rising from the horizon was like a sign to us, a symbol of rebirth.

Justin Orton

In honor of our former world we constructed a huge lion of stone. We set it into the ground mimicking the lion of the sky. Painted red like the lions of Mars, it looked magnificent staring at its celestial twin that rose from the horizon into the night sky.

By this time many of us had become settled in our new home. Children had been born and we had become stronger and more adapted to life on Earth. We attempted to educate the primitive people of the area and they proved willing students, yet despite our best efforts they persisted in referring to us as gods.

Almost fifty years we tarried in that place. Building, studying the stars, and learning the ways of the earth. It was in the autumn, the month of November to be precise, that fear once again came upon us from the skies. For two nights the sky was streaked with meteors. Shooting stars blazed across the sky in number too great to count and our senior star watchers discovered a chilling fact. The remains of the comet that had destroyed Mars had returned, and Earth was passing through its tail. Somewhere hiding in that mass of space debris lurked another planet-killer. Twin lumps of rock, iron and ice that swept by the earth never posing a real threat but reminding us of the terror that can strike unbidden from the sky.

Dardanos and I felt our work there was done. We had saved as many of our people as we could. We had built a great city, and our people were finally starting to mix with the local population of early humans. We wanted to explore more of this world and expand our knowledge, and so new leaders were elected, and Dardanos and I began our great voyage of discovery.

About three hundred of us left, taking ships along the Nile out into what is now the Mediterranean Sea. Ever we drew charts and maps recording our progress along strange and alien shorelines. We sent our drawings and the detailed chronicles of our discoveries back to Giza for careful duplication. Each document was cataloged and stored in vaults buried deep beneath the lion statue.

The people we encountered on our journey were diverse. Each a separate culture with its own beliefs and traditions. Some ran in terror from us, others met us with open hostility, but many welcomed us, providing food, information and interesting insights into their lives. Our skills grew over the years and we roamed further afield, until almost five years after our departure we encountered an island of people advanced far beyond any we had yet seen.

We had planned to stay at this intriguing place for only a month, maybe two, but the autumn passed into winter and before we knew it the spring of the New Year was passing into summer.

About half of our people left then, but Dardanos and I stayed. For us this island utopia had become our new home. As the years passed we all grew in knowledge and power until this glorious, shining city of Atlantis rivaled the greatest cities of Mars.

Inverdeer House: Inverdeer, Scotland
Friday - Present Day

Matt tossed and turned in his sleep.

One after another strange scenes whirled before his eyes—scenes he somehow knew were not the fanciful images of dreams but the tortured replaying of stolen memories, returning to him like badly edited trailers from unrelated movies.

A woman's face came first, framed with long golden hair, her pale blue eyes filled with warmth and love. She whispered Matt's name and his heart overflowed with joy at the soft lilting sound of her voice. She seemed to hover before him yet he could not reach her. Each time he tried she faded further away and then she was gone.

Terror gripped him with the next vision. A blazing hall appeared and he could feel the choking heat of the fire. Smoke swirled around the room. Bodies lay scattered amid burning beams and bloodstained weapons. Smoldering tapestries peeled from the walls to fall as blackened shrouds to the dead, sending clouds of sparks and glowing embers spiraling into the air. Matt's head was filled with the harsh cries of men, the screams of women and the roaring crackle of angry flames.

There was a sudden surge and he was being carried. Held roughly he passed along a dark passage. Behind him the blonde woman ran, her face filthy with soot and her golden hair prematurely gray with ash. He heard voices. The man and the woman were speaking, but Matt could not understand the words. The scene began to spin and Matt felt himself choking, struggling to breathe as smoke enveloped them. Figures appeared before him, and helpful hands reached out from the shadows. From behind came more men, their blades red with blood, their faces painted in garish colors. The man who had carried him turned and charged into the advancing horde. There was the sound of ringing steel, fierce cries and agonized yells, and then the man was gone, swallowed by the smoke. Grief threatened to overwhelm Matt, and he felt the hot sting of tears but knew not for whom he cried.

Next came darkness. Pure darkness, and Matt felt himself falling. He tried to force himself awake, aware this was only a dream but he could not. His breathing came in ragged gasps and then he was in a dimly lit hall where two men fought. There was no detail; all facial features were lost in shadow. For what seemed an eternity they dueled, swords flickering in the firelight, but no matter how they twisted and turned the two men stayed in shadow, nothing visible but their dancing blades. Faster the swords moved, the dull ring of steel on steel becoming an almost constant sound punctuated only by the panting and gasping of the dueling adversaries and the measured beat of their boots across the stone floor. The swords were a blur now and Matt felt his pulse increase, the blood roaring in his ears. Droplets of sweat flew from the men amid the showers of sparks as blade slid across blade. Then one shimmering sword swept beneath the other and Matt watched in horror as the silver tip curved up toward the other's throat. Crimson droplets flew like ruby tears as the blade tore across the neck and Matt gasped awake, his stomach churning with nausea.

Matt lay there staring at the ceiling, fighting to get his breathing under control. Around him the room was quiet, the breathing of the other boys the only sound. A thin line of light shone under the door of the dormitory in which they slept, illuminating nothing more than a small patch of threadbare carpet on the floor.

Slowly Matt sat up and waited for his eyes to become accustomed to the dark. A car passed by, its lights washing the room with a dirty gray before fading along the street. A dog barked in the distance. Matt watched the shadowy form of beds and lockers come into focus as his eyes adjusted.

A bed creaked and a sleeping form rolled over, burrowing deeper into the blankets. He glanced at the clock on the wall, straining to make out the time. Another car passed and he managed to catch that it was something after four in the morning.

He lay there and gazed at the discolored white ceiling above. What did it all mean? He tossed restlessly, trying to get back to sleep, but was still puzzling over the strange memories when the dormitory door opened and the click of the light switch chased the shadows of night from the room.

Tired from lack of sleep, and the stress of the previous day, Matt wearily followed the other boys to the washroom. After waiting his turn to wash, brush his teeth and comb his hair he filed back to the dormitory and joined the other boys as they made their beds, and dressed for school. They were being careful to avoid any contact with him this morning. The usual tripping on the way to or from the washroom, the pulling apart his bed after he'd made it, the ear twisting, the name-calling— all of it was absent, but still Matt remained vigilant as he buttoned up his shirt.

"Come along, boys. You don't have all day, breakfast is waiting!"

It was Mr. Carter, and he stood holding the dormitory door open as the boys filed into the corridor making their way to the dining room for their usual breakfast of watery porridge and stale toast.

"It's good to see you back, Matt," Trevor whispered, gesturing for him to join the group and patting his shoulder as he passed.

The interior of Inverdeer House had fared little better than the outside. It was a large building comprising several upstairs bedrooms and bathrooms that had been converted into dormitories for the homeless boys and living quarters for the staff. These rooms had been modernized extensively in the 1960s, at a time when little or no consideration was given to preservation of the past. As such they had lost all traces of their original architecture. Gone were the cast-iron fireplaces, the decorative ceiling moldings and the old six-panel doors. Only the high skirting boards remained and these carried too many layers of paint, chipped and scuffed by decades of careless abuse from rambunctious teenagers.

Once down the grand staircase, however, the house retained echoes of its former grandeur. The oak-paneled hall at the foot of the stairs was largely unchanged, though sparsely furnished. A grandfather clock that no longer worked stood old and forlorn in one corner, and a worn and stained rug led to the impressively huge front door. A coat stand, missing several hooks, leaned by the door and a dusty deer's head, with cobwebs adorning the antlers, gazed blindly through the stained-glass window above the door.

To the left, a corridor led off to the dining room, passing a more ornate study that now served as an office. A modern set of plastic French doors opened to the rear lawns where the children played. Opposite the staircase, another passage led away from the hall and passed a small library and storeroom, ending at the TV room where the boys were able to watch TV, play games and relax in the evening.

The kitchen, where the cook and her helper now ladled warm, lumpy porridge into bowls for the morning meal, was a modern red-brick extension located to the rear of the dining hall.

Matt followed the parade of boys as they talked among themselves, some laughing at jokes or talking animatedly about last night's TV show. No one spoke to him. They seldom did.

Matt wondered why the other boys hated him so much. Surely in this place where all the boys shared that one commonality, the lack of a loving family, friends should have been easy to make. But for him that was certainly not the case. There was just something about him that the other boys could not relate to.

Matt certainly did not consider himself a born leader, and he avoided conflict whenever possible. Overly concerned with what others thought, he eschewed any situation that would make him the center of attention. He knew a hidden reserve of confidence and strength lurked somewhere within, but it only seemed to surface when he was thrust into situations of sheer anger or desperation. Only then could he tap into this hidden well, drawing comfort or, as had happened once before, a frightening savagery that threatened to overwhelm him.

This fear of confrontation kept him from attempting to claw his way to the top of the dormitory pecking order, and a certain self-reliance and pride prevented him from following whoever the latest leader of the dorm may be. This failure to partake in the childish pranks and the frequent bullying of the "newbies" as the young kids fresh off the streets were known, kept him alone or all too often a victim of the bullying.

He passed through the door into the dining room and took a place at the table. A cracked and chipped blue bowl was set before him, half filled with a glutinous-looking glob of gray porridge that likened itself more to wallpaper paste. Cook's assistant, a cheery, overly large woman, rolled around the table to fill stained glasses with watered-down milk before heading off to the kitchen to pile a platter with dry, half-toasted bread that smelled considerably more appetizing than it looked.

A phone rang in the study across the hall and Matron left to answer it, leaving Trevor to supervise the boys. Trevor gave a startled jump as Matron's deep voice bellowed for him to join her in the office. The large dining room door swung closed. The boys were alone.

Matt instantly became alert, his body tense as he waited for something, a verbal taunt, a twisted ear, something. A heavyset boy at the end of the table looked at Matt. It was Joel, one of the heavies of the dorm. A tough kid from Aberdeen, he had reddish blond hair that had been buzz cut as short as the Home would allow. He sported a skull-stud earring in one ear that caught the light as he faced Matt.

"Morning, Runaway," Joel sneered. Passed from institution to institution and deemed by the authorities as beyond help, Joel was approaching his first anniversary at Inverdeer. Matt felt sure the kid's next residence would be the local jail. Looking at the cruel eyes that stared at him across the table Matt thought the local cemetery would be a much better place.

Matt refused to acknowledge the greeting. To do so would have been acceptance of the name.

"Hey—shithead—I'm talking to you!"

Matt's chair rocked as Grant, the kid next to him, grabbed his shoulder and pulled him up to look across at Joel. "Joel's talking to you, Runaway."

Matt sighed. This was going to get ugly.

Cook's assistant suddenly returned to the dining room, this time wearing a coat and sporting a purse and umbrella. She seemed to lean back as she walked as if she feared her girth would pull her over. "I'll be off now, Heather!" she called to the cook, then left the dining room via the heavy fire door that led outside.

"Imagine getting a piece of that," Joel laughed. "Ever wonder if that's yer mum, Run-away?" He whooped making an obscene gesture with his fingers.

A chorus of nervous laughs emanated from the other boys and Matt felt himself flush.

"So what happened to ya last night huh? Get scared outside by yerself?"

"He probably missed his ma," said Grant, nodding after the cook's assistant.

"Hey, Runaway. You met Duracell yet?" Brick joined the conversation and indicated a new kid at the end of the table. He must have arrived at the home the night Matt had left. With a bright mop of ginger-red hair and thick black-framed national-health glasses, the boy was a prime target.

"Pith off," said the newcomer, and Matt groaned. *Shit. Poor bastard's got a lisp too. He's dead.*

"Pith?" Joel suddenly got up and bent over the kid's bowl. "Thorry athhole, how about I thpit in that shit inthtead." A loud chorus of groans rose from the table as Joel hawked deeply and gobbed a large wad of mucous into the boy's porridge.

Matt looked away, his stomach churning with revulsion.

The new kid pushed his chair back to stand, "Fu—" he began but Brick now joined Joel and together they thrust the boy back into the chair. "Eat it, shithead."

The boy looked at his bowl and gagged.

"I said eat it!" and slowly Brick thrust the boy's head closer to the bowl.

Unable to get away from Joel's viselike grip on his shoulder, the newbie instead rocked back on his chair causing it to tip over with a crash. Brick cried out as the back of the chair smashed into one of his shins. "You little bastard!" and he swept the porridge bowl off the table onto the fallen kid's chest.

The boy, his sweater plastered with porridge and worse, scrambled to his feet and ran around the table heading for the door. Grant, seated next to Matt, stuck out a foot sending the boy sprawling to the floor; his glasses slid from his face and skidded across the tile, one of the lenses shattering. He rolled to his back squinting at those seated at the table and groped for his glasses.

Matt remembered all those times he had endured such torment and worse. He felt again the sense of worthlessness, self-loathing, and weakness as boys had woken him in the night pouring water over his bed; the destruction of his homework and his biggest fear of all—kids chasing him with spiders.

Matt looked down at the younger boy and saw in his place, himself, cowering and afraid, feeding the power of the bullies by his failure to stand up to them. A sudden anger burned inside.

Clenching his teeth Matt took a deep breath and stood.

"STOP IT!"

The sudden silence was eerie, and Matt felt the fiery anger inside bubbling up, mixed with a mouth-drying fear at what would happen next. "Leave him alone!" he said. "Just leave him the hell alone."

Grant switched his attention to Matt. "And what are you gonna do about it, Runaway? You can't even do that right. Runaway!"

Like a dam exploding from too much pressure, the pent up anger burst free. Matt could no longer take the beating, the name-calling, the frustration. A white fire raced in his veins and his anger burst through.

His fist caught Grant on the chin and sent him reeling back off his chair, falling over another boy who was still sitting at the table attempting to ignore all the commotion and eat his porridge. Brick and Joel looked at each other in stunned silence, then raced around the table, fire in their eyes. Matt spun to face them and sent a shocked Joel flying into the table, plates of toast and glasses of milk smashing to the floor. Time slowed for Matt and he felt more in control than ever before. His vision seemed twice as clear, his senses sharper and his reactions faster.

With a slight movement of his hips he swiveled to the left and side-stepped Brick's outflung fist. Blocking another blow with his left arm Matt struck hard with his right, straight into the chest of his attacker. By now Joel had regained his feet, and he caught and steadied the staggering Brick.

"You're gonna fuckin' die for that, Matt," Joel snarled, but Matt grinned, feeling a crazy sense of victory at the use of his real name.

Both Brick and Joel advanced on Matt, fully expecting him to turn and run, but like a knight of old Matt strode toward them. He reached Joel first and sent him sprawling to the ground again with a well-placed blow to the nose. All the other boys stood now, eyes wide in awe as the tall, well-muscled Brick and the smaller Matt faced off.

A look of doubt flickered in Brick's eyes, but fear of losing face in front of the watching boys overcame any caution from the fury he had just witnessed and he laid into Matt. The first blow slammed into Matt's shoulder turning him so the second missed. But Matt wasn't done. He straightened up, and his fists thumped solidly into Brick's stomach, knocking the older boy back several steps. A lucky blow from Brick grazed across Matt's cheek, making his ear ring and burn with sudden heat but he ignored the pain and, blocking a crushing blow to his face, delivered an attack that was savage and swift.

Staggering from the blows Brick retreated across the dining room floor, feet slipping and sliding in the milk and porridge. Behind Matt, Joel had picked himself up and grabbed the fallen chair. With blood streaming from his nose, he shoved the watching boys to one side and lunged at Matt's back, the chair raised to strike.

"Look out!"

With lightning reflexes Matt spun, reaching up even as the chair came crashing down. He ducked under the chair, stepped back and grabbed Joel's arm and hurled him into Brick. Joel screamed as his shoulder popped and the two big boys staggered across the floor toward the door that suddenly burst open to reveal a fuming Matron.

"What in the name of all the Saints is going on?" she roared. "Trevor!"

The power and energy that had burned in Matt suddenly drained away and he sagged against the table exhausted. He looked around the room before returning his eyes to Matron at the door. Porridge and spilled milk ran in rivers across the table top, pieces of smashed crockery littered the floor and the broken chair lay against the wall.

All attention turned to the battered form of the newbie as he blindly groped across the floor for his glasses. His clothes matted with porridge, he looked a pathetic and sorry sight and Matt bent forward, helping the younger boy to his feet. Nobody said a word as Matt retrieved the glasses and wiped the unbroken lens on the tablecloth.

"Here—" he smiled, and handed them back to their grateful owner.

The other boys had been sent upstairs to clean and change and were already now on their way to school, with the exception of Joel whom Trevor had driven to the local hospital. His shoulder had been dislocated in the brawl. Matt and Brick scowled at each other; they had been charged with cleaning up the dining room.

They had washed the table, swept up the broken crockery and mopped the floor. Already in a world of trouble they ignored each other, each busy with their own thoughts, most of which revolved around the further troubles that awaited them for being late to school.

Matt emptied the last broken shards of glass and crockery into the bag the cook had given him and tied it up.

"Brick, run along now and get ready for school," Matron instructed, surveying the gleaming room. "Matt!" She pointed at the plastic bag. "Take that outside, then you do the same. Fifteen minutes, boys…"

Brick grinned as he left the kitchen, leaving Matt mumbling beneath his breath at the injustice of it all as he gathered the two heavy trash bags and stumbled out the kitchen door to the large steel bins outside.

The weather promised to be reasonably pleasant. The morning sun, while lacking any real heat, made a welcome change from the rain of the past few days, and Matt felt his spirits lift at the chorus of bird song emanating from the gardens behind the kitchen wall.

He deposited the trash and turned back to the kitchen. Just then something caught his eye and he stopped. Through the slats of the garden gate he could see someone watching him from across the fence.

Myrthinus?

Matt glanced to the kitchen to make sure he wasn't observed and pushed the old wooden gate further open for a better view.

Myrthinus looked totally out of place, like some ancient druid leaning on his staff. "Come, boy!"

Matt paused, eyes narrowed with sudden suspicion. "How can I trust you?"

The man's face clouded, with anger or frustration Matt could not tell. "Have you not read me letter, lad?"

Matt ignored the question, having no idea what he was talking about. "Where's my dog?"

Matt had fallen asleep the previous night worrying about her.

"She's safe. Now grab your bag, we have no time!"

Matt took a hesitant step toward the garden. To his left was the large shed and behind that the fence panel through which he had made his earlier escape.

"Come on, laddie!" Myrthinus was clearly anxious to be moving, and Matt stepped through the kitchen gate. The shed door suddenly opened and Matt stared at the gardener who stood in the open doorway.

Deglin. A sudden chill ran down Matt's spine and he looked back to where Myrthinus had been, but he was gone.

Deglin held Matt's gaze for several moments, then stepped back into the shed. Matt watched him, puzzled, and in the brief second before the door closed he noticed something black hanging at the back of the shed, and there leaning against the corner was what Matt could have sworn was a sword. Confused, he walked slowly back into the kitchen.

"Come along, boy! No time for daydreaming!" Matron held the door into the hallway and gave him a gentle push on the shoulder as he passed. "Get changed quick as you can! We leave in five minutes!"

Matt's path to the Biology lab took him past the school library, and he skidded to a halt as he remembered the overdue book in the bottom of his bag. He peered through the window in the library door. There was no class in there this morning. He was about to reach for the door handle when a loud voice boomed along the corridor.

"Young man! Are you not supposed to be in class?"

Matt looked up to see his physics teacher approaching. The strict but friendly giant of a man moved with surprising speed for someone of his size, and he soon reached the waiting boy.

"Yes, sir. We, urrr... got delayed getting to school. I wanted to hand my book in, sir." He hung his head in mock shame, "It's late back, Mr. Jensen."

"I'll hand it in, son. You run along to class."

"Yes, sir." Matt replied and opened his bag to retrieve the book. To his surprise he saw the book was missing, and he stifled a gasp when he saw in its place a larger leather-bound book with strange markings burned into its cover. His face must have betrayed his shock because Mr. Jensen looked concerned, "What is it, boy?"

"Urrr, nothing, sir." Matt mumbled, pulling the bag closed and clutching it to his chest. "I guess I left the book behind. Sorry, sir, gotta run!" With this he turned back down the corridor and ran to class.

The remaining twenty-five minutes of Biology passed quickly as Matt copied sketches from a textbook and labeled the various parts of the human respiratory system. The bell marking recess sounded and Matt cursed under his breath as he raced to copy the final notes from the blackboard. Much of first recess had passed by the time he caught up with the notes he had missed.

Geography was his next class. He glanced at his watch—only four minutes to get all the way to the other side of the school. Snapping his books closed he grabbed his pencil case and slung his bag over his shoulder. Curiosity about the book in his bag nagged at him, but he would have to wait for lunch to examine it. He took the stairs two at a time, ignoring the shouted "Walk!" from the duty prefect, and was almost deafened by the staccato beeps of the bell as it warned the students to double time to class.

He ran through the playground waving at Nick, one of the few genuine friends he had, and passed into the new block that had been added to the school only a year ago. He raced up the stairs and joined the rest of his class waiting outside the geography room, just as Miss Spears appeared. Miss Spears was something of a fantasy among the teenage boys of the school. She appeared now with a steaming mug of coffee in one hand and a large box of folders tucked under her arm. The box had slipped and she had adopted an awkward stance to clutch them in place, causing her already short black skirt to ride higher than normal on the opposite side. How she got away with the provocative clothes she wore and her flirtatious behavior, none of them knew but there wasn't a boy in the school who wouldn't fall over himself to get her attention or perform any favors she asked. "Well, come along then, boys," she said. "Which of you fine young gentlemen is going to get the door for me?"

The class had hardly taken their seats when Miss Spears was scratching text up on the blackboard. Matt sighed; another long lesson of note taking. He opened his textbook at the indicated chapter and was captivated by the picture of bright red lava spewing from the side of an erupting volcano. "That's about as hot as she is," murmured one of the boys behind him, and Matt stifled his first laugh in days. He looked up to the board, and copied the title for the day's lesson into his notes: "Tortured Earth—Volcanoes and Earthquakes." He was almost disappointed when the bell rang for lunch.

After a hurried burger and fries with Nick in the school cafeteria, he headed through the main school building back to the library. The library was his favorite place in the whole school, a labyrinth of adventures, and research information and a haven from bullies. Apart from two giggling girls who sat off to one side, their heads together whispering behind an upraised book, the room appeared empty. Matt made for the section where he knew he was less likely to be disturbed, and took a secluded table surrounded by bibles and religious material.

Carefully he opened his bag. His palms immediately began to sweat with nervous excitement and he rubbed them on his legs. Hardly daring to breathe, he picked up the ancient book.

It was bound in worn brown leather and engraved with a flowing golden script that was, he guessed, in Latin. The pages were heavy, their edges rough cut, and each was carefully stitched into the leather binding. He opened the book and stared in wonder at the unmistakable picture on the facing page. A beautifully drawn oval frame, decorated with ivy leaves and vines outlined a sketch of Myrthinus. The old man looked almost lifelike, peering out from the page with a penetrating stare.

A red ribbon came from the binding of the book and marked a page somewhere near the center. Matt carefully opened the book at the marked spot, enjoying the musty scent and crackle of the ancient parchment as it folded back against the cover.

Between the yellowed pages was a folded scrap of paper.

Written in big bold letters across the front was a single word: "MATT."

Carefully Matt lowered the book to the table and unfolded the piece of paper. It was a handwritten note, and lying in the crease was a silver chain. To avoid any difficult questions if someone were to pass the table he stuffed the heavy book back into his bag, and started to read.

Matt, time is short. The past few days have been difficult for you, and I have left many questions unanswered. I am sorry. I thought we had more time!

If you have not yet returned to the home, do so now. I will seek you there as soon as I am able. Trust no one, Matt. You are in grave danger!

I believe you have something of mine, a medallion. Worry not, for it was my intention to give it to you. Thread this chain through it and wear it against your skin at all times.

I must end this letter now and deliver this book in to your keeping: I have great need of haste and dare not leave it where it may be found. You must guard it well for should this book fall into their hands then our greatest secret will be revealed to them.

Your friend,
Myrthinus.

PS. Mia is well!

Matt lowered the letter. Mia was okay! His dog was alive. He looked at the chain in his hand and recalled the medallion he had found under the table in the cottage. He had taken it from his torn and rain soaked jeans on his return to the home and hidden it in a small inner pocket of his book bag. He removed it now and stared in wonder at the small piece of metal that rested in his palm. It appeared to be made of lead, or maybe pewter. He turned it over and almost dropped it in surprise. It was identical to the medallion he had seen during his vision! He stared in wonder at the image of a dragon, the scales on its body and its up-swept wings all remarkably captured. The dragon crouched upon an orb of blood-red stone as if ready to take flight. As in the vision he felt the same nagging sense of familiarity; he knew he had seen it before, but where?

He thought back to the attack of the strange figure in the stone circle, the cottage in the clearing, and Myrthinus. He remembered again the key as it flew from the lock the night he had run, the knife that had sailed from the table to the "wizard's" hand, and the window that had blasted open at his command. The confused images of his dreams returned, faces of people he felt sure he should know, and then he thought again of Deglin the gardener.

There was something about the man that nagged at him, and not for the first time that day Matt wondered about what he had seen in the shed. He looked again at the letter. "Trust no one, Matt. You are in grave danger!" The words seemed to leap up at him. This was not a game. Myrthinus warned that others were seeking him. He had no idea how many of them were out there or who he could really trust. His pulse raced. He suddenly felt very small, very alone and very, very afraid. Quickly he threaded the medallion on to the chain and hung it about his neck. It felt surprisingly cold yet somehow comforting against his skin. With little time remaining before class he picked up his bag, checked again the chain around his neck, and left the library.

The afternoon's English class drifted by. The drone of the teacher's voice as she read passage after passage of Shakespeare's *Romeo and Juliet*, mixed with the rhythmic patter of rain against the window, had all but lulled him to sleep.

There had been no further opportunity to review the book during afternoon break, and he had made his way with the other boys to the sports block where they changed for soccer practice.

Soccer was Matt's game. On the field he was fast, and grudgingly respected. It was the one place he felt free to be himself, and more often than not he led the players on his team to victory.

Today had proved no exception. He had scored three of his team's four goals and he was in high spirits when, tired and muddy, he reached the shower room.

As he dried himself off and started to dress, Matt again faced the dilemma that had burdened him all that afternoon. It was now almost the end of the day and if he was going to avoid returning to Inverdeer House, despite Myrthinus's request to meet him there, he would have to decide now.

Matt pulled on his pants. Then there was the book. If he risked taking the book into the home the other kids may see it, and even try to take it. He dreaded another confrontation with Joel, Grant and Brick. They had probably spent the entire day plotting revenge, and his insides churned with fear. If he ran away again, where could he run to? It was cold now, and he pictured himself cold, wet and hungry on the streets. Surprisingly the thought was less disturbing than that of facing Brick and the others in the middle of the night.

With just his shirt and tie to put on he turned to face Tommy, the captain of the other soccer team.

"Hey Matt, what's with the jewelry?" The other boy reached up and held the medallion that hung around Matt's neck. "You know we ain't allowed to wear jewelry during PE."

Matt smiled weakly. "Yeah. I forgot to take it off."

He reached for his shirt and started to button it up, tucking the medallion beneath the thin white material.

"It's pretty cool, though! Where'd you get it?"

"Had it years," Matt replied without hesitation. Then surprising himself he added, "It belonged to my father."

As he said the words he suddenly realized where he had seen the pendant before, and waving his hand in vague acknowledgment of Tommy's goodbye he slumped to the bench.

The other boys had left, and he sat there in stunned silence as the distant memory played out before him. He could remember lying on his mother's lap, fading into sleep and seeing the dragon medallion dangling from his father's neck as the man stooped to kiss him good night. He reached up and brushed the cold metal with his fingers.

Suddenly a hand grabbed the chain around his neck and pulled, yanking Matt from his thoughts and the bench. The chain should have snapped, but this one held and Matt collapsed forward to his knees, the links of the chain biting cruelly into the tender skin of his neck.

"Hey, knock it off!" he gasped. "What the hell is your problem?" He clasped a hand to his neck, and broke his fall with the other. "You nearly broke my bloody neck!"

"Sorry, Runaway. Hurt your neck, huh? Well, after what you did this morning I'm gonna break the fuckin' thing!" Matt felt his stomach knot with fear and looked up to see Brick standing before him. There was no time to block the blow and he was sent reeling across the bench and into the lockers behind.

He struggled to raise himself from the floor but Brick reached down to grab him, again by the chain. "Nobody embarrasses me like you did, Runaway! Nobody!"

The older boy's fingers were within inches of the silver chain when a crackle of sparks seemed to fly from link to link, and with a dazzling jolt a bright blue light leaped and danced across Brick's outstretched hand.

Matt watched in stunned silence as the older boy staggered backward clutching his hand. Struggling to his feet, Matt rubbed his aching jaw and approached the bigger boy. Almost too fast to see, Matt's hand shot out to grab Brick's wrist and he held it tight, pulling the hand toward him. A bright red burn criss-crossed the bigger boy's fingers and a look of shock was in Brick's eyes. Brick tried to pull his trembling hand back but Matt's grip was viselike, unbreakable.

Slowly Matt closed his left hand over Brick's injured one and stared into his eyes. "You leave me the hell alone." He spoke in slow measured tones. "I don't know what your problem is Brick, but it's finished now. Do you understand? It's finished."

The strength of Matt's grip, the power and conviction of his voice and the majesty with which he stood filled Brick with fear. He nodded, babbling agreement and apology.

Not understanding why he did so, Matt released Brick's wrist and took the medallion in his right hand, closed his eyes and squeezed Bricks injured hand with his left. When he finally released it all signs of the injury were gone, the skin unmarked.

Chapter 5
Visitors in the Night

Passage from the Book of Myrthinus
- Atlantis

*A*tlantis! *Over the coming years the city grew into a vast and powerful center of trade and discovery. Ships were built ever larger, and roamed further, setting out on journeys of many years and returning with exotic fruits, jewels, spices, and of course the richest of all treasures: knowledge.*

Glistening pyramids and towering spires punctuated a city of soaring arches and breathtaking gardens. Spring blossoms, summer blooms, and autumn berries filled the air each season with rich scents, each gently tempered with the salty breeze that caressed our island from the surrounding oceans. It was at times otherworldly, a utopia at the center of Pangea, a world only now coming into its own; a city of color where the hues and textures of each building lent an ethereal beauty to the very structure of our home.

Alas, it was Atlantis that awoke the demon in Dardanos. Unbeknown to me he had begun to harbor plans to return to Mars. Corrupt with human desires, his greed for power was changing the man I once called friend. He knew as well as I that no people had survived the comet's impact, but that meant little to him. More important to Dardanos were the dragons—or at least dragon blood, the secret behind our longevity. His plan was to build an all-powerful Atlantean army and conquer the nations of earth that were now beginning to rise in power and threaten global stability.

Dardanos's gaze, however, stretched far beyond earth's bounds. Having achieved the impossible with our flight from Mars to Earth, he spoke now of worlds beyond our solar system, of fleets of ships that sailed not the oceans but the uncharted depths of space. He spoke of discovering and conquering entire worlds, of becoming ruler of all life—in his twisted mind he saw himself as the ultimate power; He saw himself as God.

At first his dreams were grand. Inspiring. But soon it became clear he was mad—dare I say tyrannical? The city of pyramids in Egypt had grown to a thriving metropolis and the Egyptian people were becoming more advanced with each passing season. Sadly, the survivors of Mars were becoming weaker as the inevitable union between marsonian and earthling became commonplace. It was a bittersweet time, seeing our new world prosper and thrive while all traces of my own blood became more diluted.

It was at this time that Dardanos promised a return to the grand days of old, and gathered many followers. He began using his power and influence over the weaker-minded people of the city. Dardanos and his disciples began construction of a new pattern that would act as a gate between worlds. This structure was not of the primitive kind we had used nearly a century before, but instead a powerful device that would create a permanent bridge, forever joining the two worlds.

I and others argued against him. The planet was dead—of that there was little doubt. Should the journey be attempted, certain death would befall any who set foot on that desolate world. But my closest friends warned of an even greater danger. A danger none of us had foreseen.

We tried to stop Dardanos, but in his years of study and research none understood the true fabric of space and time better than he. Porta Marsonia—the gateway to Mars—was completed and he opened the gate to great fanfare and salutation from his followers. I of course was there, despite the risks and fears of what would follow. I was drawn like others in wonder, the prospect of gazing once more on my lost world driving me against all better judgment. At his command the gate opened and the sky that only moments before had been a cloudless and pastel blue was torn asunder and we were plunged into utter darkness. The ground shook and men wailed in terror, clinging to each other in their fear.

In earlier pages I wrote of the death of Mars, and told of the comet that had become two bodies bound by gravity forever orbiting the solar system. It seems that the power unleashed in Dardanos's bridge had drawn such matter toward it, and the smallest asteroid struck the earth that day. Accelerated to unimaginable speeds, the asteroid had sped toward the earth, a massive shock wave building before it. Unchecked, the body plunged into the ocean, impacting the seabed with a shock far greater than any earthquake. Water was ejected at least three miles into the air, and waves raced from the impact point at breathtaking speeds. Although not as large as the asteroid that killed the dinosaurs or the multiple impacts that killed Mars, this impact took life to the very edge of extinction. For days the Earth staggered on the brink of planetary death.

Volcanoes erupted, sending oceans of lava across the world. Roaring tidal waves, half a mile high, sped inland from the displaced oceans clashing with the molten rock and lava in a titanic display of natural power. Mountain ranges formed in an instant. New land masses appeared almost overnight. Temperatures plummeted to below freezing and the sun was partially blocked from the sky for months. The upper atmosphere became choked with dust and debris, leading to global temperature changes. The ice caps melted, sending new oceans of water cascading over an already-tortured earth.

This was the event of which so many religions still tell. A time of global upheaval and great floods. What some would call the wrath of God. I find it ironic still that it was instead unleashed by a man who believed he was God.

Pangaea was split asunder. New continents emerged on an unstable crust. The world became unrecognizable. It took years for the earth to recover from the shock. Years of earthquakes, landslides, tidal waves, floods and volcanic eruption followed. Decades of storms and weather that made it almost impossible for life that had survived the initial impact to retain its tenuous hold.

Millions died that day. For those near the impact it was instantaneous, incinerated in a moment by the fireball of the asteroid itself, or blasted into oblivion by the crushing pressure of the shock wave. But further out it was far worse—and terrifying. After the initial earthquakes and sudden wind, walls of water reaching up higher than could be seen would crest the horizon, racing toward land and smashing into the coastline inundating forests, fields, farms, and cities. Those not drowned by these floods were swallowed by lava, or choked to death by ash, gas and smoke.

The early glory of mankind on earth is long buried now. Drowned beneath the oceans, entombed in lava, and crushed by ice; truly swallowed by the earth. Almost all of our cities were built in low lying areas, on coasts, on the banks of rivers and fertile plains. Our greatest civilizations were wiped out in an instant and the home of it all, the greatest city ever to grace Pangea, Atlantis, slipped beneath an ocean that eventually froze as the continent drifted South.

People did survive of course. Primitive folk mainly. Nomads who lived with their herds in the highlands, forest hunters and cave dwellers. Truly it can be said that the meek inherited the earth.

It took centuries before mankind rose again from the ashes. Among the first to recover, ironically, was Egypt. Survivors came from the hills to find the once-lush tropical land was nothing but barren desert. The Nile, its course altered and shortened, provided the only source of fertility along its banks. Amazingly the pyramids we had built remained, pitted and scarred by the elements though they were, and the primitive people took to them as temples. They became homes of the gods, and the dynasties to follow copied them, attempting to recreate their splendor across Egypt. They failed of course, lacking the arts we had employed in their building. Those more recent structures still stand, in ruin, built not by a waning civilization as one would think, but by an infantile one—poor replicas of the magnificent structures we had left behind.

Inverdeer House: Inverdeer, Scotland
Friday Night - Present Day

The evening meal passed without incident. There was little chatter around the table, and Matt had kept his head down and eaten quickly. Despite the many strange events of the past few days he kept coming back to fears about his father. Myrthinus had claimed to know him, and more to the point had been in possession of the medallion that Matt now believed could have belonged to him.

Did the book hold answers?

He left the table and pushed his plate through the serving hatch to the kitchen and hurried toward the stairs. From down the hallway he could hear the staccato chatter of gunfire and explosions from the old but serviceable console game, and a woman's voice drifted from the TV telling everyone the reasons why they should buy a certain brand of tissues.

There was little risk of him being disturbed on a Friday night; Fridays and Saturdays were late nights for the residents of Inverdeer House. Most would be playing in the game room, table tennis, air-hockey, console games. Others would be watching TV, and a rare few even reading. Those lucky enough to have a pass would be downtown catching the latest movie, or sneaking cigarettes and beers from drinking-age friends at the local pub.

Matron and the other staff would be around, but few of the kids would think about heading upstairs until the 11:00pm deadline. That gave Matt a little over three hours of peace and quiet to browse through the strange book Myrthinus had deposited in his bag.

Having confirmed the dorm was unoccupied, he had closed the door and jumped onto his bed. First, he opened a novel taken from downstairs to a random page and laid it to one side. Then he carefully pulled the covers back on his bed, removed the book from his school bag and laid it on the sheet.

He tested throwing the cover quickly over the book and turning his attention to the novel to make sure he could hide the book before anyone entered the dormitory. Satisfied with his subterfuge, he pulled back the covers.

His hand trembled slightly with excitement. All day he had waited for this moment and now it had arrived. Once again he was shaken by the sketch on the facing page. There was no doubt about it—the eyebrows, the hair, the face—it was identical in every detail to Myrthinus, yet the book seemed to be ancient!

Almost reverently he turned the pages. The language was strange and unreadable, yet it felt somehow familiar to him. Page after page of flowing script flicked by and then he came to a map.

It was an exquisite work of art. The map itself was not detailed, in fact it was little more than the outline of Great Britain, with several major cities and rivers marked. What took Matt's breath away were the three detailed cameos highlighting locations on the map. The first was clearly of Stonehenge. Each stone was drawn in careful detail, some highlighted by the setting sun, while others stood dark and ominous in shadow. The picture was captioned "Porta Marsonia."

The second picture referenced a location in Scotland near the city of Falkirk, and was of a Roman fort. Legionnaires were drawn up in formation before the walls and a group of mounted knights sat aloof, their eyes fixed on the third and final picture.

Matt followed the gaze of the knights across the page, to an image of a shrine that was cut back into a hillside. In the foreground a man sat on horseback, his head bowed in respect.

The picture was captioned Invalone, and Matt was about to turn the page when he noticed other letters carved in the stone lintel of the shrine. He strained to make out the words written there, sounding them out in his head; Av Allan. The words sounded almost familiar, and he repeated them aloud. Unable to recall where he had heard the words before, he shrugged and carefully flipped the page.

It was a new chapter entitled Camelon, the C being a beautifully drawn icon, surmounted by a simple crown. A sword, a glow of power emanating from the blade, passed through the crown and the letter "C". Matt sighed wishing he could understand the language.

Disappointed, he flicked through the final pages looking for more illustrations. A brief image of kneeling knights and a king flickered before his eyes and he stopped, turning back through the pages trying to find the briefly seen drawing.

There it was, occupying the bottom half of a page, and like the others drawn in lifelike detail.

The image showed a vast hall, circular in shape, with graceful columns reaching up to form arches that supported the vaulted ceiling. In the center of the picture a man stood upon a raised dais, his back to the artist, a long robe sweeping down his back to the floor, its fur-lined hem embroidered in some strange design. The hair was shoulder length and on his head was the same crown that Matt had seen earlier in the book. His right arm was extended before him, and in his hand was a mighty sword. Before him twelve men knelt, their heads bowed. All wore similar attire, long cloaks clasped at the neck with a brooch, and tunics embroidered with three circles.

Matt sat up and gasped. The man directly before the king, unlike the others, did not have his head bowed. Instead his face was lifted to gaze upon the "king," and complete devotion was captured in that image, a look of unspoken loyalty and love for the man before him.

It was this face that held Matt's rapt attention. It was the man of his recent dreams and deep inside he felt he should know him. He leaned closer to the picture and the medallion about his own neck slipped from his sweater and swung out across the page. Clutching the medallion in one hand he was struck with a sudden clarity. Could this man possibly be his father?

Footsteps sounded outside the door and Matt quickly threw the bed covers over the book and grabbed the novel. Trying to look innocent he looked up to the door, fighting the sudden fear that Joel and Grant had not gone into town. The line of light beneath the door became partially obscured as someone stopped outside. The handle lowered and Matt felt his stomach churn. Something did not feel right. Not fully understanding why, he slid off his bed and wormed under the iron frame of the neighboring bed, wriggling to get a better view of the door. Slowly and silently it opened.

From Matt's vantage point he saw two large booted feet enter the room and stand before the door. A brief rush of air passed across the floor as the door swung closed. Matt slipped the medallion under his sweater and pressed himself to the floor, the dusty smell of the carpet strong in his nose, and his pulse deafeningly loud in his ears.

The feet came toward Matt's bed. *The book!* Matt closed his eyes; the novel lay on the bed above him, testament to his recent presence. The covers would be ruffled, warm where he had been.

He could not lose the book. Matt took one more look across the floor; the figure was less than ten paces from his bed. Frozen with terror the boy willed himself to move. Just then a chorus of laughs came from beyond the door, and boys' voices could be heard getting louder.

The footsteps stopped and Matt watched the boots turn to face the door. Amazed at his own bravery Matt wriggled from beneath the bed and slowly raised his head to peer across the covers. Not more than three paces away, his back to Matt and eyes fixed on the door, stood Deglin the gardener. The hairs along the back of Matt's neck prickled and he shuddered.

What the hell is he doing here?

Matt suddenly recalled the way Myrthinus had vanished when the gardener had opened the shed, and he remembered what had looked to be a sword hidden in the dim recesses of the building. For a brief moment Matt wondered if the gardener was perhaps the friend he needed and he was right to doubt Myrthinus, but the moment passed and with heavy heart he realized he could trust no one.

Slowly, very slowly he extended a hand beneath the bed covers and felt for the book.

Don't turn around!

His fingers brushed the hard leather cover and he groped for the spine of the book. The voices outside the door grew louder and with a surprising stealth the gardener ran to the door. Matt dropped like a rock as the man took position behind the door and once again faced into the room. Horrible images of Deglin drawing his sword and butchering the boys chased through Matt's mind as he cowered beneath the bed.

The door opened and four younger boys entered the room. Matt held his breath watching them pass along the beds to the washroom at the end of the dormitory. He glanced back to the door. Deglin was gone.

Matt lowered his head to the floor and let out a long slow breath. He felt drained, only crawling out from under the bed when the flushing toilet reminded him he was no longer alone.

Matt pondered his next move. It was clear he had to leave the home again. With no one to trust he would be safest away from it all. Maybe he could find work in one of the big cities, Glasgow, or Edinburgh. For a brief moment he entertained the thought of stealing away on one of the large container ships and spending his life at sea.

The door opened again and more boys began to enter the dorm. A glance at the clock showed 10:25 pm. Matt quickly stuffed the book into his bag, grabbed his washcloth, soap and toothbrush from the locker by his bed, and headed for the washroom.

"Hey, Matt! 'Night!"

Matt looked up in surprise at the boy who had called out. It was the red headed "Newbie."

"'Night," Matt replied, and several others echoed the sentiment. For the first time since his arrival at the home, he was extended invitations to hang out with the others. These overtures of acceptance almost made him regret his decision to again escape Inverdeer.

Now in pajamas, he slipped beneath his covers, removed a notebook and pencil from his bag and set to jotting down memories of his childhood.

Lights out wasn't until 11:30pm, and he was determined to make the most of the time remaining but he found himself constantly glancing at the door. He suddenly felt too tired to focus on anything, but feared falling asleep. Around him some of the younger boys already slept and others chatted quietly.

A shadowy form crossed the bottom of his bed and he jumped before realizing that Brick had paused on his way to the washroom.

"'Night, Matt," he said. Then raising his voice a little he added, "I'll see there's no trouble, okay?"

Matt blinked in surprise. "Ur...sure...I guess."

Brick glanced around the room then leaned across the bed speaking quietly, almost whispering. "I'm sorry, Matt. I just wanted you to know that." Then he swaggered off between the rows of beds, scowling at various boys as he went.

Matt rolled onto his side facing the door and looked at the blank page of his notebook. Several thoughts raced through his mind and he jotted them down. "Sword," "Father," "Av Allan," "Medallion." He underlined "Father" multiple times.

Images of strange places, strange dress and strange customs flicked through his mind, but gradually one image above all others stood out: the man standing at the table before the sword, a medallion dangling from his outstretched hand. The man was tall and thickly muscled, handsome yet rugged. Matt suddenly remembered his father's hands—strong, powerful hands. Yet they had always been so gentle when they held him, so affectionate when they had caressed his mother's cheek. Suddenly, like a book of photographs, more images flashed into his mind.

First Matt saw a small room, his father standing before his mother. Her beautiful face was pale and her eyes were wet with tears. His father gently wiped the tears away before enfolding her in his arms. The picture changed: a larger room this time, a fireplace and crackling fire. Tapestries and skins adorned the cold stone walls. Matt could almost hear his mother's voice lulling him to sleep.

The woman's face appeared above his now. Her lips soft on his cheek, her breath warm. "Goodnight my darling." He could almost hear her whispers, then her face was gone. Suddenly he sensed strong, protective hands rest upon his head, rougher drier lips brushed his forehead; "G'night son."

Then the dragon medallion swung down from his father's neck and Matt saw himself reach for it with infantile hands. The neck and jawline of his father appeared, dark with stubble. Matt could almost taste a subtle sense of metal, horses and leather.

Matt opened his eyes and scribbled furiously on the notepad. The medallion? Had it been the same? Yes! A silver pendant in the likeness of a dragon. Matt looked down at the medallion around his own neck. It was identical. He tried hard to recall more images but could not get past a new and sudden fear. If the medallion and the sword belonged to his father, did that mean his father was dead?

Matt was suddenly aware of another presence in the room and looked up, startled, but it was only Trevor.

"Goodnight, lads."

Limp with relief, Matt laid back on his pillow. His body ached for sleep. He closed his eyes but his brain screamed for him to stay awake.

Matt forced his eyes open. The clock on the wall ticked slowly on. Muffled breathing and gentle snores arose from the beds around him. A whop-whop-whop of a passing helicopter grew louder in the sky above, then as quickly faded into the night.

Afraid Deglin would return, Matt pinched the soft skin of his arm to force himself awake, and with quiet determination resolved to sneak from his room when all was still and investigate the gardener's shed.

He lay quiet for a few more minutes and again his eyes closed, heavy with fatigue. Just a few minutes' sleep would be all right, surely? Matron would still be up. If Deglin were around he would not try anything until much later in the night. Perhaps an hour's sleep, maybe two?

It was 11:45pm Friday night, and one by one the boys fell asleep.

Matt did too.

The boys slept, oblivious to the door that swung open and the dark shadow that passed through the opening into the room.

As silently as it had opened, the door swung closed again, the faint click of the latch the only sound. The steely rasp of the sword as it slid from its scabbard was barely audible over the deep breathing of the sleeping boys.

With slow measured steps the shadow approached the bed. Reaching out a hand it took hold of the blanket's edge and with a sudden jerk pulled back the covers, raising the sword to strike.

Matt gasped and leaped up in bed, his breathing wild. Around him the room was still, and he collapsed back against the pillows. He rubbed at his eyes and shook off the last horrors of the dream. He strained his eyes to look at the clock, angry with himself for falling asleep.

It was almost 1am. Quietly he slipped from the bed and pulled on his jeans, a thick shirt, and a sweater. Taking his worn sneakers in one hand and his bag in the other, he tip-toed in his socks to the door.

Keeping his feet against the wall to avoid the betraying creak of the wooden stair treads, he slowly made his way to the darkened hallway below. There was little light to guide him. The street lamps outside were timed to switch off at midnight and the only light remaining was the ghostly blue glow from the computer monitor in Matron's office.

He paused at the bottom of the stairs, listening for any signs of life. All was quiet. He knew the home had a security system, but there was a broken window in the kitchen, the result of an overly enthusiastic soccer game. He could easily remove the taped-on cardboard and squeeze through the hole without arousing the house.

Five minutes later Matt lowered himself from the window and into the kitchen yard. The concrete was cold against his feet and he cursed under his breath. He had left his shoes and his bag on the table in the kitchen and to his dismay he realized the window was too high for him to get back in.

Ignoring the dampness on his feet, and the dilemma of getting back into the kitchen, he crept stealthily across the lawn. The moon was out, no longer full, but it gave a pale white light by which to see.

Behind him the old walls of the home looked menacing; covered in a thick blanket of ivy they towered up to the gabled attic rooms. Huge oak trees behind the house overhung much of the rear lawns and the gigantic limbs, now leafless, reached out over the shed, partially obstructing the moonlight.

Matt felt for a key but his fingers found nothing but the rusted iron key hole and latch. He reached up around the door and bit back a curse as he snagged his hand on a nail near the top of the door frame. A dull metallic knock revealed the key suspended from the nail and with relief he lifted it down and quietly slipped it into the lock.

His heart beat with excitement. He knew he would be in serious trouble if he was caught, but his curiosity about what he had seen at the back of the shed overcame his fear.

Slowly he swung the heavy door open. It made no sound, swinging back on well-oiled hinges. What little moonlight shone through the open doorway bathed the left and rear walls in a pale silver sheen.

On silent feet Matt crept to the rear of the shed. The floor was rough with dried dirt that had fallen from the gardener's boots and tools, and he wrinkled his nose against the smell of old oil and the acidic bite of powdered fertilizers.

Reaching the back of the shed he could now make out the peg board and the array of tools that hung there. There was no black cloak or long sword to be seen and Matt felt a sudden rush of relief tinged with disappointment.

Turning to leave, he caught sight of a step ladder and recalled his shoes left in the kitchen along with his bag and the precious book. The ladder leaned against a wall beneath a small window comprising four panes of glass dirty with dust and cobwebs. The window was on the opposite side of the shed to the moon so no light shone in, but what little light came through the open doorway had the effect of turning the window into a dirty mirror. Matt caught his breath, startled by his own reflection.

Berating himself for being so edgy, he slowly picked his way toward the wall, careful not to dislodge the edging shears and spade that leaned against the rusty green handles of the lawn mower.

He had almost retrieved the ladder when his reflection suddenly vanished in the window and a dark hooded head slowly walked past the glass.

Matt staggered back and sent the shears and spade crashing to the floor. He froze for an instant before stumbling madly toward the door. In his haste he snagged his foot in a coil of garden hose and fell. What little light filtered through the door was suddenly blocked and Matt felt his blood run cold and his stomach tighten in terror as a cloaked and hooded figure took a booted step inside the shed.

Justin Orton

Chapter 6
A Failed Escape

Passage from the Book of Myrthinus
- *A New Empire*

Dardanos had brought the earth to the brink of disaster. In the moments following the opening of the portal hundreds of his followers were drawn to their deaths in the shimmering vortex between worlds. Others, myself included, fled. As the earth shook from its cosmic blow I sheltered in the mountainous region now known as Scotland. I would like to say my skills kept me alive in the days that followed but in truth I fear luck played a heavy part.

The days, weeks and months that came are a blur of horror and hardship to me now. Uncontaminated water was hard to find. Food was scarcer still. Yet somehow I managed to eke out a meager existence in a strange and devastated landscape.

Over the solitary years that followed I set out to map this new world, gathering together survivors wherever they could be found. Stories

To Raise a King

abounded of global flooding, and people called it the time of the great anger, the wrath of the gods against a people that had risen too far above their station. I, with my stories of the lost cities, became outcast, seen as one of those the gods had sought to destroy. Never have I sunk so low or felt of such little worth!

Alone I continued my journey, mapping the land and coast lines, following rivers to their source, and chronicling each settlement I encountered before the people drove me away. After uncounted years of such wandering I finally found myself on a vast plain before the ruins of Porta Marsonia, or Stonehenge as it is called now. I wondered with fear if it could still be used by one who held the knowledge? Had Dardanos survived the cataclysm he had unleashed? Was he even now seeking the portal to attempt once more what he had so nearly achieved?

Years I spent in study, and gradually my knowledge grew. Others, outcasts themselves, worked with me, and I trained them in my arts, and shared my knowledge of the stars. History called us "Druids," and we discovered that like all doors, this cosmic portal to Mars also had a key. Buried deep in the center of the circle was a strange device protected by many spells. It was constructed of two crystal pyramids, each carved from Martian quartzite and polished to an exacting precision. In the base of each, a hole was bored approximately one inch in diameter, and joining them was a rod about twelve inches in length. The rod was fashioned from Martian gold, its surface an intricate design of engraved runes and flowing script. On dismantling this key, I discovered the rod was hollow, its inner surface coated in a blackened residue that I later discovered was burned blood; whose I had no idea.

I left my followers and spent the centuries that followed seeking an understanding of these strange and powerful symbols, but alas, all traces of our former societies, Marsonian and Atlantean, had been erased from the earth. With no further understanding of how the device worked I resolved to hide each piece of the key, for disturbing news had reached me.

Justin Orton

Dardanos, it appeared, had survived the destruction wrought by the asteroid's impact. Impossible it seems, but a thousand years had passed, and he had labored long, moving from one fledgling culture to another. Decades he spent in Egypt, centuries in Greece, until eventually he discovered a powerful people, descendants maybe of Atlantis itself?

I speak of course of Rome! Never taking a place of prominence in this growing nation, he instead manipulated and guided others, structuring a culture that was built for one purpose and one alone—world domination. It is no accident that this vast empire chose Mars for its god of war! Slowly the legions spread across Europe, consuming nation after nation, as Dardanos sent the might of Rome on a global conquest in desperate search for Porta Marsonia.

Thus the first legionnaires came to the shores of Britain and at last news of Stonehenge reached Dardanos.

I must pause here, for despite his evil plotting and desire for dominion, there was much good within the fabric of Rome. Britain suddenly found itself moved from the dark ages to a new and thriving golden age. Along with military might came echoes of Atlantis and the great civilization we had forged there: architecture, law and order, education, art, and music. Regions conquered were granted citizenship of Rome, and as citizens the people enjoyed greater prosperity than ever before. It grieved me to see that a twisted undercurrent of evil corrupted this otherwise great empire.

It was a testing time for me and I succumbed to an arrogant belief that with my guidance and counsel I could fix that which Dardanos had corrupted. I thought that maybe I could overthrow him, and safeguard this world and its people. I fear so many centuries spent alone, shunned by man, had made me rash and unprepared for what mankind had become. Corruption and greed were rife, and in the shadows of the magnificent cities of the empire lurked the victims of this rapacity. People steeped in poverty lived each day in hope of death. How could one man make a difference? In some ways I became like Dardanos then. I manipulated, I schemed, and played *the game of politics striving to gain a position of influence in the governing of the Empire.*

But it was not to be. Dardanos had left Rome, and was in Britain. He had discovered the theft of the key and before long I became a wanted man, hunted by one of the largest, most organized military machines in history.

It is with little pride that I confess my capture came within weeks.

Inverdeer House: Inverdeer, Scotland
Saturday - Present Day

Matt threw himself across the shed floor and felt his back come up hard against the work bench. The sudden jolt almost knocked the wind out of him.

"I mean you no harm, Matt," the figure intoned, a hand held out before him. "Come with me, we must get you away from here."

Matt glanced around for a weapon but was unable to see anything in the darkness of the shed save for an upside down crate. He pulled at it momentarily blocking the path of the black-clad intruder.

"Matt, trust me..."

Matt slid to his right trying to inch under the bench, suddenly aware that the figure before him was dressed just like the character in the stone circle.

"You cannot trust the old man, Matt—he is your enemy." The man lunged across the crate, making a grab for the boy, but missed. His cajoling tone became more impatient, angry.

"Enough of this, boy! You will come with me!" The figure kicked the box to one side, then he ducked once more to grab at Matt.

"Fuck you!" Matt lashed out with a foot, narrowly missing the outstretched hand, and pressed his back against the rough wood of the shed wall. A sudden blast of cold night air passed across his back and he felt the wall behind him move.

Mia's dog door!

The man was angry now, "Have it your way, boy!" and he dropped to his knees reaching for Matt, cursing as he struck his head on the wooden bench.

Matt rolled on to his side and struck out again, and this time his foot smashed hard against the nose of his adversary. Rolling onto his stomach, Matt wormed through the hinged wooden flap of the doggy door and clawed at the grass outside, terrified his legs would be grabbed before he was free.

"Stop!" the voice behind shouted, and Matt cried out as he scraped his back along the rough-cut edges of the opening, but then he was through, tumbling into the cold night air.

Matt scrambled to his feet. Where should he go—back to the home, or out into the night? Across the grass the kitchen door suddenly flew open and bright light blazed across the lawn. It was another man, cloaked and hooded like the first. He saw Matt and came running across the lawn.

"Matt!" a new voice called, and the boy turned. It was Myrthinus. He stood behind the fence his face a mask of rage, his voice loud and harsh. "Come, I can help you!" Myrthinus raised a hand toward the boy but two figures suddenly leaped at him from the darkness of the trees. Matt stood frozen. Which way? Myrthinus? The home? The town?

The shed door was almost torn from its hinges as the man inside stumbled out. The bottom of his face was red with blood from a shattered lip and broken nose and his eyes burned with a fury that terrified Matt. Ignoring the frantic calls of Myrthinus he ran straight at the man who had just emerged from the kitchen door. With a sudden burst of speed and change of direction Matt darted past the surprised figure and raced for the kitchen. Above it a bright blue strobe light flickered into the night, the silent alarm had been tripped and Matt knew his only safety was back inside; the police should already be on their way.

He heard a curse as the man behind him lost his footing on the grass. Matt leaped the step through the kitchen door and spun, slamming it closed.

He slid the brass bolts into place and leaned against the door, panting heavily.

The door shook as the man outside crashed against it, and he could hear the muffled voice outside. "Matt, open the door. It's not safe in there. Open the door!" but Matt had gone, already moving through the dining room and toward the hallway where the high-pitched beep of the triggered alarm could now be heard.

He was almost into the hall when another figure, also cloaked and hooded, lunged from the shadows beneath the stairs.

Deglin!

Matt jumped back into the dining room and literally threw himself through the open serving hatch into the kitchen. He hit the stone floor and yelped as his hip slammed into a steel table leg.

He looked up and saw his bag and shoes lying beneath the broken window. Reaching across, he grabbed them and ran to the larger window at the end of the kitchen. This window looked out onto the yard beside the house rather than the gardens to the rear and he hoped it would offer his one chance for a safe escape.

Jumping to the counter top he threw aside all thoughts of silence and smashed at the windowpane with his bag. The glass shattered, showering both the yard outside and the floor within with shards of broken glass.

The door behind him burst open and Deglin raced toward the window, running alongside the long steel table that stretched along the center of the room. Matt would not make it. Deglin would be on him before he could get through the window and into the street beyond. Lying in the sink beside him was a steel, the long rounded utensils used by the cooks to sharpen their knives. The boy crouched down and grabbed it from the sink and held it in front of him like a short sword.

What he hoped to achieve against a full-grown man he had no idea, but as he held the steel before him he felt that strange feeling of strength and power build within. He suddenly altered his stance and shifted his grip on the steel.

Deglin slowed his run and drew his sword. "Don't be a fool, boy—" Slowly he advanced.

Risking one more glance behind him, Matt threw his bag through the broken window toward the potting shed in the far corner of the yard, then taking a deep breath he leaped from the counter to the long steel table.

The move took Deglin by surprise and he flailed a blow at the passing boy, his sword glancing across the table top, cutting the air with a whoosh. Matt jumped back over the sweeping blade and using both hands swung the heavy steel at his attacker's head.

The sound of smashing crockery was loud in the silence of the night as Deglin fell, dragging a rack full of plates and bowls down with him.

Following the stroke through, Matt swung the makeshift sword over his head and twisted to face the gardener. Deglin pulled himself back to his feet, brushing broken crockery from his cloak. "There's no need for this, Matt," he said, jumping onto the table, sword held before him as he advanced on the boy. "I am here to protect you, not harm you."

Matt backed away from the advancing figure. "If you mean me no harm then put your sword away," but even as he spoke he raised the steel with two hands to block the sudden blow that was aimed at him.

He barely caught it and sparks flared from the steel as the sword blade was deflected. The jolt of the blow took Matt by surprise and he almost dropped the steel as the shock vibrated through both his wrists and into his arms.

Somehow he deflected a second blow but the force sent him reeling and he lost his footing. The point of the sword tore through his shirtsleeve and left a shallow cut across his upper arm as he tumbled from the table.

He dropped the steel and it clattered under a nearby cabinet. Sirens were sounding outside now, and the ceiling reflected the flashing blue lights from the police cars. Loud voices could be heard in the hallway.

Matt panicked as he fell from the table. Help wouldn't arrive in time. With a sickening feeling he realized he was going to die. He was defenseless. Pain exploded behind his eyes and his ears rang as the back of his head smashed against a heavy steel mixing bowl. Somehow he scrambled to his feet and grabbed for the fallen steel.

Broken crockery crunched beneath heavy boots as Deglin leaped to the floor. There was no time to defend himself and the steel was easily knocked from his grip.

Matt staggered backward toward the broken window barely evading the grasping hands. His head throbbed with pain yet adrenaline and fear gave him strength. A sliver of shattered glass sliced through the cotton of his sock and stabbed into his foot but he was oblivious to it.

Whether it was some trick of his imagination or another magical twist on his mind he did not know, but for a split second he was no longer in the kitchen. Instead he was one of many knights clad in royal blue on a field of green fighting desperately against an army of strangely clad soldiers, their clothing of various cuts and garish colors. The sky behind the advancing horde was a swirl of clouds edged in crimson as if the very air was on fire. Death and destruction surrounded him but the knights in blue refused to yield. As quickly as it had come, the vision vanished and bright white light flooded the room.

Two police officers were framed against the door, and Matt stood speechless as he realized the man before him with the sword had fled. He looked across the kitchen and saw the back door wide open.

A sudden pain in his left arm caused him to look down at the blood soaked material of his shirt and then he became aware of a pulsing throb in his foot.

The police officers slowly entered the kitchen taking in the sight of broken crockery, the smashed window, and the bleeding boy. One of the officers was a woman and Matt heard, as if from a great distance, her voice on the radio.

"We need an ambulance at the Inverdeer Boys' home."

Sounds were fading now; the reply that crackled from the radio became faint and the light in the room started to fade into gray. Matt felt the nearest officer grab him as he passed into unconsciousness and fell to the floor.

How long he had been out Matt did not know. A pinprick of light was the first thing he became aware of that suddenly swelled into a watery blur of bright dancing colors. He blinked away the tears.

Something tight was on his left arm and he turned his head to see the bandage. Stars exploded behind his eyes and he moaned. An ambulance attendant, wearing green coveralls and holding a form, stood to one side talking quietly with Matron and a policewoman. The officer glanced across at him. Her face showed concern.

He felt hands on his right arm and saw more stars as he moved his head to see Brick staring at him.

"Matt? Matt! Christ, Matt, what the fuck were you doing?" the big boy asked.

"Get away from him now!" Matron snapped, "All of you, come along, back to bed. Trevor!" Her shrill voice sounded like a piercing scream in Matt's head.

A door banged and the sound of rubber-soled shoes squeaked across the wooden floor, before being muffled by the rug.

"I'm here!" Carter sounded breathless.

"Get these boys upstairs at once."

"Certainly," came the reply, but Brick didn't move. He leaned in to Matt.

"You were running away again weren't you?"

Matt felt himself slipping away, but he fought the urge to fall asleep and gripped Brick's arm. "Brick, my bag..." Matt was suddenly afraid that whoever had attacked him had grabbed his bag as they fled the scene.

Brick looked confused. Tears streamed from Matt's eyes and his head pulsed with pain.

"My bag—out the window...you gotta get it."

He closed his eyes, fighting the nausea and trying to escape the swirling lights. "Hide it for me, behind the shed," he mumbled, then he passed into blissful unconsciousness.

Brick watched as Matt went limp, then reluctantly allowed Trevor to lead him away. "Settle down boys! The show's over—back to your beds!"

Brick followed the others who were chatting excitedly about the night's incident.

Trevor was beset with questions as the animated group filed into the dormitory.

"But Mr. C. ..." came a chorus of pleas as the boys begged for details as to what had happened. Trevor knew there was no getting the boys settled down without some kind of answer.

"If you all just settle down and get back to your beds I will explain," he responded.

Brick ignored the instruction and crossed to the heavy curtains, pulling them aside to look down on the driveway below. "There's an ambulance and two police cars outside!" He watched their red and blue lights painting eerie shadows across the grounds.

He felt a hand on his arm. "Brick—bed. Now!" Trevor spoke sternly but the boy shrugged the hand away and strained his neck to see the ambulance better. Peterhead General Hospital was printed on the door.

He surrendered to Trevor's commands and climbed beneath his blanket. "Peterhead General," he said quietly to himself as he watched Trevor walk into the center of the room eying the beds and checking they were all accounted for. "Peterhead General—at least I know where he'll be for a while."

Trevor was talking and Brick leaned up on an elbow to listen.

"It would appear Matt was attempting to run away again."

"Told you!" shouted a voice from near the washrooms but a loud chorus of "Shhhh" sounded from the other boys.

Trevor continued, "As far as the police could tell he slipped climbing through the window, cut his arm on broken glass, and fell back into the kitchen striking his head on the floor. He has suffered quite a cut to his arm, but the ambulance crew was more concerned about his head. He at least has a concussion, at worst a fractured skull. Now no more questions. I need you all to get a good night's sleep."

"Yes, sir."

Trevor turned to the door and looked at Matt's empty bed. He shook his head and sighed. What was going on? A social worker had already been called, and would be questioning all the boys tomorrow. He hoped they would discover what had pushed Matt into a second escape attempt in one week. Trevor glanced at Brick, who returned his gaze. *If I find your bullying led to this I will make your life here hell!* Brick broke eye contact and rolled onto his side. With a sigh Trevor switched off the lights and left the room.

Brick lay back on his pillow wrestling with his own problems. He was suddenly curious as to the contents of Matt's bag. The fact that he wanted Brick to find it and move it indicated Matt expected to be back only for as long as it took to retrieve the bag, and run away again. Brick smiled to himself. If at first you don't succeed…he mouthed the common phrase and resolved to search for the bag the next morning. What he did then would depend on what he found.

Chapter 7
Recovery

Passage from the Book of Myrthinus
- *Prisoner*

*I*nitially Dardanos treated me well. His visits were regular, and provided a welcome break from my confinement. He spent long hours extolling his virtue while regaling me with tales of his achievements throughout Africa, Asia, and Europe. It was easy to become captivated by his dreams and I would listen avidly as he expounded on the global civilization that he planned.

Of course he still obsessed about a return to Mars. He was convinced the planet had recovered in the thousands of years since the impact, that life would now abound, just as it did on Earth. Ever a gifted orator, he spoke with convincing eloquence and it was easy to see how he had swayed so many to his cause, with promises of longevity and power that would be theirs.

I remained steadfast against him and refused to be swayed into joining with him. Instead I pressed on him the dangers posed by the third and final comet fragment that would be drawn to the cosmic bridge as surely as flies to a festering wound if he should try once more to open the portal.

The Druids and I had spent hundreds of years tracking this comet. We had calculated its pathway through the heavens and accurately predicted its return each century. We watched its comma shorten with each visit and then one year it did not appear. I wondered if it had hit another planet or been drawn to some distant star.

On each date that we had calculated its return I studied the stars, and then I found it. I could trace its path across the sky by the stars that blinked off and then on again, obscured by its passing. All this and more I told to Dardanos, but to no avail.

I grew more frustrated as time passed. I demanded my release and we fought, and for my efforts he had me drugged, and banished, bound and chained to an unlit dungeon.

For months he left me there. It was hard to gauge the passage of time in that dreadful place. In almost constant darkness with little food or water my body weakened and my despair grew. I became increasingly worried that Dardanos was seeking the missing key to his portal, and I tried desperately to recall our long conversations to see what, if any, clues I may have let slip as to its whereabouts.

I exercised my mind the best I could, but deprived of light it was incredibly hard to focus one's will on anything. The chains that bound me to the wall prevented a translocation, and Dardanos had bound them with many spells that foiled every attempt I made to remove them.

Eventually he returned and my fears proved well founded for he told me he had repaired the gate at Stonehenge and was to take me with him. Apparently he had a special use for me.

Others he had brought with him, four understudies, magicians and astronomers, and he told me their studies had been unable to find the remaining comet of which I had so fervently warned. He mocked me, called me a fool and said my fears were unfounded. He blamed me for the disaster of his last attempt, claiming that I had attempted to thwart his efforts and it was I that had brought destruction to the earth, not he. Then he held before me the crystal pyramids, joined by the golden rod, and the completed device glowed with radiant power. Gloating, he raised it above his head, and with a word of command freed me of my bonds.

I must have looked a pathetic sight for him to make such a move but despite my weakened state I struck immediately. It was surprise alone that enabled me to wrest the key from Dardanos's hands. The strain proved almost too much for me, but somehow I managed to translocate myself to a stone circle in Ireland.

Dazed and weak from the effort, I was almost killed, for one of Dardanos's understudies had grabbed my robe and followed me, wrestling me to the ground.

Had it been Dardanos himself I would surely have perished, for I was tired, exhausted beyond measure. But despite my fatigue I grappled with my attacker and overcame him.

I had to act fast. Much of the military might of Rome had been withdrawn from the frontiers. Dardanos had been building a new army on the plain at Old Sarum, now Salisbury, and to swell its ranks he had stripped the legions manning Hadrian's Wall to the north. Their withdrawal had left the northern border vulnerable to attack.

If I were to act it would have to be now, and act I did. In all my years of wanderings after the asteroid strike, only one group of people had shown me any true compassion and friendship. These people were a warrior race known as the Dal-Riata, and they inhabited the Northwestern coasts of Ireland. Their leader was Fergus Mor. I spoke to him in haste of my plans and though he thought me mad, he agreed to aid me, and while he prepared an army, I returned to the north of Britain.

Many wonder at the Great Alliance between the Gaels from Ireland, Picts from the North and even Vikings from the East, and how in 367AD this barbaric host overcame the might of Rome and drove them from Britain. Uniting these nations, separated as they were by landscape, beliefs, and cultures was a significant challenge.

But unite them I did, and with the defeat of Dardanos's armies, and the ensuing plundering that followed, Dardanos fled Britain, buying me precious time. This time I sought not to hide the key but rather destroy it. Alas its unmaking almost destroyed me! Dardanos had protected it well. Once more I broke it apart. The golden rod I kept, one crystal I hid, and the other I gave to my friend, Fergus Mor, King of the Gaels and least barbaric of those who had driven the might of Rome before them.

I took Fergus into my confidence, sharing much with my friend. He swore to ever protect the crystal and keep it safe, making it an heirloom of his family. Together we traveled then to the shores of Kintyre and named this barren land Dalriada.

The Picts, wild people of the north, called these newcomers "Scots" which translates to "Raiders" in their tongue, and thus Fergus and his people became the fathers of Scotland.

As for the rest of Britain, it sadly fell into anarchy, until the Romans returned the following year but this time their stay was brief. After a mere thirty years they withdrew, called home to the final defense of their collapsing empire. Without the machinations of Dardanos to drive it, Rome had failed.

Where Dardanos had gone, none now knew.

Inverdeer House: Inverdeer, Scotland
Saturday - Present Day

It was a subdued breakfast that morning. Trevor was particularly stern as a tight-faced Matron had announced that each of them would be called to meet with a social worker later that morning. In the interim they were free to do as they wished, provided they stayed downstairs.

The skies were overcast, threatening rain, and the chances of getting out later that day looked pretty slim so those who enjoyed running around made the most of it, while several of the older kids hung around the games room eager to learn what they could of the previous night's fracas.

Brick, much to the surprise of everyone, headed to the door.

"Hey! Where you going, asshole?" Grant jibed.

Brick walked on, raising his right hand over his shoulder with the middle finger extended in reply. Once outside he made his way to the old basketball that lay against the rear wall of the home and went off to shoot some hoops.

The basketball hoop hung off the dividing wall that separated the back garden and the side yard to the rear of the kitchen. After a few minutes of half-hearted attempts at the hoop Brick deliberately hurled the ball too high, sending it sailing over the wall.

A metallic crash and clatter sounded from behind the wall as a steel trash can received a direct hit. "Oops!" Brick ran to the wooden gate in the wall, turning to grin at the boys who had looked to see what had caused the noise.

He opened the gate and looked through the small side window into the kitchen. It was empty. He spied the ball lying amongst a tangle of cabbage leaves, tea bags and two empty plastic milk jugs.

Checking once more in the side window, he ran the length of the kitchen wall and passed behind it. The broken glass had been cleaned up and a new pane sporting putty stains was already in place. Brick shook his head. If someone had been round here cleaning up and replacing the broken window, chances were Matt's bag had already been found.

A quick scan around the yard showed nothing more than a few weeds forcing their way through cracks in the concrete, a piece of rotten wood from the old potting shed in the corner, and a cabbage leaf obviously dropped en route to the bins.

He was about to turn back to retrieve the ball when a flash of red caught his eye. There in the shadows of the potting shed, behind a stack of old wooden crates, was Matt's bag.

"Yes!" Brick hissed quietly, and careful not to dislodge the pile of crates he retrieved the bag and ran back around the corner for the basketball. Ignoring the unpleasant odors emanating from the fallen bin, he righted it, and replaced most of the spilled contents.

With the bag slung on his back and the ball tucked under one arm Brick returned triumphantly to the garden and spent the next few minutes shooting hoops, surprising himself when one actually went in. Whistling to himself he made his way back inside and took the stairs two at a time, almost colliding with Trevor who was just exiting his room at the top of the stairs.

"Whoa, slow down there, son!" Trevor admonished, then recognizing Brick added, "Why are you in such a hurry?"

"Ur, nothing sir, sorry sir," Brick mumbled, pushing past Trevor and continuing to the dormitory without slowing.

Trevor locked his door. *Sir?* That was a rare salutation for Brick. He looked up the hallway in time to see Brick enter the dormitory, the red bag on his back.

"Hey!" he called, remembering Matron's instruction for everyone to remain downstairs, but was answered only by the click of the latch on the door.

Trevor glanced at his watch. "Dammit." He'd miss the bus if he didn't hurry.

He ran along the hallway and entered the dormitory without his customary knock. Brick was the only one there and he sat on his bed, the bag at his feet.

"Brick—that bag. It doesn't belong to you, does it?" Bricks face colored up, showing his guilt before he even opened his mouth to reply.

"Ur, no Mr. C." He hung his head. "It's Matt's. He asked me to look after it for him."

"Did he now?" Trevor said in a voice that did nothing to hide his disbelief. "Well, it so happens I'm going to the hospital to see him. So I think it would be best if I took it to him, don't you?"

Brick's sudden expression of relief surprised Trevor, who took the bag from him without further comment before turning back to the door.

"Mr. C?"

Trevor glanced back, again surprised at the boy's change in demeanor.

"Tell Matt I said hi, will ya? And, urrr, this wasn't my fault sir."

"Save it for the social workers, Brick."

Brick nodded.

"But I'll tell Matt you said hello. Now get your butt downstairs before I miss my bus."

Brick loped into the recreation room and slumped back on the old leather couch, hands clasped behind his head.

No one ever trusted him. *Well fine,* he thought, *I hate this shit hole anyway.* He looked through the large bay window across the lawn where leaves fluttered across the grass in the strengthening wind, and the pine trees beyond the fence swayed and creaked. The loose fence panel had been replaced; the fresh-looking post looked like one good molar in a mouth of rotten teeth.

Brick grinned. Matt had not been successful with his attempts to leave the home but Brick knew he could do better. It was time the authorities had someone else to look for, and where he was going he knew they'd never find him.

Justin Orton

Peterhead General Hospital, Scotland
Saturday - Present Day

Trevor sat waiting patiently next to the empty space where the bed should be and looked around the ward. Of the twelve beds, only four were occupied. Curtains hid three of them but he was able to see a young boy in the fourth, his suspended leg wrapped in plaster. The nurse who had guided him to the ward squeaked by on rubber-soled shoes, pushing a small trolley.

She smiled at Trevor. "He shouldn't be long now, luv."

Then she pulled one of the curtains aside and passed from view with a friendly, "Now then, Peter, how are you feeling…"

Trevor returned his attention to the magazine that lay on his lap, and idly flicked through the glossy images of cars he would never own, exotic holiday locations he would never visit, and women he could only dream of meeting. Frustrated, he dropped the magazine in the trash can.

Sounds outside the double doors to the ward made him look up to see a huge man in the uniform of an orderly, his blue jacket clearly too small to cover his bulging pectorals as he pushed a bed before him.

"Here we go, son," he said. "Back to where we started. You feeling okay?"

Trevor could not see the figure on the bed but guessed he must have nodded as the orderly gave a big grin. "That's good. Well, you take it easy now."

He wheeled the bed into the space beside Trevor. "Looks like you have a visitor, young man." He winked at Trevor. "I'll be on my way." And with a wave he left the ward.

Trevor looked at the figure on the bed. Matt was pale, and his eyes looked somehow lifeless. Trevor put that down to medication.

"Hi, Matt." He forced a smile to hide his concern.

Matt turned his head and one side of his mouth lifted in a partial smile.

"Hello, Mr. C." His voice was empty, lacking its usual enthusiasm.

"I was worried about you, son. We all are. Is there someone causing you trouble?"

Matt shook his head, and Trevor sighed.

"Can you remember what happened?"

"Yeah. I fell and hit my head."

"You cut your arm, too."

"I know."

"As far as we can tell you climbed onto the counter top and broke the kitchen window. Then you slipped, tore your arm on the broken glass and hit your head on the floor. What we can't understand is why you were trying to leave again?"

Matt said nothing.

"Look, son, I know it can't be that wonderful living in a kid's home but we care for all of you, you know? We try and make life as good as we can. I know there is trouble among the other boys, and I've seen how some treat you. If you want to talk to me you can."

Matt still made no reply and Trevor added, "I'm here because I care, Matt."

The kindness and sincerity of his words moved Matt. The urge to confide in somebody was overwhelming. But what could he say? How could he explain what was really happening? He instead changed the subject.

"Do you know how long I'll be here?"

"The nurse said maybe a few days. You have a hairline fracture and a severe concussion. But," Trevor said brightly, "I have brought you something to help pass the time." With that he reached beneath his chair and pulled up Matt's heavy school bag.

"I know you love your books and thought you might like this."

Matt looked in amazement at the bright red bag. "My bag! Where did you find it?"

"Let's say I rescued it." Trevor smiled.

Matt tried to sit up and Trevor helped, fluffing the pillow behind him, not caring he was ruining his reputation as a tough guy, should Matt relay this on his return to the home.

Matt reached for the bag. "Thanks Mr. C." Then a sudden fear grabbed him. "Did you look in it?"

The look on Matt's face startled Trevor and he suddenly wondered what was in the bag that Matt clearly did not want him to see. A horrible thought materialized. Drugs? Is this what it was all about? Not Matt, surely?

"No!" He replied truthfully, wishing now he had. "I didn't have the time had I wanted to. Do you distrust us that much?"

Matt hung his head. "I'm sorry sir." He yawned. "Thanks for bringing it to me."

"You're welcome. You get some rest and we'll see you back at the home in a few days." They both watched the nurse exit the curtain across the room and step over to the bed beside Matt's.

"You're next, young man," she said, pulling the curtain around the sleeping boy with the broken leg.

Trevor took his cue and stood, gathering his coat from the back of the chair. "Try coming and talking to me before running off again, hmmmm?"

Matt forced a smile. "Yeah. I guess I was pretty stupid."

Trevor placed a hand on his shoulder, "You're not stupid, son," he said. "Just try and have a little faith in those who really care about you." Trevor looked at the bag. "And Matt. If you're in any kind of trouble, any kind, I'm here to help." He nodded to the closed curtain beside Matt, "That cute nurse will be fussing over you any minute, so I'll come and see you again tomorrow. Try and stay out of trouble until then, okay?"

Matt forced a laugh. "I'll be fine, Mr. C. Thanks for coming." He watched Trevor walk toward the end of the ward and was a little disappointed when he did not turn and wave from the door.

Matt watched the heavy double doors swish together, then reached for his bag. With relief he saw the book was still there. He dropped the bag onto the visitors' chair and decided to wait for the nurse to finish her rounds. He hoped her visit involved some painkillers—his head hurt like hell.

He closed his eyes against the sterile glare of the ward lighting and wondered what would happen to him next. What did the authorities do to a kid that had trashed a children's home? Thoughts of a juvenile detention center filled him with dread.

The sudden rattle of the curtain announced the arrival of the nurse and she broke his train of thoughts as she busied herself taking his temperature, pulse and blood pressure.

"You're going to have to be careful with this foot, young man. That glass went in deep."

The nurse removed the dressing from his foot, and he could hear her indrawn breath.

"You heal quickly! Now let's take a look at that shoulder."

She applied fresh dressings to his injuries then made ready to leave.

"Can you leave the curtains please?" Matt asked.

"Sure." She smiled. "Now, how's that head of yours? I have some more tablets for the pain, if you need them."

"It still hurts."

"Alright then. Here we are." She handed over two small white tablets and a little plastic beaker half filled with water. "These should help."

"Thanks."

He took the tablets and handed back the beaker. He glanced at his wrist to check the time and noticed his watch was missing. He glanced down, so was his medallion! "Nurse!" Matt called out.

She poked her head through the join in the curtains, "Yes?"

"My watch, and my chain! They've gone!"

The nurse smiled and walked back to his bedside. "Relax, they're here." She gestured to the little cabinet on wheels next to his bed. "Your clothes are in the bottom, and see that little red button there?"

He nodded.

"Push that if you need anything. Someone will be straight over." She parted the curtains to leave once more and looked back over her shoulder.

"You only press that button in an emergency, you understand?" He heard the rattling wheels of her medicine trolley fade away as she headed for the doors to the ward. He was alone.

First he put on his watch and then the medallion, relieved at the cool touch of the metal against his skin.

Next he reached for his bag and removed the heavy book and then quickly surveyed what else was inside. His notebook, pencil case, a school Biology text book, the novel from the library, and one overlooked dirty sock from soccer practice the previous day.

Matt lay back on his pillow, grateful for the painkillers he had recently taken. Already the pain in his head was receding. He lifted the book and searched again for the picture of the knight with the face of his father. Finding the picture, he spent some time studying it and again marveled at the likeness. Was it really his father? Part of him wanted it to be but he had to acknowledge it was impossible.

Somewhat reluctantly he turned the page and then resumed his search for more pictures. The heavy parchment pages flicked by and he came to a new chapter entitled "Myrddin." He caught his breath. He had read enough of the Arthurian legends to recognize the Celtic spelling of the name Merlin.

Faster now he flipped the pages and finally came across another picture. This was much smaller than the earlier ones. It occupied a small oval frame at the head of one of the pages. The picture showed a man in a long flowing robe standing atop a large hill gazing out over a wide river. Hills were in the background and long grass obscured the feet of the man, who leaned heavily on a staff. The picture was captioned but Matt had no idea what the strange words meant and so continued on through the text. Another new chapter started and there was that word that had sounded so familiar the night before.

Invalone was the title, the "I" was entwined with ivy, and lilies lay around its base. In parenthesis after the word was the phrase "Av Allan." He stared at the word for some time and then marking the place with his thumb he turned back through the pages to the map where he had first seen the word.

Matt traced his finger over the map to where three rivers and an area of marshland to the north created what looked like an inland island.

"Av Allan." He whispered the words quietly, listening to the sound of them. He repeated it again, faster this time, and then as if someone had shouted it aloud he realized where he had heard it before. Avalon. Av Allan—Avalon. Could it be? Pictures of knights, a king, Myrddin, which he knew meant Merlin. And now Avalon? The fabled resting place of King Arthur, the place he had been taken after that fateful battle at Camlann?

Matt's knowledge of the Arthurian legend ran deep. He had read every book he could find on the subject and could recite the famous legend beginning with Arthur's conception at Tintagel, Cornwall. Born the bastard offspring of Uther Pendragon, he had risen to be High King of England in the early sixth century. Matt cataloged the highlights of the legend in his mind. He could recall the stories of Arthur's two swords, the first pulled from the stone declaring his right to be king, and the second, the famous Excalibur, given as a gift by the lady of the lake. He knew of the twelve incredible battles of which legend told, and he recalled how devastated he had been the first time he had read the story of Arthur's death at the hand of Mordred at Camlann. He had put the book aside for a week or more before being able to continue through the last chapter where Arthur's sister, Morgan Le Fey, had taken her mortally wounded brother to the fabled isle of Avalon and there awaited the arrival of Arthur's adviser and friend the wizard Merlin.

Legend told how Arthur did not die, but rather was left to rest in eternal slumber to return again in England's greatest need. It was one of the greatest legends of all time and Arthur had always been Matt's hero. Now, looking at the map he struggled to relate what he knew to what was shown here. Anyone who knew anything of King Arthur accepted he was not real, more likely a composite character of many local heroes. Even so, all the stories of Arthur and his Knights of the Round Table, were centered around England and in particular Cornwall, Glastonbury and even Wales. Camelot, so legend implied, was near to the Welsh border or even in Wales itself.

Matt had invested hours poring over books in the library and reading the speculations that the city of Glastonbury was the most likely modern day location of the fabled city. Yet all those landmarks were missing from this map. The only details to be found were in lowland Scotland and as far as Matt knew, Arthur, Merlin, and the legends of the past had no connection with Scotland at all.

He laid the book down on his lap and closed his eyes, trying to draw a connection between the book and the legend he knew so well. Matt sighed and slipped the book back into his bag, suddenly too tired to think.

He glanced at his watch. It was getting late, almost eleven, and the pain pills were making him drowsy. He looked out the window. A few faint stars speckled the night sky but much of the beauty of the night was lost in the glare of the city below. He flicked the white button above his bed and the reading lamp faded, leaving him lying in semi-darkness.

The soft sound of voices could be heard from the nurses' station through the swing doors at the end of the ward. No other sounds from outside filtered through the vacuum-sealed double-glazing of the windows. Matt pulled the bed covers up to his chin and welcomed the opportunity of a relaxed night's sleep—his first in several days.

He had barely closed his eyes when he heard the swish of the double doors and the unmistakable tread of booted feet.

"No," he breathed to himself. "Not again. Not here!" Matt lay frozen in shock and terror, eyes wide, waiting, listening. The footsteps came closer. He was being foolish. It was ridiculous to think those people could locate him here, but still his heart raced in his chest. The footsteps were loud now, almost at his bed.

Matt grabbed the long white cord that held the red button and jabbed it hard.

There was no sound but a red light started blinking above his bed. He lay there staring at the curtains around him. "Come on, somebody!" he pleaded to the darkness. "Please hurry!"

Footsteps sounded from outside the curtain. A feeling of relief—the nurse was here. He sat up in the bed as the curtains parted.

A tall cloaked figure approached the bed, a large purple bruise covering one side of his face. A hideous grin spread across his damaged features. "Hello, Matt," Deglin hissed.

Matt threw himself forward and heard the cotton of his pajama top rip as Deglin's black-gloved hand grabbed the thin material. He slid off the bed, grabbed his bag and bolted for the doors. He didn't stop as he raced past the unmanned nurses' station. A white button blinked on a black telephone, and a magazine was open on the desk.

With each step Matt's injured foot burned with pain. He took a side corridor to the right, and passed through another set of double doors. A green "Fire Exit" sign pointed to his left. He followed it.

Passing through a set of doors, then another, he found himself on a large landing. An elevator was to his right, and a stairway beside that. One flight led up to the left and another down to the right. The entire place smelled of bleach and antiseptic cleaner.

He ran toward the elevator, but realized there was no time to wait for it. He changed direction and bolted past two public telephones hanging from the wall and took the stairs down. Matt's foot was making wet slapping noises now and he knew he had reopened the wound leaving bloody footprints behind him.

He turned the quarter landing and took the last flight of stairs two at a time. He almost fell the last three steps and stumbled through the wooden fire door at the bottom. With a glance over his shoulder, he saw Deglin leap the last flight and catch the heavy door as it swung back toward him. A large open foyer was to Matt's right, a little parade of shops all closed up with metal shutters. Beyond the foyer were large doors that led outside. Ignoring the pain in his foot he doubled his efforts and raced for the doors.

The sign above them read Exit; he would make it, he was nearly there. But the expected hiss of the automatic doors did not occur and instead Matt crashed headlong into the safety glass. He stopped himself with outflung arms and read the little plastic sign glued to the glass before him. The letters engraved in red told the story, "Doors open 7am, Doors close 10pm."

A long red arrow pointed left: "Main Entrance." Through the locked doors Matt saw an ambulance reverse up to open doors where a number of doctors and nurses were waiting.

"Emergency" blazed from large red letters above the doors. A few brief seconds was all it took to take this in and Matt was running again. It was possible the main entrance would be locked this late, admittance to the hospital only permitted by a security guard. Accident and Emergency, however, was always open. He put his back to the doors and looked back from where he had come. Little red footprints led up the corridor. Deglin was nowhere to be seen. He glanced around. Low-backed chairs and empty tables covered the carpeted foyer. A coffee stand was closed for the night, a chalkboard beside the shutter advertising sausage rolls, Cornish pasties and hot chocolate.

He moved to follow the corridor to the Emergency entrance when from behind a pillar Deglin leaped. His heavy body slammed into Matt and together the pair slid across the polished floor, banging into a large potted plant. The plant fell against a water stand and water, soil and paper cups scattered across the floor in a wet muddy mess. Matt was pinned by the heavy body and he scrambled desperately to get away, hands clawing in the muddy water on the floor.

For a moment the weight on his back eased and then a sudden blow to the side of his head knocked him senseless. Matt slumped to the floor, limp and still.

Chapter 8
Sacrifice

Passage from the Book of Myrthinus
- *Arturius*

*A*s the Roman legions fled Britain, Dardanos returned to Europe and for the next hundred years I helped establish the fledgling Scotland— guardian nation of the Stonehenge key. My friend King Fergus had long since died and two descendants, brothers, stood in line for the throne: Aidan the warrior, who governed the new territory of Mannan in the East, and Iogenan, a gentler soul who governed the western lands from Argyle to Kintyre. Saint Columba chose Aidan to be anointed king of all Scotland and he received the crown in the year 574AD. Aidan was a good man and in his youth had been an able warrior, but it was his eldest son, Arturius, that interested me the most.

Through my friendship to Aidan I was appointed tutor to the young man and I took him under my wing. He was a handsome lad with a devilish wit. A quick and able pupil, his mind was every bit as sharp as his sword, and he soon became as versed in the art of politics and diplomacy as he was in swordplay and the tactics of the battlefield. His father withdrew to the western isles and left Arturius governor of Mannan. We, or should I say, I, had enjoyed almost a century of comparative peace, but that was about to change.

Twenty years earlier, and unknown to me, Dardanos had made his way to Orkney, just a few hundred miles north of mainland Britain. There he befriended King Canellat, the man that legend would come to know as King Lot. Lot was an island raider. He never harbored desire for conquest over his mainland cousins, but preferred instead to live off the fruits of others' labors, pillaging settlement after settlement and reveling in the thrill of battle. His longboats would return to the islands laden with stolen livestock, grain, ale, trinkets and women. Among his many trophies was a beautiful young girl by the name of Morgause, and Lot doted on her. He made her his queen and succumbed to every whim and fanciful desire the girl could dream of, including her obsession with the dark arts.

She introduced Dardanos to witchcraft and necromancy, and together they plotted and schemed to regain the key to Porta Marsonia. It began with Morgause encouraging Lot to invade the northern tribes, and while her husband was away campaigning against the Picts she spent her time closeted with Dardanos becoming his pupil and learning the power of the mind. The two grew close and an inevitable romance followed. When Lot returned at the end of his first failed campaign, he found Morgause heavy with Dardanos's child, and a few weeks later Mordred was born.

Arturius had turned eighteen when news came to us of King Lot's death, and the sudden ascension of his "Son" Mordred to the throne. What followed was an evil time, as Dardanos returned to mainland Britain with a huge force of longboats. His progress was both swift and brutal. The Pictish tribes were decimated, their people hunted down and killed like wolves. It was pure genocide and these northern tribesmen became lost to history.

To Raise a King

The northern and eastern borders of King Aidan's lands were the next to fall under direct assault, and soon Dalriada was on the brink of collapse. Sick and aging, Aidan took to a monastery in Iona and passed complete control of the country to Arturius, with myself elevated from tutor to counselor.

Alone the Scots could not hope to stand, and there was little chance of support from the lands to the south where a fragmented patchwork of petty kingdoms and clans were led by warring chieftains who vied for dominance over territories that lacked any formal boundary.

Kintyre fell the following year, and Arturius was forced southeast to the old Roman fort of Camelon near the town of Falkirk.

It was an impressive fortress for its time, and from this central location Arturius was able to defend his shrinking borders, and those of his battling neighbors. Winter gave the men a reprieve but Arturius did not rest. He spent five long months braving the storms and cold, rallying the southern chieftains to his cause and when the first green shoots of spring forced their way through the thinning snow the ranks of our army had swollen dramatically. There was something magical about Arturius that year. The men that followed him into battle loved him and after a string of stunning victories Arturius was named Dux Bellorum—war leader—of the combined kingdoms of the North. He took the title grudgingly, refusing all those that would elevate him still further to High King of Northern Britain.

A year of uncertain peace followed, and as the clans returned home, Arturius completed the construction of a massive earthwork near Stirling. It comprised a series of terraced layers, the center being a mound some eighteen feet in diameter. This mound was capped with a slab of polished granite. All those who met there were ordered in accordance to seniority. The higher their place on the mound the more prominent the leader, until you reached the granite slab where the kings of neighboring lands would stand with Arturius and myself. The Kings Knot, it is now called, and it sits *still in the shadows of Stirling's castle, its history lost, its purpose forgotten, for none now living know that we called this place The Round Table.*

Tioram Forest, Eilean Tioram, Scotland
597AD

The sudden drop shocked Matt back to consciousness. He rolled into a patch of long coarse grass and gulped painfully at the cold night air.

Unable to move, he lay shivering against the frost-hardened earth as two dark-clad figures approached. Deglin took a step across his prostrate form and threw something to the approaching men. Matt felt his stomach knot in panic when he saw it was his bag.

"Her majesty will find that of value."

Matt managed to lift his head and saw rough rope bound his feet. He tried to move, but his arms were pinned behind him, and more rope bit painfully into his wrists. He let he head fall back to the grass. No clouds hid the moon or the stars and the night was bitterly cold. Rolling hills bathed in moonlight spread out to either side, but little else was visible. Matt's shivering grew more intense. His torn pajamas offered no protection from the ground and his back felt as if it was on fire. He watched each breath stream away in ragged clouds as he struggled to control his trembling body.

"Hey!" Matt tried shouting but his voice was little more than a hoarse whisper. He tried again and instead began to cough. He managed to roll to his side feeling nauseous, afraid he was going to vomit.

"Keep still, boy!" Deglin warned.

Matt ignored the instruction and struggled to his knees, surprised to see his medallion swing free from his pajama top. He wondered why these people had not removed it. Then he remembered Brick and the sparks that had leaped from the medallion to burn the boy's hand. Could these people not touch it in the same way Brick had been unable to?

Footsteps crunched in the frost behind him.

"I said keep still!" A sudden kick to his back sent Matt sprawling. With his hands behind him he was unable to break his fall and hit the ground face first. Dirt, grass, and the copper tang of blood filled his mouth and he struggled to spit it away.

A coarse laugh rang out and Matt angled his head to see the man who had caught his bag head off up the hill. Moments later the man who had kicked him came into view. It was Deglin. The former gardener laughed at the boy's futile efforts to struggle and scooped him up.

"Save your strength, lad. It's all over for you now."

They walked higher, their feet crunching through frost-stiffened grass as they worked their way around an outcrop of lichen-covered rocks. It did not take long to reach the hilltop and Matt twisted to get a better view but there was little to see other than a gentle slope that descended toward a vast tract of woodland. His captors headed down toward the darkness of the trees.

"Where are you taking me?" Matt asked as the party came to a halt and gathered at the tree line.

"Shut the boy up or gag him." The leader snarled as he struggled to light a torch. Sparks fluttered away like angry fireflies and tendrils of black smoke rose from the smoldering rags. With a sudden whoosh and flaring of sooty flame the torch burned steadily. Matt let his head drop as they resumed their march and he passed into the forest bouncing awkwardly on Deglin's shoulder.

The scent of pine grew stronger, a somewhat pleasant counterpoint to the stale odor of sweat and ale that permeated Deglin's clothing. Needles carpeted the forest floor and the trees grew closer together. Matt was shaking uncontrollably now from shock and cold, and his neck throbbed from the constant effort to keep his head up.

He tried to relax but something caught his attention to the right of the pathway. He twisted his head to look but it quickly faded into the darkness. Matt listened for some sound but heard nothing above the labored breathing of Deglin and the steady crunch of feet on the forest floor.

Gradually Matt's eyes became more attuned to the darkness and twice he caught sight of what looked like pale eyes staring from the shelter of the thick undergrowth. If he strained his neck far enough he could discern patches of black sky visible through the canopy of trees. Here and there an occasional star twinkled.

Unable to hold his head up any longer Matt finally closed his eyes, trying to will away the burning ache in his neck while he bounced along across the shoulders of his captor. He had almost grown accustomed to the man's swinging gait when Deglin stumbled on a root and Matt jerked his head up in time to see a ghostly shadow glide across the pathway behind them. Matt watched as something leaped a bush and landed on silent feet. He twisted, trying to follow the creature but it vanished once more into the darkness.

"Keep still!" The arm around his waist tightened, crushing the air from his lungs and Matt gasped. Obediently he went limp and the cruel grip relaxed. Matt sucked in a mouthful of air, ribs aching in his chest. He did not see the shadowy form anymore, and was unable to tell how much longer they marched through the trees but it seemed an eternity before they entered a small clearing in the forest and he was once more unceremoniously dropped to the ground. Sudden light lit the ground around him and the sound of a door opening aroused his curiosity but his exhausted body, numb with cold, was too tired to move. There was no frost here, the surrounding trees providing shelter from the frigid winds, and he let his head fall to the earth. He wanted to sleep, to escape the pain and the fear. He stared into the forest and as sleep reached out to take him he thought he caught a final glimpse of those pale watchful eyes staring back at him from the trees.

Hours, minutes? Matt had no idea how long he had slept. As his senses awakened he became aware of the stiffness in his arms and legs. An experimental movement was rewarded by the chafing rub of rough rope. A coarse blanket covered his body and it prickled the exposed skin of his feet and hands. He stifled a soft groan; his foot throbbed and his arms ached, but at least he was warm.

He could hear several voices. Slowly he opened his eyes, hoping not to draw attention to the fact he was awake. The room appeared large and a smoky haze filled the air. The floor was of wood and the walls were rough cut stone. There was no ceiling, just large wooden beams, roughly squared, supporting a thick covering of thatch. It was much like Myrthinus's cottage, he realized, but sparser and less comforting. Light came from numerous torches thrust into iron brackets. It gave the room a hellish cast, and black oily smoke curled up forming an ever-darkening cloud in the rafters that slowly dissipated through an opening that served as a chimney. A man was speaking and Matt recognized the nasal quality of Deglin's voice.

"But we thought he was dead? You assured us he was dead!"

A murmur of assent confirmed for Matt that several other people were in the room. Deglin continued, gaining confidence, "Can we trust this text? How can you be sure it's genuine?"

A woman answered, her words spoken in a soft, almost lilting accent.

"I recognize his hand, but beyond that each page reeks of his presence." There was the sound of crackling parchment, and Matt could almost visualize her paging through the book Myrthinus had entrusted to him.

It must not fall into their hands.

"There is much to be learned from these pages." She paused before continuing almost reverently, "It is fortunate for us that he entrusted it to the boy."

"So you believe all this? You believe that *he* still lives? But how? The time cycle in which we are trapped was created after his death, not before. You must be mistaken."

"You dare challenge me on this?"

Matt was startled at the aggressive change in the woman's voice.

There was a long pause and then her voice settled again into the honey-smooth, almost enchanting tone Matt had first heard. "This book is not just a history, it is a message to its author reaching back across time. Just as we have to relearn all we know with the beginning of each cycle, so must he." She paused and the room hung in respectful silence, the only sound the crackling fire.

"He must have protected Arturius..."

Matt slowly slid his back along the wall until he could peer under the table that blocked his view.

This new position afforded a much better view of the proceedings. He could see a recess beside a large stone chimney. Two men stood there, partially obscuring the fire which crackled and popped in its sooty hearth.

The woman continued, "...the Dux Bellorum—he alone could unite the people against us." Another page turned and then her voice grew excited. "The rod of Dardanos! Arturius had it!"

A new voice interrupted, and Matt could hear the heavy tramp of booted feet across the cottage floor. "You are certain of this?" The voice was harsh and deep, somehow rasping as if the act of speaking caused the man pain.

The woman's voice continued, "Yes! Look. See here? It says the rod was given into the keeping of Arturius!"

"So where he sleeps, so may the rod be found?"

"Maybe so. Find the would-be king and we find the rod of Dardanos!"

A high-pitched voice interjected, "The wizard still lives, Your Majesty, and what of this boy? Can we so casually dismiss those we have toiled against for so long? Should we suddenly divert our attention to a legend? And what of the brotherhood? Could they too be re-uniting to stand in our way?"

"The wizard will come to us. The boy is surety of that."

"And the brotherhood?" the voice pressed. "What of them?"

The harsh and somewhat distorted voice responded, cutting off the queen, "They are but a memory!"

"And what of the man who almost removed your head, Lord Aldivon?" Deglin interjected. "Is he but a memory also? Remember there are two empty nails in your precious painting!"

Heavy footsteps sounded and Matt caught a glimpse of an incredibly tall figure with shoulder length black hair. Deglin cowered back against the wall and Matt watched as the giant man leaned forward, his face inches from Deglin's.

"He was outcast from the brethren. Too much a coward to take his own life, he fled. He stopped being a concern to us after the first time cycle. As for the others..." The man pulled away from Deglin and faced the others in the room. There came a hideous bubbly sound from the speaker's throat and Matt realized with horror it was laughter.

"I have personally witnessed the death of them all. The brotherhood are a memory, nothing more."

There was a low murmur of respect from those gathered and Aldivon faced the woman and continued, "With the exception of the wizard, all those who would oppose us are dead. We are but seven months away from the next alignment; time is not exactly on our side. Your Majesty, if the rod is with Arturius, he must be found."

The woman's voice was soft but filled with contempt. "Time? You dare talk to me of time?"

Matt heard the rustle of a heavy gown and saw the woman move into view. The table restricted his view and he could see no further than her waist. She continued talking, moving a little closer to Aldivon.

"Finding the rod of Dardanos before the alignment of the worlds is critical. The boy's mind is empty. What the wizard passed to him was the book, nothing more. He is of no further use to us.

"There remain but two who know the location of the rod—Myrdinn and Arturius. Why the old wizard is seeking this boy is a mystery to me. Why has he protected him for so long? What value does the boy offer? Whatever those reasons are, whatever the wizard plans, he will risk much to save him. The boy will be our bait; and when the wizard comes he will tell us everything he knows before the end."

Matt held his breath, suddenly things started to fall into place and with a sickening dread he realized what they were saying. Deglin spoke again, breaking the boy's thoughts.

"The boy wears the mark of the Pendragon. Perhaps the wizard plans for him to continue the line of the brethren?"

Matt went cold. He felt the cool metal of the medallion against his chest. The mark of the Pendragon? In Arthurian legend "Pendragon" had been the name of Arthur's bloodline. He left the thought unfinished. It was clear they intended to kill him, and right now survival was more important than speculating more on Arthur. He scanned the room looking for some way out as the woman confirmed his death sentence.

"The boy will die—" She was interrupted by the steely rasp of a hastily drawn sword.

"As you command, my Queen!" Matt cringed as Deglin strode around the table, sword drawn. The hood was pulled back and the angry purple bruise on the side of the man's head was clear to see.

Matt sprawled back across the floor as the former gardener's blade swept down toward him and then a brilliant flash and a shower of sparks momentarily dazzled him. The room rang with the clash of steel.

"Hold!" barked the man with the distorted voice, and Matt opened his eyes to see Aldivon had somehow reached across the table and blocked the blow with his own sword. The man's forearm quivered and the muscles bunched as he held the gardener's two-handed blow with only one arm. Slowly he lifted the other man's blade and Matt's eyes re-focused on the bright steel that hovered inches from his eyes. It shone like silver and caught the light, sparkling as if with some fire of its own. He looked along the blade to the man who held it. Deep-set eyes watched him and an almost mocking glint sparkled in the reflected light of the sword. "You have the look of your father, boy," he said in a hoarse whisper, and grinned. Matt noted the long scar across the man's throat and a fresher scratch to his cheek. He knew this man, had seen him before, but when? A dream, a memory?

"Put up your weapon, Deglin." It was the woman who spoke, and Matt pulled his eyes from Aldivon's unblinking stare and watched as she walked around the table. "No one hungers for his death more than I, my friend." She placed her long white hand on the gardener's arm. "You shall have your revenge, but not now, not here."

Even to Matt's inexperienced eyes there was some strange attraction to the woman. Despite the unnatural whiteness of her skin, and the thin almost bloodless lips that hinted at a hidden cruelty, an enticing air seemed to radiate from her. He felt his pulse quicken, but when she looked down at him with violet, almost black eyes, Matt shrank away from the naked hatred that burned in their depths. There was no compassion in the look she gave him and he quickly turned his head away from the malevolence of her stare.

"I trusted you," Matt breathed, looking now at Deglin. "I thought you were my friend."

"As did I," said Aldivon.

Deglin withdrew his sword and sheathed the blade, and Matt felt a stubborn surge of pride when he recalled the fight in the kitchen the night before. Deglin stood back against the wall, bowing deferentially to the queen. "Forgive me, my lady."

Aldivon fixed his former captain with a frosty stare, but the gardener had moved away.

The queen, her face devoid of any expression, withdrew a sparkling crystal pyramid from the folds of her gown. It appeared to be made of glass and as she held it so a blue-white fire flared within.

Shapes, unclear to Matt, swirled within the light.

"Already the wizard has reached the forest," she said. "He knows we have the boy. Our time grows short.

"Aldivon! See he finds the portal, then you yourself return to Tioram and prepare rooms for the wizard. Take the book with you and I shall make further study of it on my return. I would know the truth behind this Av Allan. If Arturius truly lives then he must be found. With the rod of Dardanos nothing can stop us."

"Killing the boy is a mistake," said Aldivon.

"You have your orders, Aldivon!"

"And I do not agree with them!"

Matt could almost taste the tension in the air.

The queen continued, stepping toward Aldivon. "If you value this boy's life beyond your own then persist with this insubordination! My patience with you is at an end!" Her voice lost some of its fire, taking on an icy coldness. "Do as instructed or die with the boy!"

Matt held his breath as he watched Aldivon's hand clench the hilt of his sword, then his grip relaxed. "I was wrong. Forgive me, my Queen."

She slipped the glowing pyramid back into her gown and faced the adjoining room, turning her back to Aldivon.

"Naveena, prepare the boy."

"Yes m'lady." The voice that answered was that of a younger girl and Matt watched as a new figure stepped from the shadows. She wore a long gown of the deepest green and was surprisingly barefoot. Red hair cascaded down her back in loose and natural waves. She stopped before a cabinet and reached to a high shelf. He caught a brief flash as the fire reflected from an ankle bracelet and Matt held his breath waiting for her to turn so he could see her face. There came the clinking of glass on glass, and the sound of liquid being poured. She began to turn but Aldivon suddenly stood before her and Matt felt a fleeting regret at missing the opportunity to see her face.

Aldivon reached out a hand and brushed Naveena's cheek with his fingers. She twisted her head away and Matt watched his hand slide down the front of her bodice. She slapped at his hand, stepping away.

"Mother? Please!"

Aldivon laughed and grabbed at her arm. "The phial, give it to me!"

She dropped a small glass phial into his outstretched hand and tried to pull away but he maintained his grip.

"Enough!" The queen's voice cracked like a whip.

Aldivon stared at the girl a moment longer and then released her. He threw the phial to a nearby soldier. "Give this to the boy. The rest of you come with me."

Turning on his heel he left the cottage and several men followed him into the night. Matt could not fail to notice that one of them carried the heavy leather-bound book.

Rough hands suddenly grabbed him and jerked his head back. Matt's eyes watered as the man pinched his nostrils together and poured the thick amber contents of the phial down his throat. It burned and tears stung his eyes. Coughing and spluttering, bound and helpless, Matt was dragged into the cold and was once again carried through the trees. They had not gone far before the drug coursing through his veins took effect and Matt slipped into unconsciousness, oblivious to the ghostly eyes that watched from the undergrowth.

It took several minutes for Matt to realize he was still alive. Blurred creamy images oozed into focus as if he was surfacing from a pool of milk. Whatever drug they had given him had left him feeling remote and detached from his body. There was no fear, no pain. He blinked, waiting for his eyes to clear.

He was lying down, and above him the night sky gradually swam into focus ablaze with stars. The surface beneath his back felt far away, yet something told him it was smooth and hard, like polished stone. Strangely he did not feel the cold, yet the material covering his body felt gossamer thin and flimsy. He tried to move but his body refused to respond. He should have felt panic, but his dulled senses registered nothing more than a resigned acceptance of his predicament.

There was a sound to his right, and much to Matt's surprise he found he was able to turn his head a little. Looking around he saw several large standing stones, their blue-black shadows reaching out like fingers toward the darkness of the nearby forest. Before each stone a tall robed figure stood, each with a blazing torch held before him.

The scene was bathed in ghostly white moonlight, and the eerie atmosphere was accented by the shriek of an owl. Matt rolled his head to the left and gasped.

A beautiful woman, impossible to age, stepped toward him. She wore a gown of the deepest blue, and a heavy fur-trimmed cloak hung across her shoulders. The moonlight shone on lustrous jet-black hair. He watched as she approached, unable to take his eyes from her face. She had high cheekbones and a delicate little nose above thin but sensuous lips. Her complexion was pale, almost white, and her eyes were of the deepest blue flecked with a color that made them appear almost violet. Matt dimly recognized her as the queen from the cottage but his memories were elusive and fragmented. A sudden feeling of desire, and a burning arousal brought a fleeting sense of feeling to his otherwise numb and unresponsive body.

She came and stood beside him and reached a long slender arm behind his head. When her hand came back into view she held a knife, the long blade thin and slightly curved.

Somewhere in the foggy mess of his mind the knowledge he should be afraid finally took hold. Everything around him had taken on an unreal quality, as if he was living a moment through someone else's eyes. Deep inside some awareness battered at his drugged senses trying to alert him to the peril he was in, but his body and emotions remained dull, unresponsive. He became aware of a gentle whispering sound growing louder and louder. The words were strange, the language foreign.

The whispering became a chant, a repetitive mesmerizing rhythm. He watched in morbid fascination as the woman's long slender fingers altered their grip around the knife. Slowly the blade came down toward him and he felt the cold steel touch against his neck. A single tear escaped his eye and for a few precious seconds it hung suspended on his eyelash, a glassy jewel encapsulating all the fear, pain and sadness that churned inside.

He blinked, and the tear ran down his cheek to be absorbed by the cold stone on which he lay. Matt wondered, as he waited to die, how many other tears, how much blood, had soaked into this stone before him. He felt the blade press against his chest and tensed for the burst of pain that would surely follow, but none came.

The woman started speaking and he opened his eyes. As she spoke she brought her left hand up to hover over his chest. A glowing nimbus of white light shone around her delicate fingers.

She raised the knife blade and he saw that she had hooked the chain that held his medallion. Blue fire crackled along its length but it had no discernible effect on the woman. She passed her glowing hand over the chain and uttered a single command. Without a sound the chain snapped and the medallion slid along the last few links falling in to her waiting hand.

At the removal of the chain and the medallion Matt was at once consumed by a blinding terror. The fear was so intense it was almost painful and he wanted to scream, but the debilitating effect of the drug made such release impossible.

Despite the panic that threatened to overwhelm him, his brain still registered the scene around him and he watched everything in terrified fascination as the queen held his medallion high and cried aloud, "Behold! The mark of the Pendragon!"

A chorus of cheers rose from the gathered men and as one they raised their swords high in salute to the queen.

From the shelter of the trees an archer watched as the queen lowered her pale arms and turned again to the boy. Carefully he nocked an arrow and sighted along the feathered shaft. His fingers took up the slack in the bow string and he held it taut against his cheek. It was not time for the queen to die. Not yet. He still needed her. He shifted his aim, aligning the steel-tipped arrow with Deglin's chest. Aldivon took a deep breath and let it out slowly, the bow steady in his hands. Whatever happened next, Matt had to live.

"Deglin—" the queen commanded, "to me!"

Matt had not noticed the dark figure until he moved to stand beside the queen. His hood was thrown back and he scowled at the paralyzed boy. The woman placed the broken chain and medallion around Deglin's neck and then ran her finger along the chain. The metal glowed at her touch and Matt could see the broken links had been rejoined.

"You have served me well, Deglin." she said softly. "Remain vigilant. If the wizard values this boy, his time to appear grows short."

Deglin nodded, and the queen stepped to Matt's feet. She held back her head, arms stretched once more to the sky, and began to chant.

Deglin raised his sword and laid it across Matt's neck, and the weight of the blade pressed painfully against him. Every nerve, every fiber in Matt's body screamed out in terror as the blade slowly lifted, curving back over the assassin's head ready for the final blow.

The queen continued to chant, joined by a chorus of voices from the assembled men. The cadence of the chant became faster, and with it beat Matt's heart. His chest heaved and his breath came in gasps; sweat poured from his body, and then there was a sudden and total silence.

His eyes darted from the woman at his feet to the sword above his head. He saw Deglin's arms reach back, saw his shoulders bunch as he prepared for the downward sweep of the blade. Matt turned his head, unable to watch, and from the shadows of the nearest stone, two pale eyes like those he had seen in the forest stared back at him.

He blinked, and a split second later the eyes sprang from the shadows. Like an arrow, the sleek yet powerful form of the creature arched from the ground and leaped across Matt's terrified face. Black lips were pulled back revealing a mouth full of gleaming white fangs. A low and blood-curdling growl boiled in the animal's throat, and the ruff around its neck bristled like a mane.

Mia slammed into the body of the former gardener, her front paws knocking the air from his lungs. He staggered back and the dog's jaws closed on his unprotected neck.

From the trees Aldivon stared in amazement as Deglin and the husky fell to the ground. He let the tension relax in the bow and watched the drama unfold amid the stones.

The queen screamed as Deglin fell. The man clasped his hands to his torn neck, dark blood spurting in pulsing jets from between his fingers, staining his tunic and splattering the frosted grass with crimson pearls. Deglin struggled to his knees, one hand held to his throat, the other trying to fend off Mia who had now recovered from her initial leap and stood snapping at his face, her ears laid back and her muzzle crimson with blood.

Four soldiers leaped away from the stones and ran toward their stricken comrade.

The woman backed into the center of the circle, shouting for the others to remain in place. "The wizard has come! Now is our chance—take him!"

Mia danced aside as the men approached, and lashed out at the leg of the nearest attacker. She was light on her feet and fast, very fast. She easily ducked a poorly aimed sword stroke and then spun again, her front legs stretched out before her, her powerful hindquarters bunched in preparation to spring. The growling intensified as the men tried to follow her, and with a deep and angry snarl she leaped from the ground and sent her sixty pounds of muscle crashing into the chest of another soldier. Unable to hold the husky at bay he too went down, dropping his sword and trying to protect his head and face from the snapping, foaming jaws.

Matt watched in panic as the nearest soldier chopped down with his sword toward Mia's back. The blow would have cut her in half but somehow she sensed it and leaped away. There was no time to stop the stroke and the blade bit deep into the fallen solder killing the man it was intended to save. The boy felt his stomach churn at the sudden violence and he was grateful the darkness of the night hid most of the gore.

Morgause ran toward the soldiers still standing at the stones, and with a ferocity that astounded Matt a snarling Mia leaped after her. He struggled to raise his head when suddenly a black-gloved hand slapped onto the rock beside him. Face torn and bloody, Deglin pulled himself up, still clutching the mangled remains of his throat. His eyes were dull, his wounds fatal, but hate drove him on. He grabbed the knife that the queen had let fall and lunged at Matt's chest. There was sickening thud as the end of a wooden staff crashed into Deglin's ruined face and he staggered back from the blow.

Striding into the circle came Myrthinus. The wizard seemed to radiate power and his eyes flashed fire as he caught the staggering Deglin by the chain around his neck. Myrthinus held him there for a few moments before a surge of power from his staff sent Deglin hurtling into the nearest stone, where he fell in a crumpled heap, leaving the silver chain dangling from the wizard's fingers.

With surprising speed Mrythinus crossed to the boy, placed the chain around his neck and then gently lifted him into a sitting position. At once the intense terror faded away, but the medallion's power could not protect Matt from the sickening sight of the battle around him. He fought to keep from vomiting and tried to gasp a warning to the wizard. Behind him two soldiers raced forward and the nearest swung his sword in a two handed blow aimed at Myrthinus's back.

But he never finished the stroke. The man staggered, lurching sideways, and fell, an arrow embedded in the flesh of his armpit. His comrade pivoted at the unexpected attack, raising his sword, then he too jerked backward and fell, choking, against the stone, a black-feathered arrow piercing his throat.

Aldivon lowered the bow. To lose the boy was a bitter blow, but it was far more important that Matt live. He nocked another arrow and waited for a target, ignoring the cold rising through his boots, and the cramping of his muscles.

Matt felt the rising bile in his throat and retched. The bitter taste of the poison and vomit burned his throat and he looked from the dying Deglin to the queen. The woman had stopped running and now stood to face the dog, and as Mia leaped she clapped her hands together. A wall of energy, barely visible, rippled out from her hands and the stunned dog was flung across the ground, falling hard against a rock. She yelped and lay there panting, the air knocked from her body.

Red fire suddenly danced around the woman's fingers and she closed her hand. The white flesh glowed sudden red and then she flicked her fingers open to send a ball of flame hurtling at the stunned dog. Mia pulled herself to her feet and tried to step aside but she was not fast enough. She yelped as the fireball struck a glancing blow to her side. Matt could smell the scorched fur and the singed flesh beneath. Amazingly Mia recovered her footing and leaped to avoid a second fireball. It missed, but the wounded animal lost her footing and went rolling across the grass in a tangle of legs. With the dog out of the fight the queen spun about and beheld the wizard. Their eyes met and for minutes they stood motionless, their faces creased in concentration, their minds locked in a battle of wills that no one could see. The very air between the two seemed alive with energy, and Matt could almost hear the crackle of electricity. Myrthinus was gasping, his knuckles white as they gripped his staff. Then with a blinding flash the woman and her soldiers disappeared.

Myrthinus leaned heavily against his staff, sucking in mouthfuls of the cold night air. "She grows more powerful with every meeting," he gasped.

"Mia—come." The dog picked herself up and shook the snow from her coat. She limped toward the wizard, pink tongue hanging from her bloodied muzzle.

Myrthinus looked toward the trees for a moment, searching for the unknown archer, then taking Matt in his arms he strode quickly from the stones.

Matt felt a sudden fatigue descend on him and the last thing he saw was Deglin, his ruined face a twisted mask of agony, his lifeless eyes staring at an uncaring moon.

PART TWO
QUEST

Chapter 9
Treachery and Murder

Passage from the Book of Myrthinus
- Betrayal

Some called the year that followed a time of peace. Arturius and his armies had finally stopped the advance of Dardanos but it was clear to me that Dardanos was using this time to hatch some new devilry that would sweep aside Arturius and open the road into lower Britain. I knew then that the time was fast approaching when Dardanos and I would face each other in open battle. It was a thought that filled me with dread.

I left Arturius that spring, taking from him the crystal that had passed into his care, and in its place I gave him Dardanos's rod, urging him to hide it and to never share its location even with me. Then I returned to a place I had not visited in many years. An island retreat that sat amid the juncture of three great rivers—the Allan, the Forth, and the Teith. Often surrounded in mists this isle was avoided by many save the few people who populated the small settlement of Invalone. Superstition about the place had grown over the years, much of it spread by me, for it was here I had hidden the second crystal.

This refuge was known as Av Allan, which literally means "On Allan" taking its name from the wide flowing river that made one of its boundaries. Legend calls this place Avalon, and it was here I fashioned a sword for Arturius. It was wrought from the finest folded steel with an edge that would cut through almost anything. Bound by many spells of protection, it would afford he who carried it great prowess in battle. The blade itself would not nick, mar or break, and I left it in the keeping of my maid servant Vivian who tended the chapel where both crystals now lay hid.

Toward the end of that summer I summoned Arturius to the lake at the northern edge of the isle. There I presented him with the sword. Excalibur he named it, and Vivian, appearing from the mists of the lake on a small boat, bought him a scabbard, plain in nature but like the blade wreathed in many spells. Should Dardanos seek to use his powers openly against Arturius, he was as protected as I could make him. Together he and I returned to Camelon.

'Twas then I was betrayed! I had grown too close to Vivian. In her I had seen a strength of both mind and spirit and I took it upon myself to train her in the arts of magic. She proved an able and hungry pupil, but through her Dardanos struck me once more.

While I was at court Dardanos seduced Vivian and turned her to his will. On my return to Invalone I found Vivian pregnant and like a fool rejoiced that together we would have a child. Clouded as I was by love for her, and filled with joy at the child that grew within her, I continued her studies.

How wrong could I have been? Thus was I ensnared once more by Dardanos, taken in chains to his fortress at Dunmellar. Again I was locked deep in his dungeons and I despaired, for now he possessed both crystals, and I had seen the mighty army he held poised to throw at Arturius. If Arturius fell, and fall he would, Dardanos would reclaim the rod, and all would be lost. There would be none left to stand in his way.

During my imprisonment Vivian had, at Dardanos's request, sent a sword alike to Excalibur with a letter to Morgan, sister of Arturius. In this letter she claimed to be I, declaring that Dardanos had found a way to defeat Arturius in battle, and the only way he could be saved was to place additional spells of protection upon Excalibur. She urged Morgan to bring the sword, in secret, to me at Invalone, leaving the counterfeit weapon in its place.

In innocence, and out of love for her brother, Morgan took the sword from the great hall of Camelon and bore it to Invalone. Wreathed in mists and in the depth of night she mistook Dardanos for me and handed Excalibur over.

With Morgan once more on her way to Camelon, Vivian stepped from the shadows and presented to Dardanos the crystals. Beside her came Mordred, and he took the sword from his father and swore that by month's end Arturius would lay dead at Dardanos's feet, and the golden rod would at last be in his hands.

Dardanos returned to Dunmellar with Vivian, and there began the final plans for the fall of Arturius and the capture of Camelon.

I was finally brought from my dungeon, a rope around my neck and chains about my feet. A leather hood covered my head and I was blind to all that surrounded me.

The hood made it difficult to breathe, and before long the suffocating bitterness of the leather was replaced with the sour taste of fear and the unmistakable smell of death. I was led roughly, shuffling and stumbling with uncertain steps to a high platform, and at last my head was uncovered. The chill night air made my eyes water but I savored what I knew would be one of my last breaths. With death so close, the air had never tasted sweeter. Despite the thousands of years I had lived, I was suddenly consumed by all the things I had not yet done. Rough hands held me and a rope was slipped around my neck. I could feel the heavy knot of the noose against the back of my head, and the coarse fibers prickled at my neck. It's amazing the things one feels the instant before death. It is as if one seeks to record the absolute most from every sense in those final moments.

Below me I saw Dardanos, no longer resplendent in white, but magnificent in black. He signaled a nearby herald and as trumpets sounded a ferocious-looking company of warriors with Mordred at their head marched from an adjoining courtyard. Beside Mordred rode his mother—the witch queen Morgause.

This was the first I had seen of her. Many men in that courtyard gasped as they too beheld her for the first time. Tall, with hair as black as night and skin as white as the purest snow, she had about her an allure and ripe sexuality that filled men's hearts with longing and desire. Yet to me a heavy aura of evil and malice seemed to hang like a cloak of death from the perfection of her shoulders.

Mordred dismounted and helped his mother do likewise. Taking her hand, he crossed to Dardanos and knelt before him. "Father," I heard him say, "I present your bride."

There was a gasp from the crowd as those nearby heard the words, and then all shouted as Dardanos took the witch queen in his arms, kissed her, and turned to the waiting throng.

"People of Dunmellar!" he shouted. "On this the eve of our triumph over Arturius, I stand before you as your war-chief, consort to your Queen, and thus your future King!" Cheers erupted until he silenced them with upraised arms. "I give you a token this night. A token of our coming victory and a gift!" He turned to Maugause. "A gift to you my love—behold the right hand of your enemy Arturius!" and he pointed to where I stood cold and defeated on the wooden platform above.

Mordred then drew forth Excalibur and held it high, glimmering in the cold light of the moon. He shouted triumphantly over the clamor of the crowd, "Behold—the sword of Arturius!"

The whole courtyard erupted in cheers.

Poised on that platform, looking down on a sea of hatred, it seemed an eternity before the crowd settled and then Dardanos, playing the people perfectly, turned to Morgause and held her hand aloft shouting once more, "I now take your queen to be my wife!" He raised their hands and extended them toward me and a brilliant beam of light leaped from their interlocked fingers. I staggered back against my guards as pain erupted in my chest. They thrust me away from them and for a moment I teetered on the edge of the platform before gravity overcame my efforts and I fell.

Time slowed. I felt the heavy pull of the chains snap cruelly at my feet dragging me into the void. The rush of air became a roar in my ears, and then came the sudden tightening of the rope about my neck.

Eilean Tioram, Scotland
597AD

A cold draft floated through the damp stone passageway, causing the torches to flicker and the candles to splutter.

Naveena crouched in the deep shadows beneath the stairs and watched the young guard disappear in the gloom. Had he left the gate unlocked as promised?

Holding a finger to her lips for silence, she beckoned to the woman behind her and on quiet feet they ran together toward the outer wall.

"This tunnel connects the storage rooms and the kitchen beneath the castle. There's a portal beneath the western wall." Naveena's voice was barely audible.

"What is it used for?"

"Supplies. The tunnel is sealed by a wooden door, beyond that an iron grille. I've arranged to have both opened."

"How?"

Naveena shook her head. "It's not important."

The air grew cooler in the tunnel and they could see the stout oak door before the iron gate was indeed open. It was dark outside and heavy clouds obscured any light from the stars or moon.

"Is the gate unlocked?" the older woman whispered, her eyes darting back along the passage for any sign of pursuit.

Naveena gave the heavy gate a push and it swung outward on well-greased hinges. She took a hesitant step outside, waiting for her eyes to grow accustomed to the dark. To her right a horse nickered nervously and she crept along the castle wall in the direction of the sound. The guard had done exactly as promised. Naveena cringed at the thought of what she'd promised the young man in exchange for his help, but pushed the thoughts aside and turned to the woman behind her.

"There is bread in the saddle bags, a wine skin, and a bag of oats for the horse. Should last you a few days."

The girl reached inside her dress and pulled out a small leather pouch; the coins inside made a dull metallic clink. "There's not much but it's all I could find."

The woman took the pouch and grabbed the girl, pulling her into a tight embrace. "Thank you, child."

Naveena tried to choke back the tears and brushed her fingers through the golden hair of the woman before her. "Lady Guenevere, I hope you find him."

"Come with me." Guenevere held the girl tightly. Her face was drawn with fear and her eyes glittered wet with tears. "You don't belong here, Naveena. Morgause won't be able to protect you from Aldivon forever. Besides, she has no love for you." She pulled at the girl's hands, "Please! Leave?"

Naveena let her head fall against Guenevere's shoulder. "I cannot," she mumbled. "The queen will do all she can to find me. That will put you in more danger. Already your life is forfeit." She swallowed. "I must stay."

Guenevere held the girl to her and kissed her forehead. She had come to love the girl as a daughter and the thought of leaving her brought back the crushing despair and pain she had felt when her own son had been taken from her so many years before.

"What will you do?" she asked quietly, knowing she was delaying the inevitable goodbye, and that every minute put them both at greater risk.

"I will continue to do as her majesty demands." The girl plucked at the trim of her dress and whispered quietly, "That way she protects me from him."

Guenevere shuddered. "The man is an animal." She kissed Naveena's forehead again. "Good luck child, and thank you. I'll pray to the gods for your safety."

Naveena helped Guenevere onto the patiently waiting mare and steered the horse away from the wall.

"Good luck, my lady!" she called softly, and slapped the horse's rump. She stood for a few moments more, shivering in the cold, and then wiping tears from her eyes made her way back to the tunnel beneath the walls.

Morgause hurried along the corridor, eyes fixed on the door at the end of the poorly lit passageway.

The door swung open as she approached and a servant fell into the passage, a pewter goblet smashing to the wall inches above his head. The startled man looked at the queen.

"He's mad, Your Majesty! Mad!"

Morgause watched the terrified man flee down the corridor, then entered Aldivon's quarters. The room was a shambles. In the middle of the floor lay the once-priceless painting depicting Arturius and his knights. Its frame was now shattered and the painting torn; the medallions that had hung from it were cast around the room. A chair, missing one leg, leaned drunkenly to one side amid the splintered remains of a table, while another was wedged in the narrow embrasure of the window.

Deep chips and scars in the stonework of the walls gave testimony to frenzied sword strokes, and the bolster of the bed was slashed and torn, its stuffing strewn all around.

Broken mirrors and shattered glass crunched beneath her shoes.

Sprawled on a chaise lounge was Aldivon. Unkempt, his hair a disheveled mess, he lay there clutching a wine skin, face red, eyes bloodshot.

"Get out!" he roared, staggering to his feet. His sword slid from his lap and clattered to the cold stone floor. He stumbled to one side and clutched at the chaise to steady himself.

"I had no choice!" Maugause made her way further into the devastated room. "She betrayed me, betrayed us! Is such self pity the way to deal with it?" The queen's voice was scolding. "What is happening to you, Aldivon? Where is the mighty general my late lord and I respected so much? Why abase yourself thus?"

Aldivon reached for the fallen sword and stood up, using the blade as a prop. He swayed uncertainly before drawing himself to his full height.

"I was in love with her! Two more years…" He took an unsteady step forward. "You had raised her as your own. Trained her! Why kill her now? Gods, how could you do it?"

"It is regrettable but her betrayal was unforgivable. She would have grown to be powerful, Aldivon. Maybe more powerful than I. I'd labored hard to hide the power from her but she had it, and by aiding Guenevere's escape she made her allegiance clear. Your infatuation with her is clouding your mind. I did what was necessary." Her voice rose, taking on a sharpness of tone that cut through the drunken fog of his mind like a knife.

"It's time you did the same. Look at you! You're a disgrace, General!"

He opened his mouth to speak but could think of nothing to say. He ran a hand across the stubble on his face, then rubbed ineffectively at his bloodshot eyes.

Morgause walked to the window and with surprising strength pulled the heavy chair from the embrasure in which it was wedged. She looked out into the chill pre-dawn sky and pointed at a particularly bright star.

"Mars rises. We are but months, Aldivon—months, from the alignment and you waste time wallowing in pity over a girl? If we are to achieve success in this cycle we must find the rod and remove those who oppose us."

He sagged back on the divan and held his head in his hands.

"What more can I do? My men hunt for this 'supposed' resting place of Arturius, and the Cùra dubh again search Invalone. We have lost all trace of the wizard, and now the boy. You should have given him to me when I asked." He grinned suddenly. "But have you not reminded me countless times that we have forever? In fact why rush now? If we wait, wait for the next cycle, we can use what we have learned to our advantage, and Naveena would be alive..."

"Aldivon. Things have changed. Never before have we been this close to achieving our ends. Myrthinus is doing all in his power to prevent detection; he has gone to ground, the boy with him. You know as well as I he prepares the boy to seek the crown."

"You know this?"

"No. It is a guess. They know we need the rod of Dardanos to complete the portal key. It rests with Arturius—of that I am certain. The book said Arturius has been placed in sleep, suspended outside of time. To recover the rod he must first be awakened, and the crown alone holds the power to do that."

Aldivon turned to watch the queen as she paced the room, picking her way through the debris of his rage. "So where is this crown?"

"I don't know."

Aldivon tried to push the fog of alcohol to the back of his mind. "You have the book—surely it tells where Arturius is and where the crown pieces are placed?"

"The book makes no mention of his location. As for the crown, it says nothing more than it was broken into six pieces with a fragment given to each of the kings that had allied with Arturius." She laughed, but the sound lacked any mirth. "How many of those kings have we already overthrown?" she said. "Who can tell where those pieces now lie? There are twelve possible kings, Aldivon, twelve! It is there Myrthinus has the advantage. We will be forced to search all locations, but he knows! Only he knows to whom he gave them."

Morgause turned sharply to face him. "And every hour you wallow thus buys him time!" Her voice climbed an octave. "Time we do not have!"

He hung his head at the rebuke.

She looked around the room at the scattered medallions, and spying one near her foot stooped to retrieve it. Blue sparks crackled weakly in her hand as she stroked the pewter dragon with a thoughtful finger; the red center stone seemed to pulse with an energy all its own. She cast a disdainful eye at Aldivon who blinked red-rimmed eyes, unable for once to hold her gaze.

"Sober up and rejoin your men. We need but one fragment of the crown to thwart them, Aldivon. One! Track down every king and descendant thereof from the old alliance and surely a fragment will be found. See to it."

"And what of the boy?"

"Worry not about the boy. I have already taken steps against him. He will not escape me twice."

"How can you be so sure?"

"I have employed the services of another, someone he will not suspect. The boy will not be a problem for long."

"Who is he?" Aldivon fought to keep the desperation for an answer from his voice.

"'Tis none of your concern, Aldivon. You have your task—I expect you gone by first light."

She reached the door and looked once more around the room. "I'll arrange to have *this* taken care of."

Aldivon slumped back on the divan and closed his eyes. His head felt like it was stuffed with rags and his tongue felt thick and swollen in his mouth. He raised the wine skin to his mouth but let it drop and instead staggered to the water basin in the far corner of his chamber. He splashed water on his face and regarded his reflection in the cracked mirror. The eyes that stared back at him were filled with pain and he looked away, feeling again the grief at Naveena's death. Yes he had wanted the girl, but she had a value far beyond that of the bedchamber. He sighed. It was now even more imperative he find Matt.

He pondered the queen's words. All she wanted was the location of Arturius and to exact revenge for her losses. Yes, she wanted to open the portal, but there was more. So much more. For a moment he thought of telling the queen just how costly her anger at Naveena's betrayal had been, but he stopped himself. That secret was the only thing that gave him an edge. He stumbled across the room and collapsed onto his bed. The room spun slowly and he opened his eyes, cursing the wine that coursed through his veins and impaired his thinking.

His drunken mind teased him with images and as sleep finally took hold, his last conscious thoughts were of Naveena's once-bright green eyes now dull and lifeless, set like marbles in a face pale and cold in death. Such a waste, such a loss—

The chamber echoed with his snores.

Morgause dismissed the young man. She had taken some pleasure from the act and she smiled as she watched his awkward attempt at dressing in her presence. "You have pleased me" she purred. "Your loyalty last night has been well repaid, I trust?"

The boy blushed and nodded, combing his fingers through a mop of light blond hair.

"I have another mission for you now." She let the heavy woolen blankets slide from the bed, revealing the pale nakedness of her body, and proceeded to give instructions, her voice coaching and seductive. "Please me with your reports and your reward will be waiting for you."

The young man backed away from the bed. "I will always be your loyal and devoted servant, Your Majesty," he stammered.

"Go," she smiled. "Get some rest, I'm quite sure you need it."

He closed the door behind him and made his way back to the quarters he had been assigned since his return to the castle. He walked with a swaggering confidence not known before, feeling somehow strong and invulnerable. He did not want to go back to that other life, but he would do anything Morgause asked of him.

Anything.

Somewhere West of Eilean Tioram, Scotland
597AD

Guenevere was near exhaustion.

Again she had avoided her pursuers, taking shelter amid a stand of spindly silver birch. The leafless trees, thick with bud, did little to keep her dry but they had broken the wind while the surrounding gorse and fern had helped shield her from those that followed.

She had watched them ride by over an hour ago, thankful the dark had hidden the trampled ferns where she had left the road. Her horse nuzzled her gently, and Guenevere pressed her head against the silky softness of the animal's neck trying to absorb some of its warmth, for her woolen cloak was heavy with rain and pulled uncomfortably at her shoulders. It no longer provided any protection against the pre-dawn chill. She suppressed a shudder and let her mind wander to Camelon. Did it still stand? Who controlled it now? It was there she had last seen Lancelot. He had helped her and Matt to safety, then gone to hold the tunnel through which they had escaped. Tears welled in her eyes as she recalled the abruptness of their parting in that smoke-filled hell, the din of battle fading behind her as she fled.

And for what? she wondered. She had lost them both anyway, both son and husband. Lancelot had come after her, she knew—Aldivon had gloated about that. Had he died attempting to save her?

She suddenly found herself thinking of Naveena, and prayed the young girl had not paid a similar price. It was clear her escape had not remained a secret for long. There was no other explanation for the soldiers that had dogged her every move these past two days.

Guenevere tried to push her fears aside. There was nothing she could do for Naveena now. If she let herself be captured or died of hunger, the girl's sacrifice would have been in vain.

Still trembling, she led her horse to the edge of the trees and looked at the seemingly endless expanse of moorland. A treacherous landscape of bogs, hollows and boulders that lay hidden beneath a twisted gray-green cloak of budding heather. It would be a slow passage across that wasteland, and she would be exposed all the way. She tried to recall where her crazed flight had taken her but she had lost all sense of direction. She needed to head southeast, that she knew, but which way was that? She had crossed a river during the night, and all rivers led to the sea. Here that meant west. Could she brave the road back to the river then follow it upstream, further away from Morgause? She pulled a bag from the saddle and rummaged for food but there was nothing left, just the coins the girl had given her. She stroked the neck of the horse and the mare nuzzled at her before burrowing its nose in the bag.

"I know..." Guenevere crooned. "You're hungry too."

If they survived this journey it would be a miracle. She rubbed at her prickling eyes then sneezed. "Dammit!" A jolt of pain ran across her lower back and with total disgust she wiped her nose on the hem of her cloak. "Gods! What a lady I've become!"

The horse nickered and stamped impatiently.

"Okay." Guenevere tried to rally her flagging spirits. "Let's go find that river. There will be grass for you at least." With that she pulled herself painfully into the saddle, ignoring the aches in her body and the pressure that was beginning to bloom behind her eyes. It's just a cold, she told herself, nothing more.

Justin Orton

Chapter 10
Porta Marsonia

Passage from the Book of Myrthinus
- ***Camlann***

I hung there before the crowd, to all but one of them a lifeless corpse. The rope about my neck twisted and creaked, turning me first one way and then another, and so it was I saw Vivian standing in shadow, tears streaming from eyes that were fixed not on me but upon the rope from which I hung.

I realized then how I lived. She had given her heart to Dardanos, only to see him cast her aside for another. Somewhere deep inside some love for me remained and she stood there now, employing the arts I had taught her, every ounce of her willpower taking the strain of the rope that would otherwise have snapped my neck.

She held me thus for hours while the soldiers marched away, and she remained forlorn and forgotten in the shadows of the courtyard wall.

When at last the dust of the marching host had settled she raised me once more to the platform from which I had fallen and released me from my bonds. Taking my hands she sobbed and begged for forgiveness, then exhaustion took her and she collapsed in my arms.

An emotional wreck, I remained with her, torn between love for her and love for Arturius. He had over the years become as a son to me, and each moment I tarried led him closer to mortal peril. I carried Vivian to a nearby room and left her in the care of a terror-stricken maid who saw me as a man returned from the dead. With the woman's frantic and desperate assurances that she would tend Vivian's needs, I bent my will to Invalone and vanished from that place.

From Invalone I took to horse, a mighty stallion named Dragon—a princely gift from Arturius. We rode at once to Camelon but found it empty save for servants, guards and Morgan. She welcomed me and told me she had done as I had commanded, and I understood at last how Mordred had come by Excalibur.

She told me Arturius had ridden forth three days earlier to meet Dardanos's host. Cursing, I stayed only to water and feed my horse, but before I could take my leave she brought me a beautiful staff made of ash that was easily six feet in length. Intricate carvings decorated its highly polished length and an iron shoe was nailed to the base, protecting the wood from wear. "He made this for you and bade me urge you to always carry it as a memory of him." Such ominous words made me wonder if Arturius had foreseen his own death, and in terror I bade Morgan farewell and rode like the wind in the direction taken by Arturius and his army.

I rode all the remains of that day, through the night and into the next, until late in the afternoon the distant din of battle and the swirling flocks of carrion fowl marked the site of war.

I urged my foaming mount to carry me further into the fray, but he was tired, ridden beyond the endurance of any horse, and there he fell on the banks of the river Allan, his great heart finally given out.

The battle was vast. A titanic struggle between men fighting for a cause that most did not even understand, pawns to the ultimate powers of good and evil.

Outnumbered, Arturius had been forced to fight a defensive action. No finer leader of men could you imagine, no more skilled warrior could you have seen. Tireless, he moved from company to company, rallying formations that moments before had wavered on the edge of collapse. Where he led, men followed and all that day the battle raged across the rolling hills of Camlann, but Dardanos's numbers inexorably began to turn the tide.

Approaching the field, I called to one of many riderless horses that ran wide-eyed amongst the carnage. He bore me through the fray, scattering crows and ravens already engrossed in their macabre feasting. And so at last I came to where Arturius and his knights stood besieged upon a grassy knoll.

Before me, ranks of Saxons gathered in preparation to assault the hill. Enraged, I raised my hands and with the full force of my mind I blasted a path through them, hurling men to the ground in smoking fury. In a reckless rage I rode through their lines, heedless of the swinging blades and arrows that buzzed past me like angry hornets.

As I grew closer to Arturius a wedge of cavalry broke from the rear and charged toward his flank. His line held, wavered, held again and then finally broke, and I saw Dardanos and Mordred drive their men toward Arturius and his knights.

Excalibur, clasped in Mordred's hand, gleamed blood-red in the evening sun and I watched as Arturius arrayed his Knights to cover his rear while he and a select guard turned to face this new and dangerous threat.

I tried to shout but could not be heard above the din of battle, and sick with fear I kicked those that would pull me from the saddle and struggled on toward Arturius.

As the two forces clashed so I passed through the last of the Saxon throng and found myself a short distance from Arturius. He was determined, his young face flushed, his jaw set in grim defiance, and I marveled at the speed and skill with which he wielded the false Excalibur. He moved like a dancer, his movements fluid, each stroke calculated and deadly accurate. Emptying saddles he battled closer and closer to Mordred, yet further and further from me. I shouted to him and at last he turned, a look of wonder and joy at seeing me, and then Mordred was upon him.

I leaped from my horse and ran across the muddy ground to aid him, but Dardanos burst from the surging mass of men and horses and rode me down. I fell, rolling on ground that had been churned by horse's hooves into a brown-green mire. Slipping and sliding I somehow regained my feet, Arturius's staff truly an old man's prop.

Dardanos appeared again but this time I was ready. Swinging the staff, I delivered a mighty blow that threw him from his horse. In wild and sudden madness I flew at him, and together we fell, punching and kicking in the mud, until caked with filth we stood facing each other across a small patch of ground, each aware that this would be our final meeting.

What followed was horrific. We lashed at each other with the full force of nature, and the conflict I had avoided for so long was joined with a fury that shook the earth. The sun was blotted from the sky, black clouds rolled across the battlefield and rain fell in torrents. Men fell back from each other, unable to continue the battle, their weapons falling from rain-soaked fingers as they watched lightning lash the sky like the whips of demons.

Thunder detonated overhead and where lightning struck the ground smoking craters were blasted into the earth, killing indiscriminately. There was no respite; I could not for a minute allow my concentration to lapse.

Never before had Dardanos or I been so committed and we ran the risk of destroying all around us, ourselves included, if for an instant we lost control of the primal forces we commanded.

The soldiers still standing withdrew, forming a circle around us as we faced each other, mud splattered and rain soaked. The air around us sizzled.

Every fiber of my mind and body was intent on countering Dardanos's attacks and I was totally unprepared for his sudden flight. An enormous flash rocked me back and I fell, blinded, barely aware that he had vanished. I struck my head on a fallen axe and for precious minutes passed into semi-consciousness.

Around me men of both sides cheered, each side thinking the other had triumphed and as I struggled to rise the two armies once again surged forward to end the battle that already had claimed too many lives.

Blinking away tears and pushing the fog from my mind, I struggled forward through a sea of mud, stepping over weapons and the bodies of men and horses to where I could see Arturius, now on foot, locked in deadly combat with Mordred. A shimmering blur suddenly distorted the air behind the embattled pair and Dardanos re-appeared. I called out in desperation, but even as Arturius parried a mighty stroke, Dardanos spoke and Arturius's sword burst into a thousand fragments. Unchecked, Excalibur swept down.

There was nothing I could do. I watched in horror as Arturius leaped away but the great blade bit deep, slicing across his chest, cutting a huge rent in the chain link of his mail corslet. He clutched at his chest and bright blood flowed from the wound, welling between his fingers. He staggered back, sliding in the mud, and the next blow cut deep into his side.

I heard his cry even above my shout of anguish, and I stood helpless as he lurched from the blow, and finally fell.

Mordred stood tall and victorious, Excalibur raised for the final stroke. There was no time to think, barely time to act. Closing my eyes I reached out for the sword and pulled with all the remaining strength of my will, tearing the blade from Mordred's hands. It twisted in the air and fell quivering, point first, into the muddy turf between the two men.

Dardanos turned. I must have made a pitiful sight standing there with rivulets of blood flowing from the gash in my scalp, my hair matted to my head by the pouring rain. I tried to advance but I was exhausted and it took all my strength to keep Dardanos's mental onslaught from driving me to the ground.

Pain exploded behind my eyes, and I could feel the blood flowing from my nose. I'd never pushed the boundaries of my power so far and I had not the strength to fight back, I could barely hold Dardanos at bay. A veil of red clouded my vision, and as I dropped to my knees I was dimly aware of Mordred's sneer as, certain of victory, he turned to reclaim Excalibur.

But his hand grasped thin air, for the sword was no longer there. Before him, white from loss of blood, muddied yet defiant to the end, stood Arturius, Excalibur in his hand.

My vision was fading fast; darkness encroached on me as the last of my strength gave out. I felt I was looking through a collapsing tunnel. On all fours now, I looked up one last time, and beheld Arturius as he swung the shimmering Excalibur at his enemy's head. Dardanos must have sensed the danger, because his attention snapped from me, and for an instant my torment eased. My vision became clearer and I watched as Mordred, defenseless, raised an arm against the blow and I felt the bile rise in my throat as Excalibur tore through the upraised limb and swept the head from Mordred's shoulders. Headless, the body spun from the force of the blow, and spraying blood from the severed neck it fell into the outstretched arms of Dardanos.

I tried to gather my will to strike out now and end it but I was empty, I had nothing left, but there was no need. Taking the hilt of his sword in both hands Arturius stumbled forward, and using the weight of his own body drove his blade through Mordred's headless corpse deep into Dardanos.

Dardanos turned his head to me, a hand held out imploringly, his lips mouthing words I could not hear. I shook my head, and with a gurgling sigh he toppled backward, driven into the soft ground by the weight of Mordred who remained pinned to him by Excalibur's blade.

Somehow I crawled to where Arturius lay and saw he still lived. His breath came in ragged gasps and his short beard was flecked with bloody saliva. Around us a wall of knights formed, and with a mighty roar they drove the remnants of Mordred's leaderless army from the field.

Caverns, Durness, Scotland
597AD

Matt awoke with a groan. He was painfully aware of his empty belly, but more pressing was a raging thirst. An acrid dry burning in the back of his throat brought back the terror of his brush with death on the sacrifice stone. He sat up with a sudden start, relieved he could move, even though every joint and muscle ached. He rubbed the sleep from his eyes and looked around the dimly lit space, noting the only light came from a single candle that burned with a steady radiance on a ledge next to the bed. The light reflected on a metal cup and the sharp jagged angles of what appeared to be rocky walls.

He took the cup and drank deeply, relishing the sensation of the cool water as it swirled around his mouth. He relaxed a little and became aware of distant yet rhythmic sound that echoed around the chamber. He breathed in deeply. The air was fresh and clean with a salty tang reminiscent of the sea. Matt swung his legs from the bed and looked up but the ceiling was lost in deep impenetrable shadow.

He was surprised at the feel of cool sand on his bare feet, and steadied himself against the bed that he could now see was little more than a wooden cot with a thin straw-stuffed mattress, placed on a rocky ledge. His eyes, now adjusting to the dim light, revealed his "room" was nothing more than a cave.

Soft white sand covered the floor, and footprints several sizes larger than his own led into the gloom. Unsteady on his feet and somewhat lightheaded, Matt followed the footprints to an oddly shaped wooden door set into the irregular opening of the cavern.

He pushed it open and it swung easily on large iron spikes driven deep into the rock. Bright light seared his eyes and he blinked, dazzled by the sight of the sun slipping toward the surface of the sea.

He had entered another cavern, this one larger and naturally lit, its enormous mouth open to a sandy beach where ocean waves crashed in an endless cycle of foaming water. Seaweed and driftwood marked the high tide line, and a mass of terns and other birds chased the receding water, weaving between large black rocks, stopping here and there to stab at some unseen grub. Matt watched in fascination, as the birds remained one step from the water's edge, their little legs a blur as they raced inland, and then turned once again to chase each broken wave back to the churning mass of the ocean.

He was standing on a raised rocky ledge toward the rear of the cave and noticed several rough steps cut into the rock. One flight led down to the beach, and more led upward, passing out of sight around a large pillar of rough hewn stone.

Behind him the ledge stretched back deeper into the cavern where the ceiling slanted down at an abrupt angle, narrowing to a fissure that may have opened into yet another cavern.

Matt stood and watched the sun slide toward the horizon tracing a golden-red pathway across the heaving swells of the sea. Each waves outline was etched in golden light, while the troughs between slowly darkened from shimmering blue to a cold foreboding black. Footsteps sounded behind him and Myrthinus came to stand at his side. He placed an arm affectionately across the boy's shoulders, and for a while neither of them spoke as the sun slipped lower below the horizon, pulling the blanket of night over the world like a shroud.

"You hungry, boy?"

Matt nodded.

"Come, then. Let's eat."

Myrthinus raised his staff and a nimbus of pale light illuminated the cavern. He led the way through the fissure and into a room that was much more home-like with a stout wooden table at one end and a crackling fire at the other, over which hung a large iron pot. Two small loaves of fresh bread lay cooling on a rock ledge, and beside them were arrayed a number of wooden tubs and ceramic pots. Matt's mouth watered and he would have snatched the wooden water bowl Myrthinus handed him, had he not seen the familiar shape curled on the sand before the fire.

"Mia!" Matt ran to his pet and she welcomed the boy with a tongue that left his face wet and sticky.

"Where are we?" Matt asked, wonder in his voice. He expected an echo but none came.

"One of many retreats I've had cause to use over the centuries." Myrthinus spoke from the fire where he stirred the contents of the pot. "This, I prefer to call home."

The aroma of delicately seasoned food caused Matt's stomach to growl.

"That smells really good."

Myrthinus chuckled. "Well, it's rabbit. Would have been more but"—he gestured toward Mia—"there's more than a little thief in that hound of yours!"

"She's prone to that from time to time." Matt laughed and scratched her behind the ears. "It's good to see you, girl," he said, burying his face in her thick fur and fighting back the tears of joy at being with her once again. Mia opened a bright blue eye and looked up at Matt, then rolled onto her back exposing her soft belly for him to rub.

"It seems she feels the same way," Myrthinus said, ladling rich gravy into wooden bowls. "Here..." He indicated the table. "Let's get you fed. 'Tis good to see you up at last."

"How long did I sleep?"

"Since I found you—two days."

Matt gasped. "That long?"

"Aye." Myrthinus placed the bowls on the table, then reached to the ledge for one of the loaves. He sat heavily in a chair, and smoothed out the robe across his knees. "For a while there, laddie, I thought we were going to lose you. Tell me, Matt—you look a sight better, but how do you feel?"

Matt broke a large chunk of bread from the loaf and dipped into the thick gravy in his bowl. "Starving," he answered, and they laughed together.

When they had finished eating, the wizard sat Matt before the fire and inspected his injuries. The foot was completely healed; barely a mark remained of where the glass had cut him days before, and the sword cut on his arm had faded to a pale pink scar. "Good, good," the wizard muttered to himself. "You're a tough one, Matt, no doubt about it. But are you tough enough, hmmm? So much depends on you, and there's too little time to prepare you for it."

"Prepare me? For what?"

Myrthinus picked up a large cloth and dabbed at his lips before answering.

"There's a special task, Matt, a quest if you will, that I need you to perform."

The wizard sat back, elbows on the arms of the chair, and put his hands together. He looked at Matt from across his steepled fingers and was silent for some time before continuing.

"It is time for you to learn a great secret."

Matt held his breath in nervous excitement and waited for the wizard to continue.

"It's been six days now since the night you first ran away. You asked me then who I was. Now I can tell you. My true name is Myrddin; in modern English that translates to—"

"Merlin," Matt finished for him. "It means Merlin."

The wizard nodded. "Aye, indeed. I am Merlin."

"But..." Matt's eyes widened with a mixture of disbelief and excitement. "You can't be! I mean, *the* Merlin? I've seen some crazy shit these past few days but...for real? You'd be..." He stopped as he realized what he was about to say.

"Old?" Merlin asked with one eyebrow raised. Then he laughed, a merry light dancing in his eyes.

"Ancient would be more precise, laddie, but"—he slapped the table with a wrinkled yet powerful hand, causing Mia to jump and growl at the sound—"I still have life in these old bones!"

Matt grinned.

"So tell me, lad, what do you know of me?"

"Seriously?" Matt tried hard not to stare. "Okay. Assuming you actually *are* Merlin, well, I've read loads. The legends of you and..." He stopped and his face took on a look of total surprise.

"And?" The wizard waved a hand, gesturing for him to continue.

"Arthur," Matt finished reverently. Then, unbidden, his eyes glistened with tears.

Merlin slowly raised himself from his chair and walked around the table to place a comforting hand on the boy's shoulder. "Come now, lad. What troubles you?"

"I've been remembering things, like you said I would. In your book there was a picture, a picture of a king and knights. One of the things I remember is a man like one of those in the book. He had a medallion." Matt clutched at his chest and lifted the dragon pendant up to Merlin.

"He had one of these. I thought he might be my father but then when I was captured in the cottage I heard one of them speaking. A large man, Aldvan or something like that..."

"Aldivon," Merlin said quietly. "So he was there?"

Matt nodded. "He seemed to know me. Said he'd killed all the knights of the brotherhood. He said I looked like my father." The tears he had refused to cry for so many years came now, large salty blobs that seemed to scald his eyes before tracing fiery tracks down his cheeks. He looked at the now-blurry wizard, struggling to suppress further tears. "How could my father have been there all those centuries ago? And if he was, and Aldivon has killed them then that means..." His voice broke, but he managed to complete the thought. "...that means my father is dead too."

Merlin pressed his hands against the boy's shoulders. "I'm sorry, Matt, truly sorry. If only we had had more time at the cottage for me to explain things to you." He looked hard at the boy, eyes filled with compassion.

"The picture you refer to is of Arturius, he you know as Arthur. He's depicted there with the men your history has named Knights of the Round Table. Each of them wore one of those." Merlin indicated the medallion Matt wore. "It's a Pensilis Draconum, or hanging dragon. Arthur's knights referred to themselves as the Pendragons.

"Many of them fell with Arthur one thousand four hundred and twenty years before your time, at the battle of Camlann. Those that survived were later hunted down and killed by Aldivon. With the exception, I hope, of the man in the picture—who was indeed a father to you."

Matt stiffened but held the wizard's penetrating gaze. "Was a father to me? So not my actual father then?"

Merlin looked away from the stricken look in Matt's eyes. "He raised you as his own son, Matt. He believed you to be his, even though others doubted the truth of it."

"And you? Do you know the truth?"

"Not all of it, no."

"But you believe he still lives?" Matt was unable to hide the pleading in his voice.

Merlin's shoulders slumped. "I'm not willing to accept that he is dead, and until we know otherwise, you too need to hold to that thought." He pulled himself upright, using the table for support, and crossed to the large iron pot. He poured another serving of rabbit stew into his bowl and returned to the table, his face somehow shadowed with doubt.

"These are dark times, Matt. Your father loved you very much. All your life he fought to protect you, and everything the Pendragons stood for."

He took a spoonful of stew and then continued, "It has been many years since I last saw your father, and for the past four months I've been searching for him. When I spoke that night in the cottage I was deeply concerned that the enemy had found him. Aldivon is a dangerous adversary and he hates your father. When you fled the clearing I was torn with indecision. Should I follow those who attacked us, continue my search for your father, or take a third course and return to you? My decision was made for me when our attackers proved too persistent in their efforts to capture me. Hunted mercilessly, I was forced to attack and it was then I learned of the risk to you at the home."

Matt sat, intrigued, and waited silently as Merlin took another mouthful of stew. Dabbing at his beard the magician continued.

"I returned to the stone circle and passed to your time, arriving at the home late at night, just as you were leaving the shed. Alas, you would not come to me." The wizard sighed. "I understand your lack of trust, but had you come to me then things would have been much better for us both."

Matt hung his head and Myrthinus smiled. "Don't be hard on yourself, boy. I made mistakes that night too. I should have followed you, but instead I pursued Deglin, anxious to find what he knew, but he eluded me. Too late I followed you to the hospital, but you had already been taken and the trail was cold.

"Fortune smiled then, for I intercepted two guards and gained from them an understanding of what was happening. Mia and I then tracked your whereabouts. The rest you know."

Matt shook his head, overwhelmed by what he was hearing. "So what happens now?"

"You must put your childhood behind you, and become a man. I had hoped for more time, but now they have my book—" Merlin waved away Matt's attempt to apologize. "Over the next four weeks I am going to train you as best I can. It is too little time, but all I dare spare. The rest"—he paused—"the rest you will have to pick up as you go. But, before we can begin you need to know what it is we are fighting for, and who it is we are fighting."

Matt sat and watched as Merlin rose from the table. His heart and mind were racing and he was not sure if what he felt most was giddy excitement or abject terror.

"Come, lad. Don't just sit there, it's time for you to learn the true story of your King Arthur."

They passed onto the cold rocky ledge and took the upward steps Matt had seen earlier. The chill wind hurried the pair along until they rounded a rocky column and arrived on another ledge. A subtle glow suddenly flared from the wizard's staff and Matt was able to see the steps continued upwards, but how far he could not tell. The ledge was dry, untouched by the ocean waves, and the rocks around them were scoured smooth by windswept sand. To his left the darkness of the sea stretched into the night and he would have stayed longer, mesmerized by the regular hiss and swish of the unseen waves against the shore, had Merlin not beckoned him through another door.

"Come, laddie! Out of the cold."

Matt was not prepared for the cavern into which Merlin led him, and he gasped in wonder.

"Wow!" How far the cavern stretched Matt could not tell, for the faint glow from the wizard's staff illuminated only a circle no more than ten feet around them, yet in that space Matt could see a comfortable chair, part of a fireplace and a towering bookcase. The wizard crossed the stone floor and propped his staff against the wall. Their shadows curved like giants on glimmering rock walls.

Merlin pointed a finger toward the pile of wood in the fireplace and a single flame danced on his fingertip. Matt watched in fascination as he casually flicked it into the hearth and the cavern was at once lit by the warm orange glow of the fire.

"Too cool!" Matt looked around; the walls were criss-crossed with veins of limestone, quartzite and other mineral deposits. He could hear running water and noticed a small stream spilled from a crack in the rock into a natural basin set back in the wall. On a rocky shelf adjacent to the pool sat several drinking bowls of various sizes, and across from the spring a natural chimney drew smoke from the now-roaring fire high into the darkness.

A low table, two comfortable chairs, a large divan, and a footstool occupied the center of what could only be called a room, and animal skins and thick rugs provided a welcome break from the sand-covered floors of the other caverns. Two additional bookshelves, smaller than the first, were set across the cavern, their shelves covered with an assortment of books and scrolls.

Matt's eyes were immediately drawn to a huge iron-bound chest that lay between the two bookcases, its lid firmly closed. Suspended above it was a large map of Britain, and above that a map of the ancient world.

Merlin stepped across to a high-backed and strangely patched armchair and kicked off his boots. He dropped into it with a sigh.

"Had this chair nearly four hundred years, my boy," he said. "Never be another like it. Now then, relax, make yourself at home."

Matt gestured toward the divan. "Can I?"

The wizard nodded, and while Matt busied himself with an assortment of cushions, Merlin removed a long thin pipe from a fold in his robe, and after a few puffs was sitting back, feet up on the footstool, a look of pure contentment on his old and careworn face.

"Filthy habit," he said, grinning, "but impossible to break at my age. So while I savor this"—he took another puff—"you tell me what you know of Arthur."

Matt lay back on the divan and gathered his thoughts. *Where to start?*

"I've read the legends, seen most of the movies. I dreamed of being an archaeologist, the one to find Arthur, and maybe even Excalibur, proving he really existed." Matt laughed nervously. "That all seems kind of pointless

To Raise a King

now. I mean, I'm talking to Merlin!" He rolled onto his side propping himself up on one elbow. "I still don't understand how this is possible."

"That will all become clear soon enough, but first tell me what you understand of Arthur. Leave nothing out. I need to know what you have to unlearn."

Matt began slowly, his excitement building as he told all he could of King Arthur and his knights, relaying the fabled story of Arthur's conception at Tintagel, the sword in the stone, Camelot and his crowning as king.

"His final battle is said to have been at Camlann, where he defeated the army led by Mordred but was himself mortally wounded. Some say he fell because you were not there, others say it was because Morgan betrayed him. Either way he fell and was taken to Avalon to be healed by the monks. Some say Arthur did not die, but lays in sleep, ready to return at his country's greatest need."

They sat for several minutes, Matt lost in the stories of his hero, and Merlin gazing intently at the boy. It was the wizard who finally broke the silence as he eased himself from his chair and shuffled slowly to the stream. For the first time he showed signs of his age, old and bent, as if carrying the weight of the world on his shoulders.

Speaking quietly, his voice barely audible over the crackling fire and the trickling stream, he turned to Matt.

"That last is true, Matt. Arturius, or Arthur as he has become known, still lives. Of all the stories and legends, that last piece is closest to the truth. He sleeps now, waiting to be woken when called, and that time is drawing near. We need him Matt, and events are moving faster than we can match. I fear that soon it will be too late for even him to save us."

He filled a bowl from the stream and took a sip.

"But we must try, and there's the problem. The means to waken him are now lost." Merlin returned to his chair and sat down heavily. "But you, young man, are going to find them."

Matt sat in stunned silence until a loud crack from the fire startled him. He suddenly felt very immature, and very alone. How could he, only seventeen, hope to carry out some mysterious quest?

"Will you be coming with me?" he asked, aware of the slight tremor in his voice.

"No." Merlin leaned back in his chair. "I have another task before me, but take heart, Matt. Before you embark on this quest you will possess skills you never dreamed of. I have much to teach and you will need to work hard!"

"Am I to learn magic? I thought at the cottage you said I was too old!"

"No, Matt. Not magic, but more basic skills. Survival, language, riding, swordplay, herb lore. You have a quest before you, but first I must tell you a story and complete what we began to discuss in the cottage.

"Do you recall my telling of my people, and the loss of their world?"

Matt nodded. "You said their world was destroyed."

Merlin watched Matt's face carefully. "Aye, that it was. We were Marsonians. My home was the planet Mars."

Chapter 11
The Broken Crown

Passage from the Book of Myrthinus
- *An Endless Sleep*

*M*organ *found me on the battlefield, caked in blood, mud and filth beside the body of her fallen brother. She had followed me from Camelon, arriving shortly after the battle and had made her way through the dead and the dying to where we rested beneath a stand of Rowan trees.*

She set a group of nearby soldiers to work fashioning a bier and bade them escort herself and her brother back to Invalone.

Tired beyond measure, I returned to the scene of the epic struggle between Arturius and Mordred to retrieve Excalibur, but the sword and the bodies of Mordred and Dardanos had gone. Morgause, it seemed, had claimed her dead.

I was too exhausted to do more that day, but the next I traveled to Invalone where Arturius hovered on the brink of death.

It took all the skills I could muster to aid his recovery, and for months Arturius struggled for his life while the regional kings gathered in council. Impressed with his victory at Camlann, they had agreed to elevate him to a loftier station. No more would he be their war-leader, but upon his recovery they would crown him High King of all Britain.

I shared these aspirations with Arturius but he refused them, and instead implored me to take another path. He argued that with Morgause in possession of the two crystals, all she required to open the portal to Mars was the Rod of Dardanos. The Rod that joined them was lost to me, for at my behest only Arturius knew of its location. He begged to now take that secret to his grave, preventing the portal from ever being used again.

I told him it was unnecessary. For the key to work the device must be infused with the blood of a Marsonian. With the death of Dardanos I was the last of that bloodline. Only I could open the portal and that was something I would never seek to do.

But Arturius disagreed. Who was to say Dardanos had not sired others? What descendant of his may once more threaten the very future of the world in a crazed attempt to open the portal? What if Morgause knew of the blood and had taken it from the body of Dardanos or Mordred? Only with his own passing would the secret of the rod pass from the world.

But this too I challenged. The Rod could still be found, I said, but he would smile mockingly. "If one such as you has not found it, then surely it will never be revealed."

I finally ceded to his wishes and agreed to end his life.

But I could not do it. I instead betrayed his trust. Rather than kill him, I cast him into an eternal sleep and moved his slumbering body from Invalone to a secret location. Thus hidden, I used my arts to suspend the passage of time around him. So entrapped he would not age, but would remain always at rest, until called upon once more.

I then told the world that Arturius had succumbed to his wounds, and gradually I wove the story of his life into a tapestry of legend, myth and deceit that would forever carve the name of Arthur and his Knights in history.

But Morgause was not done with us. Arturius had been right to council against her. She threw her forces against us the following year, driven with a desire to exact revenge on those who had robbed her of son and husband.

Lancelot led us then. While maybe a little brash and quick to anger, he was the obvious choice to take the vacant title of Dux Bellorum. He was a great tactician, better maybe than Arturius, and a respected leader on the battlefield. The two had been the closest of friends until their love for the same woman had soured their bond. It was this falling out, what some even saw as a betrayal, that led several of the kings not to answer Lancelot's call. Hard pressed by Morgause's forces, Lancelot was pushed ever back until the onset of winter drove each army to its keep and its soldiers to their homes.

Caverns, Durness, Scotland
597AD

How many hours had passed since Merlin began his tale Matt did not know, but he had lain entranced, captive to every word. The man certainly had a gift when it came to storytelling, for Matt did not just hear the words, but somehow felt each emotion as if he too lived each epic moment. He lay now quietly absorbing the story while Merlin smoked in silence.

"So this Morgause—she seeks the rod of Dardanos?" Matt finally broke the silence.

"Aye. The portal cannot be opened until Earth and Mars are aligned and the three parts of the key are made whole. That time draws near and so time for us grows short. Morgause now knows that Arthur lives. She will assume the rod lies with him. When she finds it does not, she will attempt to wrest its location from his mind. The only hope that remains for us is to prevent her from reaching Arthur and to do that we must move him. Sadly, the very spells designed to protect him also prevent him from being moved."

Matt felt a tingle of excitement course through his body, and with his voice barely above a whisper he breathed, "So first he must be awakened?"

"Aye," Merlin answered gravely. "'Tis time for Arthur to return, and that is the quest that lies before you."

"But how? You said earlier I had to find something. Can't you just…" Matt waved his hand as if he were casting a spell.

The wizard shook his head and looked at Matt with eyes that had seen a thousand lifetimes. "I wish it were that simple! But alas it is not. I bound the spell of sleep to an object, and now I just pray there is time for you to find it."

"Find what?" Matt asked quietly.

Merlin walked to the large chest that sat beneath the map against the far wall. He passed his hands across the lock and there was an audible click as it snapped open.

Lifting the lid, the wizard reached inside and retrieved something that Matt could not see. He stood but Merlin gestured for him to remain where he was.

Curious, Matt waited as the old man closed the lid and returned to the table bearing what looked like a small piece of gold.

"The northern kings had fashioned a crown for Arthur, but with his passing it was broken into six pieces. Each king took a fragment and it was agreed that when a man worthy of the title should come forth, they would make the crown whole once more and anoint him High King of Britain.

"It was into these fragments that I set the spells of sleep and awakening, and with the joining of the six fragments Arthur will awaken and once more stand as the last line of defense against all that is evil."

He held out the piece of dull metal and Matt could see it was a cross of the purest gold. Thin it was, joined to a broken band of thicker gold that was perfectly smooth on one side and engraved with strange marks on the other.

With trembling fingers Matt took the proffered piece of metal and turned it in his hands, marveling at the smoothness and the weight of the historic fragment.

"You are holding the front section of Arthur's crown. Five more pieces there are, but where they rest I no longer know. That crown is our last hope, Matt, and you can be assured you will not be the only one seeking it. Morgause has my book, the only true account that exists of what happened all those years ago.

"She knows that the rod lays with Arthur, or at the very least that Arthur knows its location. Furthermore she is driven by a burning desire to see Arthur, myself, and you dead. The odds are all in her favor, Matt. You must find the five fragments of the crown to succeed—she needs but one to thwart us."

"Why me?" Matt asked. "You've told me nothing about me. Why does Morgause want me dead? Why do you need me for this? I don't even know who I am or where I belong."

Merlin stroked his beard for a few moments then answered slowly. "It is hard to know where you belong now. You were born here in the sixth century, but you do not know this world. You were sent away shortly after your fourth birthday, and the children's home is all you have known. You have lived the majority of your life in a time and place completely alien to me. You tell me, Matt—where do you feel you belong?"

"I don't know. I've never felt I belonged anywhere." Matt sat quietly watching the fire for a while and then continued. "If I was born here, then I belong here right? But this time, this place is as alien to me as Mars! What of my parents? You told me my father may still be alive, that my mother was taken. Who were they? Where are they?"

Merlin sighed. "Your mother was taken by Aldivon when you were four. I do not know if she still lives."

Matt gasped. "And my father?"

"I do not know."

Matt felt his throat tighten.

"I have memories, Merlin. I see things. Things from the past, but I don't know who the people are. I see the man you call my father, and there is a woman. She's pretty. Tall, with long blonde hair. I think she's my mother?"

Merlin pulled himself up from the chair.

"There is much I do not know for certain. Some of what I tell you is mere conjecture, but I will tell you what I can, and then you must concentrate on your training and the quest. Can you agree to that?"

Matt nodded and Merlin continued. "The woman you have dreamed of is indeed your mother. She is the lady Guenevere." He raised a hand to silence Matt's outburst, and continued. "Your father, or to be more precise, step-father, is Lancelot. History has twisted the truth of these two to make for better storytelling."

Matt's mind raced. "If Lancelot is my step-father, and my mother is Guenevere does that not make Arthur my father?" His eyes were wide, and his heart suddenly hammered with the excitement of discovery.

"Morgause believed that to be so, but your father was not Arthur."

"How can you be sure?" Matt's crestfallen look tugged at Merlin and he continued quickly.

"Lancelot saved your mother's life from a raiding party and brought her to Camelon. Over time they fell in love and were to be married, but the Lord Arturius had also fallen for your mother. The two men became rivals for your mother's affection. Unwilling to come between them she left Camelon. Where she went, none knew."

Matt watched as Merlin paced back and forth on stockinged feet, presenting his tale like a lecturing professor.

"A few months before the fateful battle at Camlann, Guenevere returned to Camelon. She was heavy with child, but whose she would not say.

"After Arthur's fall Lancelot took command of Camelon, but without full control of the armies he was unable to repel Morgause for long. Camelon became an island, a solitary outpost held against the forces of the enemy. For four years neither side gained an advantage over the other. It was a dark time.

Raiding parties would destroy the crops and livestock of our people, and Lancelot had insufficient men to protect them all. For every estate, farm or croft he saved, two more would burn.

"It was then that the son of one of the western kingdoms came to Camelon. A handsome man, strong and proud. He pledged the support of his father's kingdom in the fight against Morgause in exchange for a place in the brotherhood of knights. His name was Aldivon. He and Lancelot became instant adversaries, contesting for leadership of Camelon. The knights became divided, their loyalty split."

Merlin had made his way to the spring and paused to sip from a bowl, and his lined and weathered face clearly showed the anguish of the memory. He offered a bowl to Matt but the young man shook his head.

"I left Camelon to learn more about this young prince from the west. That proved a most terrible mistake, for while I was away Aldivon stole into your family's chambers and took both you and your mother prisoner. Your lives were threatened and Lancelot was forced to resign from the Pendragons, relinquishing control of the order to Aldivon. He surrendered both his sword and medallion in exchange for the lives of you and your mother. As your family prepared to leave Camelon in exile, Aldivon finally revealed himself for who he truly was: consort to Queen Morgause. He betrayed the knights and slew many of them, but not before Lancelot had almost killed him in a fierce duel in the great hall of Camelon. The fortress was put to the torch and your mother escaped the flames with you and a small handful of survivors."

Merlin had made his way back to his chair and he lowered himself into it, his gaze locked on some distant scene only he could see.

"Having learned of Aldivon's treachery I returned to Camelon, only to find it in ruins. The once-great fort had been burned to the ground and nothing but a blackened stone shell remained. Of Lancelot I found nothing save his medallion and sword. Both you now possess."

Matt fingered the medallion about his neck.

"And my mother?"

"You and your mother were starving. She and her small band of followers found their way to a small community and took shelter within a church. It was there Aldivon found them."

"What happened?"

"Something strange. Aldivon took your mother, yet spared the settlement. Stranger still, he left you there! Morgause believed you to be the son of Arthur and sought your death as vengeance for the loss of her own son. Aldivon would have gained much favor by bringing you to his queen."

Merlin paused to add fresh tobacco to his pipe.

"Is she still a prisoner?" Matt asked.

A small flame appeared on the wizard's finger and after a few experimental puffs he blew out an aromatic cloud of spicy blue smoke and watched it waft toward the upper reaches of the cavern.

"I do not know. Fearing that Morgause would raid the community to capture you, or Aldivon would return at her instruction, I took you from that place and brought you home with me. But then what was I to do? I could not pursue your mother with a young child in tow and I had no one I could trust to care for you."

"So you took me to the boy's home?"

"No. Not then. Up to that time we lived a single reality. There was no 'future' to take you to. Before that chapter of your life began, Morgause did something truly terrifying!"

"To my mother?" Matt's voice shook with horror.

"No. No boy—not to your mother. To us all. She attempted to do the impossible. She tried to turn back time, to alter history, taking us back to before the death of Dardanos."

"No way!"

"Truly. But such a thing is beyond comprehension. History cannot be changed. The passage of time can be slowed around an object, as it is around Arthur, but turned back? Think what that would entail, lad! You would have to stop the passage of time for all creation. For every star, planet, and universe you would need to somehow pause all existence and then roll it back. It is an impossible task, for who knows all that exists? Yet she tried, and in her failure she split time around us, spawning an alternate reality. In one reality time marched on, but this new reality was like a bubble on the timeline of history. It begins on the bloody battlefield of Camlann at the instant of Dardanos's death and ends on the day that Morgause dies. The end point is not fixed in history for her death occurs at different times, and the years that elapse between are different with each cycle. This is why I wrote the book. In your reality I have surely died and am nothing but dust and legend. But here I am forced to live the same life over and over, and with each restart I have no knowledge of the cycle that passed before. The book became a message to me across time so I could be ever vigilant and prevent Morgause from finding the Rod of Dardanos." His voice became very soft, almost a whisper and he fixed Matt with a terrible look.

"If she should succeed in opening the portal then the world will be destroyed, and should the world be destroyed in either reality, then so it will be in the other."

Matt sat stunned, fixated on Merlin's every word, eyes locked on the magician's face. Merlin drained his water bowl and rubbed at tired eyes.

"I have no knowledge of what happened in the history of your time, Matt. Clearly Morgause failed in her undertaking and the components of Dardanos's key must still be lost, for the world clearly still exists. But here, for us trapped in these repeating cycles, Morgause grows closer to achieving her goal. She keeps her own history of events and it is but a matter of time before she locates Arthur. As your sole guardian, I was unable to both care for you and do what was necessary to counter her machinations. I fashioned a portal—a bridge if you will—between the two realities, and carried you into what we shall call real-time. I have endured much in my lifetime. Lived on two worlds, and seen the rise and fall of countless nations, but nothing prepared me for your world. I was terrified. I all but abandoned you to the boys' home and fled back here."

Matt sat silent for a moment, struggling to digest all he had heard.

"So…" The boy paused, then continued. "If I go back to the boys' home, back to 'real-time' and this cycle ends, what would happen to me there?"

Merlin chuckled.

"To be honest, lad, I have no idea! You may live, or you may just blink into nothing with the rest of us."

Matt's face went deathly pale.

Glenhurich, Scotland
597AD

Guenevere was almost delirious with fever.

After evading the patrol, she had successfully made her way back to the river and followed it upstream, not keeping to the water, but rather moving from one tract of woodland to another, mindful of those that hunted her. The going had been slow, her cautious route adding miles to an already-ambitious undertaking.

By midday she had been overcome by hunger and had spent hours laying on the riverbank tickling for trout. Her efforts had eventually been rewarded and while the horse grazed, she had eaten the fish raw. The night had been spent on a bed of bracken, screened by fern and juniper bushes.

That had been two nights ago.

Now she was desperately sick, tired beyond anything she had known before. Sleep had become almost impossible, the nights spent shivering miserably beneath the stars, while her head throbbed and her throat ached. Each morning she had forced herself to rise with the sun, pressing onward only to become increasingly frustrated by a landscape that seemed to block her every move east.

Impassable lochs seemed to stretch as far as the eye could see, and she had no idea of the best direction to take around them. Mountains rose on either side, hemming her in, and she was forced to follow the lower valleys making her way through one of Scotland's many beautiful glens; but the grandeur of the scenery was completely lost on her.

Each hour had become a constant struggle. It took every ounce of strength just to stay astride the horse, and she swayed wearily in rhythm with the lazy plodding of the mare.

A racking cough spread pain through her chest and lower back, and she clutched at the mud-encrusted gown that hung on her gaunt frame. She spat off to one side, and wiped her mouth with her sleeve. The pungent reek of stale fish was the only thing that penetrated the congealed mucus and congestion that made her head feel like it would explode. Any other time the odor would have made her nauseous, but now it awakened the hunger that seemed to gnaw at her gut endlessly.

She wondered vaguely where the trail she followed would lead. It appeared to be a drovers road but she had seen no sign of cattle. These lands still belonged to Morgause—of that she was sure—and if a settlement lay ahead it would have soldiers. Would she be recognized? She laughed to herself. Doubtful. She'd barely recognized her own face in the reflection of the stream from which she had drunk that morning.

On she rode. The piping song of birds stabbed at her brain, and the midmorning sun seared eyes grown overly sensitive to light. Its warmth on her face was pleasant but it failed to still the bouts of shivering that shook her. Her throat burned horribly and she fumbled with her water skin.

Swallowing hurt, and the water seemed to go down in painful lumps. She knew flushing her system was the best she could do to purge herself of the malady but the frequent drinks came at a price, requiring strength-sapping stops to either urinate or pick her way up to one of the many creeks and streams to refill her depleted water skin.

The mare stopped to rip at the long stems of the roadside grass but Guenevere didn't force her on. She sat slumped in the saddle and waited for the rolling gait to continue. They continued this way, passing stands of trees dappled with buds that waited patiently to unfurl into a wondrous canopy of green. Occasional herds of deer, returning from the low lands of the glen to the heights they frequented in summer, watched her pass. Had she a bow and the strength to pull it she would have tried hunting one, but that was futile in her present state.

The unexpected bark of a dog pulled her from the half doze she had fallen into, and she looked through dry and crusted eyes to see the sun was high in the sky, preparing to cross to the west and drop below the towering peaks that surrounded her. She rubbed her eyes and tried to stifle the cough she knew would rack her chest with pain. She failed and hacked loudly.

"You don't look so good, m'lady."

The man had emerged from the trees beside the trail and stood beside her, a large deer slung across his shoulders and a bow in one hand. A dog sat patiently beside him.

"What place is this?" she croaked.

"Hurich."

Guenevere swayed in the saddle. She had never heard of the place.

"Does this road lead to Camelon?"

"This road leads to the priory, 'tis all. The glen ends there."

Guenevere looked around in dismay. She had expected the glen to cut a path through the mountains.

"There's no way through to the east?"

"Nay. Least not an easy one, and then it would take you nae further than the great loch of Linnhe."

She tried to turn her horse to retrace her steps, but she coughed again, another racking bark that seemed to tear at her lungs. She hunched against the pain, but the fit would not stop.

"Lady!" the hunter dropped the deer and stepped forward just in time to catch Guenevere as she slipped from the saddle.

Chapter 12
An Unexpected Companion

Durness, Scotland
597AD

M att had been slow to rise after Merlin had shaken him awake, and he now rubbed at gritty eyes as he stumbled from his room. A chill breeze swept in from the sea, carrying with it the tangy salt of the ocean and a freshness he could taste. It was early, the sun not risen high enough to paint the landscape in color, and the faint light of early dawn left the water looking cold and gray against the washed out white of the sky. Matt shivered as he watched the gathered seagulls rise and fall like feathered rafts on the morning tide.

Below him Merlin stood on a wide stretch of sand. The golden powder was burnished bronze where it met the water's edge, and Merlin beckoned for Matt to follow.

Matt felt strangely despondent as he walked toward the wizard; he almost missed the regimented mornings of Inverdeer House. The tired old home with its rattling pipes was at least warm, and his iron-frame bed with mattress was luxurious compared to a straw-stuffed canvas perched on a rocky ledge!

His stomach rumbled.

"No breakfast and no hot shower!" he mumbled to himself as his feet sank into the soft sand.

"I'm coming!" he yelled in response to Merlin's shout to hurry.

Merlin had strode some distance from the cave entrance and stood now on the firmer ocean-washed sand of the water's edge. Matt was breathing hard by the time he joined the wizard.

"We need to get you fit, boy!" he said in a not-too-gentle tone. "Fit and strong. It will take all you learn here to survive the trials ahead. Courage you have, but courage will not suffice! You'll need skill, wits, and an overwhelming desire to succeed!"

The cold wind chased away the foggy remnants of sleep and Matt felt a spark of anger at the insinuation he had none of the virtues just listed. Trying to ignore the cold, he scowled.

"I barely slept!" he groused, stifling a yawn. "So what exactly will I be learning?" Matt wanted to add "How to build sandcastles?" but bit off the sarcasm and instead looked at his feet, shoulders hunched against the chill sea breeze.

"Everything I can teach in the limited time we have," Merlin answered. "First—you need to gain physical strength, endurance and agility. Every morning you will run, swim and climb, building stamina. Each day we will learn new skills, and hone those already learned. Your evenings will be spent in study. You have much to learn, lad—language, herb lore, tracking and more. Much more."

Matt felt a sudden surge of excitement at the wizard's curriculum, and tried to shake off his early gloom. "So what's first?"

"See that outcrop of rock?" Matt looked along the beach, where a series of rocky outcroppings swept down from the grass-covered cliffs to cross the sand like the fingers of some giant rock monster. The first such outcrop was about a half mile distant and it extended into the sea where waves broke around the tip in a white-capped frenzy.

"Yeah?"

"Good. Now I want you to run to it, swim out to the end of the rocks and then climb from the water to the top. Follow the ridge until you find a path. Follow that and it will lead you to the top of the cliff. I'll meet you there with breakfast."

Matt looked from the heaving swells to Merlin with a look of pure horror. "You want me to swim? In that? Now?"

"You'll be fine, laddie—now off with you."

"I'll freeze to death!"

The wizard's lined face crinkled into a smile. "Try not to, boy—'tis only your first day."

Matt searched for a reply, but a firm push between the shoulder blades sent him forward.

"Go, off with you—and remember—be aware of your surroundings, regardless of where you are or what you are doing. Be observant! The enemy will use every opportunity to stop you."

"There's no enemies here though, right?" Matt asked.

"Only me, boy. Only me. Now—go!"

Matt nodded and started the jog toward the distant black rocks. To the casual observer the beach had appeared one long stretch of empty sand, but as he ran he saw it was covered with sea shells, mermaid purses, partially buried rocks and crab carcasses picked clean by the ever-present gulls. From his starting point the outcrop had looked like little more than a broken pile of boulders protruding into the sea, but as he drew closer he was alarmed to see it comprised of gigantic slabs of jagged black rock, its lower half coated in yellow seaweed that made the surface slick and treacherous. By the time he reached the outcrop his legs ached and his breathing came in ragged gasps. He stood to catch his breath and the chill sea breeze quickly cooled the sweat from his run. After a few minutes his breathing was back under control and he took a hesitant step toward the water.

"Screw it!" he said. "There's no frickin way." And Matt turned to climb the outcrop.

"I'm disappointed, lad!" The wizard's voice was close and Matt dropped back to the sand in surprise. Merlin stood just a few feet away, watching him.

"'C'mon! Is the swim really necessary?" Matt asked.

The man nodded. "Aye. It's not the swim itself, lad, but a test of your commitment. A test you failed!"

The wizards face became stern as he continued. "Will you always turn aside when the path ahead is not to your liking? If so, we have already failed. Seriously, lad, a little water never hurt anyone."

Slowly Matt eyed the water as it swirled around the base of the nearby rocks. "I guess that means drowning is painless," he muttered to himself.

"Your father always had a saying, lad. *'The battle's not over till it is won'* You should remember that!"

Matt took a cautious step toward the waterline. Water oozed from the sand around his feet as he skirted a number of small rocks. A large pool separated him from the last few feet of sand and his eyes were drawn to a crab, whose frantic burrowing clouded the water with sand.

Matt looked to the end of the outcrop where another wave exploded in a spectacular burst of spray.

"The battle's not over till it's won, huh?" Matt took a deep breath and jumped the pool, then without pause chased the receding water into the sea. "Here we go!" he yelled, then gasped aloud at the biting cold of the water. He pressed on, making his way along the outcrop. The water was not as deep as he had expected, only coming to his knees, but he could see the next wave rolling toward him fast. The sea level rose quickly, a frigid caress moving up his body and sweeping along the outcrop. The seaweed fanned out across the surface of the sea, lifted by the incoming swell. Matt battled on, racing the oncoming wave, his tired legs dragging as he fought against the resistance of the water.

The wave arrived with the force of an avalanche and Matt was knocked from his feet and carried back toward the shore like a piece of discarded debris.

Drenched to the skin, he tumbled in the wave. The weight of his clothes dragged him down and he kicked furiously to stay afloat. Then the roiling water suddenly settled around him and he rubbed the stinging salt water from his eyes and allowed the retreating wash to carry him, coughing and spluttering, back out along the outcrop. Eyes clear, he looked up to see another wave sweeping toward him, but this time he ducked beneath the swell, then struck out with his arms until he reached the spur of granite that marked the end of the rocky promontory.

Spray from the waves erupted over him as he struggled up the eight-foot wall of rock. Twice he slipped, barely maintaining a hold, and the second time he felt the sudden burn of salt water on his knee and knew he'd torn his jeans and cut the skin beneath. Clenching his teeth, he clawed his way to the top then stood there, hands on thighs, panting. His clothes clung to his skin and he felt totally miserable as he picked his way along the jagged and treacherous rock, fighting the suck of vertigo as the drops blurred by on either side.

As the wizard had said, Matt found a small pathway at the end of the outcrop and he briefly stopped to examine his knee. It was cut and grazed but not badly. Satisfied the sea had cleansed the wound, he began the arduous walk through the coarse tufts of yellowing grass to the top of the cliff.

It took him about twenty minutes to reach the top, and he stopped to gaze out across the landscape. The sun had risen now and the olive drab of the cliffs had been painted a brighter emerald, with explosions of gold here and there where the hardy gorse clung to their last few clusters of flowers. Beyond these grassy headlands the land extended into a vast boulder-speckled moor. An undulating landscape of greens and browns that drew the eye to distant mountains, their smoky gray bulks shrouded in cloud. Above him speckled patches of pale blue sky attempted to rally together against the relentless flow of flat-bottomed clouds that drifted inland before a stiffening morning breeze.

A shrill cry made him turn and he gave a scream and dropped to the grass. A gigantic bird, bigger than any he had seen, swooped above his head, wicked talons reaching for where his head had been only moments before. Matt rolled across the grass and caught a flicker of gold from the eye of the brown-feathered bird and watched in horror as it banked sharply. Like a dive bomber it once more hurtled toward him.

"Holy shit!"

Matt rolled again and felt the wind of the bird's wings against his face. Twice was enough. He didn't hang around to watch the bird make another pass. Ignoring his aching legs and burning lungs he rolled onto his feet and ran, head down, along the cliff top angling away from the edge and heading inland. The sudden beating of wings caused him to dive to the ground again, and he closed his eyes as the bird whooshed once more across his back. He lay still for several minutes and when no further attacks came, he opened his eyes.

Rabbit droppings carpeted the close-cropped grass inches from his face. Matt groaned and rolled on to his back. "This is shaping up to be one shitty morning."

With no further sign of the bird, Matt stood and brushed futilely at the grass and soil that stuck to his wet jeans. Fresh blood welled from the scrape on his knee and he carefully picked the grit and dirt from the cut.

Dejected, wet and cold, he looked across the expanse of cliffs and spied a small building across the hill. A tendril of smoke rose from the roof, almost lost against the dramatic backdrop of towering mountains on the horizon.

"Wow!" The landscape was breathtaking and he took a moment to follow the impressive skyline before looking back to the building where Merlin now stood, waving in his direction.

"What kept you, boy?" the old man asked as Matt dropped to the ground beside him. "I see you met the Skua. I was sure you'd lose a little hair at least." Merlin touseled the boy's head.

"The what?" Matt asked between breaths.

"The Skua. 'Tis a large breed of sea bird. Very territorial. Now, lad, let's get you fed."

Matt pulled himself up. His whole body felt battered and bruised. Moving stiffly, he followed Merlin into the shack. Built of stone, with a turf roof and bare dirt floor, the single room was lit by a large hole in one wall and a crackling fire at the far end. Matt wrinkled his nose at the musty smell of decaying wood and earth, and felt his eyes water a little from the pungent smoke that failed to completely escape through the rough cut hole in the roof. He shuffled toward a stool set before the fire and relished the sudden warmth.

Merlin's deep voice filled the small room. "Come, laddie, dry yourself, and I'll get breakfast."

Matt took the offered cloth, stripped off his clothes and dried as best he could. Wrapped in a thick woolen blanket, he spread his clothes before the fire and watched as Merlin placed several thick slices of bacon in a pan that already sat smoking over the fire.

"You did good out there, laddie." Merlin gave the boy a smile. "You feel okay?"

Matt thought back to the exciting adventure stories he had read and looked down at his mud-streaked jeans steaming before the fire. He felt totally drained from the unusual morning exercise, his knee was starting to stiffen and throb, and he was still unnerved by the attack of the Skua. Reality, it seemed, was very different from the stories and he suddenly failed to see how he could achieve this impossible quest.

"I'm not sure I can do this."

"You have to. As I said before, lad, there is no one else."

With despair Matt predicted he would be dead before the week was out. He wanted to get up, walk away, but where would he go? With sudden fear he realized he had no idea where he even was.

Matt watched the wizard. He seemed harmless enough, kind too, but had last night been for real? In the cold light of day it seemed too incredible to accept. The epic tale no more than a fantasy, a bedtime story told by a lonely old man.

"You can do this, Matt. Trust me." Merlin seemed to read the boy's hesitation. He flipped the bacon and it sizzled and popped in the heavy iron pan. He added two thick slices of bread and Matt felt his mouth water.

"Each day you will grow stronger, more confident, and ready for the task ahead."

"You have more confidence in me than I do!" Matt knew he was whining and tried to rediscover the determination that had sent him plunging into the ocean.

"That will change, laddie. Here—" Merlin pulled a cloth wrapped bundle from a nearby sack. "Take a wee dram of this. It'll wake you up and light a fire in your belly."

"Wake me up?" Matt felt his mood lighten, and he said with a grin, "Like the swim this morning didn't?" He watched as the old man unwrapped a glass bottle almost full with a pale amber liquid. Myrthinus removed the stopper and passed the bottle. "Geez! What the hell is this?" Matt's eyes watered from the burning fumes.

Merlin grinned and flipped the bread in the pan. "Whisky."

Matt had just been about to take a sip. "Whisky? Are you serious?"

"Aye. 'Tis a fine single malt, distilled by me no less, and blended with a delicate mix of herbs, heather-honey, and a special cordial. Will give you strength, stamina, and endurance. Now drink."

Matt sipped at the liquid. A rich smoky flavor filled his mouth with a sudden warmth, followed by a subtle burn to the roof of his mouth. He swallowed and found the initial bitter spiciness of the drink was tempered by a smooth sweetness that he found himself rather liking. A deep glow spread through his body and radiated through him.

"This is pretty good," he said, taking a second, larger swig.

Merlin grinned and took the bottle. "Aye, that it is." He lifted the steaming pork from the pan and placed it with the bread on wooden platters.

Matt was suddenly ravenous and he relished the taste of the thick salty bacon, and the crisp bread that had been fried to a dark golden honey color. Whether as a result of the food or the drink he didn't know, but already he was starting to feel better.

Merlin watched the boy eat. "So," he said around a mouthful of pork, "Do you know how to ride?"

Matt's physical exhaustion had melted away at the prospect of learning to ride. Blue dominated the sky now. The clouds had floated far inland and the orb of the sun rose above the hills chasing away the early morning chill. It was much warmer, and breakfast had left Matt feeling ready for anything. He took a deep breath of pure sea air and followed Merlin.

The horse, his reddish brown coat glistening in the morning sun, was grazing, flicking at flies with his long tail. As the pair approached the animal stopped his chewing and regarded them with eyes of the deepest brown. He stamped a foreleg and snorted indignantly.

"He's a little bigger than I expected," Matt said.

Merlin grinned at the boy's obvious discomfort.

"Come Matt, meet Kamen. He's a small enough horse, and gentle too."

Merlin caressed the horse's neck, and it settled, allowing Matt to walk up and stroke its velvet-soft nose. It fixed a watery eye on the boy awhile and then nuzzled him affectionately.

"There. He likes you."

Matt smiled nervously. "So when do I get to ride him?"

"No time like the present, boy. On you get."

"But—" Matt paused. "He's got no saddle, or reins!"

"Indeed not, my lad, and that's how you're going to ride him."

"But—" Matt started to argue when Merlin interrupted him.

"No butts, Matt. Now listen. The journey before you will be far from easy. You will be traveling in a land and time that is alien to you. While horses are aplenty, most folks lack the wealth for saddle and tack. You must master both ways of riding, for should you find yourself with the luxury of a mount, more oft than not it will be without saddle."

With that he began whispering to the horse, and despite his age he easily lifted Matt onto its back. Apart from twitching its ears and a low snort, the horse remained still.

"Now," Merlin began, backing away from them, "relax yourself and move with him. Make no attempt to command him. Learn how his body feels beneath you, learn to adjust your balance to his movements."

"How do I get him to go where I need to?" Matt asked, all too aware of how far the ground was below him.

"I will be controlling the horse," Merlin replied.

Matt looked at him questioningly. "With what?"

"I can speak to him, Matt." The boy's eyes widened in wonder.

"And yes—once you are comfortable on his back, once you can predict his moves and stay on, then you will learn to communicate with him too."

"You mean I'm going to learn to talk to animals!" Matt exclaimed.

"No—just horses. We have not the time for others."

There was no time for further argument as Merlin's brow furrowed in concentration and the horse suddenly turned to the right and started walking across the grass.

Matt gave a sudden cry of alarm as the horse moved, and with the grace of a sack of grain swayed first to the left then to the right and slowly toppled to the ground, landing in a tangle of arms and legs in a patch of thistles.

Kamen stopped and looked at his fallen rider. Huffing, the horse turned a deep brown eye on the wizard, who stood shaking his head.

"It's going to be a long day," the old man muttered to himself, and then louder, "Up you get, lad. Let's try that again, only this time let's go a wee bit further before you get off."

Matt threw him a dark look, and using a nearby boulder pulled himself awkwardly onto the horse, hoping his tugging on the mane did not hurt the animal. Settled on Kamen's back he gripped a handful of mane and squeezed his legs together to help hold on.

With a sudden surge the horse leaped forward, and Matt was immediately catapulted off the rear of the animal. He landed on his back this time, the air knocked from his lungs by the fall.

"Didn't I tell you not to jab with your feet and legs?" Merlin asked as he pulled the gasping boy to his feet.

"No—you—didn't!" Matt gasped painfully between gulps of air.

"My mistake!" Merlin grinned.

Matt rubbed the back of his head as he watched the horse turn around and come back to them. "You're enjoying this aren't you?"

"Not at all," the old man replied with a perfectly straight face. "Now up you go, and remember—don't grip with your lower legs. Grip with your thighs and hold on to the mane. Move your body in balance with his movements."

As Matt once more mounted the horse he heard Merlin mumbling strange words.

"What did you tell him?"

"Just to keep away from the cliff edge, as you seem a wee unsteady."

"Gee, thanks!" Matt retorted and then quickly faced forward as Kamen set off once more.

This time Matt stayed on and even started to enjoy himself. The horse followed the instructions Merlin gave, and Matt began to differentiate between the various movements of the animal's back, neck and head.

"He'll speed up in a minute," Merlin warned. "Ride with him. Hold the mane with two hands and keep balanced. Let your body flow with his, don't just sit there like a rock."

"Okay!" Matt shouted back. "I'll just hit the ground like one instead!" But he laughed as he said it, excitement buzzing through him.

Merlin shouted a command and the horse quickened its pace. At first Matt bounced around on the horse's back, each jolt jarring his spine until he began to feel the rhythm of the horse.

Gradually he learned to feel each powerful bunching of its muscles and time the up and down motion of its back as the animal angled toward the stone shed at a gentle trot.

Running into the sea breeze Matt suddenly felt a freedom he had never known. He relished the feel of the wind through his hair as the horse quickened its pace further.

For a moment boy and horse moved as one, and Matt yelled in elation as the grass whipped by under the pounding hooves.

Then Kamen stopped.

For the third time that day Matt fell, this time sailing across the horses head. He barely had enough time to curl into a ball before his shoulder struck the springy turf and he was sent rolling several feet, coming to a stop in a sandy hollow.

Merlin ran up, his face a mask of concern, "You alright, boy?"

Matt sat up, spitting sand and blood that welled from a cut lip. He fixed the magician with a wooden stare. "I guess telling me he was gonna stop slipped your mind too?" The boy suddenly laughed and pushed himself to his feet. "I think it would be best if you taught me how to tell him to go and stop—that way I'll be a little more prepared!"

Merlin agreed and patted the boy on the back. "You've done well for your first morning. A couple of tumbles but no real harm done. Now, how do you feel about learning to use a sword?"

The next six weeks raced by for Matt, and despite the grueling routine he was surprised at how much he had enjoyed himself. As Merlin had told him he would, he had grown fitter, stronger and more confident than ever before.

Each morning Merlin had sent him running on the beach, extending the distance gradually until Matt could now reach the furthest outcrop almost two miles away, climbing each intervening barrier along the way. Every day he had swum to the end of the final outcrop with the exception of four mornings when inclement weather had prevented the swim.

He had quickly become an accomplished rider, and the time spent with Kamen had soon become the highlight of each day. The sheer thrill of racing across the cliff tops with the wind in his hair and the horse's hooves pounding beneath was exhilarating.

Matt had taken to sword play like a natural too. That first morning, when he had taken his sword from Merlin's hand, he had felt again that surge of strength and confidence he felt when facing Deglin in the kitchen of Inverdeer House.

The late afternoons and evenings had been the hardest, but under the careful guidance of Merlin Matt had gained a rudimentary understanding of the political situation of sixth century Scotland and become somewhat fluent in Gaelic. Most often the pair conversed in that ancient lilting language, switching only to English when there was a need to explain something new or complex.

Several times Matt, Mia and Merlin had left the caverns and hiked deep inland, the wizard teaching Matt the secrets of navigating the vast expanse of Scotland's bogs and wetlands, and the basics of survival in the wilds. Three nights they had spent beneath the stars, and then his lessons had begun to include the study of plants and herbs, and their roles in cooking and healing. Matt learned new skills daily as Merlin strove to give the boy a crash course in survival, teaching him the basics of how to hunt, fish, and forage for food and water.

The training was hard, and if not for the patience and assistance of Merlin it would have been impossible, but as each day passed so Matt changed, passing from boyhood into a young man developed beyond his years in strength, knowledge and ability.

The youth rested now in the comparative peace of his cave-room and idly ruffled Mia's thick fur. His entire body ached. Merlin had worked him hard with the sword for hours until his shoulders, arms and wrists screamed in protest. He looked at his forearm, and clenched his fist; it was noticeably thicker with muscle and he felt a stir of pride.

He could fight with some skill, although Merlin had focused on teaching him defensive sword work. "You're not going to wage a war, lad!" he had said over and over again. "Your greatest asset is your speed, boy. Speed and stealth. There is no shame in running from danger, but better yet to avoid it altogether."

Matt laughed at the memory. Where had that advice been his first day when Merlin had chided him for seeking to avoid his first Atlantic swim?

Slowly Matt swung his aching legs from his bed and placed a foot on either side of Mia. The dog sat beside the bed wagging her tail. Matt took her head in his hands and looked deep into her pale blue eyes. *Time to try again* he thought, and he gathered his thoughts and reached out with his mind, trying to project an image into her head.

Merlin was right. Learning to communicate with Kamen had been incredibly hard, and that was a horse used to hearing the commands of the wizard. Merlin had told him he would not be able to break into the somewhat limited mind of his dog but Matt had continued to try, often long into the small hours of the morning.

"C'mon, girl," he whispered quietly. "C'mon, NOW." As he spoke the last word he pushed with all his will, trying hard to pass an image to Mia of her sitting beside him on the bed, one paw on his lap. Beads of perspiration broke out on his brow and he closed his eyes, trying hard to form a link, however tenuous, between his mind and the husky's.

The bed suddenly dipped beside him and a large white paw pressed against his thigh.

Matt opened his eyes and nearly wept with joy to see Mia sitting beside him, one of her paws resting on his leg and her long pink tongue lolling from the side of her mouth, just as he had pictured in his mind.

"You did it, girl!" he shouted, ruffling her head with both hands. "Good girl! You did it!"

Immediately he felt foolish. Had she really obeyed his command, or was it purely coincidence? His head hurt from the effort, a pulsing ache behind his eyes, but he decided to try again. Kissing her muzzle and receiving a long sticky kiss in return he closed his eyes and pictured the dog standing by the cavern door. Holding the image in his mind, he then reached out once more and attempted to project the image to her.

It was easier this time, the link now forged, and he felt Mia leave the bed. He watched her cross the cavern floor and stop to look back at him over her shoulder tail wagging, a slightly confused look in her eyes.

"Yes!" he cried. "Yes!" Then pointing to her he snapped his hand back to himself and called, "Mia, come!" and she trotted over to the bed resting her head on his knee.

"Good girl!" he said again. "Good girl." He tossed her a piece of dried rabbit meat in reward, and she gulped it down before circling a number of times and then laying down, head resting on her paws.

Smiling weakly, Matt lay back on his bed. His head was pounding now and he pressed a hand to each temple. It had taken hours of instruction from Merlin to explain to Matt how to "talk" to Kamen by passing instructions in the form of images to the horse. He had mastered it only recently, and each session had led to blinding headaches from the intense concentration. The effort of the brief communication with Mia had exhausted Matt, and he collapsed back on his bed watching the shadows flicker over the rocky roof of the cavern. He let one arm hang limply over the edge of the bed so he could fondle Mia's head as she settled down for the night and a wet nose nuzzled his palm. As Matt relaxed he fingered the medallion about his neck. The Pendragon. The name "Pendragon" had always been associated with Arthur and his mythical sire, Uther Pendragon. Matt had listened entranced as Merlin had told him the truth behind the name. The brotherhood of knights, those famous men of the round table, had been members of an elite group—the order of the dragon—and each was given a pewter medallion depicting the fabled beast crouched, wings spread, atop the planet Mars. Merlin himself had made them, infusing each with a power to aid their keeper.

Matt caressed the soft metal, enjoying the coolness of its touch. As always it calmed him and he felt himself relax. Gradually the headache faded and his thoughts strayed unbidden to his mother. Was she still alive? Merlin insisted it was unlikely but Matt refused to accept that. He would recover the crown fragments and return them to Merlin, but then he would hunt for those who had taken his mother.

The candles in the cavern suddenly danced wildly as a draft stirred the air. Matt looked to the door, and propped himself up on one elbow as Merlin stepped toward the bed.

"Tomorrow, lad. Tomorrow you will begin."

Matt's mouth went dry and his stomach suddenly knotted in fear.

"You are ready, lad, as ready as I can make you."

"But there's still so much to learn..."

"There's always things to learn, laddie. To stop learning, is to give up on living. Here—" Merlin leaned the sword against his bed and placed a hand on Matt's head. "I've cleaned and oiled your sword for you. Now you must rest, for tomorrow will be a busy day."

Matt watched the grandfatherly figure leave, then took up his sword. To think this weapon had been given by Arthur to Lancelot, and now it was his. He studied the flickering candlelight reflected in the blade. The dancing gold light became his mother's hair blowing in the wind.

"I'll find you, Mum," he whispered. "Find you, or avenge you." Then with a deep sigh he sheathed the weapon and passed into a deep and restful sleep.

Justin Orton

Inverdeer Park, Scotland
Present day

They stopped close to the edge of the trees overlooking Crabtree Park. It seemed a lifetime since he and Mia were last here but only six weeks had passed since the pair had fled the boy's home and plunged into an adventure that would lead him who-knew-where.

Matt was a young man now, barely recognizable as the boy Merlin had rescued from the stone circle. His clothes were totally out of character and would have drawn many a strange look had anyone seen him. Tucked into brown boots of supple leather he wore coarse woolen leggings cinched firmly at the waist by a thick leather belt that also secured his money pouch, a travel pouch and small dagger. A fine chain mail corslet hung over a thick cotton under shirt and a brown woolen cloak covered all this, fastened at the throat with a plain wooden toggle.

At his side hung his sword, and a large pack was slung on his back bulging with essentials for his quest. He pulled the small knife from his belt and gently cut a thick tuft of gray and white fur from the dog.

"To remember you by," he said, smiling at the bemused-looking animal.

In the park below, children played in the afternoon sunshine. They were from the home and Matt recognized several faces. Younger kids hung from the monkey bars or soared screaming into the sky on the swings while nearby a group of older boys played soccer under the watchful eyes of Mr. Carter and another man Matt did not recognize. Beside them a boy sat at the edge of the playing field looking completely dejected. It was Brick. Matt grinned to himself.

"I wonder what he did this time?" Matt wondered aloud, not knowing that Brick had only recently returned to the home. The older boy had been reported missing a week after Matt's own strange disappearance from the hospital. He had not explained why he had returned, or where he had been, and he was now being watched closely, as both the police and Inverdeer staff strongly suspected Brick and Matt were caught up in some kind of drug trafficking.

Matt ruffled the thick fur at the back of Mia's neck and squatted to press his cheek against hers. She made no move. Much of her playfulness was gone. Obedient and loyal, she had been a constant companion to Matt throughout the grueling training of the past few weeks, and like him, she had matured beyond her years.

He kissed the side of her muzzle.

"I'm gonna miss you, girl" he said, the sickening feeling of grief flooding his stomach. Mia licked his cheek in reply, but there was sadness in her blue eyes.

Matt had planned to take her with him on his quest but Merlin had spoken against it, and after a spirited argument Matt had finally conceded she would be better off returning to the home, where at least she would be tended to, safe from the perils that lay ahead.

He watched the children play, absentmindedly fingering the medallion about his neck. What chance did he really have on this quest? He shrugged. That didn't matter now. What mattered most was trying. An unsuspecting world went about everyday life while a few hundred miles and fourteen hundred years away a woman was set on a course that would wipe them all from existence.

A heavy paw found its way into his lap and he stroked it, tears spilling from his eyes.

"You be a good girl now, you hear?" he asked. His voice choked with the emotion of an unwanted goodbye. Since making a mental connection with the dog the day before, a bond now existed that surpassed the love they already shared.

Mia nudged him gently with her head, wiping the tears away with her fur, and he buried his face in her chest and cried quietly, absorbing the warmth, the smell and the memory of her.

A church clock slowly rang out 4pm. It was time to go. Wiping his eyes and pulling away from her Matt began to picture the boy's home in his mind, building an image to pass to the dog so she would understand where it was she was supposed to go.

Carefully he searched for the link to Mia's mind and pushed the image into her head, biting back the tears as he breathed the command, "Go home, girl. Go home."

Mia stood and slunk to the edge of the trees. Matt waited for her to leave but she turned and padded back, smothering his tear streaked face with kisses.

"I love you too, Mia, but you can't come with me. You gotta go, you hear? Go home!"

The dog whimpered but obediently walked from the trees.

Matt watched her go and swallowed back the tears. Reluctantly he turned his back on the park and picked his way through the trees to the path that led to the stone circle where Merlin waited patiently for him, but he had not gone many steps when a crashing in the undergrowth sounded to his left.

A moment later the burly figure of Brick came bounding through the ferns and brambles. "I'll get it!" he yelled and Matt dropped to a crouch but too late—he knew he had been seen.

"Hey! Wait!" he heard Brick call. "You see our ball?"

Matt hoped Brick would turn away, but the burly boy took a hesitant step closer, then his eyes opened in wonder at the sight of Matt.

"Holy shit! Matt? I thought…" then he suddenly became aware of Matt's garments, "What the fuck are you wearing?"

Matt fled. The heavy pack bounced on his back and the straps bit into his shoulders as he ran.

"Matt! Wait!"

Matt glanced behind. Brick was giving chase, his arms waving wildly as he called for Matt to stop.

A sudden commotion to his left caused Matt to change direction and from the trees plunged two men. Matt had no time to take in the details of their garb, the drawn swords told him all he needed to know. Branches snagged at him as he ducked around the trees and then he caught his foot on a moss-covered stump and fell, crashing to his knees.

Matt rolled quickly, sitting back against his pack. With no time to get to his feet he struggled to draw his sword.

"Shit!" Brick rounded a large oak tree to see Matt lying on the ground, sword raised defensively. The woods reverberated with the sudden high-pitched ring of steel on steel as Matt parried a blow from a large figure clothed in black leather pants and jerkin. A second figure closed in on the pair and then like a silver bullet Mia returned, launching herself from the undergrowth and knocking the sword from Matt's attacker's hand. The man cried out and fell heavily against a tree, and his companion turned to face this sudden new threat.

Matt swiftly took advantage of the man's distraction. He swept his legs out in a roundhouse kick that sent his assailant reeling, then Mia leaped at the fallen man, snapping and snarling as Matt staggered back to his feet.

"Mia—come!" Together they turned and ran.

Brick stood for a moment in open-mouthed astonishment until one of the figures in black pulled himself from the ground and fixed the boy with an ice-cold stare. The man bent to retrieve his fallen weapon and Brick followed the fleeing Matt, cursing all the way.

Matt glanced behind and saw the bigger boy, face red with exertion, pounding after him with the two attackers close behind. Matt was only minutes from the edge of the trees. Should he plunge on into the portal and back to the sixth century, or stand and help Brick?

Cursing, Matt spun around and raced back to the panting boy. "Brick, keep running!" he called. "I'll hold them off."

The attackers slowed when they saw Matt now stood his ground, sword held confidently before him. In moments he was joined by a menacing Mia, who crouched low, ears flat and fangs bared.

The soldiers advanced with caution and Matt raised the point of his sword threateningly.

A large rock suddenly sailed over Matt's head and smashed into the face of one of the men. The stunned soldier cried out and fell to his knees both hands raised to his bloody face. Another rock whistled past and barely missed the other man, forcing him to duck.

"Matt, there's two more!" Brick called and hurled another rock through the trees.

Matt disengaged and fell back to the waiting Brick. The closest attacker made to pursue but Mia leaped and bit down hard on his arm. The soldier dropped his sword and beat at the dog with his other fist but she refused to release her grip. She growled noisily as her teeth ground down hard, tearing muscle and grating against bone.

"Mia! C'mon!" Matt yelled and the dog gave a last snarl before releasing her hold to follow the fleeing boys.

The trio burst from the trees just as more black-clad figures appeared behind them. They angled away from the trees, racing to the stone circle where Merlin could be seen, his white hair whipping in the wind.

"Matt, quickly!" he called.

"What the hell is going on?" Brick demanded, but Matt was laughing. "Now I know why they call you Brick! I've never seen anyone sling a rock like that!"

Brick grinned in reply.

Merlin raised his hand, palm outward. Two men who had run from the trees crumpled to the ground and did not move. But two more appeared behind them, these dressed in flowing robes. Merlin again raised his hand but this time his attack was blocked as a shimmering force expanded from the crossed wrists of one of the newcomers. The other robed man pulled a strange device from his robes and sent a bolt of sizzling energy hurtling into the stone ring. Merlin reeled from the sudden attack.

"Matt, you must go! These are Cùra dubh. I cannot fight them and hold the portal open. Go! Now!"

Between a pair of standing stones a gray mist floated in the autumn sun like a cloud trapped between two giant rocks. Matt ran toward it and leaped into the mist. There was a flash and a fleeting moment of weightlessness accompanied by a sickening sense of vertigo, and then he tumbled forward into a soaking rain.

He gazed in wonder at a landscape wreathed in mist, as rain fell in sheets around him. A cordon of stones, shiny with wetness, surrounded him and knee-high tufts of grass grew from the springy turf in random clumps, giving the valley floor a mottled look, a two-tone carpet of green upon the valley floor. A brief disturbance in the air beside him caused him to scramble to one side. There was a momentary blurring and for a split second the air seemed to tear. A blast of warmer air surged from the rip and then Brick, closely followed by Mia, flew into the stone circle.

Brick said nothing, staring first at the rain, then at Matt, his face a mask of shock and surprise.

"You're not going to believe this..." Matt said, "but you've just gone back in time."

Chapter 13
Dunadd

Southwest of Kilmartin, Scotland
597AD

"Okay! That's it! I ain't movin' another step until you tell me where the hell we are!"

Brick was cold and unsettled from his recent experience. The boys had been forced to take shelter from the driving rain and they stood pressed against a large stone as wind-driven rain cut their view to a few yards.

Matt burrowed in his pack and pulled out a thick woolen tunic.

"Here."

Brick quickly took off his thin jacket and gratefully took the proffered garment, then stretched his jacket back over the bulky wool. He had plunged through the portal wearing nothing but sneakers, jeans, a sweatshirt and a lightweight windbreaker tied around his waist by the sleeves. He stood beside Matt red faced, his thick mop of hair plastered to his head by rain.

"So, for the hundredth time, are you going to tell me where we are?"

The landscape here was barren. During his training with Merlin Matt had become accustomed to the sweetness of an air totally devoid of pollutants, and the peace of a landscape without the many marks and scars of civilization. To Brick they had just fallen into a totally different, almost alien world.

Matt glanced behind the stone and saw the sky behind it was brightening as the storm blew east, one last reminder of winter before the full warmth of spring chased away the cold and returned life and color to the hills.

"We're about a mile South West of Kilmartin, in Argyle—" Matt began.

"Oh right, 'course we are!" Brick sneered. "We just ran out of a forest and managed to cross all Scotland in ten fucking minutes! I haven't heard a car since we arrived here." He looked around as the rain eased.

"Like I said," Matt tried to explain, "we've gone back in time."

"That's impossible!"

"Oh come on, Brick! Look around! There are buds on the trees! It's spring here! You were probably getting ready for Guy-Fawkes back at the home, right?"

Brick nodded. "Yeah. Fireworks night next Tuesday."

"Right!" Matt said. "Look, you saw the old man in the stone circle, right?"

"Yeah?"

"Well..." *Crap, this was gonna sound insane.* Perhaps if he spoke quickly it wouldn't sound so bad, and so Matt continued in a rush, "He's a wizard and the cloudy thing you saw between the stones was a portal, a gateway between our time and his."

Brick's expression just showed stunned disbelief. "And the men with swords?"

"Bad guys." Matt answered quietly.

"What did they want?"

Matt threw the bigger boy an incredulous look and failed to bite back the sarcasm. "To play football, dumbass!" A few seconds passed and then he snapped again, "What do you think they wanted? They were trying to kill me, you bloody idiot!"

Brick bunched his fists, his face suddenly angry, but he stopped as soon as Matt's hand slid to the hilt of the knife in his belt.

"I'm sorry." Matt sighed and rubbed a hand through his rain-soaked hair. "I'm sworn to secrecy, but I guess circumstances are a little different than we expected..."

Matt proceeded to tell Brick a dramatically abridged version of his quest, deciding it was probably best to drop any reference to the Arthurian legend. Time travel to an alternate reality was a big enough shock to deal with.

"So—a comet or asteroid is gonna hit the earth if you fail?" Brick said.

"Yeah."

"You mean like in Armageddon?"

"The movie? Yeah. Like Armageddon." Matt suddenly grinned. "I guess that makes me Bruce Willis!"

Brick shook his head. "Hope not Matt, he died." The pair stood in awkward silence before Matt continued.

"So like I was saying, the stone circles can be used as gateways through time."

"You mean any time? How do you pick where, errr, when?"

"No, not any time. Just between our time and here, the sixth century."

"What's so special about the sixth century?"

"There's this powerful witch who plans to use..." Matt swallowed. Boy, this sounded so farfetched. "...Stonehenge as a portal between Earth and...and another world."

"Oh, sure. Right. I can buy that." Brick sneered, "Not!"

"I know. It sounds crazy, but it's true." Matt plunged on. "The magic used to open the portal will draw the comet to Earth. I've been sent back to find some things that the wizard can use to stop her."

"You actually believe this bullshit?" Brick looked at Matt with wonder.

"Yep, I do. Trust me; I've seen enough strange crap these past few weeks to believe anything!"

"Why you?" Brick asked. "Why have you got to be the one to do this?"

Matt slowly withdrew the medallion from beneath his shirt and held it out for Brick to see.

"You remember this? Back in the changing rooms at school?"

Brick stepped back and rubbed at the hand that had been burned and then miraculously healed. "Yeah. I remember…"

"There has been a group of people trying to prevent this witch from opening the portal, but one by one she's killed them all. That's why me. I'm the last descendant of their line and it falls to me to get this done."

Brick looked at the smaller boy for several minutes. He had always thought there was something special about Matt; it had antagonized him at first, but now he regarded the kid with a kind of grudging respect.

He shrugged, "I don't believe a fuckin' word of it, Matt, but what the hell. You do, and if any of it's true I won't be getting home without you. So what's next?"

"I dunno. We'll make it up as we go, I guess." Matt looked critically at his companion. "First we need to find a way to make you blend in. Jeans and a windbreaker is not exactly sixth century clothing!"

Brick grinned back. "You mean I've got to look as dorky as you? So where are we headed from here?"

"A castle, a place called Dunadd."

"Where's Dunadd?"

"'Bout three miles south of here as the crow flies. There's a settlement there. Doesn't really exist anymore." Matt stopped and looked at Brick. "This is getting confusing. What I mean is, it doesn't exist in your time anymore, but now we should find a market town and small castle there. Home to the king of these parts."

"King?"

"Yep. Back in the sixth century Scotland was lots of little kingdoms. So was England, actually. Once we find what I'm looking for we have a longer trek—thirty miles to Kintyre."

"Thirty miles!"

"Uh huh."

"We've got to walk thirty bloody miles?"

Matt smiled. "Yep, thirty bloody miles! But don't worry. After that we've got even further to go!"

"Can't we just catch the bus?"

Matt slapped his companion on the back. "Sure. If you don't mind waiting a thousand years!"

The rain had stopped, and the wind had abated somewhat. Around them smoke-gray clouds began to lift, revealing deep green hills on either side. Matt's spirits rose with the clouds. He had been dreading his journey to the past. Despite his training and the skills he now possessed he had not relished the thought of being alone.

Now he had two unexpected companions.

"C'mon!" Matt said, and despite his heavy pack and the knee-high grass that soaked his leggings, he set off south whistling *Mull of Kintyre* as he went.

Dunadd, Scotland
597AD

"Is that it?" Brick breathed. "When you said a castle I thought…well, you know…"

Matt nodded. He too had envisaged something a little more spectacular than this.

"It's so small," said Brick.

"I know. Little more than a stone keep on the hilltop, and an outer wall."

The two boys lay concealed in the long wet grass nestled between two gigantic boulders. They had made their way south, keeping as often as possible to the vast tract of woodland that followed the glen, an amazing expanse of oak, ash, and birch that was alive with birds and the frequent sign of deer.

Matt studied the township before him.

Dunadd was the most densely populated settlement in the region, and home to the kings of Dariada. From here the Scots nation would later arise, yet looking at it now it seemed hard to believe.

The rich fertile glen of Kilmartin was significantly different from the typical glens of the Scottish interior. Instead of the narrow passes, towering mountains, and cascading waterfalls, Kilmartin Glen was a wide flat expanse of rich fertile land and dense forest, enclosed by gently rolling hills. It was cut by the sinuous course of Kilmartin burn, the creek that joined the wider river Add from which the settlement took its name. The southern end of the valley was dominated by a solitary hill around which the river curved sharply to the south. The community had taken root beneath the protective bulk of the hill, and the enfolding arms of the sweeping river bend.

"How you getting up there?" Brick pointed to the circular stone keep that rose from the top of the hill.

"I don't know." Matt indicated the stone wall that seemed to encircle the hill about a third of the way down from the keep. "Getting past that is gonna really suck!"

"No shit." Brick said. "And we ain't even got into town yet!"

The bulk of the population lived in a poor assortment of stone and wooden houses clustered at the base of the hill. Smoke curled from the fireholes in an assortment of reed, thatch, and sod-covered roofs.

"The bridge is guarded." Matt pointed to a pair of wooden towers that stood perhaps fifteen feet tall, part of an incomplete wooden palisade that provided the first layer of defense to the sprawling settlement. Soldiers could be seen standing on the platform watching the rivers only crossing point.

"So I guess we can't just walk into town?" Brick asked.

"I don't know. Normally we could, but these are unsettled times. If the people we're opposed to hold the town it may not be wise."

"Is there another way?"

"Not without heading miles upriver."

Beyond the hill, farm land stretched to the west following the rich flood plain of the widening river to the sea.

Merlin had warned him of the risks here. Given Morgause was actively engaged in uniting Scotland under her banner, these far western kingdoms were the last outposts loyal to the former Camelon.

"It's almost dark—we'll wait a while and see what happens," Matt declared. "If we can't cross the bridge we may be able to cross beneath it, then sneak around the palisade."

He looked toward the west where the sun had almost disappeared beneath the distant hills.

"So we're just going to lay here in the wet?" Brick grumbled.

Matt looked at his companion, face expressionless. "I'd rather be wet than dead."

Brick looked back at the town and scratched at the back of his neck. "I'll be dead soon anyway," he griped. "There are things living in these clothes! I'm getting eaten alive here!"

Matt allowed himself to grin. "You needed to blend in. We had to get you something and that was the best I could find."

"Yeah. So you said." Brick pulled at his new garments. "I feel stupid!"

Matt patted him on the back, his hand sinking in to the coarse woolen fleece he had stolen. "If it's any consolation you smell even worse."

Brick playfully slapped his arm away and grinned back. "You could have pilfered the clean linen pile."

Their banter was interrupted by a distant rumbling that grew quickly into a rhythmic pounding. Moments later a large body of horsemen swept along the road toward the bridge.

"Dammit!"

"What is it?"

"Bad guys." With a finger held to his lips Matt signaled for Brick to be quiet.

The horsemen drew up at the bridge in two rows and sat waiting, their horses steaming in the evening air.

"What are they waiting for?" Brick whispered.

"I don't know." Matt responded. "Wait and see."

They soon heard the rattling of heavy wheels and the clinking of harness as a carriage came into view. Behind it two heavy wagons followed, four horses straining to pull each through the muddy ruts of the road. Both boys gasped. The wagons were piled high with bodies, and the fading light mercifully hid the more gory details from them.

The carriage passed between the lines of horsemen and a large gate in the wooden palisade opened, allowing it to pass inside, but the wagons with their grisly loads turned from the road to follow the river.

They came to a stop before the small knoll where the boys lay concealed, and the drivers climbed down and unhitched the horses. Within minutes each had mounted a horse and were leading the others into town, the horses' hooves making a hollow clattering on the bridge. The heavy wooden gates closed behind them with a thud. The wagons and the dead were left alone in the gathering dark.

Lightning flickered across the sky to the west and the first heavy drops of rain splattered to the ground before them.

Matt pulled his eyes from the wagons and looked at Brick, breaking the uncomfortable silence. "This doesn't look good."

Brick looked again at the wagons parked no more than a hundred feet from their hiding place.

"The weather or the wagons?" he asked.

Matt pulled his cloak about his shoulders as the rain began in earnest. "Both."

"Look!" Brick pointed across the bridge to the gates. A single door within the gate had opened and through it came a number of women, children, and elderly men some of which led pitifully thin donkeys, or dragged heavy hand carts behind them. The little procession crossed the bridge making their way to the wagons, oblivious to the rain that soaked them to the skin and threatened to quench their spluttering torches. Several of them pulled carts.

"They've come to bury their dead," Matt guessed, and the two boys watched in horror as the corpses were dragged from the wagons to lay on grass that quickly churned to mud, as the women and children wandered from body to body looking for their husbands, fathers, sons or brothers.

The mournful group worked in silence until the first body was identified. The stricken wife fell to her knees, clutching at her dress and crying into the night. Children gathered around her, their heartbroken sobs racking their little bodies. More wails and moans of grief filled the night as those who had clung to the brief hope their man still lived were confronted with the awful reality of death.

Matt's face became grim. His hand clenched tightly on the hilt of his sword. He looked to Brick and was surprised to see him openly crying, making no attempt to wipe away the tears that streaked with the rain down his cheeks.

Matt placed a hand gently on his shoulder. "It's this kind of thing we're here to fight," he said. "Come, we need to mingle with them and take this opportunity to get into the town—I'll do the talking."

As the boys and Mia moved from the trees, torches leaped into flame along the town walls, and the windows in the castle blazed with warm inviting light, making a mockery of the sorrow below.

Matt approached an elderly man who had limped away from the main group of mourners and was struggling to lift the body of a man several times his size onto a cart. The man's wisps of silver hair were matted to his head by the rain, and his toothless face was twisted in grief. He was pathetically thin, his arms little more than bones encased in hanging flaps of parchment-thin skin.

Matt laid a gentle hand on the man's trembling shoulder and with the aid of Brick they carefully lifted the heavy body onto the cart.

The man looked at them, his sunken eyes pools of grief and anguish that still somehow managed to convey thanks and surprise.

"Wh-who—" he stammered, "—are ye?"

"Mata," Matt answered giving the Gaelic rendition of his name. He gestured to the people around him and the body they had just helped move. "What happened here?"

The man glanced at the town wall where soldiers could now be seen, and whispered quietly. "Several weeks ago the witch queen from the North invaded our lands."

"Morgause?" Matt asked.

The man gasped and made a sign to ward off evil.

"Ye are clearly not of these parts, lad—'tis evil to speak her name!"

"Forgive me."

"The king marched against her over a week ago. We beat off her advance troops but the king was slain. She came again with more soldiers and again our people marched against her." The old man's voice broke and he looked at the body on the cart.

"Would that it was I lying there, nae my son." Tears ran down his face. "I pressed him to stay but he would have none of it."

"I'm truly sorry." Matt's heart went out to the grief-stricken man and he hated the empty sound of his words, wondering if anything he could say would truly bring much comfort against the horror that surrounded them.

Matt thought fast. The king he had come to see was dead. So what had become of the crown fragment? He sought for the correct words that Merlin had drilled into him and continued, the Gaelic flowing from him as easily as his native tongue.

"Does the body of the king still abide here?"

"Nay. He was laid to rest in the burial chamber of his ancestors." He looked once more at his son and shuffled through the mud to the handles of the cart.

"I must go now and tend to my son. 'Tis not fitting for him to lay here like this."

Distant screams issued from the town and the man's bony hands gripped the cart with surprising strength. "Already these bastards take our daughters as spoils of war. Please, I must go—my granddaughter will be needing me."

Matt placed a hand on his arm. "Sir, please. I do not wish to intrude upon your grief, but could you provide some shelter to my friend and I?" He pulled aside his cloak revealing the hilt of the sword beneath. "I can offer protection for your grandchild in payment. You can then tend to your son without fear for her safety."

The man looked at the boys for a moment. "The wolf with you too?"

Matt glanced at Mia who sat patiently nearby, and nodded.

"Little Eleanor would like that."

Straining with the heavy cart the two boys followed the old man and the straggle of mourners back to town, leaving behind several wailing wives and a number of still-unclaimed bodies.

The home the old man took them to was little more than a hovel. Stones formed the structure, with mud and peat used to plug the holes. Rough-cut wood made a weak frame for the roof, which was comprised of thin thatching covered with coarse heather weighted down with stones. A hole at one end allowed smoke out but the rain in, and the floor inside was nothing more than damp earth covered with dirty straw.

Matt and Brick sat before the peat-block fire, shocked by the brutal reality of war. They had helped Donald prepare his son for burial by removing the clothes and washing the body. Matt wondered if he could ever draw his sword again after seeing the horrible mutilation it could wreak. Brick had gone outside, unable to continue, but Matt had remained and helped bind the body in sacking. When the task was complete he had staggered outside into the cold night air and been violently sick.

Brick had helped him inside and the pair now sat draped in blankets while their outer garments dried. Donald remained with his son. In the far corner of the hovel Eleanor, his twelve-year-old granddaughter, lay snuggled against Mia upon a pallet of old blankets and straw. The poor child had cried herself to sleep with her tear-stained face buried in the dog's thick fur.

"So what do we do now?" Brick asked quietly.

"I've gotta get into the castle." Matt said. "The king had something that I'm supposed to get."

"But the king's dead."

"I know, but the item may still be in the castle."

Brick stood up and tested their clothes.

"They're pretty much dry."

"Good," said Matt, crossing to the fire and pulling on his tunic. "I hate putting on wet clothes."

"Yeah, me too," said Brick. "So you got a plan for getting in the castle?"

"No..." Matt hesitated. "Brick, I need you to stay here."

"Why?"

"'Cos I promised Donald we'd look after Eleanor."

"And you expect me to do what exactly?"

"If anyone comes, just look mean. You used to be good at that." Matt tried a smile. "Here." He reached into the shadows by the fire and pulled out a somewhat rusted short sword. "Keep this handy."

Matt crossed to Mia and crouched down beside the half-sleeping dog. Her tail beat lazily on the floor and he rubbed her head with both hands. Closing his eyes, he reached for the dog's mind to convey to her the need to protect Brick and Eleanor.

She licked his hand in understanding and he slicked her ears as he stood to leave. "Good girl."

Matt buckled on his sword and pulled his cloak tight. He paused at the door and nodded at Brick, who raised a hand in farewell. With a deep breath Matt stepped into the night.

The street, if you could call it such, was a narrow track between the buildings, churned to mud by hooves and the passage of feet. Matt found himself wishing it would rain again. A good downpour like the one earlier that evening would be sure to keep all but the most zealous guards under cover.

Moving with as much stealth as was possible in the glutinous muck of the street, he ducked into a narrow side alley between two houses and looked up toward the castle.

Strains of music and laughter could be heard drifting into the night from the candlelit windows of the keep, a stark contrast to the occasional sob and cry that had issued from the pitiful hovels he had passed.

He made to move from the alley but stopped when he noticed a small group of men gathered before the gates of the outer wall. Their raised voices carried clearly; they were demanding the return of their women.

A coarse laugh sounded overly loud in the night, and a black-clad guard lashed out with a foot to send one of the more vocal peasants sprawling into the mud. "Crawl back to your sties, rabble! The Lord Teagan has imposed curfew. Return on the morrow, and he may deign to hear your grievances then!"

Matt watched as two of the protesters stooped to help their fallen comrade but a third drew a dagger and lunged at the guard.

He did not get far. After two steps he staggered awkwardly and then dropped to his knees. Matt saw the arrow in the man's chest and the stricken look of shock on his face before he slumped to the ground. Matt slipped back into the shadows as the dead man's companions fled. Clearly Matt would have to find another way up to the keep.

Working his way between the houses Matt eventually found himself in a stone wall enclosure, home to a number of sleeping pigs, goats and chickens. The rank smell of animal dung, stirred by the recent rain, was thick and cloying, and Matt ran with one hand over his mouth and nose as he slipped and stumbled through the mire. The animals not sleeping watched his passage with mild curiosity, and Matt had almost reached the outer periphery of the pens when a blood-chilling hiss erupted behind him. He spun to face the sound, just in time to see a winged monster racing toward him, wings outstretched, head down and beak extended like a spear. Matt turned again, gained the wall in a stumbling run and leaped blindly, landing amid a dense patch of ferns and nettles on the other side.

The goose that had attacked him continued to honk and hiss its way along the wall, while Matt crawled away in the dark to a nearby boulder where he made a half-hearted attempt to scrape the filth from his boots and allow his racing heart to settle.

The angered goose continued its honking, but after several minutes it gave a final half-hearted "rronk" and silence settled once more upon the town. Composure restored, Matt began his cautious climb toward the outer stone wall of the castle.

It seemed to take an eternity to reach the wall. The coarse grass was slick from the rain, and the hill far steeper than he had realized. For every few steps he climbed he seemed to slide another back. *Geez. Those damn rocky outcrops on Merlin's beach had nothing on this!* Finally Matt slumped against the wall and spent precious moments waiting for his labored breathing to ease.

Seen from the woods that evening, and even from the small town below, the castle had not appeared that impressive but now, standing below its outer wall, it was imposing and—as far as he could tell—impregnable.

Carefully Matt skirted his way along the wall looking for some alternative entrance. The going was easier now, and as he approached the side furthest from the town he soon became aware of a growing stench, a disgusting reek of rot and human waste.

Again Matt was forced to cover his mouth and after a few more steps he found the source of the smell—a chute, about five feet above the ground, built in to the wall angling upwards into the castle. It was small, no more than fifteen inches wide and maybe two feet high. From the smell and look of the ground its purpose was clear—it was an outlet for the castle privies. Matt swallowed. "Dear God, let there be another way!"

Taking care to avoid the cesspit and its foul contents he continued around the wall, gagging as he went.

He was at the far side of the castle now, and here the walls had been built on the very edge of the rocky outcrop. He pressed his back against the wall and inched along the ever narrowing ledge until he felt he could go no further. Before him the night seemed to pull at him, threatening to draw him away from the safety of the wall and send him plummeting to the vale below. He started to retrace his steps, then recalled Merlin's words on the beach his first day of training. *Will you always turn aside when the path ahead is not to your liking? If so, we have already failed.*

Matt took a deep breath and faced the wall. Once more he began to inch his way along the ledge, now no more than half the width of his foot. He wanted to scream from the tension. His fingers throbbed from the effort of clasping at every crack or protrusion of the wall he could find. His cheek burned from the steady rasp against the coarse rock and he could feel the emptiness behind him sucking at his pack, the heels of his boots, his cloak—then to his relief the ledge widened into a small plateau and light spilled out across the grass.

Above him, Matt could see a large opening cut into the castle wall. The aroma of roasting meat, rich gravies and bread wafted from the windows and Matt guessed he had found the kitchen.

Until then his entire focus had been on getting past the outer wall. How he was to reach the keep at the top of the hill he had yet to figure out, but now he realized his good fortune. The outer wall stretched around the hill at a much lower level than the keep, shielding the various castle buildings, but toward the back of the hill it had climbed steadily, following the rock face of Dunadd hill. Here at the highest point, the kitchens were built directly into the outer wall, and connected directly to the keep itself!

Matt worked his toes into a small gap in the stone beneath the window and reached up for something to grab. His searching fingers found the edge of a wooden shutter and with a heave he was soon sprawled on the sloping ledge that angled back to the window.

The actual opening into the kitchen was little more than a foot wide; scarcely enough room for him to squeeze through, but he felt a sudden elation. He had found a way in!

Now, who's in the kitchen?

Matt stretched along the ledge and peered into the space beyond. A spitted pig lay steaming on a grease-stained table, and another smoked above a fire at the end of the room. Hot fat splashed in mouth-watering bursts on the smoking pan beneath.

Matt inched his way closer, searching as much of the kitchen as he could see. *Seriously? The kitchen's empty?* He waited, every nerve alive, eyes darting around the space beyond. The roasting pig would surely not be left unattended for long; it would burn. A woman's high-pitched giggle followed by a man's coarse laugh drew his attention to a curtained arch in the far wall. "Bailoch...the pig, it needs turning!"

"Aye, woman, and so do you! The pig can wait..."

"Bailoch—" The woman's voice became suddenly muffled.

Matt closed his eyes for a second in a silent prayer, and squeezed through the opening. More of the kitchen came into view, thankfully devoid of people. Nervous excitement sent the blood racing through his veins as he lowered himself to the cold stone floor and inched his way along the table toward a platter piled high with glistening chicken quarters.

His stomach growled. *Should I?* He glanced at the curtain. *God knows when I'll get a chance at food like this again!* Matt grabbed a chicken leg and bit into the succulent meat. Juices ran down his hand and he relished the smoked flavor of the crisp yet oily skin. Quickly he threw the bone out of the window and glanced again toward the curtain.

A soft feminine moan and the sounds of labored breathing came from the alcove beyond, and Matt allowed himself a grin. At least someone was having fun.

Spying a pile of sacks against the wall, Matt took one and stuffed a nearby loaf and some chicken pieces into it. Behind him pork fat hissed and sizzled in the pan. *Screw it!* He stepped to the table and hacked two generous slabs of pork from the steaming pig and added them to the sack.

The woman's moans rose in volume and, blushing furiously, Matt darted to the window and threw the sack into the night, then ran quickly toward the stairs at the end of the room, licking the salty pork grease from his fingers as he went.

The music that had been faint before now grew louder, and Matt soon found himself in a wide hallway. A narrower stair continued up, and in front of him a heavy tapestry hung across an arched opening. Edging forward he inched the tapestry to one side to peer into the room beyond.

Before him was the main hall of the keep. The center was lit with two gigantic iron candelabras while roaring fires at each end provided warmth and additional light. Servants scurried to tend the tables while others waited in watchful attendance from the perimeter where the only light came from flickering torches held in brackets on the smoke-blackened walls. Long tables, piled with food and decanters of wine, were lined with nobles, wealthy farmers and other people of influence from the area. They were seated on rough wooden benches and a babble of voices competed with the music from the little band of minstrels seated on a raised platform at the lower end of the hall. Matt's stomach growled at the aromas of roasted meat, pungent spices and aromatic wine and he wished he had taken a larger piece of chicken for himself.

The floor was strewn with fresh reeds and straw, and large wolfhounds lounged near the benches waiting for a bone or a carelessly dropped tidbit.

Beyond the tables people danced before steps that led up to a wooden stage where a large man presided over the assembly. Matt guessed this was the Lord Teagan.

Obese, pale faced, he sat sprawled in a high-backed chair that could barely contain his giant bulk. His neck was lost beneath the roll of his jowls and he held a goblet in one swollen hand, the short pudgy fingers bedecked with gaudy rings. He was deep in conversation with a man clad in a long black robe.

A door opened across the stage and Matt cowered back against the wall stifling a startled cry. Regaining his composure he again peered from behind the tapestry. There was no mistaking the man who strode toward the stage.

"My lord," Aldivon croaked, and the distinctive rasp of his voice sent shudders up Matt's spine. "You sent for me?"

"Lord Aldivon!" Teagan's voice was deep, guttural, and the words sounded as if they were forced around a sluggish and oversize tongue. The grotesquely overweight man heaved his body from the chair and the two men embraced.

"I trust your business in town is concluded, my lord?" Aldivon inquired.

Teagan's answering smile was twisted and sadistic. "Ahh! Yes my good friend, to complete satisfaction." He turned and clapped his hands.

Two large doors at the end of the hall opened and a number of soldiers ushered in a line of women. Matt's eyes opened in shock. It was not the fact they were bound and strung together like slaves that shocked him, but the fact that they were totally naked. They shuffled into the room hunched over, trying without success to retain some dignity.

Aldivon's eyes widened in surprise and a number of women in the hall gasped, some standing in stunned and open-mouthed astonishment, hands raised to their throats.

In stark contrast the soldiers in the room cheered and thumped their tankards and goblets on the table. Some even threw coins at the pitiful parade, until Teagan silenced them with upraised hands.

Matt's attention was caught by a sudden movement to his left. He caught a brief view of a pretty young woman who skipped briskly past his hiding spot toward the lower end of the hall. The girl seemed to take great care to remain in the shadows, and Matt could hear the whisper of silk and feel the faint breath of air as she passed his hiding place. The subtlest of perfumes reached him and he followed her with his eyes until she reached the end of the hall. She stopped there and glanced back over her shoulder, then gathered her skirts and ran to the stairs, dainty feet tripping lightly over the cold stone flags.

"Wow," he breathed quietly to himself, unable to shake off the image of the girl's long red hair cascading down her back.

With the girl gone from sight Matt returned his attention to the stage. Teagan was talking. "...and I commend you for your victory, my friend. A reward is in order, so I insist you pick the first of these lovely treasures." Teagan lurched to the line of women and beckoned to Aldivon. "Come, Lord Aldivon! Which wench pleases you the most, hmm? Let us choose together, then determine the fate of the others. Hung for sedition perhaps?" He sneered at the chained captives, then announced to the hall in a loud voice, "or given to our loyal captains for sport? What say you?"

The soldiers roared their approval, ale horns and tankards sloshing their frothy contents as they were banged on the table or raised in salute. The landed gentry and senior tenants guesting at the main tables, however, looked openly horrified, yet none dare speak out—to do so would be a sign of protest they could ill afford.

Aldivon's face was expressionless as he approached the huddle of women, but Teagan's was filled with lustful anticipation. "What of this one, hey?" He pointed toward the nearest woman, a tall brunette partially obscured from Matt's view. The big man groped toward her but reeled back when she leaped at him, spitting in his face and screaming in rage. Face red with anger, Teagan struck out with the back of his hand. One of his rings left a trail of bloody beads across her cheek, but the woman refused to be cowed and lunged again, this time pulled short by the rope about her feet. She tripped and fell. Tears of fear, hate and despair sparkled in her eyes.

"Sword!" Spittle flew from Teagan's enraged face and a nearby guard stepped forward, presenting his blade. Teagan took the proffered weapon and stepped to the fallen woman. Matt held his breath along with everyone else in the great hall. The room had suddenly grown deathly silent.

"My lord..." Aldivon stepped forward but stopped at Teagan's upraised hand. He watched as Teagan lightly ran the cold steel tip of the sword along the woman's spine.

"You will pay for your insolence, whore—"

Matt let the tapestry fall closed. He could watch no more. This evil had to be stopped. He thought of the bodies in the wagons, of Donald's mutilated son, and the bound and helpless women in the hall who waited for a fate worse than death. Angry and sickened, Matt turned away and climbed the narrow stair that circled the outer edge of the keep.

How long he had wandered along drafty corridors and dimly lit passages he did not know but he was getting frustrated. The scene in the great hall had rekindled his anger from earlier that night, and now his failure to find the chambers of the old king was wearing at his already-frayed temper. His mood became blacker as he realized the lost crown fragment would probably not be in the chamber even if he found it. He increased his pace, becoming less cautious with every aggravated step. Despite his training and Merlin's insistence to remain "uninvolved," he had the overwhelming desire to hit something.

Rounding a corner he entered a familiar passage and ran headlong into a startled page boy. The young man was probably no older than fourteen and he stopped in stunned surprise.

"Who—"

Matt did not let him finish but leaped at the boy, pressing him against the cold stone wall, his knife hovering inches from the boy's throat.

"Where are the king's chambers?" He pressed harder against the boy. "Tell me! Duncan McFarlane's chambers!"

The page's eyes were filled with fear but he could not move. Matt had him pinned and he could feel the cold steel of the knife against his neck.

Matt eased his grip but kept the knife close. "Which way?"

The page pointed back along the corridor.

"Show me!" Matt leaned in close. "And make any attempt to flee or cry for help and I'll kill you, I swear! Now move."

It soon became apparent that the castle was divided into two main wings, the north side and the south. Matt had spent the past ten minutes wandering around the northern wing, which was the confine of minor land owners and senior household members. The king's quarters were on the south side, and to get there the page led him back down the tower and through a maze of dimly lit passages to the far side of the great hall. A wide wooden stair led upward, spears, swords, animal skins, and deer heads adorned the walls to either side. The page bypassed this and led Matt to a smaller stone stair reserved for the servants that waited on the king's pleasure.

They followed the twisting stair up, passing two floors until they reached a small landing area. Through an ornate archway a passage traveled the length of the south wing and wax candles burned on the walls in place of the smoky torches. Several stout wooden doors led off into various rooms.

With the knife pressed to his back the page walked slowly forward until he reached a turn in the passage. He stopped beside an alcove that housed a statue of some ancient monarch and pointed around the corner. Matt pressed against the wall and peered into the adjacent corridor. A small opening led to an antechamber and beyond that three wide steps led up to a large iron-studded door. To Matt's surprise the door was open, but even more surprising was the body slumped on the steps, a thin steel blade embedded in his neck. A sticky pool of blood had gathered around the dead guard and two red footprints led into the kings chamber.

A raised voice, deep and rasping, growled from the chamber, and there was the distinctive sound of a body being thrown against a wall. A woman's cry was quickly cut off and the voice asked again, "Where is it?"

Matt cringed. *Aldivon! Again?* He ducked into the alcove behind the statue and dragged the startled page in with him. "Not a word!" he breathed, and the boy nodded.

They both winced at the sound of a slap.

"You know of what I speak, don't you?"

The woman must have nodded, as Matt heard no reply, and Aldivon continued.

"Good. So tell me. Where is it now?"

Matt barely caught the reply.

The woman's voice shook with terror. "It was just a piece of broken gold, lord. 'Twas buried with him. That's all I know, sir. Please..." Her voice trailed off into a string of broken sobs.

Matt heard footsteps approach the door and then they paused.

"I will be missed and must return to the hall. Take two men and guard the tomb. I shall come at first light to open it." He gave a hoarse laugh. "It would seem our task was easier than we expected!"

Aldivon's men acknowledged his command and Matt pressed back into the shadows as two guards marched past.

"What about her, my lord?" a third voice asked.

"Do with her as you will, but first dispose of this!" There came the sound of a boot connecting with something soft and Matt guessed the dead guard had just received an unnecessary kick.

Matt pressed deeper into the shadows of the embrasure and cringed as the tall figure strode by. Matt kept his blade pressed against his prisoner's neck and waited until the clatter of boots had faded down the wooden stairs, then he looked at the terrified page. The boy probably had little if any love for Aldivon or Teagan, and was just another victim trying to keep out trouble. Matt sheathed his dagger and quietly drew his sword.

The boy's eyes widened in terror.

"I need to help her." Matt gestured to the king's rooms. "Can I trust you to remain here?"

The boy nodded emphatically.

Matt held the boy's gaze a moment longer, then crept from the cover of the alcove. Careful to avoid the blood, he skirted the body on the steps and stepped into the room, sword held before him.

A serving maid, her dress torn and tattered, sat huddled by the door. Her raven-black hair was a mess and an angry bruise was already showing on her face. One eye was puffy and a thin trickle of blood ran from the corner of her mouth. The other occupant of the room, clad in the familiar black robes of the Cùra Dubh, had his back to Matt and stood over the abused woman, his sword drawn and held to her throat.

The woman saw Matt and opened her mouth to speak. He tried to silence her with a wave of an outstretched hand but it was too late. Her eyes had betrayed his presence and with lightning reflexes the man spun around, his sword arcing up in defense.

Matt cursed. *"There's no shame in running,"* he could almost hear Merlin say. *"You're not there to fight a war."* But Matt couldn't leave this poor wretch to whatever horrors fate had in store. Hardly pausing, he swung his sword, knocking aside the guard's blade, and crashed into the man shoulder first. Dropping his sword, Matt continued his run, flinging his arms around the man and driving him into the wall. The air left the man's lungs with a *whoosh,* and with a viciousness born of desperation Matt drove a knee hard and fast into the man's unprotected groin. The man crumpled to the floor gasping for air, hands clasped between his legs.

Stooping to grab his sword, Matt reached out a hand to the woman. "Quick. Come with me."

Clutching the torn dress to her breasts, she let Matt help her to her feet. "Thank you, sir!"

The page was still hiding behind the statue and Matt left the woman with him. "Wait here! Both of you!" Then Matt darted back into the king's chamber.

The soldier was struggling to his feet, but Matt had yet to kill and did not relish starting with an unarmed man. He had seen enough death this night. With no more time for reflection he lashed out with his boot instead. There was a crack as the man's head struck the wall and the soldier fell senseless.

Matt pulled the black cloak from the inert form and spied a money pouch on the man's belt. He tugged it free then returned to the couple outside. The woman was shivering and Matt draped the heavy cloak around the woman's shoulders and then emptied the money pouch into his hand. The page's eyes opened in astonishment; he clearly had never seen so much money before.

Matt held up two of the larger coins, one silver, and one gold. "Get us back to the kitchen undiscovered, and these are yours." He returned the rest of the coins into the pouch and handed it to the woman. "They owe you more but this is a start."

She clutched the bag and looked at him totally speechless; finally she leaned forward and kissed his cheek. "God bless you, sir!"

Matt's face colored in embarrassment and he waved his sword in the direction of the stairs, gesturing to the page. "Come. Get us out of here."

Chapter 14
Innocence Lost

Kilmartin Glen, Scotland
597AD

"So what do you think they'll do now?" Brick asked as the rickety old cart disappeared into the night.

"Head south, probably," said Matt. "Heather said something about an uncle on Skye, and now she's got the money to get there safely."

"And Donald and Eleanor?"

"She promised to take them both."

"That's a long way to go." Brick took a bite from the chunk of pork he carried in a pouch at his side then waved the meat at Matt. "I won't forget the look on Donald's face when you showed up with that sack of food and Heather in tow."

"Me neither!" Matt smiled. Donald had clearly not eaten so well in months, and little Eleanor had taken to Heather, the maid he had rescued, almost immediately.

They had shared a wake-feast that night with Donald recounting tales of his son and the happy years before the troubles began. Before long, little Eleanor slept and only then did Matt press Donald to leave Dunadd.

"Teagan will turn the town upside down looking for whoever broke into the castle. I cannot stay," Matt indicated Brick and Heather. "We cannot stay, and you should not either."

"Aye!" Heather had supported him. "I'm known tae all of 'em up there. They'll want me dead fer certain noo. Come wee us, man!"

With the death of his son Donald had nothing to gain by staying, and eventually he had agreed. It had taken little time to gather his meager belongings and load the simple two-wheeled cart Matt had stolen from the farm. Thankfully the goose had missed his crime.

A sad specimen of a donkey had pulled them to the gates at the bridge, with Brick and Matt hidden beneath sacks alongside the body of Donald's son. Mia had lain protectively across them and maintained a low threatening growl as Heather had bribed their way past guards clearly reluctant to leave the warmth of their guard room.

The heavy rain of the previous night had long since abated and the storm had headed east, leaving behind tatters of cloud and an intermittent drizzle.

Out of sight of the town, Matt and Brick had helped bury Donald's son. It had been a shallow grave on a small wood-covered hillock, and they piled it over with stones. Heather had taken the grieving Eleanor to the wagon, leaving the old man to say his last farewells to both his son and the town that had been his home for almost seventy years.

Before climbing up to join Heather on the wagon, Donald had retrieved a bundle from the back and given Brick some additional clothes, thanking the boy for his care and help. When Brick had tried to return the sword Donald had shaken his head.

"I'll nae be using such a thing again, laddie. May it serve yea better."

To Matt he had given a twine bracelet with charms of highly polished wood and bone. It had belonged to Donald's wife, a wedding gift made by her father. It was a family heirloom, said to bring good fortune and love to the wearer. Matt realized it was a priceless gift and had taken it only grudgingly.

Looking at it now he laughed quietly to himself; love and good fortune, he thought. What time had he for love? A fleeting image of the pretty girl who had run by him in the castle intruded on his thoughts, but he pushed the memory aside. Love would have to wait, but he would certainly take any luck that chanced his way.

Matt adjusted his pack and looked back toward the sleeping town and keep above.

"I doubt we have long before they raise the alarm. We should be going."

Brick nodded, throwing a piece of pork fat at Mia and wiping his greasy fingers on his tunic.

"Okay. I'm ready."

Despite their fatigue the boys made steady progress. Neither of them had slept much in the past twenty-four hours but the knowledge that Aldivon would ride to the cairns in the morning spurred them on. From the town to the burial cairns was a journey of less than four miles and the going should not be too difficult, but for the boys there was the constant fear of pursuit.

"We should leave the road," Matt said. "If we follow the valley floor, we'll be harder to spot."

Brick agreed, and the pair crossed the fertile farmland of the valley and followed the sluggish Kilmartin burn that meandered lazily toward the river Add behind them. Gradually the land became more wild and rugged. A hill to their left, covered in shoulder high bracken and stunted trees, rose toward the night sky before falling away to the sea while the ground to their right rose more dramatically. Forested foothills climbed steeply beside them, the trees eventually thinning out to boulder-strewn slopes above.

"Which way?" Brick indicated the small trail ahead of them that led back to the north road or up toward a wooded hill.

Matt pointed to the left where the trail bridged the stream by means of several heavy planks bound together with rope.

"Great!" Brick said. "More uphill. My feet are soaked, and my legs are killing me."

Matt gave a wan smile. He felt the same way but said nothing as he led the way across the stream to pick his way through a maze of boggy pools black with peat and tough stands of highland cotton. Insects buzzed around them and the two boys constantly slapped at the blood-sucking fiends that relentlessly homed in on hands, face and ears.

Distracted by the bugs and with little light from above, they soon wandered off the trail and the ground beneath them became wetter and springier with each step.

Mia leaped lightly ahead of them, angling upward until she found the trail. There she looked back at them, a dark shadow with wagging tail.

"Keep your feet on the grassy tussocks," Matt called behind to where Brick was picking his way between the deep black pools and the thick mud of the bog.

"Easy for you to say—these damn things wobble!"

Brick let out a startled cry, and would have fallen had Matt not turned and caught hold of an outflung arm. Brick's left leg was sunk almost to the knee in thick mud and he swayed alarmingly, trying to regain his balance.

"This bloody expedition of yours gets better by the hour!" Brick groused, pulling his leg free and looking at the glutinous mess that clung to his leggings like treacle. "I can't believe I agreed to this!"

"Hey!" Matt retorted, "I never asked you to come!"

"Whatever!" Brick mumbled, clinging to Matt's arm until he had regained his balance. They looked upward and could see they were much closer to the trees now. Slipping and sliding and grabbing at stout heather roots, the boys gradually pulled themselves to drier ground and regained the path above.

They stopped to drink from their water skins and catch their breath, and Matt nibbled absently on a crust of bread. Mia looked at him expectantly and he threw the dog a piece of pork. She gulped it down hungrily, then gave her attention to Brick in anticipation of another morsel, but the boy was staring up at the sky.

The clouds had finally dissipated and the sky above was a sparkling array of stars, a million diamonds scattered across a dust-flecked velvet cape.

"Doesn't look like that back in our time, does it?" Matt mused. Brick made no reply; he was in much poorer shape than Matt and was still breathing hard. Despite the chill of the night his face was flushed, and beads of sweat sparkled in the moonlight. He shivered and Matt stood, pulling him to his feet.

"Come. We shouldn't stop now—we'll stiffen up, and it's not far to the burial mounds. Once I've got what I'm looking for we can find a place to hole up and get some rest." Reluctantly Brick allowed himself to be pulled to his feet, and taking a deep breath he followed Matt toward the trees.

Giant oaks and silver birch stood stark and naked in the night, leafless branches reaching out with skeletal hands. Their mighty trunks were covered in green moss and their thick roots crossed the trail like ancient bones.

Where the pathway entered the trees, two flat stones smooth as glass lay glistening from the earlier rain. Meaningless swirls and cups were etched upon one, but the other seemed to stare at them from a pair of deep carved eyes.

"We have to go in there?" Brick asked, his voice strained with fatigue and nerves.

"Yeah, the burial chambers are in a clearing halfway up the hill. We just need to follow the trail."

"You said it was guarded."

"So?"

"Well how do you know the guards are going to be at the tombs and not hiding somewhere in the trees along the path?"

Matt pointed at Mia. "She'll smell 'em before they see or hear us."

"Good point," Brick conceded, but he noted Matt had drawn his sword; nervously he drew his own.

Matt gave a reassuring smile. "We'll be okay."

"I hope so—I haven't got a damn clue what to do with this." He waved the sword in a clumsy fashion and almost dropped it.

Matt grimaced. "Hopefully you won't need to. But if it comes to a fight just try and stop the other guy's blade from hitting you!"

Brick swung the weapon a few more times and then followed Matt who was already fading into the darkness of the trees.

They took their time along the pathway. Brick clung to Matt's back pack and Matt kept a firm grip on Mia's tail, as what little light had filtered down from the moon was lost almost completely beneath the trees. Relying on the dog to keep to the path, they picked their way slowly and quietly through a thickening press of holly, juniper and fir.

They continued this way for a quarter mile, and then before them the trees suddenly opened into a broad clearing bathed in soft silver moonlight. A spattering of stars twinkled above.

Matt crouched behind the trunk of a fallen tree and surveyed the clearing. Four large mounds, each about forty feet in diameter, were surrounded by a small ring of standing stones. Rough-cut sod and coarse heather lay over piles of rock forming each dome-shaped tomb.

"There should be a sealed passage into each of them. It will be no more than two or three feet wide. There's probably several chambers beneath each one."

"How do you know all this?"

"You wouldn't believe half what I've learned recently. C'mon, follow me." Matt darted from the trees to the upright stones that stood around the nearest mound.

The whole atmosphere was eerie. The cold penetrated their clothing and the moon cast a ghostly pallor across the scene. Their breath hung in clouds of moisture and the stone against Matt's back seemed unnaturally cold. He shuddered, pushing aside the thought of long-dead kings, their spirits reaching out to ensnare those that dared disturb their slumber.

He edged his way around the circle, Brick close behind. "How do you know which one to look in?" Brick whispered.

"It will be guarded." Matt suddenly stopped.

"What is it?" Brick asked, his voice too loud with fear. Matt shushed him with a stern look and was surprised to see Brick's pimpled and usually red face was deathly white. The boy's gaze darted around at the swaying trees, the silent mounds and moon-cast shadows. "Sorry, Matt," he whispered, "but this place gives me the fucking creeps!"

Matt pointed to Mia who lay a few feet in front of him. She had dropped to the ground, fur raised about her neck and ears pricked forward. Her long muzzle twitched as she tested the air with her nose.

"Smoke," said Matt. He strained his eyes into the darkness but could not make out any tell-tale signs of fire. "I think it's the next mound."

Brick simply nodded and swapped the sword from one hand to the other, wiping sweaty palms on his leggings. The mud from the bog had dried crusty and hard but he was totally unaware of any discomfort. Every fiber of his body tingled with fear.

Matt closed his eyes, reaching out for Mia's mind. Silently he sent her commands and soundlessly she darted across the gap between their mound and the next. They watched as she leaped the fence of standing stones and, belly low, climbed to the top of the mound.

Matt looked at the startled Brick. "I want you to go around that way, and I'll go this. With luck they'll be asleep." Brick's gaze, however, was still fixed on the shadowy form of Mia.

"You okay?" Matt asked.

Brick nodded again, looking in wonder at the dog. "Why'd she do that?"

"I told her to.... C'mon, let's go." Matt crouched low and ran for the cover of the next mound, pressing his back to the stones of the burial chamber.

Brick followed, curiosity burning within. *Told her to? How the hell'd he do that?*

Matt had already disappeared around the mound by the time Brick reached the cover of the stones. With heart hammering, he slowly skirted the mound in the opposite direction, fearing at any moment the looming presence of a guard.

What would he do? He wanted to be brave but did he have it in him? It was one thing beating up on little kids back at the home, but this was different. This was real. With sickening dread he realized he could die.

Fighting the desire to turn tail and run, he tightened his grip on the sword and continued on. *How big is this thing? And where the fuck is Matt?* His thoughts were suddenly interrupted as he rounded the mound and saw the guards. Moments later they saw him too.

A small fire burned before the closed entrance to the next mound, and huddled close to it were two men, barely visible in their dark cloaks. A wide stretch of coarse grass stretched toward the trees and two horses grazed there, darker shadows in the darkness of the night.

Brick stood frozen in sudden terror but the men responded instantly, leaping to their feet and shouting. Brick tried to run, but his feet refused to obey. He caught his heel on a boulder and fell back against the mound. He raised the sword awkwardly, but the nearest guard swatted it aside, and with a flick of his wrist sent it spinning to the ground.

Brick's mouth went dry and he pressed against the mound, straining to keep the guard's sword from his throat.

"So you're the little bastard we were warned about!" spat the tallest of the guards. He placed a rough hand on Brick's shoulder and spun him around, holding his head against the coarse heather that roofed the mound. He sheathed his sword and drew a dagger, holding it to the back of Brick's neck.

"Lord Aldivon wants you alive, but you so much as move, boy, and he'll have you dead." The guard turned to his companion. "Get a rope!"

Brick watched the other soldier run toward the horses, and tried to ignore the ice cold steel pressed against his neck. He made to move his feet but his assailant jabbed a knee into the back of his leg preventing any further movement.

Where was Matt? The other man had reached the horses now and was fumbling in a bag. *C'mon Matt! What are you waiting for?* He tried to move and was rewarded by increased pressure from the guard.

"Not a muscle, boy!"

Brick went limp, his gaze fixed on the other man, who rummaged through his pack for a rope.

Unseen, behind Brick, Mia stalked her prey.

Leaping silently from the top of the mound, she had crept closer and closer to the pair and now lay there, concealed in shadow, only feet from the man who held Brick.

"Got it!" called the man, brandishing a length of rope, and he jogged back to the mound.

C'mon Matt! Brick felt panic rising. *Where the hell are you?* But Matt was waiting. He could not take the risk of the guard at the horses taking off and summoning help, he needed the man closer. "Hang in there, Brick," he whispered to himself.

The man with the rope came back and bent low to bind Brick's feet together. Mia struck.

With the speed of a snake she lunged forward, jaws snapping closed on the calf of the man holding Brick. The soldier screamed in pain and tried to turn but Mia hung on, digging in with her paws and pulling backward. His leg gave way, tendons and muscles ripping as the enraged husky twisted her head one way and then the other.

The man with the rope leaped backward, startled by the ferocity of the sudden and unexpected attack.

"Gods!" he screamed, "A wolf! 'Tis a fuckin' wolf, man!"

"Get it off me! Get it off me!" His fallen companion squirmed on the ground beating ineffectively at the bloody foaming jaws that snapped at his face.

Free of both men, Brick turned to run, but stopped as Matt leaped from the mound above, smashing the man with the rope to the ground. The two rolled across the ground in a tangle of arms and legs.

The man beneath Mia finally got two hands on her head and with herculean strength began to lift the dog away from himself. She scrabbled furiously at his arms with her feet, and one of her paws caught him in the eye. The man screamed, his head exploding in pain. Lurching upright, he flung the dog to the ground. Blood and water streamed from his damaged eye but he somehow held Mia at bay with his sword.

She danced from side to side, head held low, ears flat and teeth bared, growling and snarling, always just out of reach of the wildly swinging blade as the man hobbled on his damaged leg.

Matt and the man with the rope crashed into a standing stone and struggled to their feet. Matt whipped the knife from his belt but the man head-butted him, sending the boy reeling backward, multi-colored lights bursting behind his eyes. A heavy boot lashed out at his hand and the knife flew from his grasp, spinning across the grass. Matt staggered several paces and then fell as a powerful fist slammed into his chest.

Having the upper hand, the man flung the rope to one side and drew his own sword, slashing down at the squirming boy. Matt rolled, barely avoiding the blow.

Brick at last broke free of his trance and looked around for his fallen sword. He saw it lying against the stones of the burial mound and reached for it. He glanced at both Mia and Matt. There was no way he could give the sword to Matt and he doubted his ability to take on Matt's attacker.

With barely a pause he charged toward the man that held Mia at bay. The ruse worked. The guard raised his sword to easily deflect Brick's poorly aimed blow and it was just the opening Mia had been waiting for. She sprang, jaws closing about his neck in a deadly grip. His scream was cut short as her lower teeth crushed his windpipe and he fell to the ground choking.

Brick had never seen anyone die before and he dropped to his knees, heaving and retching, unable to look away from the grotesque and tortured face of the man before him. Mia, however, didn't wait—she spun and raced across the open ground to Matt, who had somehow grasped the guard's hand but was fighting a losing battle to keep the sword from pinning him to the ground.

Mia leaped again but the man had seen her coming. He swung an arm, sending his gloved fist smashing into her head. She howled and rolled across the grass.

Matt had no time to draw his own sword so instead lunged forward, driving his head up and into the stomach of the soldier. Once again they both fell to the ground, this time Matt on top. Somehow the soldier retained his grip on his sword and flung his arms about the boy, who managed to get a forearm across the throat of his fallen adversary but lacked the strength to finish him.

Matt was exhausted, every muscle screaming in protest, his head throbbing with pain. He knew he was no match for this man and could do little more than lie there trying to hold him down while the man rained blows upon his back.

Gasping for air, Matt cried out as the man beat him again and again with the pommel of his sword, unable to rotate the weapon for a killing blow. Matt's right hand was pinned beneath his enemy and as he struggled to work it free his fingers brushed across the hilt of the man's dagger. Ignoring the agony of the blows to his back, he slid the blade from its scabbard.

Time slowed as he held the knife between them. He had the means to end his torment now, and his senses sharpened. He could feel the tip of the blade catching in the coarse woolen fabric of the soldier's clothes, feel the heat of the man's breath, smell the odor of stale ale, wood smoke, and sweat. Another blow crashed down on his shoulder, and with a feeling of unexpected regret and rising nausea, Matt drove the dagger home. The man stiffened as the steel bit deep, and Matt vomited when he felt the knife scrape across bone, catching stiffly for a moment before sliding to the hilt.

The blows to his back stopped, and he let go of the knife and pushed himself away. Beneath him the man lay still, arms at his sides, eyes wide with surprise. Matt rolled back and wiped the bitter vomit from his mouth.

Mia struggled upright, shaking her head, and shambled over to sit beside him. She licked his face. His cheeks were smeared with dirt and the left one was grazed just beneath the eye. Tears ran from his eyes and he blinked them away as Brick came to stand beside him.

"I killed him." Matt said. He felt dirty, ashamed. "I—I killed him!" He knew with sickening regret that he would probably have to kill again if he were ever to defeat Aldivon. He suddenly wanted to quit. Lying back on the grass he let the scalding tears flow, blurring the stars above, aware that with each tear ran the last of his childhood, the last of his innocence.

Matt's bruised and battered back felt as if a mountain had fallen on it, and he looked again at the body of the man he had killed. Deep wracking sobs shook his body as the enormity of what he had done took hold, but then he thought of Merlin, his mother and the man he thought of as his father.

He saw again the Pendragon swing from his father's neck. Matt reached for the cold medallion beneath his tunic and pulled it free. Closing his eyes, he recalled the words of the wizard. Gradually the thumping ache in his head began to ease and the agony in his back receded.

A calm reassuring detachment washed over him, and he rolled to his knees and pushed himself to his feet. Brick looked up from the seat he had taken against the mound.

"You all right?" he asked, voice hoarse.

Matt nodded. "I'll be fine. C'mon, we don't have long. It must be nearly four in the morning now." He looked at the heavy stone across the passage into the tomb. "Can you get that rope for me?"

Brick went to fetch the rope and Matt limped over to the entrance to the burial chamber. The stone was heavy and refused to budge.

"Mia! Come!"

Obediently she trotted over and sat patiently while Matt removed his belt. "Brick, give me your sword belt."

The older boy looked at him confused but removed the belt and passed it to Matt. Matt worked quickly. Using his knife he cut a length of rope and separated the strands, and used them to bind the leather and fashion a primitive harness for the dog. Satisfied with his work, he passed one end of the rope through the rig, made a loop and slipped it over the top of the rock door.

"Brick, help me push." The two boys stood either side of the stone and pushed forward. They felt the tiniest of movements. "Mia! Pull!" Matt commanded and watched as the dog dug in with her back legs and threw all her strength and weight into the task. She only weighed sixty pounds, but no other dog could match a husky when it came to pulling power. Her paws flew at the grass, dirt showering in all directions, and her muscles bunched and rippled under the thick rolls of fur.

The boys pushed, straining the muscles in their backs and legs. Matt gasped in pain as his body protested this new round of abuse.

Imperceptibly at first, the stone began to move, and then with a muted thud it fell to the ground. Behind it the mouth of the tomb gaped open, black, silent and waiting.

Mia collapsed to the ground panting hard, long pink tongue lolling from her mouth. Her ribs rose and fell like bellows and she did not move her head when Matt approached her. A look of concern crossed his face, to be replaced with relief when the tip of her tail twitched in greeting. He knelt beside her, rubbing her ears and praising her efforts. "Good girl, Mia, good girl!"

He pulled the water skin from his belt and shook it. Much of its contents had spilled during the fight but there was some left, maybe a quarter. He ran back to the mound and retrieved his pack from where he had hidden it before the fight. He set a wooden bowl, taken from the castle kitchen, on the grass and poured water for Mia to drink. She eyed the water gratefully, lapping it up before laying her head on the grass once more.

Matt left her to rest and returned to the open tomb.

Brick looked at him and slowly shook his head. "I ain't going in there. Hell no."

Matt nodded in understanding. "Look after Mia, and if you can, drag those out of sight." He pointed at the bodies of the dead guards. "I'll be back soon."

He removed a smoldering branch from the guards' fire and picked up an unlit torch from the soldiers' bundle. Taking a deep breath he dropped to his knees and crawled through the opening into the tomb.

Within minutes he felt as if the stone walls were narrowing, pressing in to crush him. Matt could not breathe and felt the rising panic of claustrophobia. He struggled to overcome the desire to scurry back outside, and crawled a few more feet into the tunnel. He gagged. The air was suddenly fetid, filled with the sickening sweet smell of decay. The king had been laid to rest four weeks earlier, and Matt realized with horror what lay ahead.

What would the body be like now?

Pulling his cloak to cover his mouth and nose, Matt crawled on a few more feet until it opened into a domed chamber, the floor of which was nothing more than dry dirt.

Matt held the smoking brand above his head and looked around him. There were three small openings; one of them would lead to the king. "Be methodical," he said to himself, speaking out loud and gaining a small measure of comfort from his own voice. "Right hand wall, keep following the right hand wall."

He checked his brand—plenty of wood remained. Ducking the huge stone lintel to the opening he wormed his way along the first smaller passage. He expected it to open into another chamber and it did, but what took him by surprise was the drop. The floor had been dug out by about five feet and he tumbled from the passage, dropping the torch.

The brand hit the dirt floor, spluttered and went out. Matt was instantly plunged into pure and absolute darkness. In a panic he groped around for the fallen branch.

He was trapped and his imagination kicked into high gear. He thought of Aldivon catching Brick outside, resealing the tomb and leaving him here to die, alone in the dark. His terrified mind began populating the tomb with all manner of horrifying things: rats, spiders, snakes and worse.

He flailed around for the fallen torch, smashing his elbow against something hard and rough. Then his fingers brushed something wooden. He felt again and cried out in pain as he grasped the hot brand. Ignoring the burn, he grasped the wooden torch and desperately blew on the end. A faint red glow was followed by a spark that fizzled and died. Again he blew, willing the flame to catch hold. Nothing. Sobbing, he blew again and this time a tiny flame danced before his eyes. He gently tilted the wood so the flame spread until gradually it grew and once more the torch burned brightly.

"Thank you," he breathed as the suffocating shadows were burned away. He looked around the chamber. On three sides embrasures had been cut into the wall, and each held a skeleton. He shuddered, half expecting the skulls to creak around and gaze at him through empty eye sockets.

Small clay pots, poorly decorated, stood around the chamber, and in the center was a large stone upon which stood little wooden statues. Matt guessed they were the carved effigies of ancient gods.

His torch was burning low now so he cast around looking for the second brand, which had fallen when he tumbled into the tomb. He found it lying beneath one of the openings that housed a skeleton, and reached out a foot to pull it toward him. He hooked a heel over the brand and slowly drew it close. A bony hand suddenly flopped from the ledge, skeletal fingers grasping at his leg. Matt screamed.

After what seemed an eternity he regained his composure, realizing he must have caught the fragile bones with his knee. He laughed nervously, waiting for his racing pulse to settle. Having retrieved the fallen torch he spent several minutes lighting it, and once it was burning satisfactorily he sought a way out of the chamber.

Brushing the wooden statues from the center stone he dragged it across the floor and used it as a step. Somehow he managed to squirm his way back into the passage, and moments later returned to the central chamber.

He used his nose this time, noting the sickly smell was stronger from the third passage. Steeling himself for what possible horror lay ahead he continued on. This time he was prepared for the drop and upon reaching the chamber he let himself down carefully, checking first for a stone or suitable way up again.

The king's body lay immediately opposite, the two remaining embrasures unoccupied. Mercifully the body was still clothed although noticeably bloated, and Matt tried hard to avoid looking at the head, most of which was covered in thick red facial hair. A heavy woolen robe of dark tartan weave wrapped the body, and sparkling on its chest, held in two decaying hands, was the crown piece. Matt's pulse raced. He had found it!

Gently, with trembling hands, he gripped the golden fragment and eased it from the grip of the king. Bile rose in his throat as the cold dead fingers slid wetly from the cool metal, and he hurriedly backed away clasping the treasure to his chest.

Holding the torch high he carefully examined the fragment. It was not as heavy as he expected. Two jagged ends showed where it had been broken, but the bottom edge was smooth and polished. Carefully Matt deposited it in a pouch on his belt and then replicating the method employed in the first chamber he scrambled from the tomb.

When he finally emerged from the chamber he was surprised to see Brick asleep, head slumped on his chest leaning against the nearby mound. Mia had recovered from her efforts and she rose from Brick's feet and walked over to meet him, sniffing at his legs and wagging her tail.

Matt gently shook Brick awake, envying the sleep his friend had enjoyed, however brief. He indicated the nearby bodies.

"Let's get these inside, it's getting light."

Already he could make out more of the surrounding trees, the sky turning from black to dirty gray.

Brick yawned and helped Matt pull the corpses of the guards into the passage.

"You find what you were looking for?"

Matt grinned. "Yep! One down, four to go."

They pushed the second body into the tunnel and contemplated the fallen stone.

"You want to put that back?" Brick asked.

"You think we can?"

"I thought you'd want to try." Brick pointed to two large branches he had dragged from the surrounding trees.

"If we use these like a lever and pivot we might manage it."

Matt grinned. "Mr. Jensen would be proud of you!"

Matt used one of the swords to chop a wedge on the end of the longest log and using the other as a pivot they heaved and strained to lift the stone. Somehow they managed it, the heavy stone rolling back against the passage opening, once again sealing the tomb.

Both boys were exhausted by the time they were done, but they hurried to pick up their packs and check around the site one last time. It was impossible to hide their presence. The grass was torn and scuffed where Mia had dug at it, and a deep divot marked where the stone had fallen.

Stumbling with fatigue Matt led off toward the tethered horses, calling over his shoulder to Brick, "You ever ridden a horse?"

"No!"

Matt laughed. "Well now's your chance!"

He reached for the reins of the nearest horse and handed them to Brick. "Here, take these." The horses eyed the boys nervously and shied away. Matt stroked their necks, speaking softly and soothingly until they settled down. Stooping once more, he gathered the second set of reins and prepared to swing himself into the saddle.

Only then did he see the girl.

Chapter 15
Pursuit

Kilmartin Glen, Scotland
597AD

The horses raced along the road. Clods of mud sprayed from their flying hooves spattering both horse and rider. The morning sky was free of clouds, and although the sun had yet to clear the horizon the day promised to be free of rain.

Deer had gathered at the stream in the half-light of dawn and they raised their heads to watch the riders as they thundered along the northern road. As one the deer turned and ran, their white tails bobbing as they bounded gracefully up the hillside to vanish in the trees.

Aldivon led the way, his face a mask of fury. The man Matt had knocked senseless in Teagan's quarters had been taken to the infirmary where he had spent the remainder of the night. No one had seen fit to summon Aldivon.

He slapped the reins against his horse's neck and kicked savagely at her flanks, urging greater speed from the foaming mount. He replayed the morning's conversation in his mind, convinced the man had lied to him.

"It was one of the townsfolk, my lord, I swear."

"And what of the woman?"

"He took her."

"And what did this *townsman* want?" Aldivon had barely held his anger in check.

"He never said! To kill the Lord Teagan maybe? The town simmers with anger at the loss of their king!"

Aldivon felt sure the man was holding something back. Had there been a townsman, or was the fool too embarrassed to admit he had been bested by a woman?

The road curved ahead and the riders startled a pair of ptarmigan that clucked loudly as they skimmed across the heather.

There were too many possible scenarios, each equally plausible. Aldivon clung to the hope that the guard had told the truth, that his assailant had in fact been a supporter of the old king making a desperate bid to kill the new Lord of Dunadd and incite an uprising.

And if it had been the woman? His tight-lipped smile twisted into a sneer. He should have kept her for his own amusement. A wench with that kind of spirit would have been much more entertaining than the pathetic peasant he had taken to his bed.

Still, he could not discount the possibility that either Merlin, Matt or both had begun the search for the crown. As a precaution a detachment of soldiers had been sent into the town to begin a house by house search for anyone fitting their description. Any brown-haired boy was to be arrested and taken to the keep for questioning. If they were still in Dunadd they would be found.

"How much further?" Aldivon yelled over his shoulder, refocusing his attention on the task at hand.

"Little more than a mile to the bridge, my lord..." The answer was all but whipped away by the wind of their passage. "...'tis then but a short climb through the trees to the tombs."

Aldivon tightened his grip on the reins and wondered what awaited him at the king's chamber.

Before him the mountains of Argyle stretched eastward, but his attention remained focused across the valley where a small wooded hill rose to his left.

He pointed ahead. "There it is! I see the bridge!"

Reaching the intersection between the road and the trail that led to the clearing they slowed their mounts to a walk, dipping down into the valley toward the bridge.

The girl lowered the cross bow and slid the thin wooden peg through the trigger lever, a primitive but effective safety. Not once did she glance away from the boys.

With the weapon no longer aimed at his chest Matt relaxed. He had spent the last few minutes explaining his and Brick's presence at the tomb. The lowering of her weapon at least indicated she no longer felt threatened, and Matt took the opportunity to study her a little.

It was impossible to determine the girl's age. She was clothed in men's leggings, which were clearly too big for her, and an equally oversized woolen tunic. About her shoulders hung a heavy cloak of deep forest green, and its hood hid most of her face in shadow. The outfit did nothing to reveal her figure, and only her voice had betrayed her gender.

"So, I've explained why we are here. What about you?" Matt asked.

The girl shrugged. "I came to pay my last respects to Lord McFarlane; beyond that I had no plan other than head south."

"Then our paths lay together." Matt eyed the rapidly brightening sky.

Last thing I need is another person tagging along, but... "We are anxious to be on our way—you are welcome to ride with us."

Better than having her questioned by Aldivon.

She tipped her head to one side as she contemplated the offer and a red curl escaped the hood she wore. She brushed it aside and for the first time he caught a glimpse of her face. Her features were delicate and soft pink lips parted in a hesitant smile. Bright green eyes held his for a moment and he felt a fleeting sense of recognition before she adjusted the hood, hiding her features once more.

Matt took a risk. "I haven't been completely honest with you. We are wanted for attacks on Aldivon's soldiers—"

"Jesus, Matt!" Brick looked aghast. "You can't—"

Matt raised his hand. "Aldivon is coming here and if we are found it will be death." He pointed back at the fire. "I told you we came here just as you did, to pay our respects to the king, but now we must go!"

"So you do not support the witch queen?"

"No, I do not!" Matt fixed the girl with a firm look, then lowered his eyes to the crossbow. "And if you don't either, then *that* will not be enough to protect you. Three would be better than one on the road south. Come with us."

"I am more than able to take care of myself!" she replied.

Matt shook his head and held up his hands in supplication, "Okay, fine!" He turned to Brick, who was looking at the horse with some trepidation, and helped the other boy up into the saddle. Assured his friend was safely seated Matt swung himself easily onto the second horse and once more faced the girl.

"I'd appreciate you keeping our meeting to yourself," he said, and without looking back spurred the horse toward the trees.

Brick gripped the reins as if his life depended on it, which given the way he lurched in the saddle it probably did. Fighting to keep his balance, he somehow remained upright as his horse followed Matt's.

"You just gonna leave her there?"

"Yeah."

"But what if she—"

"Wait!" the girl called from behind them, running back to her own horse. Matt reined in and grabbed at the halter of Brick's mount that, unchecked by its rider, tried to continue on.

"Pull back on the reins to stop!" Matt yelled at Brick as he watched the girl climb easily into the saddle and canter her horse to join them. Despite the bulky clothes he could see she was athletic and accustomed to horses; clearly not a regular girl from town, and no peasant either. He filed the thought away for further consideration. An explosion of wings pulled his attention from the girl. Wood pigeons and crows rocketed from the trees at the southern end of the clearing and rough voices carried on the morning air.

"Come on!" Matt yelled and the three of them pushed their horses into a mad dash across the clearing and into the trees beyond. Mia gave one last look at the pigeons then bounded after them, her wolflike muzzle fixed with a lopsided grin.

They drove their horses hard, weaving through the trees and the occasional rocky outcrop until they emerged into the valley below the hill. The sun had risen now, and the sun sparkled on the wet granite of the distant mountains. The girl pulled her horse to a stop alongside Matt's. "So where exactly are we going?"

"I have no idea! Ultimately south, but we need to rest."

"Rest? I thought you spent the night at the mounds?"

Matt silently swore to himself. *I'm too damn tired to lie convincingly!*

"We didn't get to the clearing until the small hours of the morning. There was little chance to sleep."

The girl raised an eyebrow but let the explanation stand. "There are caves east of here," she said.

Matt thought for a few moments. More than anything he needed rest, but could this girl be trusted? "I don't even know your name," he said, trying to draw the girl into revealing more about herself.

"Nor I yours," she replied simply.

Matt sighed. "I'm Matt, he's Brick."

"Brick? That is a strange name."

Brick said nothing, concentrating his efforts on staying upright in the saddle. He raised a hand in a friendly wave but snapped it down again to clutch the reins as his horse swerved to avoid a large boulder.

The girl laughed at Brick's obvious discomfort on the horse. "I'm Valina." She pulled the hood from her head, allowing her hair to cascade down her back in shining auburn waves. "Let me lead from here. I'll take you to the caves." Both boys stared first at her and then each other.

"Wow!" Brick breathed as Valina led her horse across the valley floor.

Matt grinned. "Concentrate on your riding, my friend."

Brick reluctantly looked away from the girl. "She's hot," he mouthed.

"Yeah, beautiful," Matt agreed quietly, desperately trying to break through the fog of fatigue that stood between him and the nagging feeling he had seen her before.

Valina waved a slender hand at them. "You coming?"

Brick looked at the bemused expression on Matt's face and risked releasing the reins long enough to punch his arm.

"You can sit there and stare all you like Matt, but where she leads I'm following." And with that he kicked at his horse with his heels.

The startled animal leaped after the girl and then continued on past her, Brick's elbows flapping like stubby wings. Matt laughed at Brick's terrified cries for his horse to stop and nudged his own mount into a trot to catch up. Gathering his concentration he issued a telepathic command to Brick's horse, bringing it to a gentle halt.

Valina cantered up the slope to join the boys, her eyes bright with mirth.

"Come on," she laughed, and the group trotted across the valley and into the desolate foothills of Argyle.

The heavy stone crashed to the ground for the second time that morning as the soldiers heaved it from the entrance. Two men ducked into the passage, then quickly returned.

"They're dead, my lord!"

Aldivon looked coldly at the bodies as they were dragged into the clearing.

Dammit! He kicked the nearest corpse.

"'Tis Merlin and the boy!"

"My lord?"

"Look!" Aldivon pointed a shaking finger at the torn throat and savaged leg of the nearest body. "That's the work of an animal."

"Aye, lord! Others have spoken of it. They say it's like a wolf and possesses strange powers. 'Tis Merlin himself, some say, transformed into a beast!"

The soldiers took an unsteady step back from the bodies and looked nervously around the clearing.

Aldivon fixed the speaker with a dispassionate stare. "'Tis a dog, man. Nothing more," he said, then crouched beside the remains of the fire. He passed a hand over the blackened wood and ran a stick through the piles of powder-white ash. It was still warm and orange sparks drifted into the sky as he allowed fresh air to tease the heat into new flame.

"They cannot have gone far," a soldier observed.

Aldivon returned to the entrance of the tomb and crouched before the passage.

"Search the clearing for tracks. Someone is with the boy. I doubt the lad could have done this alone and"—he pointed back across the clearing—"both horses have gone."

Aldivon held out a hand, "Fetch me a torch!"

A soldier ran over with a stout brand and, using the newly awakened fire, lit it. Taking the torch Aldivon turned and disappeared into the tunnel. He already knew the crown piece would be missing but he had to be sure.

Argyle Highlands, Scotland
597AD

Matt came awake with a start. Brick lay off to one side sleeping soundly, and beyond him the three horses stood close at the rear of the cavern.

Warm and dry, Matt felt surprisingly comfortable despite the hard surface of the cave. It would be so easy to close his eyes and drift back to sleep, but then he remembered the girl.

He propped himself up and looked around the dimly lit space. She was nowhere to be seen. In a panic, Matt threw aside his blanket and looked into his belt pouch. He breathed a sigh of relief at the sight of the pale yellow metal. *Arthur's crown!*

Careful not to disturb Brick, Matt gathered up his sword and walked quietly to the mouth of the cave.

Valina sat just outside, gazing over the desolate landscape beyond. Beside her, head in the girl's lap, Mia lay stretched out in the afternoon sun. The girl toyed with the animal's neck, running her fingers through the thick layer of fur.

Matt watched her for a while. Her hair was pulled back, revealing delicate un-pierced ears and a neck as smooth as porcelain. Her nose was tiny, slightly upturned, with a fine dusting of freckles. It was hard to tell but he guessed her age at about eighteen. Again he was struck with a vague feeling of recognition, her hair and the...

She turned and he blushed, guilty at being caught watching her. "I just woke up." He indicated the rocky ledge beside her. "May I?"

Her smile could have lit the darkest room. "Of course!" She patted the ledge. "You've been asleep for hours."

He stepped over the sleeping dog and slid to the ground beside the girl. He tried hard not to stare, but was very aware of the fluttering pulse at her throat and the downy soft hairs that ran up the back of her neck.

With an effort he forced his attention to the wide expanse of scenery before them. The hills were cloaked in color. Lichen-speckled rocks of various grays punctuated a landscape rich in green; grass-covered slopes of olive and khaki were cut here and there with dark scars of emerald that spoke of unseen rills and streams running deep in their moss-covered beds. Gorse, broom and bracken grew in abundance, greens so dark they were almost black in the shadows of the lower hills, while in the distance vast tracts of Caledonian pines marched across the hills to the smoky haze of the horizon.

"Beautiful, isn't it?" Matt said.

"Aye. That it is." Matt found himself captivated by the soft melody of her voice and was pleased when she continued. "I've never taken the time to just sit and look before. Always so many things to be done."

Valina reached across him and withdrew a water skin from a cleft between two boulders.

"Water?" she asked, then hesitated when she saw the astonished look on Matt's face.

"What is it?"

The faint trace of perfume as she had reached across him had been impossible to forget and now he recognized her, seeing not the manly clothes she wore but the long evening gown that had flowed around her as she had fled the hall the night before.

Matt looked into her eyes, noting flecks of gold and brown that matched the freckles on her nose.

"I've seen you before!"

Matt saw the momentary fear in her eyes.

"Last night," he continued, "you ran from the great hall when Taegan brought in those women."

Her face flushed. "You were there?"

"Aye." Matt gestured to her clothes. "So why is a lady of the court dressed this way, and what are you doing here?"

Valina sighed and looked down at her hands. She picked idly at the burrs and dirt matted in Mia's fur. "I am the niece of Lord Morton. My father was loyal to the late king and as a minor noble was regularly at court. When the witch queen began her campaign against us my father arranged for me to live at the castle.

"Our home lies north of here. As a child I would ride with my father when he went hunting."

A faraway look came into her eyes and he could see she was struggling to continue. "My father died last year."

"I'm sorry." The words sounded somehow insufficient and Matt wondered how it always sounded so sincere and appropriate in the movies.

Valina continued as if she had not heard him. "Father was murdered by his brother. The two had always been bitter rivals, with my uncle maintaining he was the lawful heir to our lands, him being the eldest son. But he was illegitimate and grandfather had willed the land to his younger son, my father.

"They fought over everything." She paused, and a look of disgust crossed her face. "Over land, and my mother."

"That's terrible!" Matt found his heart going out to the girl, amazed she would reveal so much of her personal life to a stranger.

She raised her gaze to his and gave him a bitter smile. "It does not end there. With the death of my father our lands were held by the king, and when the witch queen began her attacks on our borders my uncle fought alongside Aldivon." She looked at Matt with something akin to desperate pleading. "My uncle promised me to Aldivon in exchange for more titles, more land."

"So that is why you left?"

"Aye! When those poor women were brought into the hall my uncle was distracted. I fled to my chambers, gathered some belongings and left."

"You said you were heading south. Do you have other family there?"

"My mother has a sister in Ireland. I thought to head south and buy passage across the sea." Her bright green eyes sparkled with moisture but she proudly blinked the tears away. "There is nothing for me here."

Matt was moved. He knew he could not divert his attentions from the quest but for now his path also led south. He did not know what he was feeling but there was something captivating about the girl that transcended her obvious beauty. All he knew for sure was he wanted to spend more time with her. He gave a reassuring smile. "I would be honored to escort you at least some of the way." Matt blushed and stammered, "If that would not be improper?"

She lowered her eyes, hiding them behind lustrous lashes while she pouted in mock contemplation. Matt held his breath, hoping she would agree, and with a bright little laugh that sent his heart skipping and racing in ways he had never known she carefully moved Mia's head and stood to give a dainty curtsy. It should have looked absurd in the oversized costume, but instead sent Matt's pulse racing even more wildly.

"I would be delighted to accept your gallant offer, sir!" She laughed, mimicking the formality of his words, and Matt found himself grinning. Despite the horror and stress of the past few days, he realized he was at last looking forward to the journey south.

Brick awoke to the smell of cooking. His stomach growled and he threw back the blanket, stretching noisily.

To one side of the cavern he saw Matt and Valina sitting close before a small fire. Two rabbits slowly roasted on makeshift spits and the fire hissed and cracked with each drip of fat. The smell of cooking meat made his mouth water.

Mia had gone hunting earlier in the day while the boys had slept, and now she lay with head on paws watching her catch cook. She too licked her lips in anticipation.

Running fingers through the tangle of his hair, Brick stepped around the fire to join them. "Sure smells better over here," he joked, casting a thumb in the direction of the horses. "It's getting a bit ripe over there."

Valina smiled but cast a questioning look at Matt, "What is the language your friend speaks. Briton?"

Matt searched for a suitable reply, suddenly aware of the difficulties the language barrier might cause. Of course trade with Europe was commonplace, and northern England and post-Roman Scotland were involved in extensive trading with France. While Gaelic was the common tongue of Scotland, many spoke French. English had yet to emerge even in the south where a mix of languages were spoken—Cumbric, Briton, Latin.

Brick solved the problem for him by responding in fluent Gaelic, "I am sorry." He grinned. "The horses, they stink."

Now it was Matt's turn to look in consternation at his friend. In English he asked, "How the hell do you know Gaelic?"

"I was born on Skye; it's pretty much the native language there."

"But I thought..." Matt left the obvious statement referring to Brick being a child of the streets unfinished.

Brick shook his head. "There's a lot you don't know about me, Matt. Dad married a woman from Newcastle and she hated me. Only time she wasn't beating up on me was when she was too drunk or when Dad was home. We moved to Aberdeen when I was little."

Matt sat in open-mouthed astonishment as Brick went on. "Dad was a soldier but I hardly knew him. He was killed in Ireland. My step mum didn't give a crap about me and took all her drunken frustrations out on me. I ran away from home when I was seven. Spent time with this tramp who only spoke broken English but fluent Gaelic. Rest is history."

Matt smiled at Valina and then looked back at Brick. "We tell her we speak Cumbric. That will do as an excuse, but from now on we'll stick to Gaelic, okay?"

Brick nodded and switched into the ancient lilting language of the Scots. "So where'd these rabbits come from? I'm starving!"

The remainder of the day was spent resting and preparing for the journey south. Matt estimated it would take two full days to cover the thirty miles to Clachan, the fortress on the West Coast of Kintyre where, he hoped, the next crown piece was located. He had picked out a circuitous route, planning to take a wide detour east of Dunadd during the night, then angling south into Kintyre.

Only one patrol had passed near their hiding place during the day but he did not want to take the risk of passing too close to town during daylight. With Aldivon in charge this small kingdom was now hostile territory.

As the sun set and a few bright stars appeared in the sky, the three companions left the shelter of their cave. Rested and refreshed they began their journey south.

Chapter 16
Traitor

Glen Airigh, Scotland
597AD

The night's journey had begun well. They had kept to the upper slopes of the low-lying hills in an effort to avoid the difficult and sometimes treacherous terrain around the small lochs and boggy pools of the lowlands.

Twice they had been forced to retrace their steps, finding themselves on ground too wet and soft to accommodate their horses. Despite these setbacks they had made steady progress eastward, curling around Dunadd and leaving the town several miles behind.

With sufficient distance between them and the town Matt had changed course, angling more to the south, but their pace had slowed as the land began to rise more steeply and the gentle heather hills gave way to boulder-strewn slopes.

Here they were forced to dismount and lead their horses, skirting the shoulder of Sidh Mor, the highest peak in the region. Picking their way carefully over the mountain's treacherous slopes they eventually descended, foot-sore and weary, into the forested depths of Glen Airigh.

The first major check to their journey came just before midnight when they encountered the river Add some five miles upstream of the town. The river was wide and fast-flowing, its banks steep and the water inky dark. The map Matt carried had shown the river as a thin blue line, but the swirling water before them was impossible to cross. Forced to follow the river, they continued to lead their horses, walking in single file as they made their way through the dense trees, taking constant care to avoid the tangle of roots that reached for the water like giant tentacles.

For almost two miles they tripped and stumbled their way upstream before the trees at last gave way to stone-shattered moorland. Here the river curved sharply to the north, its steep banks finally leveling out into wide gravel beds. The water here was shallow and made an ideal crossing point.

"There's little shelter, but fresh water. Shall we stop here for the night?" Valina asked.

Matt's legs ached and the prospect of resting the remainder of the night was tempting, but that would leave them exposed with nothing but open ground ahead when day dawned.

Matt shook his head. "We should press on and find a more sheltered spot to camp." Noting the dejected expression on both faces he added, "But we can rest here a bit. The water's cold and the horses will need drying lest they come up lame. We'll cross here, then rest an hour."

They had refilled their water skins and allowed the horses to drink, drying them off and rubbing down their legs, giving them time to recover from the shock of the ice cold river. Matt had kept watch, and both Brick and Valina had to be shaken awake before they could resume their journey south through the glen.

The ground of the glen was dry and firm and the going much easier. Behind them the steady roar of the river faded away and the night became a world of silent mystery. Huge oak trees and towering pines rose around them and the horses forged an easy path through the thick bracken of the woodland floor. For the first time they were able to pick up speed, and Valina nudged her horse closer to Matt's.

"I'm glad to be free of the river! My feet hurt tripping over all those wretched roots!" She raised a hand to cover a yawn. "The rest was good, but you woke me far too soon. Are we to ride all night?"

Matt smiled. "We'll stop soon."

They rode in silence and Valina allowed her horse to fall back alongside Brick where she could study Matt a little. Despite his obvious fatigue he was still very alert. His eyes were never still, constantly scanning the trees around them and the path ahead for hidden danger. Several times she had caught him looking in her direction and then he would blush and look away when she caught his gaze. The attention pleased her, for she liked the young man and it was obvious he was attracted to her, although equally obvious he was unsure of the ways of women.

"Tell me, Brick," she said, "how old is he?"

Brick shrugged. "Seventeen or thereabouts. I never really knew him that well until recently."

"Really? So what brings you both to these parts? Have you been here long?"

Brick winced as his horse turned to avoid a fallen tree and he tried without much success to find a more comfortable position. He had finally grasped the basics of riding but his thighs, back and arms ached terribly from his efforts to stay on the horse. He recalled his first long journey on a cycle—the discomfort he had felt then was nothing as to now. This journey gave a whole new definition to *saddle sore*.

He looked at the girl, making no effort to mask his appraisal of her. "That's a secret you best ask him about. I'd rather get to know you a little better instead."

She shrugged. "Later, maybe," and after a few moments of silent riding she pulled her horse beside Matt again.

"You never did tell me where we're going," she said. "We talked mainly about me in the cave. As a lady traveling with two strange boys I think it's time you told me something of yourselves." She tossed her hair and gave him a sidelong grin. "Well?"

Matt inwardly sighed. The last thing he wanted was to lie to the girl. She had been so open with him and yet how could he ever explain the truth to her? Brick had found it hard enough to accept the truth and he came from a world of books, movies and technology where fantasy and science fiction were but a mere step from reality.

This girl—he gave her a quick glance—woman, he corrected, of the sixth century would never comprehend what was really happening; he chose to improvise.

"Brick and I live a long way from here."

"That much I'd figured out already! But why have you come here? And what is your argument with Aldivon?"

"Our lord wishes to aid the remains of the old alliance against the witch of the north." That was almost true, he thought. "I have urgent business with King Moy of Kintyre."

Her eyes widened in surprise. "You are openly challenging the queen?"

"Atrocities like those at the castle last night must be stopped!" Matt felt his face flush with anger.

"I would agree, but that was the work of Aldivon and Teagan, not the queen. What is this alliance of which you speak?"

"Decades ago there was an alliance between the free kingdoms that stretched from east to west. They united to fight the Picts in the north who were led by a fearsome and evil man known as Dardanos."

Matt was concentrating on the trail and missed Valina's sudden intake of breath.

"Dardanos was defeated and the alliance dissolved. Its leader was a prince. A man named Arturius." Matt glanced at the girl. "Surely you've heard of him?"

"I have heard stories. Few speak of him with love and many of the younger folk and those from the northern villages say he was a butcher, a brutal warrior under the spell of an evil magician named Myrdrin. They say he used the people of Scotland to exterminate those who practiced the magic arts and posed a threat to his darker designs! You speak of evil times, Matt, and evil people!"

Matt was stunned but made no reply as Valina continued. "I've heard stories of how Arturius and his soldiers led raids into villages, murdering old women, accusing them of witchcraft and putting to the sword men and boys who stood in their way—innocent farmers, shepherds and crofters. Aye, many mothers threaten their bairns with tales of Myrdrin."

"You can't believe such stories!" Matt was aghast. "You yourself have seen the brutality of Aldivon—and he's a servant of the queen. Arturius was their enemy, and therefore our friend!"

Valina fixed him with a cold stare. "Aldivon, aye, he is a monster! But by all accounts so were Arturius and Myrdrin." She paused, noting the confusion in his eyes. "Morgause promises salvation from poverty; she talks of riches and greatness to all the people of Scotland and tells of a new world order where all will prosper under her banner. Many believe in her."

Matt found it hard to hide the anger in his voice and snapped back at her, "You sound like one of them! Back at the mounds you said you came to pay respects to the very king Morgause and her army have overthrown! Her army killed your father, for god's sake!" Matt's knuckles were white as he gripped the cold leather reins.

How could she be saying this?

Valina looked startled at his sudden outburst and responded hotly. "King McFarlane was like a father to me. His death grieves me still, as does the loss of my father. But I know little of politics, Matt. I've heard people say the king took arms against the queen, who had approached him in peace with nothing but offerings of friendship and unity."

She fixed her eyes on the trail ahead. "And it was my uncle in league with Aldivon who slew my father, not Morgause. This land is torn asunder with war and drenched in bloodshed. I have no family now. I just want to live in peace and safety, away from war, away from Aldivon, and yes away from Morgause, but you should not be so fast to judge those you do not know."

Matt rode in silence trying to make sense of her words.

Not be so fast to judge? Well that's rich! How about you heed your own fucking advice! To hear his lifelong heroes Arthur and Merlin branded as brutal and evil monsters made his blood boil. Matt wanted to shout, wanted to be angry, but something held him back.

You want her to like you!

Matt suddenly realized he was developing feelings for the girl that confused him.

You're a romantic idiot if you think she's gonna be interested in you. Part of him had been looking forward to spending the journey south with her. *Shit!* His emotions were in turmoil.

She laid a delicate hand on his forearm and felt him tense at the touch, *Gods, he's well-muscled!* "You should not deliver your message to King Moy, Matt. It will only lead to further conflict, more loss of life, and to what end? Aldivon is evil, and maybe Morgause too but is it not a greater evil to cause men to die to protect a myth? Some legend of the past? Perhaps it is time for a new order."

Matt fought for something to say but was distracted by the heat of her hand on his arm. *Her skin's so warm, so soft!* His head was spinning, and finding nothing to say he shrugged her hand away. "I need to scout ahead for somewhere to camp," he said and spurred his mount forward, calling to the dog who ran to catch up with him.

Valina watched him go and pulled her horse to a stop to wait for Brick who had lagged behind.

"Where's he going?" he asked, bringing his mount to a stop and standing in the stirrups to rub his aching legs and buttocks. "My backside feels raw," he griped.

Valina smiled but the smile quickly faded as she watched Matt depart through the trees. "I think I upset him."

Brick shrugged. "Well I ain't galloping through here in the dark. He can just bloody well wait for us."

Valina giggled.

"So—like I said before, how about you and me get to know each other better?" said Brick, and the two continued on following the trail of broken bracken that marked Matt's passage through the trees.

Loch Airigh, Scotland
597AD

Matt had cut bracken for bedding and fashioned three makeshift beds on the sandy shore of Loch Airigh. His blanket was already spread across one and he sat now gazing out over the dark still waters of the loch. Mia was already asleep, curled in a hollow beside a large boulder, her paws twitching occasionally and a long string of saliva dangling from the pink and black of her lips.

Matt's thoughts turned to Valina. Was he right to be so angry at her comments? Had she really branded Merlin and Arthur as butchers or had he misinterpreted her words? Replaying the conversation he realized that he may have gotten it wrong. He kicked a pine cone sending it rolling into the loch.

Or was he simply making excuses, trying to twist her words because he liked her?

The more he thought about the conversation the more he began to realize she had expressed nothing of her own opinions beyond a desire for peace. The words that had angered him had been echoes of the thoughts of others. He picked up a stone and massaged it in his palm, seeking to relax his mind and let his thoughts drift anywhere but the girl. But it was useless—either her voice, her eyes or that wondrous mane of auburn hair would creep to the forefront of his thoughts. He saw her smiling and laughing, the flash of perfect white teeth, the mocking glint to those slightly upswept eyes. He recalled the heat of her touch the moment before he had so rudely brushed her away.

"Forget her!" he mumbled into the night. "In a few days she'll be gone anyway, and I have a job to do." He angrily tossed the stone into the water, shattering the reflected orb of the moon into a million sparkling drops. He watched the ripples spread across its surface and cursed himself for acting immaturely.

Lying back on the sand, hands behind his head, he gazed up at a sky now ablaze with stars. What would she think of him now? How could she possibly know the truth behind Arthur and Merlin? He had more than a thousand years of history to look back on. He had met Merlin, but she had none of that. No newspapers, radios, books, libraries or education. Her sources of information were little more than village gossip and hand-me-down stories. He had acted like a fool. Would she let him put things right?

He closed his eyes, pushing her once more from his mind. What would tomorrow hold? He thought of the route they would take and wondered how far behind Aldivon's soldiers were. How would King Moy react to his arrival?

Holy cow! A king! How the hell will I react meeting an actual king?

Matt's thoughts were broken by the sound of voices and he sat up to see Brick and Valina, locked in conversation, trot from the trees onto the beach. He felt a momentary twinge of jealousy when he saw her laugh and touch

Brick on the arm, but he forced it away. He had already acted stupidly enough in front of her.

Eilean Tioram, Scotland
597AD

The raven perched on the window ledge and pecked at a large rat pinned beneath its feet. The giant bird's bill looked like a wooden dagger, varnished in blood, as it stabbed down again into the stricken rat. Beady eyes glittered in the light of the flickering candles arrayed around the room, yet the chamber itself seemed strangely absent of light.

Morgause was clad in a rich gown of purple velvet, and her midnight-black hair was pulled back, layered upon itself and held at the back with a silver clasp. Her unblinking stare was fixed upon a mirror that stood upon an otherwise bare table.

But this mirror cast no reflection. Its burnished surface did not reflect, but rather absorbed light, drawing it into its depths, swallowing it like starlight pulled into a black hole.

Deep inside the inky darkness of the mirror an image finally formed. Stars swam into focus, brilliant yet tiny reflections in the surface of a lake.

A figure sat huddled behind a fallen tree, eyes fixed on a small mirror held cupped in its hands.

"Why have you taken so long to contact me?" the queen's voice was cold, almost painful in the listener's head.

"It was not safe." The voice was nervous, almost hesitant.

"Is it now?"

"Yes. But I dare not stay long."

"What news then? Be swift!"

The figure glanced over a shoulder before turning again to the queen.

Morgause's face was a mask of concentration as she held open the mind link between herself and her subject. Her pale face looked deathly white in the faint light of the room and her violet eyes hungrily searched the image in the mirror. She could make out a beach beside a loch, and trees stretching as far as she could see.

"Matt has found the first fragment," said the voice of the informant. "It was buried with MacFarlane at Dunadd. Aldivon was there and we barely escaped in time."

"Did he follow you?"

"Yes but we hid. We are not being followed now."

The queen pondered this for a moment. "I need to know where you are and where you are heading. Does the boy suspect you?"

"No, he does not suspect me. I am safe for now. We are currently camped near a loch in southern Argyle, not far I believe from Loch Fyne. The others are asleep and with respect, Your Majesty, I too am tired. I have been through much these past few days."

"Others? There are more than just you and he?"

"Yes, my queen. There are three of us now, and the dog."

The witch queen's voice was cold, emotionless. "Where do you go from here?"

"Matt says we will leave early in the morning and head south into Kintyre. We are making for the castle of Moy but I do not know the route or what he plans to do when we arrive."

"Then find out! And watch for Aldivon. That man has his uses but I do not trust him. His army already moves on Kintyre. You will probably find the road dangerous."

"We will be careful, Your Majesty."

"Good." The queen smiled, her lips thin and bloodless. "Remember what I promised when you left me last. You will be rewarded for your efforts and you have pleased me well thus far. Report when you can but do whatever you must to remain above suspicion. I am counting on you."

"Yes, Your Majesty. Thank you."

The queen waved her hand over the mirror and the room was suddenly bathed once more in the warm glow of candle light. Morgause considered her reflection for a moment then placed a black velvet bag over the mirror and crossed to the winding stairs that descended the tower.

The raven croaked and launched itself from the ledge, landing on the queen's shoulder with a ruffle of feathers. She kissed its bloodied beak and it fixed her with a cold stare, eyes bright yet unfathomable. She stroked its wings and crooned. So far everything was progressing perfectly. One crown fragment was all she needed and one was as good as in her grasp. All that remained now was to find Arthur's location, and the rod of Dardanos.

Chapter 17
Tolnech

Tolnech, Scotland
597AD

They had been riding since sunup. The remainder of the night had passed without incident and after a makeshift breakfast, which consumed the last of their rations, they had set off.

The morning was bright and the day full of promise. They had followed the loch south, keeping to its beach of sand and water-smoothed stones before passing once more into the dense woodland of the glen, a mixture of bud-rich trees and majestic firs.

The air was filled with the sweet scent of pine and birds chirped loudly, flitting from branch to branch, feeling the first stirrings of spring. Deer had watched them pass the southern end of the loch and Matt had been forced to restrain Mia who had looked on them with hungry eyes.

"Well I don't know about you two," said Brick, "but I'm lost. Exactly where are we?"

"Approaching Loch Fyne," Matt replied. "I plan to follow its shore until we reach Tolnech."

"Tolnech?"

"Yeah. It's a fishing village. We should be able to resupply there and then head west to rejoin the north-south road into Kintyre."

"Is that wise?" asked Valina, who had hardly spoken that morning. She had seemed somehow withdrawn and Matt guessed she was a little unsure after his behavior the night before. He was angry at himself too, for failing to make amends, but did not know where to start. Never one to feel comfortable around girls, he found himself feeling foolish and flustered whenever she looked at him.

Brick had called her hot but to Matt the term seemed crude, derogatory somehow where she was concerned. Valina was more than that. He was aware of her in a way he'd never been aware of a girl before. In a single look he saw the sparkle of sunlight on her hair, the flurry of tiny freckles across her nose, the way her tumbling red locks fell against the green-colored wool of her cloak. He wanted to say sorry, wanted to explain, but right now didn't trust himself to speak. She turned and held his gaze with her own. A tentative smile played across her lips.

"I heard in the castle that Aldivon was already moving his forces south to take Kintyre," she said. "Depending how fast they have marched we may have an army to pass through."

"Yeah!" interjected Brick quickly. "While we've been creeping through the hills and glens, you can bet Aldivon has spread word of us south by road."

Matt pulled his eyes from Valina and reined in his horse.

"We'll approach with care. If the place is crawling with soldiers then we'll have to rethink. If the place seems okay we'll head into town, replenish our supplies and gain whatever information we can from the locals. At this stage I think it's worth a little risk. Depending what we learn, we can adjust our plans accordingly."

"I think that's a mistake, Matt," pressed Brick. "We should stay away from populated areas."

Matt glanced at Valina but she said nothing. She sat quietly, head to one side studying him. *Why was her approval suddenly so important to him?*

"Well?" she asked.

"We're going to Tolnech." Matt kneed his horse and quickened their pace through the trees.

Brick and Valina sat for a moment and then Valina urged her mount forward. Brick brought up the rear, his expression one of anxious concern.

Tolnech, they soon learned, was more like a small town than a village, dramatically different from the hovels and pens of Dunadd. Located on the juncture where Loch Fyne curved from the east before beginning its journey to the sea, it was home to a people that thrived on a healthy fishing industry and enjoyed good quality soil for farming.

The crystal waters glistened in the noonday sun and the loch's glassy surface was dotted with fishing boats, some wallowing low in the water, heavy with herring and oysters. The sea-loch stretched for over forty miles, and from the fishing docks to the far shore it was almost three miles wide.

The mountains that formed the backbone of Kintyre had shed their winter snow, and waterfalls cascaded down their slopes feeding the loch below and seeming to trim the forest-clad hills with tendrils of foaming lace.

The people were proud of their town. Meadows that in summer would be abuzz with bees and insects and speckled with sweet-smelling flowers stretched from the water's edge to the narrow dirt road that followed the winding river to join the main north-south road further inland.

Matt and his companions emerged from the trees and skirted the fields where farmers struggled with primitive plows and others, bent double, planted potatoes.

Old men and boys paused in their work to watch Matt's little group pass, but a black collie raced from a nearby cottage, barking excitedly at the travelers.

Mia looked at Matt and he nodded. "Go on, girl. Go play," and the dog leaped off to frolic with the noisy emissary who had welcomed them to town.

"There's a wagon coming." Valina pointed into town where two stout donkeys could be seen rounding a bend in the road. A scrawny dog chased the rattling wagon, barking and yapping at the driver.

"Is it normal for wagons to carry armed guards like that?" Brick asked, and Matt turned from watching Mia play to observe the wagon as it rumbled along the road. Two men clad in leather armor sat atop the heavy load of straw. Each held a crossbow.

"They look like soldiers."

"Or they could be townsfolk protecting their goods from brigands," Valina said.

"Maybe." Matt gently brushed Valina's arm with the back of his hand and pointed to the fields. "But see how the common folk turn away, eyes down, focusing on their work. You may have been right about Aldivon's men being here."

She shrugged. "So what would you have us do?"

"Leave, if you want my opinion," mumbled Brick.

"No." Matt shook his head. "Aldivon is heading south for sure, but he has an army to lead. They've recently fought and taken Dunadd, so that army will need supplies the same as we do. They cannot move as fast as us, and we have the lead on them. He may have advance units here purchasing supplies from the town, and maybe not, but it's unlikely he or even a description of us has got here any sooner than we have. There's a risk, but it's a small one.

"I say we continue"—Matt looked again at the townsfolk working the fields and the wagon as it rumbled out of sight—"but let's just be careful and ready to run."

Large houses, a mixture of wood and stone, lined the main street leading into town. Tended vegetable plots, some partially dug, lay behind many houses, and here and there a cow, pig or donkey could be seen, although many pens they passed were unoccupied, and the fodder bins empty. A few chickens pecked at the dusty road, snatching every fallen grain they could find, but they scattered noisily when Mia ran to join them.

As they approached the docks they passed more businesses. These were much poorer buildings built more for function than any ascetic look.

"Not much activity is there?" Matt observed.

The smells and sounds told more of each building's purpose than could be seen. Pungent smoke rose from the smokehouse where fish were being dried, and the odor of leather and animal pelt, along with the buzzing of flies, marked the tannery. Animal hides were draped over rails drying in the late morning sun, and across the street the rhythmic pounding of a hammer on steel indicated the blacksmith, at least, was at work.

Stacks of weathered lumber came next, and the sweet resinous smell of pitch was a pleasant counterpoint to the salt tang of the loch that lay just beyond an orderly row of incomplete fishing boat keels and the bed of a wagon that waited patiently for wheels at the carpenters shop.

The road curved here, bending away from the loch to cross a small but rapidly moving stream whose bubbling waters drove the mill wheel of the granary before tumbling over a final course of rocks to join the waters of the loch.

"It's like a totally different world!" Brick whispered. Matt glanced at Valina but the girl had not heard. "In fifteen hundred years this will be all gone or replaced with steel and concrete," Matt said. "Seems sad somehow."

Last came the pottery with the unmistakable kiln, and here the road at last opened into a central market where folks bartered for the various goods of the tradesman. Matt reined to a halt.

"Looks okay. Do you see soldiers anywhere?"

Brick shook his head.

"Over there," Valina pointed quickly, "I thought I saw—"

Matt followed her gaze. "At the tavern? Did they go inside?"

"No. They passed beyond the stables there. Was probably nothing."

"Okay. Let's stay wary. The tavern's the best place to get news, and supplies, but..." he left the thought unfinished. They were taking a significant risk here.

Perhaps we should have avoided the town.

Committed, they rode into the square. Few of the townsfolk spared them a second glance but Matt noticed a few who seemed to look upon them with more than passing interest.

Had a description of them reached here?

There seemed to be an unusual tension in the air, the people on edge. Matt loosened his sword and his pulse quickened, his mouth suddenly dry, but Valina felt the most self-conscious of all.

It was not common to see a girl riding a horse, and even less so for her to be dressed in men's clothing. Women looked disapprovingly at her while men gave overly appraising looks that earned them a sharp elbow or sharper tongue from nearby wives.

They passed a large barn where a stable boy watched from a hay loft, and Matt looked around for the soldiers Valina may have noticed earlier. He helped her dismount and spied two figures leaning together in a conspiratorial pose watching them from the shadows.

"Be casual..." Matt leaned in close to Valina and his breath caught in his throat at the musky scent of her. "Look behind me. Are they the men you saw?"

Valina unstrapped her travel pack and discreetly searched the shadows of the barn.

"I can't tell."

"Okay. Well, let's try and get a meal and some information."

"I can't go in there!" Valina said. "It's not fitting for a lady to venture in such places."

Matt gave a sudden laugh. "Is it fitting to be seen in leggings? Trust me one wouldn't mark you as a lady right now."

She blushed, "Well that's charming! But—"

Matt suddenly took one of her hands. "Valina, look. I'm sorry about last night. I acted—" *childish, like a fool,* "—badly." He looked into her eyes a moment longer. "It was wrong of me. Just because our opinions differ, that was no excuse to be rude."

He was blushing now and with reluctance he released her hand, slowly, so his fingers trailed along the outer edge of her palm. An electric tingle danced through his fingers at the contact. Valina caught her breath at the unexpected touch, but before she could answer Matt had turned away.

"Come. We'll skip the common room and see if we can get something to eat and maybe rooms in which to change and freshen up."

He opened the door and allowed Valina to pass in front. Brick hurried up behind him.

"There's a bunch of men across the street. They've been watching us since we rode into the square."

"I know," said Matt, and he looked back at the barn. The two men there had gone.

"Keep an eye on the horses and I'll order us some food. We'll stay only as long as we need to. You guys were right, I'm thinking we shouldn't have come."

Brick shrugged and led Valina to an empty table with a view through the window to the stables. Matt told Mia to stay by the door and made his way through to the common room.

The room was empty, which was hardly surprising given the time of day.

"And what ken I be servin ye young sir?" The innkeeper was a stereotypical figure, tall and balding with a hefty paunch that threatened to spill out from behind the grubby white apron he wore. The man's voice was booming, almost overbearing and his eyes burned inquisitively on either side of a plump, almost purple nose. Tiny red veins traced spider web patterns on a face that was permanently flushed.

Matt smiled nervously; he was unaccustomed to pubs and the smell of ale and poorly distilled spirits burned his nose and made his eyes water. He struggled to sound older than he was and inquired after rooms.

"We have three rooms lad, but only one vacant for now."

Matt handed over a selection of coins and asked if hot water could be brought to their room. He guessed Valina would like to bathe and there was no doubt that he and Brick should freshen up.

"Do you have anything to eat?"

"Nae much lad, but I'll bring what I can. Would you be wanting anything to drink?"

Matt shook his head and the innkeeper took the order, somehow maneuvering his bulk through a door into the kitchen where Matt's request was relayed in booming tones to whoever prepared the meals. Matt quickly exited the common room and joined the others at the table.

"I managed to get us a room and water for bathing. We'll have food shortly."

They did not have long to wait. A rich broth, a few cold cuts of venison, and a freshly baked loaf soon arrived and they eyed the food hungrily. "So what brings you three to our fair town?" asked the innkeeper as he transferred the platters from his tray to their table.

"Just passing through on our way to Kintyre." Matt gestured to Valina, "I'm escorting my cousin to Tayinloan. She's taking ship to Ireland."

Valina raised an eyebrow but remained silent.

"That would be a good day's ride from here the best o times. With all the troubles could tek you a deal longer. Will you be staying just the one night?"

Before Matt could answer Valina interrupted, "What troubles?"

The innkeeper eyed the girl and his expression became grim. Wiping his hands on his apron and tucking the empty tray under his arm he leaned forward, knuckles on the table.

"Murderin' savages from up north hev tekken Argyle, an they didnae stop there. Their army marches on Kintyre. Soon ne'er a bit of Scotland will be left unsullied by the witch o' the north."

Matt silenced Valina with a sharp look and a nudge of his foot. He looked up at the red-faced innkeeper. "Has the army already passed here?"

"The main body no, but their lead elements have fer sure, thievin bastards! You'd be eatin' better fare noo had they not. Cleaned out the town's remaining stores of last year's vegetables and meat. You got some of the last right there."

"They did not pay you?" Valina sounded surprised.

The man shook his head. "'Less you consider keepin yer life and home a payment, nae. Not a bronze sceat!"

"How long ago was this?" Matt asked, suddenly aware that the men across the square were beginning to disperse.

"Two days. They took wagon loads o' fodder, our food and other supplies with 'em. There's a bunch of 'em back in town today takin' more hay from the barns for their horses. It'll be a meager year for us, I tell ye."

The innkeeper stooped to peer outside. He let out a low whistle. "They your horses?"

Matt nodded, his mouth full of venison and warm soft bread.

"They look like soldiers' horses." The innkeeper gave a worried look at the boy. "Yer not with—"

Matt swallowed his food, "No. We're not with them"—he lowered his voice—"and we'd prefer to avoid contact with them if possible."

"Well that I understand, make no mistake. Yer likely be conscripted or worse." He cleared his throat and nodded toward the window, "I'd get those horses moved if I was you. I ken find ye room in me own stable. Not that it's my business, but ye should consider staying here awhile, give them bastards time to leave the region. There's little fare in town, but the loch's well stocked. You could maybe fin' work and then move on. 'Course up to you but I'd be happy to see you stay."

Matt mumbled his thanks and waited as the innkeeper cleared the empty platters from the table and headed back to the kitchens. "You be needin' anything more give me a shout. That water you asked for should be ready shortly—Martha will tek it up to ye; rooms first door on the right, top o' the stairs." Then he disappeared into the common room beyond.

"I told you there'd be trouble on the road!" said Brick. "Now what do you plan to do?"

"Perhaps we could get a boat tomorrow and head down the loch first thing in the morning," Valina said. "If we leave today it will mean another night outside, at least here we could sleep well." She looked at Matt.

"That's not a bad idea," Matt agreed. He felt frustrated at the possibility of another delay on their journey, but what other options did they have? Moving on foot through a hostile army would be dangerous. He wiped the last of the broth from his bowl with a piece of bread and then wiped his fingers on his tunic.

Brick stood up. "I'll take a look outside and see what happened to those men and get the horses in the stable for the night. You want a hand with those packs up to the room?"

"No, I'll be fine." Matt slid some coins across to the older boy. He gathered his own pack and Valina's lighter traveling bag then led her up the narrow stairs.

The room was welcoming, and more comfortable than Matt had expected. A small wooden tub, half filled with steaming water, sat behind a screen made of woven cloth, and beside it sat two buckets, one half filled with fresh hot water and the other brim full with cold. Two beds occupied the remainder of the room and being a corner room, there were two small windows. One looked out over the meadows behind the inn, where coarse grassland stretched to the wide expanse of the river. The other, on the side of the building, looked toward the barn just across the street from the tavern.

Matt leaned from the window and caught sight of Brick in conversation with a man at the stables. The boy pointed back at their horses and the man nodded.

A splash behind caused Matt to turn and he gasped. Valina had already removed her clothes and was kneeling in the tub rubbing coarse and strangely scented soap over her shoulders. The tub and the soapy water hid her from the waist down and she shielded her breasts with an arm, but Matt was seeing far more "girl" than he had ever seen before and he colored up, stammering an apology.

"Well don't be shy." Valina said with an uncharacteristic playfulness. She looked over one shoulder and grinned impishly. A long tendril of hair had fallen across her cheek and a devilish glint appeared in her eyes. She stretched out the arm that had until then maintained her modesty and held out the cake of soap. Suds and water dripped from her shapely arm to the wooden floor. "Scrub my back for me?"

Matt stood rooted to the floor as he gazed at her sleek and glistening body. He couldn't imagine wanting anything more than to do as she asked. He took a step toward her, pulse racing, face flushed, and then with a herculean effort he moved to the door. "I'll check on the horses!" he croaked and left the room with Valina's bright laugh loud in his ears and the image of her delicate rose-tipped breasts forever burned in his mind.

Matt paused at the bottom of the stairs and struggled to regain his composure. With his emotions swirling he walked from the inn, one part of him congratulating himself for such chivalrous behavior while his teenage hormones berated him with every step he took for failing to take advantage of such an opportunity.

He looked around for something else to focus on and noted that their horses were gone and the square was rapidly emptying of people. *Where was everyone going?* Matt looked toward the barn, calling for his dog.

She ran from the center of the square where she had been playing with what looked to Matt like large hunting hounds. She trotted up now, tongue lolling from the side of her mouth and tail arched high across her back.

"Good girl," he touseled her head as he looked around the square.

Where's Brick?

There was no one at the stables where he had seen him last. He looked around. The whole area appeared deserted.

Something was wrong. Matt could sense the danger. He took a hesitant step backward and then from behind the tavern four men rushed toward him shouting for him to stay where he was. They all wore swords and two carried heavy wooden clubs.

Matt spun and raced back into the tavern taking the stairs two at a time. "Valina!" He shouted to the girl as he ran, then tripped and smashed his shin on the topmost stair. Pain exploded in his leg and cursing he stumbled to the door, wrenching it open as footsteps sounded on the stairs below. Mia darted inside and he slammed the door closed and locked it behind him.

Valina sat upright, startled, water cascading in all directions. Matt tore a blanket from the bed and threw it at her. "Quick! Cover yourself and grab what you can. We're leaving!"

He grabbed a chair and wedged the back against the door handle then limped to the window. "Shit!"

"What is it?" Valina pulled a long homespun dress from her bag and threw it over her head.

A crash at the door sent her scurrying across to the side window. She struggled into woolen hose and grabbed her leather boots while Matt donned his pack.

"It's too far to jump!"

Matt looked across to the barn, the wagon with its load of hay was still tethered to its horses.

"Mia!" Matt shouted as another crash all but splintered the door.

He ran to the rear window and dropped to his knees, pressing his head against the dog's. He forced the pictures into her head as fast as he could. His brain throbbed with the effort but a long wet tongue acknowledged her understanding, and Valina gasped as the dog jumped through the window and onto the small roof that partially covered the kitchen yard below. Without pause Mia leaped to the ground and landed hard, rolling in the dirt before regaining her feet. She paused to shake and then raced toward the barn.

"Valina, get out there quick!" Matt tried to blink the sudden wash of tears away. A searing pain from the extended link with the dog burned behind his eyes and he staggered. Pinwheels of colored lights blurred his vision.

Valina was through the window now. "My bag!" She reached out and took the bag from Matt. "What is the matter with you? Your eyes?"

Matt shook his head, fighting the rush of nausea, but thankfully his vision began to clear as he clambered through the window.

"It'll pass, I'm fine."

Behind him the door burst open and fragments of the chair skittered across the floor.

"Back up!" Matt yelled to Valina, and drew his sword clutching at the window shutter as he fought to regain his balance on the steeply sloping roof. A man reached the window and swung at Matt with a club. Matt ducked the blow but lost his footing and sailed out over the yard hanging on to the shutter. His back slammed into the wall, the shock absorbed by his pack. The man lunged again, grabbing at Valina, and Matt kicked at the wall behind him, swinging back onto the roof. He cuffed the man on the side of the head with the hilt of his sword and the man dropped like a rock.

Matt released the shutter and backed away along the narrow roof holding his sword in one hand and Valina's trembling arm in the other.

Below, Mia was busy in the barn. Her razor sharp teeth tore savagely at the leather straps that tied the wagon to a nearby post. One already lay in the dirt, wet and sticky with the dog's saliva. The second trace snapped and the dog turned on the horses, baring her teeth and growling. Terrified, the horses lurched forward, straining against the heavy wagon desperate to avoid the dog that danced between their legs snapping and snarling.

Slowly the wagon began to roll from the barn. Matt glanced from his dog back to the window from which they had escaped. A soldier's head appeared and Matt lashed out with his blade. Glass shattered as his sword struck the window frame, and the head was hurriedly pulled back inside.

"Matt, look!" Valina pointed to the far side of the barn where two more men ran toward the tavern; one carried a heavy bow and was already fitting an arrow to the string.

"Shoot him!" came a shout from the window, and the archer took aim.

Startled by the noise above, the innkeeper rushed into the street, wielding a cudgel. His wife, Martha, a giant of a woman, followed from the kitchen with a rolling pin clutched in one hand.

"What is this?" the innkeeper roared, then stopped as the archer fixed his aim on him.

"Drop the club!" the archer ordered while the second soldier moved toward the two, sword held ready.

Matt looked across to the barn. The wagon was rolling now and Mia ran beside the horses, herding them like sheep and steering them away from the barn. The wagon, piled high with hay, passed beneath the narrow roof. There was no time to shout a warning. Matt simply grabbed Valina and jumped, pulling the girl with him. She screamed briefly before landing in the hay to roll heavily against one of the side boards, her long wet hair covered in hay and dust. Matt noticed a shallow scratch across her cheek but her eyes burned with anger.

"You could have warned me!" she yelled, then noticed that Matt was clutching his head where he had struck the tail board of the wagon. It felt as if he had been hit with a sledgehammer and his ears rang from the blow.

"You okay?"

Nodding, he scrambled over the hay to the reins that hung in a loop over the bench seat. Matt pulled the wagon around in a tight turn away from the tavern and shouted over his shoulder, "Do you see Brick?"

Valina looked around and shook her head.

"Look out!" she cried as the wagon bounced around toward the innkeeper and his wife. The archer dropped his bow and dove out of the way of the horses, and Martha suddenly swung her rolling pin in a vicious attack on the swordsmen who had turned to watch the wagon. The blow slammed into his temple and he spun around before folding into a heap on the ground.

"Good luck, boy!" yelled the innkeeper, waving his cudgel. "Your friend is over there!" He gestured to the far side of the barn and Matt saw two men run from the barn and grab Brick, who had been kneeling in the shadows.

"Hold tight!" Matt yelled to Valina, and pulled on the reins turning the horses into the street between the tavern and the barn. As the wagon passed beneath their room one of the men above attempted to jump from the side window but the wagon was rolling faster now and his timing was off. He landed heavily, clipping the wagon with his shoulder. One of his legs folded beneath him and snapped like a twig. The rear wheel of the wagon struck him next, crushing his ankle, and he screamed. Valina looked away, her face ashen.

Behind the barn one of the men holding Brick released the boy and fumbled with a bow strung across his back. A sudden twang and crack sounded behind Matt and a crossbow quarrel zipped over his head. The bolt struck the man in the chest and he staggered back, his face a mask of stunned surprise as he slumped against the barn. Matt glanced behind to see Valina struggling to reload her tiny crossbow. "Good shot!" She smiled grimly and Matt glanced back to see Brick twist and kick frantically at the remaining guard. The man struggled to hold him and the older boy kicked again this time striking the knee. The man lost his grip and Brick tore himself free, racing to intercept the wagon as Matt steered it to the open meadow behind the barn, and the bridge beyond.

"Where are you going?" Valina gripped the sideboards as the wagon turned.

"The bridge! It's the only crossing point into Kintyre without moving north. They'll put guards on every crossing now! Brick! C'mon!"

Behind them black-clad horseman suddenly appeared from between houses at the edge of town. In front, two bowmen ran toward the wooden bridge that spanned the river, supported on twin columns of stone. One of the riders bore down on Brick, drawing his sword and urging more speed from his mount.

It became a race to reach the boy. The horseman was faster, but the wagon closer. Matt slapped the reins across the horses' rumps, urging them to greater effort. Behind him Valina dropped her crossbow as the wagon jolted across the uneven field.

"Grab the reins!" Matt called, and she clambered to join him. Matt pulled a rope from beneath the seat and looped it around his foot then the backrest of the seat before leaning out over the spinning wheel toward Brick. The boy was running as fast as he could, his face red with effort and eyes wide with terror. The horseman was closing the gap, the beat of the hooves audible over the creaking wagon.

Brick jumped and clutched at the side panel. He hung there a moment, then scrabbled with his feet to find something against which to propel himself over the wagon's side. Leaning precariously, inches from the spinning wheel, Matt reached down and grasped his arm. "Christ, Brick! Climb, dammit!" Matt pulled with all his strength. His shoulder burned in protest and his arm muscles stretched to the breaking point, but somehow he hauled the bigger boy into the wagon and they fell back against the hay breathing hard.

Behind them the horseman did not slow. His black cloak billowed behind like demon's wings. The wagon was now racing as fast as its horses could pull it, and the jolting ride sent clumps of hay falling over the side. The occupants held on to whatever was at hand as they approached the river at breakneck speed.

Valina lacked the strength to turn the horses and she threw the reins at Matt. "Turn them!" Matt pulled hard to prevent their headlong dash into the river while Valina dove back into the wagon to retrieve her fallen crossbow. She grabbed a quarrel from her bag and loaded it into the groove of the weapon, then strained to pull back on the string until it clipped over the trigger catch. It was a small weapon, only good for close range work.

"Slow down!" she called and Matt hauled back on the reins, grabbing the braking lever as he did so.

The startled horses slowed and the rider behind was taken by surprise as the gap narrowed at an alarming pace. Bracing herself against the jolting wagon, Valina took careful aim and fired. The pursuing rider was too close to miss and the bolt flew straight and true taking the rider in the shoulder. His startled mount, feeling the loss of control in the reins swerved to miss the wagon, passing within feet of the now almost stationary vehicle.

Brick grabbed a pitchfork and swung it at the swaying rider, who despite his injury fought to regain control of his horse. The wooden handle snapped as it struck the rider's back and the man toppled from the saddle. The horse bolted, and with a foot caught in the stirrup the wounded man was dragged across the meadow for several yards before the animal came to a nervous stop at the river's edge.

Matt released the brakes and cracked the reins, guiding their team in a wide turn toward the road. A loud buzz sounded by his ear and then an arrow suddenly thudded into the seat beside him. A second fizzed past his head.

He looked to the bridge where the bowmen on the road were already fitting fresh arrows to their strings.

"Brick! Drive!" Matt shouted.

"What? How!"

"Just grab the reins and keep 'em straight."

Mia had seen the archers and she streaked across the meadow, ears flat, tail straight and legs a blur. The dog was giving it her all but Matt could see she would not reach them in time. Behind him Valina stood tall, unable to load her crossbow due to the violent lurching of the wagon. Matt grabbed a second pitchfork and threw it like a spear but it fell short and both archers fired together.

Matt flung himself from the seat, reaching out for the girl in a desperate attempt to pull her to safety. She fell into his arms and he felt her wet hair brush against his face. The first arrow skipped on the hay inches from them and sailed over the sideboard falling harmlessly to the grass, but the second found a mark.

Valina fell back into the hay. Her eyes filled with tears and fear as she saw the arrow protruding from Matt's shoulder.

"Matt! No!" she cried, but Matt's eyes clouded with pain. He fell heavily against the girl then rolled from her as Brick somehow hauled the careering wagon onto the road toward the bridge.

The archers never had a chance to fire again. Mia's flying leap slammed the first into the hand rail of the bridge. The other yelled in terror and dropped his bow, grabbing for a knife in his boot top. He was not fast enough. Mia went in low, snapping at his ankle, and in desperation the man flung himself over the rail and into the water. Mia leaped in after him.

The wagon bore down on the bridge at a crazy pace and behind it four more horsemen galloped from the town.

Matt pulled himself to his knees and saw the riders racing from the town. His left arm hung useless at his side, the pain almost unbearable. A red hot burning coupled with the numbing ache of a heavy blow was accompanied by a searing shock each time he tried to move his arm. His face was white and his eyes glazed. There was a violent jolt as the wagon struck a rut in the road and the shaft of the arrow caught on the side of the wagon. Matt screamed as he felt the tip move in his shoulder.

Valina crawled to him and held him up with her arms. She followed his eyes and saw the riders racing ahead of a cloud of dust.

"We can't outrun them in this!" she cried.

The tone of the wagon's wheels suddenly changed into a hollow roar as Brick took them onto the bridge.

"Stop the wagon," Matt croaked through gritted teeth. "Tell him to stop the wagon."

Valina looked from his face to the riders. "You're giving up?"

A look of angry defiance flared in his eyes. "Fuck no! Just get him to stop the wagon now, while we're on the bridge."

Valina did not understand but she shouted up to Brick.

"What?"

"Stop the wagon!"

"How?"

She let go of Matt, making sure he could support himself, and climbed over the hay. Fumbling for the brake lever she pulled hard, jamming the wooden brake blocks against the wheels. "Pull the reins!" she cried. "Hard!"

Matt fought against the sickening pain in his shoulder and kicked the wooden restraining peg that held the side of the wagon up. Turning he kicked the second peg and the side panel folded down with a crash. Hay spilled out onto the road.

"Uncouple the horses," he instructed and then pulled his tinder pouch from his belt. It took both hands to stroke a shower of sparks across the oily cord. He almost passed out from the pain but gasped with relief as a tiny tongue of flame flickered on the cord and he touched it to the hay. It caught almost immediately. A wall of flame leaped before him.

With the horses free of the wagon, Valina ran back to Matt who slid from the wagon bed and leaned drunkenly against the guard rail of the bridge, watching the approaching riders through the swirling heat haze of the flames. The wagon bed caught next and wisps of smoke curled from the blackening timbers of the bridge.

Valina steered Matt toward the horses; the boy was weaving drunkenly, his legs barely supporting him. The terrified animals neighed loudly and shied away from the smoke, their eyes rolling wide. It took all of Brick's strength to hang on to them and guide them away from the wagon.

"We can't mount them, they have no saddles!" Valina shouted above the crackling roar of the fire. Matt was swaying now, dragging the girl down, his strength almost gone.

"Brick!" she called, "Bring them closer to the wagon."

"You out of your mind?" Brick heaved on the reins to drag the tormented animals even closer to the fire, and Valina pushed Matt onto the wagon steps. The heat of the fire grew intense, the flames spreading faster than Matt could have imagined. Brick succeeded in pushing one of the horses close and Valina grabbed a handful of mane and swung herself onto its back. The animal trembled beneath her but remained steady. Matt somehow found the strength to climb onto the horse behind her and slipped his good arm around the girl's narrow waist. He let his head fall against her shoulder.

She nudged the horse away from the wagon and joined Brick who had somehow managed to climb the railing of the bridge and swing astride the second horse.

"What about the other two?" Brick shouted to be heard over the roar of the conflagration behind them.

They looked back and saw the riders from the village rein in their mounts. Thick black smoke and angry red flames rose in to the air as the wagon and the bridge became fully engulfed.

Valina pulled her horse into the lead. "Bring one with us, and cut the other loose," she said, then led them across the bridge, leaving the road and taking a gentle hill up and into the woodland beyond. Mia scurried up the river bank to join them, her coat slick from the swim, and covered with green weed and straw.

Matt slipped in and out of consciousness as Valina led them into the trees. He was almost becoming accustomed to the pain now, but for some reason was finding it difficult to stay awake. As if from a distance he heard Valina speaking to him.

"You saved my life, Matt!"

He felt a sudden rush of reckless bravado as the heady concoction of adrenaline and fear began to fade. "I had no choice," he laughed deliriously, oblivious to the trees that continued to blur by on either side. "Not if I wanted see you bathe again."

He never heard her reply, as unconsciousness finally took him and he slumped heavily against her shoulder.

Chapter 18
Cavern of the King

Tolnech, Scotland
597AD

Smoke still rose from the shattered remains of the bridge. Charred timbers extended from the far bank, their jagged ends reaching out to the stone supports that now stood alone, their tops blackened from the blaze. The fire had consumed the center section entirely and the roadway from the town hung from the river bank into the swirling black waters below.

A makeshift ferry now carried passengers and cargo across the river. Stout ropes anchored to the forlorn stone columns prevented the raft from being swept downstream while horses on each bank dragged it across the river. A chain gang of soldiers handed supplies pillaged from the town down to the waiting raft while a similar gang waited to transfer its cargo to the wagons on the far shore.

Aldivon watched the last wagon of supplies depart from the town square. The merchant stalls were gone and the marketplace was now full of soldiers.

Two stakes had been driven into the ground and the innkeeper and his wife now stood tied to them. Townsfolk watched, many from the safety of their homes, although those braver ones stood at the edge of the market square. The innkeeper's face was bloodied and one eye swollen closed. Before him, fingering the thick coils of a whip, stood one of Aldivon's captains.

"You gave them food, shelter and supplies!" The man's eyes flashed with anger. "You expect me to believe they told you nothing of their plans? Now I'll ask you again. Where were they going?"

The innkeeper barely had strength left to shake his head and the soldier had to lean close to hear the whispered reply.

"Go fuck yourself."

The soldier's face flushed and he spun on his heel, pulling his arm back as he did so. The whip straightened across his shoulder and as he turned he brought it whistling back—not this time at the innkeeper, but at Martha, his wife. She screamed as the thin end of the lash cut through the material of her dress, leaving a bloody scar across her shoulder and upper arm.

Despite the pain of the blow she defiantly jerked her head away as he approached and he slapped her hard, snapping her head back to face him. He grasped her about the jaw with an iron grip and pressed her head against the rough stake. He looked into her terror-filled eyes.

"There were two boys, yes? What about an old man, was there an old man with them?"

Martha struggled to shake her head and between her crushed lips managed to blurt, "There were three of them. Two boys and a girl, they were going to Kintyre." Aldivon stepped forward and pushed the soldier to one side. Angry red impressions marred the woman's face where the man's fingers had gripped her.

"A girl?" Aldivon rasped, eyes intent.

Martha glanced across at her husband who hung weakly beside her, his considerable weight held only by the ropes that bound him to the stake. Aldivon slowly turned the woman's face back to his. "The girl?"

Martha did the best she could to describe Valina but she had barely seen the girl, catching nothing more than a fleeting glimpse of her as the wagon had careened past on its way from the village.

Martha answered Aldivon's questions as best she could and embellished where memory failed. No more blows were struck and she slumped with relief as he turned away.

Aldivon lost interest in the interrogation. Martha and her husband clearly knew nothing about their quest. But this girl? Could she be the same serving girl from the castle, who had vanished from the king's chamber? Was that important? He had been continually frustrated at Matt's ability to stay one step ahead of him. Another thought stirred in his mind, but he quickly dismissed it—even she wouldn't step that far, would she?

Aldivon looked at the tavern and the group of soldiers who loitered outside.

"The inn. Is it empty?"

"Aye, my lord." They pointed to the wagon that swayed heavily as it approached the river, piled high with barrels of ale and casks of wine. "That's the last of it."

Aldivon nodded. "Burn it!"

Crossing the market square, he did not stay to watch the flames that burst from the windows of the inn, but swung himself into the saddle of his waiting horse. Two officers who had been standing nearby ran up to him. "Lord Aldivon. Your orders?"

"Send riders to block all roads from here in a twenty mile radius. Guard every bridge and patrol the river banks. If they are found they are to be brought to me, unharmed." His horse backed up, skittish, as it felt the nervous excitement of its rider. He hauled viciously on the reins and the horse whinnied. Turning the mount, he fixed the men with a cruel stare.

"If they are harmed..." he leaned forward in the saddle, his eyes almost level with theirs.

"They will not be harmed, my lord. Where will we find you?"

"Kintyre. I'm taking the army south…" His lips curled in a sly grin. "We have an appointment with a king." He spat the last word, and with a crack of the reins he jabbed at his horse's flanks with his heels, leaving the market in a thunder of hooves.

Eilean Tioram, Scotland
597AD

Three times she had read the book and always she returned to the same paragraph. Morgause let her eyes scan the page, the words already committed to memory.

His body we took in secret, and placed beneath the seat of the king, there perchance to rest forever; for only with the rejoining of the crown could the spell of sleep be broken.
I left him with heavy heart, for he had become as a son to me. The fragments of the broken crown I gave into the keeping of five kings, all save one; that I kept for myself.

She flicked back the pages to the map of Britain and studied it before rising and crossing to the nearby window. Clouds obscured the partial moon and the smell of rain was on the air. She pulled the shutter closed and the candles flickered wildly for a moment in the sudden draft.

"Beneath the seat of the king," she echoed aloud the words as she pondered yet again their meaning. Arthur had made the old Roman fortress of Camelon his home. It was from there his legendary knights had ridden on countless sorties against her husband. Its central location near the market town of Falkirk was ideal for easy and rapid deployment east to west, north to south.

But all that land is mine now.

She looked again at the map. A few hours' ride from Camelon was the volcanic outcrop of Stirling, atop which sat the watchtower and warning beacon of the kingdom of Mannon. Further to the east sat the port town of Din Eidyn, Edinburgh as it would later be known. It too nestled beneath volcanic hills with a similar watchtower and beacon.

Her eyes followed the winding road that made its way from Camelon, skirting the swamps and marshes and passing into the rich and fertile farmland south of Stirling. There beneath the shadows of that craggy peak stood the King's Knot. The round table, a giant earthwork of several tiers topped with polished granite. It had been Arthur's meeting place.

But no more!

She had taken the granite slab, its shattered remains thrown into the sea.

Of the fort at Camelon nothing remained but the charred and shattered remnants of barracks, stores and stables. Aldivon had destroyed it years ago. Its capture had cost her dearly and she had razed it to the ground rather than allow it to fall once more into enemy hands.

So where had Merlin taken him?

She had men searching the rubble of Camelon now. Perhaps some underground chapel or chamber had been missed?

"The seat of the king," she repeated quietly to herself, and then slammed the book closed.

"He wasn't even crowned!" Her outburst disturbed the raven that sat perched upon a nearby stand. The bird gave a tentative *"caw"* and adjusted his wings, watching the queen as she paced the room, her anger and frustration mounting, violet eyes afire in the ruddy glow of the candles.

She reached the wall and turned again, the heavy velvet gown sweeping across the floor.

Arthur holds the secret to the Rod of Dardanos, and Merlin holds the secret to Arthur's resting place!

It should not have been this difficult. She felt the first involuntary tremble of her lip and the fragile barriers she had erected against the memories of the past weakened as her frustration mounted.

No, not now...I need to think...need to solve...

Unbidden, the first tears gathered on the lush lashes beneath her eyes, and then with the unstoppable flow of water from a bursting dam the memories overwhelmed her and she stood helpless against the flood.

Orphaned at age three, Morgause had seen her mother and father brutally cut down by island raiders. She had hidden beneath sacking and only crawled from the building when the flames and smoke had become too intense. Not a single villager had survived the raid and the young girl would have died too had she not been found, wandering and forlorn, by Morag, an old crone who lived alone in the forest.

Morag had been both respected and feared by the people of the village. Her herb lore and healing powers were local legend, but many suspected her of being a practitioner of darker arts. She gave to Morgause not only a home but something her peasant parents could never have provided—an education. By the age of seven the girl could read and write, both Latin and Gaelic, and she understood the runes of the ancients. She became adept at working with plants and primitive medicines, and by nine was blossoming into a girl of uncommon beauty, ambition and power. Her mind was quick, and marveling in the girl's ability to absorb knowledge Morag taught her all she knew of the ancient craft. Then Morag had died, and not yet fifteen years old Morgause found her world turned upside down again.

She returned to the village of her former home, which over the years had been rebuilt, but the people there shunned her. They branded her the daughter of a witch, the offspring of some tryst with the devil. It was almost a welcome relief when once more the mighty longships of the island kingdoms came ashore and the raiders from afar ransacked the village, raping and pillaging as they went.

Morgause made no attempt to hide. This time she stood ready to embrace death, but that was not to be her fate.

Lot, leader of the war party, son of Orkney's king, was struck by her raven-haired beauty, and he took her to his ships and into his service. He was an ambitious man, young and reckless, and Morgause saw in him an opportunity to rise. Her progress from servant to confidante was rapid, and she played Lot like an instrument using her skills of language, her knowledge of herbs and finally the pleasures of her body to manipulate a place at his side.

Lot had easily fallen to her ambitious machinations but his aging father was less easily won. The kindly old monarch seemed to see right through her, and despite all her womanly charms she had failed to win past his mistrust. Lot had repeatedly requested the right to marry her but his father ever contested the match, stating she was not of their blood, not fitting for a prince.

"Bed her as you will, boy. But no offspring of her womb will ever sit the island throne! You will marry another!"

And so a steady stream of suitable girls had been found, each more lovely and purer of island blood than the last.

Morgause had put an end to it. A simple cocktail of herbs mixed by her own hand had finally removed the obstinate king, and Lot and Morgause had been married shortly after his ascension to the now-vacant throne.

Initially Morgause had been content to be the wife of an island king. To the people Lot was their ruler but it was she who guided his hand. In return Lot spoiled her, lavishing the teenage queen with gifts but never showing her the attention she craved. One thing had been lacking all her young life—love. She wanted, ached for something, some deep inner need. She called it love, but how was she to know what love was?

She turned nineteen during her second year as queen, a woman of devastating beauty, fiery and passionate with an equally flaming temper. Left alone for countless weeks while her husband expanded his realm left her bored and lonely, and so it was she returned to the earlier teachings of Morag—witch craft—a practice forbidden in Orkney.

The thrill and the danger of the dark arts both sickened and excited her, but the illicit rituals performed in the name of the earth-gods captivated her, satiated those burning desires of the flesh. It was then, in the deepest shadows of the night, that Dardanos had found her.

Oh how he had used her, and how she had loved him for it. The more twisted and decadent she became, the more power he gave to her. Finally she had found a new outlet for her desires. Not the simple incantations, potions and herb craft of the common witch, but the true power of the mind. Dardanos's magic was like a drug and she swiftly fell prey to its addiction. Only he could bring release to the insatiable desires of her mind and her body. She knew not the difference between love and lust and gave herself completely to Dardanos. From that dark union came her first son, Mordred, and she lavished on him the love that had been stolen from her as a child.

Mordred! My son! Do you watch over your mother now?

Morgause staggered across her room and called for the raven. She took a seat at her desk as the heavy bird settled on her shoulder. The memories would not stop. She knew they would run their course, but still she fought against the burning pain of loss, slamming her hands against the desk.

The candles spluttered in their bronze holders and hot wax splashed across her hands but she ignored the momentary pain, trying desperately to picture her son in life, but all that came was the heart-wrenching image of his body pinned to her lover by Arthur's sword.

You took them both from me, Arthur! You stole their lives, stole their love!

She tried to think back to before the terrible battle, to the night Dardanos had taken her to be his wife, the night that had culminated in the conception of her second child. She felt a rush of heat in her belly at the memory. That night had been like no other. Merlin hung! Arthur but a day from destruction! And Dardanos. Oh gods, Dardanos! She pressed a hand against the heat between her legs as she lived again the magnificence of that night. He had touched her soul, filled her with love, and together they had planned their future. A future full of magic and wonder, not a nation to share, nor a world, but a multitude of worlds.

Immortality! Such a legacy they would have made for the child that had been planted in her womb that night.

But it had come to naught!

She picked the drying wax from her skin and looked again at the jagged scars across her wrists, the only flaws on an otherwise perfect body. Tears dripped from her eyes, scalding drops on scars that burned with the memory of the blade that had cut them. Aldivon it was who had found her and stemmed that crimson flow.

"Your unborn child, my queen! All is not lost!"

She had clung to him and he had held her until morning.

Then he had brought her to me! Merlin's whore!

I should have killed her then -

But Aldivon had stayed her hand, for Vivian also carried a child – the child of Dardanos.

Fresh anger fueled her hatred as she recalled the mockery of that birth.

A girl!

Why not a son? Though not of her body she would have loved the child nonetheless, but a girl?

But such a son would have been a threat to your own unborn child -

Out of love for Dardanos she had allowed the child to live, but Vivian had received no such charity. Her death had been slow, a lingering game of vindictive pleasure. But those pleasures had been cut short by the tragic birth of her own child.

And it had been a son! Dardanos's son!

The birth had been difficult and the midwives had taken the child to a side chamber while they tended their queen. She had recovered, but the child had not.

In the days that followed her despair had deepened. She had confined herself to her tower, and in her madness had tried to alter time. Using all the power she could command she had manipulated the very fabric of creation, attempting to cast back time and undo the horrors she had endured; to restore her lord and love to her.

But that too failed!

She had instead, ripped apart the very fabric of reality, creating a rift in time. Like a parallel universe the earth knew two realities. In one, she aged, and died, bitter, twisted, defeated. New civilizations came into being and the passage of time marched on, she and all those of her time lost to legend. But in the other, she and all who lived in that instant were trapped in a constantly repeating cycle.

The memories passed. Exhausted and weakened by grief, Morgause pulled herself up and wiped the tears from her bloodless cheeks. All that mattered now were the deaths of Arthur and Merlin, and the opening of the portal to Mars.

Opening that portal would change everything. She could lead her people to a new world, the world of Dardanos, and there she would claim that which lay at the heart of his people's power. The dragon stones. The stones that gave longevity, and power, power even over death. She *would* take Dardanos home. His embalmed body waited now beneath this very chamber. With the dragon stones she would restore him to life! They would be united again for all time.

Immortal! We will be as Gods!

With trembling hands she reopened Merlin's book.

His body we took in secret, and placed beneath the seat of the king, there perchance to rest forever; for only with the rejoining of the crown could the spell of sleep be broken.

I left him with heavy heart, for he had become as a son to me...

Glenhurich, Scotland
597AD

Guenevere opened her eyes, blinking at the brightness.

"Matt?"

"Lady?"

She regarded the boy through watering eyes. He moistened her lips with a wet cloth, then touched her brow with a gentle hand.

"Your fever has finally passed."

She felt a rush of sorrow. It was not Matt.

But I saw him!

No. It had been a dream...

She let her body relax and closed her eyes.

"Where am I, lad?"

"The monastery of Finnian, lady."

"Finnian? The Christian?"

"Aye, the Christian."

"How? How did I get here?"

"Aidan, our huntsman, brought you here. You were very sick—"

"And you aided me?"

"Not I, lady. Brother Marcus has been your healer. I am but his acolyte. Rest, and I will fetch him now."

Aidan? The hunter?

Then she remembered. She had escaped from Morgause, then fallen sick.

"The man with the deer? I was lost..."

Naveena? What had become of Naveena?

When no answer was forthcoming Guenevere opened her eyes. She was alone. Slowly she struggled to sit and took stock of her surroundings.

I'm so weak!

The room was tiny, more like a cell, and the white walls were devoid of any decoration save a simple wooden cross on the far wall. Other than her bed the room was empty. A coarse woolen blanket had covered her but it had fallen around her waist when she sat, and she noticed she was dressed in a loose brown robe of simple homespun wool. The wide neck of the robe had gaped open and she was startled to see how wasted her body had become. The once-proud breasts were shrunken, and the rack of her ribs was clearly visible. She pulled the robe tight and sighed.

"I wonder what happened to my clothes?"

"Burned, my dear. Burned."

She started and looked to the door. She had not even heard the monk approach.

"I am Brother Marcus. Kanich told me you had woken, praise God."

"How long? How long have I been here?"

"Four days, child. But for Aidan and the grace of God you would surely have died."

"Then I thank you, sir."

"Friar, lady. There are no knights here."

"Then I thank you, Friar."

"'Tis all God's work, child. Now tell me, how came you to our glen? Few trouble us here."

Guenevere leaned back against the wall and sighed. She was somewhat familiar with the Christian God, for both Lancelot and Arthur had converted to his ways, baptized by none other than Columba himself. If these were Christians then she was probably safe for a while. Morgause and her followers decried any that followed that faith. While many had adapted their own beliefs to fit with the gods of Rome, many more had retained their Pictish ways.

"I was a prisoner."

"A prisoner? And what was your crime?"

"There was no crime!" Guenevere felt her temper flare. "A prisoner of the witch queen. 'Tis a long story..."

"Then you will tell it. All."

Guenevere looked at the monk, startled by the unexpected firmness of his tone.

"We have little love for the queen, but nor do we wish to incur her wrath. Tell me your tale, then together we shall seek God's guidance on what to do next."

Din Eidyn, Scotland
597AD

Merlin sat in the darkness, a thick woolen cloak furled around his shoulders. Below him the infant city lay; a mere town compared to the sprawling metropolis it would become.

Few buildings betrayed their presence with flickering candles or crackling fires. Most lay in silent slumber nestled beneath the giant crag of the extinct volcano. In the star-speckled sky above a crescent moon sketched a silver outline to the fishing boats that clustered around the wooden docks.

Few sounds reached him here. The distant bark of a dog, the lonely cry of a gull. A baby's cry floated by, faint and distant, barely carried by the wind, and he gripped the staff that lay across his legs. His thoughts turned to Matt.

Where are you, laddie?

Almost a week had passed since he had traveled west.

By now Matt should have recovered the first crown fragment from Duncan, and be well on his way to Moy. Moy was the tricky one. The other three would be easy. They were closer to home and Merlin himself had checked in on them from time to time. Matt would pass all three kings on his journey back to Din Eidyn. Sending him fresh to the most distant location had seemed a good idea. But it was also the closest to Morgause. Did she already move south? With northern Scotland and much of the central and Eastern highlands under her sway, the west coast was the last remaining redoubt.

Merlin thought of the challenges that lay before the boy and wondered if the only sign he would ever have that the quest had failed would be a blazing ball of fire streaking across the sky.

Perhaps I should have gone in his stead. Could the lad have remained here and stood guard over Arturius?

No. Morgause now knew Arthur lived. Sooner or later they would discover his resting place and Merlin would be all that stood between them. He would have to trust—to hope—that Matt would succeed. The magician stood and put his back to the town.

Be careful, boy. May all the gods, old and new, be your shield and guide.

A subtle sound brought the wizard alert. Ears straining, he slowly placed one hand on his sword, while the other clutched his staff.

He saw nothing, but he was sure he had heard something. Carefully he picked his way through the ferns and gorse and crouched behind a large boulder. There, part way across the rabbit-cropped grass a highland wolf sat, head raised to the sky. A blood-curdling howl escaped its throat and then it sat, head to one side listening, waiting for a reply. None came. Three more times the wolf howled, and when no answer came it slowly picked its way down the hill to the forests below.

Merlin watched the animal depart. By the 7th century these wolves would be all but extinct in Britain. He felt a strange empathy with the creature as it paused before the stunted trees that clad the side of the hill. Seldom seen this far south, he wondered if it sought a lost mate, or a cub? With a rush of anguish Merlin thought of Vivian.

I should have returned for you my love.

He watched the wolf lope his lonely way into the trees, then Merlin too picked his way back down the slope, working his way around the hill toward Arthur's resting place.

It took him an hour to reach the hidden entrance, and there he waited a further hour, patiently watching to see if he was followed or observed.

Confident his presence was undetected, Merlin slipped into the tiny fissure that led deep into the heart of the extinct volcano. Once inside he was plunged into complete and absolute darkness.

He felt no fear. With one hand on the rough rock walls and his staff held before him he made his way forward.

Roots dangled from above, brushing his hand and face like cobwebs, and although unseen he knew thousands of bats hung no more than two or three feet above his head.

His fingers became his eyes, feeling for the indentations he had chipped into the rock many years before. He reached the sixth marker, the point he had deemed enough twists and turns of the passage would prevent light escaping into the night and betraying the tunnel's existence.

Merlin muttered a word and a flame danced upon his fingertip. He smiled.

Matt had always taken a simple delight in that.

Stacked neatly against the wall was a pile of brands. Merlin selected one, lit it, and took off down the passage. The tunnel was an ancient volcanic fissure, a lava tube, the path taken by molten lava that had spewed from the side of the volcano hundreds of thousands of years ago.

The walls were rough and hard, but unlike many caves these tunnels were completely dry. Merlin passed a large open chamber, the remains of a magma bed, and continued to follow the widening tunnel while shadows danced ahead, leading him deeper into the hill.

Ahead a softer light spilled into the tunnel and Merlin extinguished his torch, rolling it in the ancient volcanic dust of the cavern floor.

He took a deep breath and paused a moment. He had not been here for many years and with heart pounding he stepped into the blazing heart of this subterranean cathedral.

Here there was water. A giant lake stretched across the central floor of the cavern. Undisturbed, this lifeless pool lay like a giant mirror, reflecting the towering dome of the rock above. The effect was one of immense depth, with the floor of the cavern plummeting into a rocky bowl below. Huge stepping stones seemed to float in mid air, making a path across its glassy surface to a small wooden bridge suspended across a gaping chasm.

Beyond the bridge the rough rock of the cavern had been carved into sweeping steps of polished obsidian that climbed to a single slab of unadorned granite. Dozens of candles surrounded the slab, banked in tiers they fanned around the slab like spectators in a giant auditorium. Yet these candles did not flicker. The shadows did not dance. Each flame was frozen in time, its light filling the cavern with a strange ethereal glow. To cross that bridge would be certain death for anyone not protected from the spells that encapsulated the figure that lay upon the granite slab.

Royal blue robes embossed with golden thread covered Arthur's body. Only his head was visible. Shoulder length chestnut hair spilled over a crimson pillow.

Behind the body a wooden stand held a corslet of chain mail, polished and glittering, untarnished by time. An empty scabbard hung from the belt; polished leather trimmed in silver. Merlin sighed. The last time he had seen the missing blade, Excalibur had been in the hand of Aldivon.

Slowly, Merlin made his way across the lake to a single stone column that stood just before the bridge. The column stood no more than waist high and atop it lay a cushion of deep blue velvet. Carefully, Merlin reached into his robe and removed the crown fragment he had kept. He bowed to the recumbent form of Arthur and placed it reverently on the cushion.

"One..." he whispered into the hollow emptiness around him, and wondered again if Matt would return with the other five.

Slowly Merlin made his way back across the stepping stones to the rear of the cavern where a much smaller chamber was closed off by a hanging curtain. The space beyond was meagerly furnished. A sleeping pallet lay against one wall, and barrels of dried food stood against the other. A tiny rivulet of water trickled down the back wall of the cavern, gathering in a naturally carved basin before seeping into the bowels of the earth below. Beside the stream a large pitcher for gathering water stood dry and unused.

Merlin let the curtain fall behind him, and took a step toward the water bowl.

The attack was lightning fast and the old man froze at the press of steel against his throat.

Justin Orton

PART THREE

ARTHUR

Chapter 19
Capture

Eilean Tioram, Scotland
597AD

Morgause focused on the swirling threads of multi-colored light that gradually coalesced into an image. She studied the scene as it formed in the mirror.

Towering pines appeared first, their rust-red trunks seeming to sprout from the moss-covered boulders at the water's edge. The river foamed white, cascading over rocks worn smooth by time, and high above, the moon cast an eerie light upon her contact's face.

"Speak!" Morgause commanded.

"Matt grows delirious with fever, Majesty. Would you have me return with the fragment recovered at Dunadd? I could leave tonight..."

Morgause pondered the request. It would be easy to command her contact to kill Matt then return with the fragment, but she had wanted that pleasure for herself, and besides...

"No. You must stay. According to Merlin's writing only Arturius knows the location of the rod of Dardanos. You must see Matt lives and leads us to him. Much rests upon you now."

The figure slumped, and Morgause could see the unease cross her informant's face.

"Then with your permission I will return to camp."

"Wait!" The queen's voice was urgent. "He wears a medallion. It is an object of power infused with the ability to heal. Wake him, and encourage him to use it, he will know what to do. You should also know that Aldivon's men are already in Kintyre, you can afford no further delay."

Morgause watched the figure scramble carefully across the boulders down to the broken gravel of the river shore, then gradually the image faded away.

Matt opened his eyes and felt a panic when everything remained dark.

I'm blind!

He tried to sit but his body was stiff and unresponsive.

A shape loomed above and a sticky wet tongue lapped at his face.

"Mia?" his voice was barely a croak.

He let his eyes close, trying hard to escape the blossoming pain that threatened to overwhelm him, but footsteps sounded close and he forced them open again.

"Who—?" His tongue was thick and swollen and he could not form the words. He groaned as waves of pain assaulted his body, yet somehow he managed to roll slightly toward the approaching footsteps.

Valina came toward him, her thick cloak pulled tight around her. She carried several rags, still wet from where she had washed them in the river, and on her shoulder hung a skin full of fresh water. She quickened her pace when she noticed he had rolled, and dropped to his side.

"Matt? How do you feel?"

He tried to reply but his throat was dry.

"Here—" Valina slowly dripped water into his mouth and he swallowed gratefully.

"Thank you."

The girl smiled and stroked a hand across his forehead. He shivered at her touch.

"I'm cold."

"You have a fever." Her voice was soft and soothing, and he felt a pleasant detachment from the pain as her fingers wove through his sweat-dampened hair.

"I need to cleanse your wound."

"Where's Brick?" Matt asked, clenching his teeth as she rolled him fully on his side.

"We went to the river. I to wash rags, and to fill the water skin. Brick took a rod and went downstream to fish. He should return shortly."

Valina gently pulled the blankets from Matt, and he cried out as she unbound his wound. In the two days since the attack it had clearly begun to fester.

She looked now at the unpleasant mess. Much of his shoulder was bruised, the skin shiny and purple, but the puncture itself was what concerned her most. Partly crusted, the wound still wept, and the skin around it was a fiery red. She had snapped the shaft off the arrow to prevent movement causing further injury, but the head was still embedded in the shoulder.

Her previous attempt to remove it had been a disaster. Poorly made, the arrow had become detached when she tried to draw it, the clinging muscle and tissue of his shoulder holding the barbed steel firmly in place.

She squeezed water from the freshly washed rags and attempted to clean the wound. Matt groaned and slumped forward, his breathing labored. Fresh watery blood stained the rags and trickled down his arm and back.

A pungent aroma filled the air as Valina removed the lid from a wooden pot of thick green ointment and applied a thin layer across the wound. She knew enough of healing to keep wounds clean and freshly bound. She also knew which plants made the best ointments for fending off infection, and reducing pain.

She rocked back on her heels and sighed, for she also knew that without removing the arrow Matt's condition would worsen and eventually he would die.

She leaned across the boy and her hair swept across his drawn and sallow face. Moonlight glimmered on the chain about his neck and she cradled the Pendragon in her outstretched hand. She turned it carefully, and passed a thumb across the dragon emblem and the strange red stone within.

"How's he doing?"

She looked to see Brick stumble into the clearing, a wooden pole across his shoulder and three large salmon hanging from his hand.

"Not good," she said. "The arrow *has* to be removed."

Brick dropped the fish and came to kneel beside the girl.

"What are you doing with that?" Brick indicated the Pendragon.

"It's beautiful. I wonder where he got it."

Brick eyed the medallion carefully. "It's dangerous." He looked at his hand then back to the medallion. "Maybe it can help him. C'mon, let's get him awake."

Valina looked at Brick and raised her eyebrows questioningly, "How can a pendant help him?"

"Trust me." Brick smiled, thinking back to the locker room incident. "But we will need his help with this."

It took time, but with the application of the potent green ointment to Matt's top lip and the gentle force feeding of water the boy coughed and gradually came awake.

Valina and Brick spoke quickly, explaining to Matt how the arrow was lodged in his shoulder and had to be removed.

"I can't get to it," Valina said. "The skin has partially closed and it's in too deep."

Matt breathed hard, eyes glazed and staring, then with clumsy fingers reached for Valina. She took his shaking hand and with surprising strength he pulled her close. She lowered her head to his face and he breathed in the scent of her hair, enjoying the softness of her skin next to his lips.

"Take my knife," he instructed. "Cut the skin and follow the path of the arrow into the wound. The knife will widen the opening. When you reach the arrow have Brick remove it, then clean the wound and stitch the skin together."

Valina's face blanched at the thought of doing what Matt was asking. "I don't want to hurt you further!"

Matt tried to grin but it was more of a grimace. "Neither do I, but it is necessary."

Brick pointed to the medallion and leaned closer to Valina. "Tell him about the medallion. He can use it!"

The girl nodded and looked into Matt's deep blue, pain-filled eyes. She felt something awaken inside of her, a gentle compassion for the boy before her. She gently kissed his forehead, her lips lingering longer than she intended and she pulled back embarrassed. Blushing, she held the medallion before Matt's eyes.

"Brick feels this can help you. Do you understand what he is saying?"

Matt's pulse quickened.

The Pendragon. Of course!

Merlin had told him how it could be used to accelerate healing, and ease pain. He tried to reach for it with his left hand but the arm hung useless at his side. His face contorted with the pain of it and Valina's eyes narrowed in concern.

"What is it?" she asked, stroking his cheek.

"I need to hold it. When I appear to sleep begin with the knife."

Valina gently lifted the chain from around Matt's neck and pressed the medallion into his right hand, closing his fingers about it. She watched Matt for a moment, and then taking a deep breath she slipped the knife from his belt.

"Brick, we need a fire. I have to heat the blade to make it clean."

"But we've avoided a fire since we got here. If the river is patrolled we could be seen!"

"We must take the risk."

Scowling, Brick gathered wood and stones, and built a simple fire. He pulled a blanket from his pack and using two stout sticks constructed a crude but effective screen between the fire and the river. "That may mask the fire's glow but there is nothing I can do to hide the smell of smoke."

Valina nodded, saying, "It will suffice," and she plunged the knife into the heart of the flickering flames, watching as the bright steel blackened.

Beside them Matt clasped the pendant and fought the pain in his body, seeking the calming effects of the mental exercises Merlin had drilled into him. Gradually his mind cleared and he began to focus on the Pendragon. In the same way he had touched the minds of animals, he felt for that strange other presence in the medallion. To start with it eluded him but then he found it, a tingling vibration deep in the heart of the stone. He could feel a warmth to it now, and there was almost a pulse.

Gradually a spinning vortex appeared in his mind, a swirling patch of bright light in the darkness, and holding the image he gradually imagined the pain in his body being drawn away. He relaxed, the pain subsiding. The medallion was hot now, a wheel of fire in his fingers.

Valina and Brick stared in wonder at the red glow coming from Matt's hands and then the boy slumped forward, all tension leaving his body. If it weren't for the shallow breathing they would have thought him dead.

Brick looked at Valina and nodded. With trembling hands she pulled the glowing knife from the fire and cooled it with water from the skin, then holding her breath Valina sliced open the shoulder. Blood, water and pus oozed from the wound and she wiped it away with the rags. Matt's body trembled beneath her fingers.

"Hold him!"

The wound was fully open now and she fought down her rising nausea and pressed the knife into the flesh. Slowly she worked the blade in deeper feeling for a resistance or some indication she had found the arrow head.

Matt's breathing became ragged and Brick could feel him trembling beneath his hands. Valina pressed the knife deeper, grateful for the darkness, relying more on feel than sight. She struggled to keep her hands steady and then felt the blade grate against steel.

"I found it!"

With two fingers she pulled the wound open, pushing in one direction with the knife and pulling in the other with her fingers. Dark blood ran freely from the wound, thick rivulets coursing down Matt's back.

"Now, Brick!"

But Brick did not move.

"Brick, get the arrow!"

Brick was shaking, his face ashen.

"I can't! I can't put my fingers in there!"

"He'll die!" Valina thought for a minute. "Can you at least hold it open for me?"

Brick nodded and carefully replaced her hands on the knife and on Matt's bruised and battered back. He turned his head away. "Do it. Do it quickly."

Valina closed her eyes briefly and then with teeth clenched she felt inside the wound. The muscle seemed to clench against her fingers as she slid finger and thumb along the steel of the knife. Her thumb was almost completely in the opening when she felt the rough steel of the arrow head. She reached past it until she could get a finger and thumb on either side of the flat of the arrow.

She took a breath and pulled. There was no movement and she fought the tears of frustration as she felt her blood-slick fingers start to slip from the arrow.

Matt's body was starting to convulse and the glow from the medallion began to fade.

"No," she breathed, "Come on...please..."

She pulled again, her fingers slipping, and then with a horrible wet tearing sound the arrow came free. She rocked back on her heels and cried tears of relief as she saw the bloodstained arrow tip in her hand. "I got it," she cried, "I got it."

Brick carefully pulled the knife from Matt's shoulder and smiled at the girl. Then he ran to the edge of the clearing, barely reaching the trees before he started to vomit.

Valina washed the wound and stitched the skin together as neatly as she could using a fish bone needle and twine from her bag. Finally she smeared a generous amount of the precious ointment across his shoulder and bound the wound with fresh rags.

When she was done she felt drained.

They took turns watching Matt through the remainder of the night. He came to only once, a little before dawn. Valina held his hand and stroked his cheek, offering him the medallion, and once again Matt entered that strange trance-like state, the beautiful dragon emblem glowing in his hands until once more he drifted into sleep.

By noon the next day the fever had broken, and as she changed the dressing Valina was stunned to see the angry red skin had paled to a more healthy pink; the bruise had faded to a mere discoloration and scar tissue was already forming around the puckered skin of the stitches.

As evening descended once more on their camp, Valina prepared their meal. She had wrapped the salmon in leaves and buried the fish in the ashes of the fire, leaving them there for most of the day. As she unwrapped the lightly baked fish and broke it into portions she heard movement behind her.

Matt was awake and had rolled onto his side. He lay there watching the girl, and he smiled weakly when she looked at him. "That smells really good," he said.

Her eyes shone bright with tears as she handed him a generous portion of the pale pink meat.

"Welcome back, Matt."

It was several hours before noon when they finally broke camp. Brick and Valina led their horses south, while Matt rode and Mia trotted faithfully alongside. Five days had passed since the attack in Tolnech. Valina had spent most of her time tending to Matt, but she had managed to patch several rents and tears in their clothes and had worked with Brick to shorten the overly long wagon-reins into something more manageable. The rest had been hardest on the horses. With no food for the animals Brick had spent several hours each day leading the animals in search of grass.

Matt's fever had gone, and thanks to Valina's ministrations and the power of the Pendragon the wound had healed at an unbelievable rate. Still weak, Matt knew it would be some time before the use of his left arm was fully restored.

If it ever will be?

He pushed the dark thoughts from his mind and concentrated on the horse beneath him, trying to ignore the discomfort in his shoulder for now the skin was tight and itched.

They followed the bubbling, tumbling river upstream, higher into the tree-clad hills. At times the trees seemed to close around them oppressively, but the occasional break would allow glimpses of Loch Fyne far below, its waters dark beneath overcast skies.

They had been traveling for almost two hours when they finally emerged from the trees onto the upper slopes of the mountain. Far below, the dirty smudge of the north-south road followed the shoreline of the loch, whose cold black waters were flecked with white as a bitter wind swept down from the hills, herald of the coming storm.

"You feeling all right?" Valina asked for the fifth time that morning.

Matt smiled weakly. "I'm fine. But we should rest the horses before heading downhill."

The companions gave the animals time to graze and drink while they themselves ate a quick meal of cold salmon. They talked quietly about the journey ahead, but when thunder rolled in the distance and lightning flickered across the sky they quickly packed, mounted up, and continued south, keeping to the rills and valleys of the hillside, angling ever down toward the road.

"Storm's getting closer." Brick said after the last crash of thunder finished echoing around the hills.

"Yeah." Matt pointed in the distance. "Rain's coming too."

The far shore of the loch was lost in a curtain of gray as the clouds began to shed their heavy burden. Matt pulled his horse to a stop and watched the rain spread across the loch, driven toward them before a strengthening wind.

"In less than an hour we'll be at Tarbert. It's a strip of land less than a mile wide separating Loch Fyne and Loch Tarbert. It's a perfect place for Aldivon to watch for us. Beyond Tarbert lies Argyle." His face looked pained and he looked directly at Valina. "It's but twenty miles from there to Tayinloan. My plan was to escort you there and then cross Argyle to Carradale and the shores of Kilbrannan." He looked into her eyes and his stomach bunched in sickly knots. Despite the heavy gray skies Valina's eyes sparkled with their own inner light, starbursts of gold set amid the softest green. Her red hair flared around her shoulders, streaming in the wind.

Matt turned away, all too aware of the hollow empty feeling of impending loss.

I'm gonna miss her. Her smile, her voice, her face.

Would she stay if he asked her to?

But we'd have to say goodbye eventually.

The longer they spent together the more painful the parting would be.

Valina nudged her horse alongside Matt's. She touched his arm. "What is wrong?"

Matt's pulse raced at both her touch and the lilting softness of her voice.

"You are barely recovered from your wound, Matt. Come with me. Leave this land of violence and war. Come to Ireland, we could..." Her voice faded away and she blushed.

"I can't." Matt suddenly wanted to tell her everything, but she would never understand, "I just can't."

Matt pulled his horse around and pointed southeast to a wooded hill slightly lower than the one they were on. "From there we should be able to see across to Tarbert. We'll decide then how to proceed into Argyle.

"Those trees may also give some shelter from that." He nodded his head in the direction of the advancing storm. "Come, let's ride."

They made good time despite the thick heather that carpeted the hills, hiding hollows and boulders from view and making the footing treacherous for the horses.

"Here it comes!" yelled Brick as the first drops of rain began to fall.

"Almost there!"

Valina's voice was swept away on the wind and with a mighty crack of thunder the heavens opened.

The trees gave little shelter from the downpour, and the companions huddled close forming a circle with the horses drawn up around them. The wind was cold, and before long they were soaked to the skin, and their clothes hung heavy with water. Beside Matt, Valina shivered constantly.

"Some shelter this is," moaned Brick, and Matt agreed.

"Let's move. We can't get any wetter."

Dejected and miserable, hair plastered to their faces and rain dripping from ears, noses and chins they led the horses through the stand of trees to the far side of the hill and looked down toward the flat expanse of land that divided the two lochs. They could see nothing. Tarbert was still a mile distant and the heavy rain hid the valley from view.

"What now?" Brick asked, shivering in the cold. "You want to wait, or head down there? We can't see a bloody thing, so they sure as hell can't see us."

Matt looked at Valina but she said nothing.

"Let's go," he decided, and they picked their way downhill, following a stream that tripped and tumbled its way through the coarse grass.

If it weren't for the bark from Mia who had walked ahead, they would have missed the unexpected drop that yawned before them. The stream tumbled in a waterfall, falling twenty feet into a pool before continuing down the hill. They dismounted and backed their horses, turning away from the stream and looking for a more gentle way down. The horses trembled as their hooves constantly slipped, and their frantic pounding churned the grass to mud. Twice Brick fell, and by the time the group reached the bottom of the hill their feet and legs were caked in mud.

Mia looked equally bad. Her coat was matted flat, and her legs and belly were black with mud and grime. Her tongue hung from the side of her mouth, and the shine had left her eyes.

"I'm in no hurry to do that again!" Brick gasped, as they slowly picked their way through the pools and wild lowland cotton bogs.

"I'm sorry," said Matt, leaning heavily against his horse. "We should have stayed up there, waited for the storm to pass. It was foolish of me."

Valina gave a wan little smile and patted his arm. She was limping, having turned an ankle in a hole halfway down the hill.

"It's okay," she said, "and look! The rain's easing!" So intent were they on their footing they had failed to notice the gradually brightening sky and slackening rain. Minutes passed, and the rain stopped and the group gave a collective gasp as the flats of Tarbert appeared through the thinning veil of highland mist.

Valina's hand shot to her mouth and her eyes reflected the horror of the sight before them. Brick pulled his horse to a stop and looked across the mud flats. "Mother of God," he breathed, and looked at Matt.

Matt's mind raced and Valina pulled her horse beside him. He felt the trembling of her thigh against his, and the tension in her hand as she reached for him. "What do we do?" she asked.

Matt felt his blood run hot. The sight before them was horrifying, but the sounds were truly sickening. He reached across and pulled at the reins of Valina's horse forcing the terrified animal around in a half circle. Pushing as hard as he could he sent an image to the horse urging flight, back along the road. Stealth no longer mattered. He drew his sword and slapped the rump of Brick's horse with the flat of the blade.

"Run! Both of you!" he shouted. "Run!" and then he turned his gaze to Mia.

"Protect them!" The now-familiar pain blossomed behind his eyes at the forced mind contact with the animal, and he swayed a little in his saddle as he faced the carnage across the inlet.

He did not look back. He knew Valina's horse would not stop, and he trusted Brick would stay with the girl. He could hear her cry drifting back to him on the wind—"Matt, please..."—but he pushed her voice from his mind and kicked his tired horse forward. With a yell he raised his sword and charged.

Chapter 20
Seeds of Doubt

Cavern of the King, Din Eidyn, Scotland
597AD

Merlin remained perfectly still, careful not to alarm his assailant. He let go his staff and the wooden prop made a dull, almost hollow thud as it fell to the cavern floor. Behind him his attacker loosened the grip about his neck.

"Turn. Slowly."

Merlin turned gathering his will to strike, but immediately the tension drained from his body and his eyes sparkled with joy as he beheld the face before him.

"Lancelot! My dear Lancelot!"

Lancelot hesitated, his sword still held between them while his eyes searched the old man's face. "Merlin?" There was doubt in the warrior's eyes.

"Aye, my friend! Who else? It is I." Merlin reached out a hand, but Lancelot retreated a step and there was an awkward silence as the two men held each other's gaze.

"I guess the last years have been less than kind to me?" Merlin said, and Lancelot finally relaxed.

"You've changed," he agreed. "You look older, yet somehow wiser."

Stepping forward, he sheathed his sword and pulled Merlin into a tight embrace. "It's good to see you old friend. Come,"—he grasped the wizard's shoulders and steered him from the cave—"let's eat."

Merlin had not eaten so well in weeks. Slow roasted haunch of lamb, seasoned roots, fresh bread, and a rich broth all washed down with several flagons of pleasantly spiced ale. While Lancelot had cooked, Merlin had talked, bringing his friend up to date with the happenings of the past year, culminating with the recent discovery of Matt, the boy's training and the quest to recover the broken crown.

"So tell me, old friend," the wizard asked, concluding his tale, "Tell me of yourself. I feared you were captured or dead. You made no move to find me?"

Lancelot cut a generous slice of lamb from the spitted roast and the fire popped and cracked as fresh drops of grease splattered on the logs. He refilled his tankard from a nearby cask and returned to his position by the fire.

"I had set out to find Guenevere but the trail was cold. Eventually I found my way to Eilean Tioram but was almost captured. My likeness has been well reported, I am a wanted man."

Lancelot spoke at length, and several more brands were thrown on the fire as he relayed the tale of his search for Guenevere.

Lancelot's eyes filled with sadness and his voice took on a somber tone. "Rumor came that Guenevere was dead, put to death by Aldivon. I would not believe it, but as the days passed I confirmed she had been tortured and the existence of Matt revealed. I should have asked more questions of the torturer but I was incensed. I killed him and began a mad quest for vengeance.

"At the ruined abbey of Invalone I gathered many men. Those still loyal to Arthur. From that sacred place we launched harassing attacks against the queen's supply columns, intercepted messengers and anyone who supported the queen or Aldivon. Our numbers increased and I grew brash. We attacked a large war party heading south but we were defeated, driven into the hills and scattered. I lost many men that day, and I myself was wounded. Invalone became watched and the ruins of Camelon are guarded. Aldivon's forces have grown strong, Merlin. They are disciplined and great in number, surpassing even the army that Arthur once led.

"Since then we have dared not attack again. Instead we listen and watch. I first learned something was afoot three months past when we heard rumors of another world, a search for some special artifact, and for the first time in almost a year the mention of your name.

"I spread word to the southern kingdoms that an invasion was underway and then bent all my energies to defending this place, as I guessed it would be but a matter of time before Morgause learned that Arthur still lives."

"You have prepared defenses here?" Merlin was surprised. "I saw nothing on my way? I was not challenged."

Lancelot smiled, his blue eyes sparkling in the fire light. "I gave instructions you be allowed to pass."

Merlin's eyes widened and he licked his lips thoughtfully. "I would see these defenses." He leaned forward and squeezed Lancelot's shoulder with an old yet powerful hand. "I am truly sorry for your loss my friend, but all being well we will end this soon. We will have vengeance."

Merlin stood and retrieved his staff. "Come, let's meet your men, and—Lancelot?"

Lancelot stood and buckled on his sword belt.

"Yes?"

"'Tis good to see you again, my friend. Good indeed!"

Tarbert, Scotland
597AD

From their vantage point in the foothills above Tarbert, Valina and Brick watched the encampment. Several hours had passed since their mad flight from the mud flats up into the boulder-strewn hills. They lay close, concealed behind a large boulder, trying to ignore the discomfort of the wet ground on which they lay.

Valina had said very little since they had raced from the battlefield. The sight of Aldivon's soldiers as they roved among the bodies of the fallen, clubbing or hacking to death those that still showed signs of life had sickened her, but it was the pitiful band of women and children being chained and pulled into the camp that had led Matt into making his crazy ride onto the field. She had watched him fell the guards, releasing the children, but they had just stood in shocked bewilderment until fresh soldiers had overwhelmed Matt and pulled him from his horse.

"Looks like they're loading supplies on those boats."

Brick pointed to the five ships that lay beached on the shoreline, their heavy prows buried in the mud.

Soldiers sat in groups about the camp and exchanged idle banter, while others organized the prisoner parties who continued the grisly task of recovering the bodies from the previous day's battle, carrying them to one of two pyres that sent plumes of oily black smoke into the cloudy skies.

"Looks like we'll get more rain." Brick tried again to draw Valina into conversation, but when she continued to ignore him he rolled away. "I'll check the horses."

The horses had been tethered on the backside of their hill, concealed by the thick gorse and broom that crowned its summit.

"Hey Mia! How ya doin', lass?" The dog lay sulking, head on her paws. Since arriving at the hilltop she had become withdrawn, preferring to stay near the horses than join Brick and Valina on the hilltop.

"He'll be okay," Brick tried to reassure the husky and she flicked the tip of her tail at the sound of his voice, but her eyes remained dull and she gave a pathetic whine.

"Never knew a dog could look so sad," Brick muttered as he returned to Valina.

A flurry of activity from below caught his attention and he watched as several horsemen cantered into the far end of the camp.

"Aldivon!" Despite their distance from the camp there was no mistaking the figure as he dismounted and passed the reins of his stamping mount to a nearby youth. Valina drew a sharp intake of breath and squirmed against the boulder as if in an attempt to burrow deeper under the rock.

Brick watched the girl. She brushed a wet strand of hair from her face, and he felt his pulse quicken and his throat tighten at the sight of her. She really was a beauty. He rolled across the springy heather to lie against her.

"Brick—" Valina looked at him, eyes wide, and attempted to pull away but he stopped her, wrapping his arm across her shoulders. He was intently aware of the warmth of her body next to his, and his voice betrayed his desire as he hunted for something encouraging to say.

"I'm sure he'll be okay." He spoke quietly and brushed another strand of hair from her face, caressing her cheek.

"Please—" Her voice was cold. "Don't touch me like that." She wriggled from beneath his arm and pointed below. "Aldivon is down there now. Do you know what that means? He will kill him. You know that as well as I. We have to do something!"

A rush of anger at the girl's rejection was almost immediately replaced with a surge of jealousy over her obvious concern for Matt.

She hardly even knows him!

Yet she clearly had an interest that seemed to go beyond mere friendship.

Why'd you have to be such a fuckin' idiot, Matt?

"I can't believe he went to save those kids. They were too damn stupid to even try and run!"

"He wanted to help..." Valina's face looked pained.

Brick rolled away from the girl. He wanted to get back at her and a thought occurred to him.

"Why do you even care about him so much anyway?" he snapped. "It's not as if we've had anything but trouble since you joined us!"

Valina looked startled and she fixed Brick with an icy stare. "What is that supposed to mean?"

"We were doing fine until you appeared at the tombs. Then look what happened. Aldivon and his men started chasing us, and they've been right behind us, or worse one step ahead ever since. It's almost like they know where we are. The village, the bridge, and now here. How do we know you're not on their side, leading us to them!"

Valina's face went ashen. "How dare you!" Her usually soft and pretty voice took on an edge and her eyes narrowed dangerously. "I could say the same of you! Every time we've run into trouble where have you been? Just before the attack in the village you were talking to those men at the barn, and then at the woods when Matt was so sick you were always sneaking off on your own."

Brick raised his voice, his face flushed with anger. "To fish! We had to eat, dammit! And sneaking? Seriously? You're the one who's always sneaking off. Sneaking off to bathe, or get water, or some such lame excuse. Matt came here with me and I don't trust you!"

"I saved his life!" Valina yelled back, her eyes burning with anger. "You didn't even want to help!"

Just then Mia barked, and joined them on the ridge, teeth bared. Brick and Valina stopped their arguing and glanced down the hill. Soldiers were scouting the lower slopes working their way methodically across the hill and up toward their position.

"I suppose I signaled them our position too, did I?" Valina spat sarcastically. Then she crawled back to the horses. "I'm not staying to get caught—come if you will, unless you're waiting for your friends." And with that she grabbed her horse, slipped its tether from the boulder and led the animal down the opposite side of their hill.

Brick looked at Mia. "Thanks for the warning, lass," but the dog ignored him, and trotted after Valina.

"Great!" Brick muttered to himself, "you bitches stick together then," and he returned his attention to the camp, keeping a cautious eye on the soldiers that searched the hillside below.

The men were getting closer and with a curse the boy realized they would find him if he stayed. He grabbed his own horse and quickly stumbled down the reverse slope of the hill following Valina who had already disappeared into the sanctuary of the trees below.

Matt was exhausted. The fog of sleep was slipping away and he tried to hold on to its tenuous sanctuary for a few more minutes.

I don't want to wake up!

What horrors waited in the cold light of day he shuddered to think, but sleep left him and with a groan he opened his eyes.

At first glance the tent appeared empty. The animal skin walls were stretched tight, allowing light to enter, and he was somewhat surprised to see his sword, pack and other belongings in easy reach of the sleeping pallet on which he lay.

What the hell?

A quick glance beneath the blanket showed the medallion was still around his neck. He had been bathed and dressed in an almost full length linen robe.

Cautiously he sat up, rubbing the last of the sleep from his eyes.

"Ah! He wakes!" a deep, gravelly voice came from behind. Matt lurched away from the bed and turned. Aldivon was seated on a wooden box behind the bed and Matt dove for his sword.

"Matt, wait!" Aldivon barked and Matt stopped, surprised the man had made no move of his own. Slowly Aldivon unbuckled the heavy sword belt around his waist and dropped the sword on the bed. "I mean you no harm, boy. I just want to talk.

"You have led me a merry dance up and down this accursed country. Come..." and he extended a hand.

Matt was scared but there was nowhere to run. A brief glance through the opening in the tent had shown many soldiers milling around outside. To run would be certain death. With his heart in his mouth he moved away from his sword but obstinately placed his hands behind his back.

"Hungry?" Aldivon asked letting his hand drop to his side.

"No." Matt lied, unwilling to accept any more hospitality than he had to. He looked again at his sword and pack, and wondered if the crown fragment had been found.

"Suit yourself, but I will eat. You may accompany me, or wait here, that is your choice." Aldivon stepped to the tent flap and turned again to face the boy. "Shall I wait for you to dress, or do I eat alone?"

Curiosity burned within Matt.

Why was Aldivon so cordial?

Matt moved to the bundle of clothes that lay rolled against his pack. "I'll come," he said.

May as well eat than die on an empty stomach.

Having dressed he pondered his sword, and on a whim buckled it on. He would test just how far this relaxed manner of Aldivon's would stretch. Stiff and sore from the abuse of the past few days, he stepped outside the tent and crossed to Aldivon who stood a few paces away talking with two other soldiers. One, Matt noticed, was a boy little older than himself.

At his approach Aldivon dismissed the others and beckoned to Matt. "Come, we have some fine wines and ales if your thirst is more than your hunger. For food we have apples, a little soft but palatable, fresh baked bread, cheese and a roasting pig. A meal almost fit for a *king,* huh?"

Matt walked beside his adversary, head racing with a thousand questions, while behind them, the young soldier Matt had noticed earlier watched the pair from across the camp.

Sure he was unobserved, the young soldier slipped between the tents and disappeared into the trees.

Matt and Aldivon walked in silence to the northern edge of the encampment. Many soldiers sat here and the buzz of coarse conversation settled into a respectful silence as Aldivon passed. Matt was surprised to see obvious devotion and dedication in the faces of these men.

These men do not appear to be led unwillingly, or held in service through fear.

What kind of man would follow someone like Aldivon?

A large pavilion was raised beyond the soldiers, and crude tables and benches had been placed so Aldivon and his captains could eat protected from the rain. Two other men sat here and both had finished eating. They left at Aldivon's instruction and he indicated Matt should sit, while he himself loaded a wooden platter with food.

Licking greasy fingers, he inclined his head to the boy and took a bite from an apple. "You sure you won't eat?"

Matt shrugged. The smell of the pork made his mouth water. He reluctantly stood, stepped to the table and cut a generous slab of meat, took some bread and a small piece of cheese then followed Aldivon to the table.

They were alone and Matt felt very aware of the sword strapped to his side and the fact Aldivon was defenseless with the exception of a small eating knife that lay on the table by his plate.

He let his fingers slide to the hilt of his sword. Could he reach the man and cut him down before the guards got to them?

Maybe. Then you would die and the quest would fail.

The quest failed the moment you rode out on the sands. What were you thinking?

Matt let his fingers slide from his sword and placed his platter on the table.

May as well find out what the man wants...

They ate in silence for several minutes. Matt was the first to speak. "You said you wanted to talk."

"Aye. Indeed I do." Aldivon responded around a mouthful of bread. He washed the food down with a large gulp of ale and belched, then wiped his fingers on his tunic and regarded the boy through blue and thoughtful eyes.

"So. What lies did Dardanos weave for you?"

Matt could not hide his surprise. "Dardanos? Dardanos is dead."

Aldivon leaned across the table and fixed the boy with an iron stare. "Dead? Do not mock me, boy. He was in perfect health when you left him last."

Matt stared at Aldivon, his eyes registering complete confusion. "Dardanos died at Camlann. Slain by Arthur. What are you talking about?"

"The old man that trained you, boy. 'Twas Dardanos. Did he claim to be another?"

Matt's mind raced. What was happening? Was this some kind of trick? He opened his mouth to speak but no words came. He licked his lips and just looked at Aldivon, his face bemused.

"Merlin died years ago, Matt. Dardanos killed him. I was there when it happened and that day haunts my dreams still."

"You lie!" Matt found his voice. "Arthur killed both Mordred and Dardanos at Camlann. Merlin was there, he told me!"

"You have been misled." Aldivon's voice took on an urgency and he leaned across the table. "There are many in this camp I cannot trust, lad. I am not who you think I am. There is much to set straight between us and little time. I have not the patience or the will to play games.

"Merlin is dead, and it was Dardanos who trained you, manipulated you, played you for a fool. He used your love for Arthur and Merlin to his own advantage. I would know his goal!"

Matt reeled at the words and desperately sought a counter argument, but Aldivon continued.

"If Morgause knew my true identify I would have died long ago. For years I have debased myself and pandered to her every whim but now my time approaches."

"Who are you?" Matt's voice shook with uncertainty.

Aldivon's reply came in slow and measured tones, each word striking Matt like a physical blow. "I am Arthur's brother."

Chapter 21
Unexpected Allies

Loch Fyne, Tarbert, Scotland
597AD

The dark waters of the loch lapped gently against the stones of the shore. The young soldier pulled his cloak against the breeze that blew unchecked across the water.

He knelt behind a fallen pine and peered through the tangle of roots toward the encampment he had recently left. There was no sign of pursuit and he knew no patrols were scheduled to pass this way.

Trembling, he pulled from his pack the mirror the queen had given him and breathed on the glass as she had instructed. Once the glass had misted he dipped a finger into the loch and allowed two drops of water to fall upon the mirror.

"Morgause," he whispered, and stared fixated at the glass. Several seconds passed, then the droplets expanded into oval pools, the water darkening, taking on a deep violet hue. He gasped as he found himself locked in the gaze of the queen, her eyes staring at him from the mirror.

His pulse quickened and his stomach tightened as it always did in her presence. He was captivated by her, and that one night in her chamber had left him with a burning hunger he could not suppress. His voice shook. "Your Majesty. I have news."

"What news?" Her voice didn't come from the glass but purred in the depths of his head.

"You asked me to tell you if there was news of the boy, Matt. Well he is here, my queen. Aldivon has him."

He felt the hiss of her indrawn breath and could almost taste the anger. But there was something else? Fear?

"Has he been harmed?" The purring tones were now replaced with a brittle edge, and he wanted to reassure her, to comfort her, but more than anything to please her.

"No, my queen, quite the opposite. Aldivon is treating the boy well. In fact, he seems to be making an effort to befriend him. The two have been closeted away in conversation for almost an hour now, all others dismissed from their presence. He's even allowed the boy to remained armed."

There was an icy silence in his head and the eyes in the mirror narrowed in thought, focusing on something he could not see. He waited, holding his breath, then once again her attention returned to him, her eyes boring into his. "You remain above suspicion?"

"Yes, Your Majesty. The lord Aldivon trusts me completely." His voice shook with trepidation. "Was I right to report this, my queen? I pray I have not disappointed you."

"No, you have not displeased me. Aldivon is up to something and I must know what. My trust in him has waned since Matt was found. There will be danger here, but you must find out all you can. Will you risk all for me?"

"I would risk my life for you, my queen."

She smiled. She had known his response even before he spoke it. It never failed to amuse her just how much power she could wield over the weak with the promise of her body. She licked her lips in delightful anticipation and caressed the young soldiers mind.

"Your loyalty will not go unrewarded," she promised, and then she was gone.

Brother!

Matt was stunned. How could this be true? His mind raced to process the information but he could not believe it.

Couldn't, or wouldn't?

He stared at Aldivon through confused, tired eyes. He searched for something to say, and unbidden the words escaped him.

"Prove it."

Aldivon reached across the table to place a hand on Matt's arm but the boy snatched it away. Aldivon sighed, his distorted voice somehow conveying concern.

"Matt, there is not time to tell you everything, and even if there were how would words prove anything to you?

"You would have my story and the tale of Merlin, or should I say Dardanos. How would you discern one from the other?"

The man stood and placed a hand on Matt's shoulder. "Come. There is another way," he said, and with that Aldivon led the dazed boy across the camp back toward his own pavilion.

Seated on a large cushion Matt waited as Aldivon retrieved his sword from the tent in which Matt had slept. He felt far less comfortable now that the imposing figure was armed. On edge, Matt watched as Aldivon crossed to a small iron-bound box.

With a key removed from a fold in his tunic Aldivon unlocked the box and withdrew a crushed velvet bag. Closing the chest he returned to Matt and sat before him.

"Do you remember when you were captive in the cottage?"

Matt nodded, recalling the hatred in Deglin's face and the sword that had swept toward him.

"I saved your life." Aldivon said quietly and Matt remembered the clash of steel as Aldivon's sword had caught the gardener's blade.

"You said I looked like my father." Matt recalled, and Aldivon smiled.

"And so you do. You may also recall I challenged the queen about the logic of having you put to death."

Matt shook his head. "I don't remember that. I had other things on my mind at the time."

Aldivon nodded, understanding.

"Can you remember the ceremony at the standing stones?"

Matt shuddered and his face blanched. "I will never forget it."

"You would have died that night too, had I not shot those who would have cut you down."

Matt had forgotten that, but the horrors of that night now came flooding back to him. He remembered Mia's courageous battle to protect him, how Merlin had rescued him from the cold stone slab, and the flight of arrows that had cut down the two soldiers. Something did not, however, make sense, and he challenged Aldivon.

"Morgause and Merlin fought that night. If Merlin was Dardanos as you claim, she would have recognized him. They were married!"

"Not so," Aldivon responded quickly. "Dardanos and Merlin always looked much alike, and Dardanos is gifted at twisting people's minds to see what he wants them to see.

"Morgause believed she was confronting Merlin. Dardanos has no use for her now. He uses everyone, Matt. Everyone and everything. He serves none but himself."

With a flurry he drew his sword and Matt tensed, half rising, but Aldivon reversed the sword and passed it hilt first to Matt. "Behold Excalibur."

The last time Matt had seen this blade it had hovered inches from his face. He had marveled then at the cold brilliance and naked beauty of the weapon. Now with trembling hands he took the sword from Aldivon. It was light, lighter than his own, yet so much bigger.

The blade seemed to resonate with a life of its own. Not a mark marred the highly polished steel and Matt felt overcome with emotion as he stood there holding Arthur's legendary sword.

A tingling in the medallion about his neck startled him and he felt a subtle malevolence emanate from the sword itself. He almost dropped the weapon then, but the feeling passed and he felt tired, almost drained. As he passed the sword back to Aldivon, he felt a presence inside his head and he staggered, pushing back against the crushing pressure in his mind.

Aldivon took the sword, a look of concern on his face as he helped Matt back to the cushion.

Matt looked up at the man, his face a mask of fear.

"I heard a voice, there was something, someone..." He looked at the sword. "It came from that!"

Aldivon frowned. "What did you hear?" his voice growled, but with anger or concern Matt could not tell.

"Words, but I could not understand them. It was if they came from a great distance."

Aldivon passed the boy a wooden mug half full with water. "Here, drink this and relax."

Matt took the proffered drink and tried to relax. Aldivon studied him a moment, then confident the boy was paying attention he indicated the velvet bag.

"I have something more to show you," his voice took on an almost reverent air.

Matt watched intently as Aldivon reached into the bag and then he gasped as Aldivon withdrew the crown fragment Matt had recovered from the tomb only days ago. The man placed it on a table, then reached into the bag and to Matt's complete astonishment withdrew four more fragments, placing them alongside the first.

"You were sent to recover these, yes?"

Matt, numb with shock, simply nodded.

Aldivon leaned forward and pushed the fragments toward the stunned boy. "Search no more. I have them, and willingly surrender them to your care."

Matt stared at the crown fragments, his mind awhirl with what he had learned.

Had Merlin really lied? What could Aldivon possibly hope to achieve by giving him the crown?

Taking a deep breath Matt reached out his hands, but with the speed of a snake Aldivon struck, pinning Matt's arms to the table. The man leaned forward, eyes burning with an intensity that startled the boy.

"Wait!" Aldivon commanded. "To take these, you must first listen to what I have to say. You are filled with doubt. Who should you trust? What should you believe?

"Before I can let you go from here, I need to know that I can trust you. Will you listen to me now, with an unbiased heart and an open mind?"

Only after Matt had agreed did Aldivon relax his grip and sit back. He passed his fingers through the thick black waves of his hair and yawned. "I'm tired, Matt, tired beyond imagination, but hopefully, together, you and I can end this madness. Now listen carefully, for this is what we are going to do..."

Shores of Loch Fyne, Scotland
597AD

Valina pulled a third bolt from the quiver on her belt and struggled to reload the crossbow, cursing the hurried shot that had so narrowly missed. Two soldiers had fallen to their unexpected attack, but with the element of surprise gone they were now outmatched. Two more men advanced on Brick.

Loading the bow, she watched the burly boy fend off a flurry of blows from the nearest swordsman while Mia danced in front of the other, keeping him at bay.

Brick was clumsy, his strokes purely defensive. To an observer he either had no skills with a sword or was going out of his way to not harm the soldier. He risked a glance in her direction and the move proved almost fatal.

The nearest soldier lunged at him and Brick stumbled as he jumped away from the blow.

With a fury Brick's assailant pressed home the attack, and the outclassed boy stumbled again, this time crashing heavily against a tree. His pack took the brunt of the force yet Brick yelled with pain and lurched away from the tree as if struck.

He staggered toward his attacker and dropped his sword.

With no time to take proper aim Valina raised her bow and fired. The shot took the soldier in the arm and he reeled from the blow. His sword clattered to the ground as he clutched at the dart now buried in the muscle of his upper arm. Brick seized the moment and lashed out with his legs, dropping the wounded man to the ground.

Brick retrieved his fallen sword and backed toward the girl, feet slipping and sliding on the wet undergrowth.

"C'mon!" he yelled, his voice hoarse. "Run!"

Mia, who had blocked the second soldier from getting close to Brick, stopped her snarling and turned to race after the pair. Valina hesitated a moment longer and then backed into the trees toward their horses, her voice shrill as she shouted to the fleeing boy.

"You should have finished him!"

The wounded soldier was pulling himself to his feet, his face drawn in pain.

"They will alert others to our presence now. We will never escape!" Valina was angry.

"I rate my ability to run much higher than my ability to fight. We will be long gone by the time they reach camp and return with more men."

Brick crashed into the clearing at a dead run, and the startled horses shied away rolling their eyes and snorting loudly. He lost several minutes getting his horse under control but eventually managed to pull himself awkwardly onto the animals back.

Valina threw the boy a dark look. She was clearly aggravated. Slinging her bow over her shoulder she swung herself with athletic grace onto her horse and pulled the animal around in a tight circle. She jabbed with her heels and sent the horse weaving through the thinning trees in pursuit of the fleeing Brick.

As Brick had predicted the soldiers did not pursue. He and Valina had ridden for almost thirty minutes, angling down the heather-clad slopes toward the loch. With the army behind them Valina had argued the road would provide a faster route, and be safe to travel, but Brick had refused to head toward the camp and the two companions now stood facing each other on a small sandy beach.

"I will not leave him to die!" Valina snapped. Her eyes had narrowed and there was a determined set to her jaw.

"I don't want him dead either!" Brick snarled. "Trust me—without Matt I have no way home, but we can't just march through an entire army and rescue him!"

"So what do you suggest?"

Brick hesitated before responding. The argument earlier on the hillside, and the obvious mistrust between them, had unsettled him. He watched her pace across the sand, mesmerized by the sway of her hips and the way her wet hair clung to her tunic. He would hate to see her go but he needed her gone from the group. He had to see this thing through, and the accusations she had made on the hillside were dangerous. Matt may just decide to continue on his own if he couldn't trust either of them.

Assuming he ever makes it out of there.

"Look. I know you worry about Matt but he's my concern. You were going to leave us in a day or two anyway. I would suggest you leave us now. Head to Tayinloan. The journey west should be safe for you. As for Matt, I'll see what I can do to get him out of there."

Valina hung her head and went to where Mia sat, gazing south along the loch. In the far distance she could discern tendrils of smoke rising above the trees. The air was chill and evening was fast approaching.

She scratched the dog's head and ruffled her ears as she had seen Matt do a thousand times. Mia licked her hand and gave a little whimper, her eyes once again staring downstream toward Aldivon's camp.

"I don't want to go to Ireland now," she said softly. She remembered Matt's carefree smile, and the innocence of his eyes. He had shown her nothing but trust, respect and friendship and she felt an aching sadness in the pit of her stomach at the thought of not seeing him again.

She turned to Brick. "We have to find a way to get him out of there. Together."

Brick's face grew sullen as he realized the girl meant what she said.

"Okay. Let's picket the horses here and you stay with them. I'll follow the loch to the encampment. It will take me at least two hours so it will be dark by the time I get there." He looked at the still-cloudy skies. "There will be no moon tonight. I'll sneak into the camp. If we can perhaps find our way back to the soldiers we killed today I can take their tunics and blend in as one of them. I'll find Matt and get him out of there."

Valina watched as Brick explained his plan.

"We should go together," she said quietly.

"No." Brick was adamant.

"Why? Because you don't trust me?" She raised her eyebrows questioningly. "Because ever since I've come along you've had nothing but trouble?"

Brick flushed but made no answer; instead he ignored her and moved toward his horse.

"Do you think it safe to leave me here alone when I could slink off and alert the camp to your approach? Or perhaps you don't want me to see you being welcomed by your friends?"

Brick heard the metallic click of the crossbow ratchet and turned to see Valina sighting at him down the length of the bow, her last remaining bolt locked against the string, its deadly barb aimed at his chest.

"You don't trust me Brick, you've already made that clear, and I don't trust you either. We go together."

Brick's mouth was uncomfortably dry and he raised his hands in the universal sign of surrender. "All right." He licked his lips. "We'll go together, no need to get violent about it."

Keeping the bow aimed at the boy she inclined her head toward the horses. "Take our packs and hide them here, then muffle the tack on the horses with pieces of cloth. We must approach with as much stealth as possible. On a still night the sound of a harness travels a long way."

Brick quickly untied their packs and placed them in a sandy hollow on the loch shore. He pulled a few large stones and a length of sun-bleached pine across the hollow and stood back to admire his work. In the darkness they would be completely invisible unless you knew where to look.

"There," he said, approaching the girl and standing a foot from the still-leveled weapon. "Are you ready?"

She lowered the crossbow, but did not remove the bolt. Instead she slipped the wooden peg through the trigger mechanism, locking the safety.

"Is this how it will be from now on?" Brick asked, relieved the weapon was at least safe.

"Until we can put this nonsense behind us and work together, yes."

"If we get Matt out of there alive, then you will have earned my trust." Brick tried a smile. "Hey, I may even apologize."

"*When* we get Matt out of there I'll accept it," she said, and together they led their horses onto the darkening road.

Above them the clouds remained thick, masking the sun as it slipped below the ridge line to the west. Darkness soon followed and in muffled silence they continued along the road, eyes straining for any movement, ears alert for the slightest sound. The soldiers they had fought earlier would surely have reached the camp by now, and if Aldivon sent out patrols they wanted plenty of warning.

To their left the dark waters of the loch kissed the stony shore, a soft rippling caress, while to their right a shallow rock cliff rose fifteen feet or so before leveling off to a gentle heather-clad slope. Walking in silence, they both wondered when the road would open up again. Should soldiers approach them now there was no place to hide.

They continued in silence, eyes fixed on the ghostly form of Mia who led the way, nose to the ground, tail arched across her back.

Suddenly she stopped.

"What's up with her?" Then Brick heard it too. He grabbed Valina's arm, pulling her to a stop. "Listen!" he hissed, and together they held their breath; there was no mistaking the distinctive sound of approaching horses.

Chapter 22

Gathering Forces

Tarbert, Scotland
597AD

Aldivon stood on the prow of the ship and looked across the growing expanse of water to the far shore. Dark shapes flitted amongst the trees, their silhouettes stark against the multiple camp fires. His men were breaking camp. Coarse shouts and curses drifted through the night, punctuated by braying donkeys, the ring of steel, and the rattle and creak of wagons. He smiled. His order for a night march had come as a surprise, but the men were loyal and rested from the battle two days prior. Despite their grumbling they worked feverishly to collapse the tents, load the wagons, and prepare for the arduous journey east.

Behind him, toward the center of the loch, the other four boats were already unfurling their sails, while oarsmen shattered the dark waters as they angled the heavy vessels southward before the wind. The ships were laden down with the advance guards and their essential supplies. The water lapped inches from the gunnels and they wallowed like pregnant beasts.

The vessels were a mixture of Roman and Viking craftsmanship, based on the Norse raiders, with double banks of oars, a single large center sail and a smaller sail or spinnaker at the bow. Each carried one hundred and forty men, and most of these now manned the oars, their shields slung on the sides of the ship.

Aldivon's army was on the move. The cavalry had left an hour earlier, over three hundred horsemen moving along the road in tight formation, their orders clear: ride north, skirting Loch Fyne and loch Long, the two immense bodies of water that prevented a direct route east. If they pushed their horses hard, he estimated the cavalry would arrive in the open flat lands west of Din Eidyn three days hence. This would put them no more than a day behind his advance guard, who would secure a perimeter at Camelon before marching on Din Eidyn.

The rest of the army would follow only a day behind, the foot soldiers marching south to where they would be ferried by multiple ships to a staging location at the head of the river Clyde. To save the army from making the long march east, Aldivon planned to stop off at the many fishing villages and small towns as he took his little fleet to the Clyde. He would engage the townsfolk, having every fishing vessel and ship capable of carrying men move his forces east. Separating the army in this way was considered risky by most tacticians but it was a maneuver Aldivon had perfected. Moving his advance guard and cavalry forward in rapid and unexpected advances, he was able to secure favorable ground and often capture the enemy by surprise. If ever unable to overwhelm a force he maintained sufficient strength to make a rugged defense while the main body of his army would arrive on the field striking the enemy from behind or crushing them in a devastating flanking attack.

Now, with the priceless information Matt had given him, it was time to play for the ultimate prize. All the pieces of the puzzle were at last coming together. He suppressed a chuckle as he pictured the old man waiting at Arthur's resting place. Waiting for Matt to blindly hand over the crown fragments. The old fool had plotted so well, but not well enough.

Aldivon finally turned away and faced the men crowded onto the boat deck. Those spared the duty of rowing slept, but a small body of men sat alone. They were his officers, and amongst them was the promising young guard he had recently taken into his service.

Picking his way through the mass of men Aldivon walked to the young man and placed a fatherly hand on his shoulder.

"Ithius, come with me."

The young man got to his feet and followed Aldivon to the rear of the ship. Here a raised deck, reached by wooden stairs, was home to the three most important men on the boat. The two steersman who handled the giant navigation oars, and the captain, who was busy barking instructions to the rowers and those struggling to haul the heavy rawhide sail aloft.

Beneath this raised deck was a small cabin, no more than five feet wide at the door, tapering back to a mere foot at the stern. The ceiling was so low that both men were forced to stoop. The cabin was the only one on the ship, reserved for the captain's use or that of a higher ranking passenger. A single bunk nestled against the port side, hidden by a large animal skin curtain, and other than a lantern suspended on an iron spike above, there were no other furnishings in the room. In the starboard wall a small hatch was fitted, leather straps acting as hinges. Aldivon pulled this open and took a deep breath of the fresh night air.

"You relayed our destination to the queen?"

Ithius nodded, and swallowed hard. He was nervous, and had every right to be.

It had been he who had betrayed Naveena after helping in Guenevere's escape. The girl had broken their bargain, refusing to sleep with him, and in anger he had relayed her actions to the queen. He had not known Morgause would kill the girl over it, but neither had he been prepared for the pleasures of that night, when Morgause had given what Naveena had denied. He had become her devoted servant and spy.

He pushed the pleasurable memories from his mind, and focused on the imposing black clad figure before him.

"My lord, I did just as you instructed, telling her of Matt's capture and death, and that you are taking the crown fragments to the old chapel at Invalone where Merlin guards the body of Arthur. You will meet her there."

"And the army?"

Ithius could feel the beads of sweat on his brow. "I told her nothing of the army, my lord. She knows not that we march on Camelon." Ithius was lying, and hoped that the flickering light from the lantern above did nothing to betray the anxiety in his face, and the fear in his eyes.

Even now he could see Morgause as he had seen her last, lying in her bed chamber. He could feel again the warmth of her body, and he shivered with the memory of her touch. He would never betray her. He loved her, was devoted to her, and had told her the truth—not the false message that Aldivon had requested.

"Thank you, Ithius. You have pleased me well. Tonight this cabin is yours." Aldivon pointed to the curtain, saying, "Enjoy the comforts of a bed for the night," then he left the cabin, closing the door behind him.

Aldivon smiled. Following Naveena's murder it had not taken long for Aldivon to discover the role Ithius had played. He had spared the fool's life only when Ithius had confessed that the queen had instructed him to spy for her. Aldivon had given him a simple choice: turn traitor, feeding the queen the information Aldivon wanted, or die.

In the cabin Ithius let out his breath and relaxed.

He doesn't know!

The young man kicked off his boots and unbuckled his heavy sword.

The queen will be pleased.

He pictured her naked before him as he loosened his tunic, and pulled the curtain aside, eager for a night of warmth and relative comfort.

He had no way of knowing it would be his last.

Eilean Tioram, Scotland
597AD

Beneath the shadows of the castle walls, officers barked instructions to their men. Congregating in the main square of the keep, Morgause's personal guard prepared to march. Riders had departed an hour before, racing to the towns and outlying posts to raise more men and bring to the field the garrisons of several outlying forts and castles.

Morgause paced angrily in her chamber.

She knew she had been right to send Ithius to spy on Aldivon. For months now she had suspected something about her most trusted adviser, but open rebellion against her was unexpected. And why had he killed Matt?

Ithius had not seen the body, only reported that Aldivon had told him to pass the news to her. Was it a lie? Did he still have the boy with him? She cursed again and went to the perch where her raven sat, its beady eyes following her every move. It squawked and flew to her upraised hand, pecking at her for the morsel it knew would be hidden between her slender fingers.

So Aldivon moves the army east, to Camelon.

Ithius had been clear, declaring Aldivon's intentions to lure her to Invalone, while he took Camelon himself. But why Camelon? Arthur could not be there. The ruins had been searched countless times. Was it a feint, to draw her and her forces to the wrong location? She glanced through the embrasure to the courtyard below.

I can ill afford a battle with Aldivon.

He had marshaled the majority of her strength in his campaigns to unify the kingdoms of Scotland under one banner, and she doubted the ability of the forces at her command to best him in open battle.

She stroked the dark feathered head of the raven, and pondered her other dilemma.

Why had her other spy been silent since Matt's capture?

Her plans were coming unraveled and she had to regain control. Voices sounded in the passage outside her chamber and she opened the door before the guards had time to announce the arrival of the Cùra Dubh assembly.

"Your Majesty." The elected spokesman bowed low.

"Is the pattern complete?"

"Yes, my queen, and the men sent to Camelon report construction there is almost complete also. If all goes well you can begin moving the army at noon, but it will take all of our strength to hold a portal that large for any length of time.

"I must warn you our ability to aid you after the portal is closed will be somewhat limited."

Morgause scowled. "Aldivon cannot reach Camelon for at least four days, and when he does his men will be exhausted. You will have time to rest."

"Aldivon's forces still outnumber yours, Your Majesty."

The queen passed another bloody square of meat to the raven.

"Aldivon is not my concern. Locating Arthur is. If we can secure Arthur before Aldivon arrives I can extract the location of the rod from him even while he sleeps. Aldivon will need to awaken Arthur to get the same information. That is why he retains the crown and seeks to delay me. Yet something is still amiss with this."

"My queen?"

"To awaken Arthur, he will need the aid of a magic user to undo the spells that hold him in slumber. Where do you propose he plans to get one of those? Aldivon has made his first mistake. He has shown his hand too soon."

"What of Merlin?" the senior magician asked.

"He will be no match for our combined strength. Now go. Rest. I will need your very best tomorrow."

The men bowed before her and she ushered them from the room.

As soon as the door had closed she walked quickly to her desk and removed the heavy velvet cover from the mirror. Despite the confidence shown to her supporters she felt nothing inside but a growing anguish. So much depended on her finding Arthur first. Closing her eyes, she bent all her thoughts to the mirror and attempted once again to summon the one she had sent to watch over Matt.

Almost an hour had passed and in the courtyard below yet another company of men marched through the giant castle gates to the staging area beyond. Above them the pennants and banners on the castle walls flapped loudly in the growing wind.

A scream of anguish and frustration sounded from the tower above and every face looked to the queen's window in time to see the raven launch itself into the night, climbing high into the star-filled sky. With powerful beats of its wings the huge black bird banked across the moon, and curved south to race toward Argyle.

Alone in her tower Morgause sat hunched before her mirror. Its burnished surface remained dark. Once more her servant had failed to answer the summons.

Din Eidyn, Scotland
597AD

Merlin swung himself into the saddle of the snowy white horse. Beside him Lancelot handed up the wizard's staff.

"You should not leave him unprotected. Let me go in your stead."

A growing wind tugged at Merlin's wiry white hair and pulled at his beard.

"I need to see this for myself!" he replied. "I will be gone three hours, no more. You must gather your men. Our only chance to hold her will be at Camelon. Leave only sufficient here to hold the cavern."

Lancelot nodded. "Good luck, old friend." He smacked the horse across the rump and watched as Merlin galloped west.

As soon as Merlin had disappeared into the darkness Lancelot turned and ran back through the trees to the small encampment nestled beneath the towering black crags of Arthur's Seat, the famous upthrusting of rock beneath which the town of Din Eidyn slept. Wrapped in a coarse woolen blanket lay a man, pale from loss of blood.

Lancelot knelt beside him and placed a gentle hand on the man's brow. "Gerard, tell me again what you saw."

The man licked dry and cracked lips and looked at Lancelot through eyes of the deepest brown. Merlin had tended his wounds, and eased some of the pain but it was unlikely the man would live. It was a miracle he had made it this far.

When he spoke his voice was soft, his breathing shallow. "Her servants appeared from nowhere. They just appeared in the remains of the great hall. We cut down three of them but they used some fell devilry and we were forced to flee. I and two others took to the trees and watched from a distance."

Lancelot noticed the spittle on the man's lips was flecked with blood. The man did not have long to live. He stroked Gerard's head and bent lower to hear the whispered words.

"They began the construction of a strange device. Its purpose I cannot tell. They were erecting stones in a circle. More men arrived then and they sent scouting parties into the woods. We were discovered and fled."

"Were you followed?" Lancelot asked, fearful the dying man may have unwittingly led their enemies here.

"No, my lord. Despite my injuries I was careful to cut my trail and double back to ensure I was not pursued. I hope I served you well, lord?"

Lancelot smiled. "Aye, Gerard. You served me well. Now rest."

The man closed his eyes and took several rattling breaths. "I would rest lord, my eyes grow heavy."

"Rest," Lancelot breathed, and then sat quietly, waiting, until the shallow breathing beside him ceased. Gently covering the dead man he mounted his horse and rode to gather what men he could.

Over thirty miles to the west a solitary rider galloped wildly toward Din Eidyn. His horse's hooves clattered loudly on the stones of the old Roman road and the rider blessed again his grandfather and the men of the legion in which he had served.

The road followed the Antonine wall, the northernmost of the two walls built by Rome to separate the wild men of the north from the more civilized cities of the south. Several hours still lay before him as he urged his mount to greater speed. His message *must* get to Lancelot.

It was only by chance he had seen the five large ships sailing up the Clyde. Aldivon's army was coming to Din Eidyn.

Shores of Loch Fyne, Scotland
597AD

The sound of approaching hooves grew louder, and together Valina and Brick mounted their horses, pulling the animals around to face back the way they had come. With nowhere to hide, they would be forced to outrun the approaching riders until they reached a place safe enough to take shelter. Once more they prepared to ride, but Valina paused, beckoning Brick to wait. "Listen!" she ordered.

"What?" Brick's tone was agitated. "Wait here to get caught?"

"No!" Valina threw the boy an angry look. "Listen—it's a single horse."

"So? One or a hundred? Let's get out of here." The boy kicked at his horse, and with a groan of frustration Valina followed.

The two companions pushed their horses hard and it was all Mia could do to keep up as she raced up the road behind them.

Before long they reached the sandy dell beside the road where they had hidden their packs and here they pulled their horses to a halt, walking the animals onto the beach and turning them to face the road. Mia collapsed to the ground beside the sweating horses, her tongue swollen and her flanks heaving.

"What now?" Brick whispered, "You want to spring another ambush? I'm tired of fighting!"

"Be still," she hissed. "We'll let him pass then try again to reach the camp. It's probably a scout looking for the patrol we attacked earlier."

Brick said nothing but loosened the sword in his belt.

They didn't have long to wait. The beat of hooves grew louder, and then with a blur, the horse thundered by, the rider lying low against the horse's neck, the powerful animal pushed to a full gallop. Before the dust had even settled on the road, Mia leaped to her feet and despite her exhaustion she gave chase, high-pitched barks punctuating the night.

Brick struggled to control his excited mount, and turned to look after the dog. "What the fuck's got into her?" he yelled. But Valina kicked her own horse and with a clatter of stones and soil crested the bank and onto the road.

"It's Matt!" she cried. "Get the packs! C'mon - it's Matt!" Then she too was gone.

Chapter 23
Return to Tolnech

Shores of Loch Fyne, Scotland
597AD

Matt had never ridden so hard. The horse Aldivon had given him was fast and the journey from the camp was passing in a darkened blur of trees and flashes of moonlit water. He was still confused by all he'd learned but his mind kept coming back to Aldivon's final warning.

"Ride hard, Matt, and do not seek your friends. One of them is not to be trusted—it would be better if you traveled alone."

But Matt knew otherwise. There was one he could trust, one he would not abandon, and that was Mia. He had planned to set out after the cavalry had departed, but as soon as the two men had arrived at camp and given news of the fight with Brick and Valina, he had determined to leave right then. Now as he approached the area where they had last been seen, his thoughts turned again to which of them had been sent to spy on him.

Brick or Valina?

He knew deep down it could not be Brick. The boy's presence here had been a complete accident, but still he sought for a reason to blame him, unwilling to entertain the idea that Valina could betray him. His emotional attachment to the girl was overriding his common sense. He'd never been in love—hell, he chided himself, how was he to even know what being in love was? He'd hardly known what it meant to be loved himself, yet he knew he felt more for her than just a passing friendship. The thought of never seeing her again brought a dull, aching pain that sat like lead in the pit of his belly. He had grown accustomed to her presence, her smile, and her voice. She made him feel strong, confident, and in a strange way somehow complete. He pushed the images of her from his mind and tried to think rationally about the girl.

Was she really on the run from Aldivon and the castle at Dunadd, or was that a convenient cover story? He had to confess that things had started to go wrong after she had joined them, but there was one thing that didn't fit the picture. She had remained adamant she was to leave Scotland and take ship to Ireland. Surely if she were the spy Aldivon had warned about she would be anxious to stay with him? He felt a surge of hope that perhaps the girl could be trusted after all. He put the thoughts of her bright green eyes, and lustrous hair to one side and began a similar analysis of Brick.

He thought back to what seemed an eternity ago, when he had said farewell to Mia by the park, and Brick's arrival coinciding with that of Morgause's Cùra Dubh. The attack in the town, launched on him and Valina when Brick had conveniently gone to the barn. The only thing that didn't fit was how a boy from the children's home could have any connection to Morgause? He had lived at the home in twenty-first-century Scotland—the sixth century was as alien to him as the surface of Mars. But then again, who would have suspected that Deglin was actually one of Aldivon's most trusted captains? If he had been sent to the home by Aldivon as a spy, could Brick have not been sent as a servant of Morgause? That would explain so much.

Gaelic! That's how he can speak Gaelic!

Urging more speed from his horse, Matt leaned forward in the saddle. If he found his companions he would need to remain careful, to stay on his guard, but he'd definitely keep a closer eye on Brick.

Near Camelon, Scotland
597AD

Merlin sat on the crest of the wood-covered hill, and peered through the trees toward Camelon. It was too dark to discern the details of Arthur's ruined fort, but the stone circle being constructed in the open fields was clear to see. Torches and fires illuminated the scene in an eerie glow, and Merlin shuddered as he watched the completion of the portal.

While the stones were not as impressive as many used in stone circle construction, the diameter of this circle was huge. Gangs of men, taken from their homes in nearby towns during the night, worked feverishly, digging holes and struggling to maneuver the heavy stones into the ground. Using ropes and pulleys, giant wooden levers and brute strength, they raised the stones and held them upright, while others pounded the soil around them, planting them firmly in the ground.

It was clear Morgause intended to move significant bodies of men through the portal, and Merlin marveled at the thought of the power it would take to hold such a gateway open.

Clouds scurried across the otherwise starry sky and he looked to the heavens where an almost full moon rode high, its brilliance failing to diminish the pin prick glow of a rising Mars. He frowned. The power to move Morgause's army here was nothing compared to the immense forces locked within Stonehenge. A power that if unleashed would establish a bridge to another world, but a bridge that would last only as long as Earth. The painful memory of the impact that had destroyed his world came flooding back, and the last major asteroid to strike Earth had sent his beloved Atlantis beneath the sea.

He pushed the thoughts aside and focused on the dilemma at hand. If Morgause was coming, then she must know the location of Arthur. That meant she had either divined the location from the book, or more likely that Matt had been captured. Merlin retreated back through the trees and retraced his steps toward Din Eidyn.

They had only one chance now to safeguard the location of the rod of Dardanos. All hope rested in the defeat of Morgause as her army arrived through the portal. Allowing her full strength to be brought to bear would result in guaranteed defeat for Lancelot's small force. If Morgause remained undefeated, then only one course of action was left open.

Merlin felt a sickness at the thought. Only Arthur knew the hidden location of the golden conductor that would complete the key to unlock Stonehenge's power. If Arthur's location was finally known to her, then Merlin's last act as guardian of earth would be the hardest act of all. Arthur would have to die.

Tolnech, Loch Fyne, Scotland
597AD

The road narrowed as it curved closer to the shores of Loch Fyne, and in the darkness of the night Matt felt he was racing into a tunnel with no end. The waters of the loch flashed by on his right and the almost sheer earth embankment to his left whipped by at breathtaking speed.

Wind ruffled his hair, and his cloak billowed behind him like a sail, and despite the uncertainty in his mind, part of him took time to relish the ride. He had never ridden such a powerful horse; it seemed tireless, and the miles passed effortlessly beneath its pounding hooves.

Moving as one, horse and rider rounded another bend and then the road opened up again, boulder-strewn slopes on his left and the shoreline of the loch falling away to stone and sandy beaches on his right. There was a brief flash of moonlight on metal. It took a moment for the fleeting image to register, but then he was past, the strides of his horse carrying him away.

What had he seen?

He straightened in the saddle, and pulled the horse to a trot. The animal snorted in protest at the break in speed, and then Matt heard the barking.

He pulled the horse around in time to see Mia, tongue lolling, muzzle flecked with foam, come limping along the road behind him.

"Mia!" he cried, and with an overly enthusiastic pull on the reins hauled the horse to a complete stop. The horse whinnied and stamped, backing up along the road until it understood its rider's instruction to stop.

Matt slipped from the saddle and fell to his knees as Mia reached him. The dog jumped, slamming into his chest and together the pair rolled in the road, Mia smothering his face in sticky wet kisses.

"Okay! Okay!" Matt laughed, tousling her thick neck and trying to hold her away. "Settle down, lass!" Mia backed off for a moment and lay on the ground breathing hard while Matt petted her, but the moment he stood she again leaped up, dancing on her hind legs and thrusting her muzzle to his face.

There was a pounding of hoofbeats and he looked up to see Valina swinging from her horse and running toward him.

"Matt!" her voice cracked with emotion. "Oh, Matt, you're alive!"

The boy freed himself from his dog and looked up at the girl. He tried to study her face, looking for any sign that she was Morgause's spy, but there was barely time to see the moonlit sparkle in her eyes and the open-mouthed smile before she was in his arms.

He stood awkwardly for a moment, not sure what to do. Her arms felt like bands of fire around him, and the softness of her breath against his face was like an angels kiss. He could feel the breathless rise and fall of her chest against his, and he pulled her close, all thoughts of betrayal gone as he felt the warm trickle of tears from her eyes caress his own cheek. For a fleeting moment he saw her again in the bath at the inn, and he felt himself flush. Ashamed, he took a step back but didn't let his hands leave her arms.

"I missed you," he whispered, his voice catching in his throat.

"And I you," she replied and the soft lilting accent was the most beautiful sound he had ever heard. Her gaze held his, searching, and then her hand caressed his cheek, and the softness of her fingers was almost lost in the burning exhilaration of her touch.

"Are you all right?" she asked, and he nodded.

"How did you get away? What happened? Tell me!"

Matt studied her face a moment watching the movement of her lips as she spoke, her delicate tongue flicking across white and even teeth. He wanted to kiss her, wanted to take her in his arms and tell her he was sorry for doubting her, for believing she could possibly be a servant of the enemy, but he blinked the urge away and instead replied, "I will. But first, where's Brick?"

"He's coming," she said. "Matt, I'm worried about him, there's something you should know—" but she didn't have time to finish, for Brick's horse clattered to a stop beside them and the older boy looked down on the pair, his face flushed.

"Matt! Holy shit! It is you! How did you escape?"

Matt stood for a moment and there was an uncomfortable silence as he looked at Brick. The older boy's eyes narrowed and Matt threw him a quick smile.

"It's a long story," he said. "I'll tell you later, first we must get away from here. Aldivon's cavalry are little more than an hour behind and riding hard. We have a long way to go. I'll tell you more when we reach the inn at Tolnech."

Brick looked at Valina but she just stared back as if daring him to say something. He shook his head. "The inn?"

"Aye! We're going to Din Eidyn. If we can get a boat across the loch we'll save almost a day on the journey."

Matt and Valina remounted their horses and Matt watched Valina. He knew, if she still resolved to journey to Tayinloan, that their parting was imminent. He had but three days to cross almost a hundred miles of inhospitable terrain. He could not ask her to go with him, but neither could he escort her further south.

She saw him watching and smiled. It was infectious and he shook off the gloom and smiled back. He climbed into the saddle and glanced once more at her, then jabbed his horse forward, doubting he would ever know a more beautiful girl in all his life.

They rode north in silence, their pace reduced to allow the travel-weary Mia to keep up with them. It was almost midnight when they reached the charred and blackened remains of the inn.

Tolnech, Scotland
597AD

Matt stifled a yawn and circled the ruins one last time. He had hoped to find the friendly innkeeper and enlist his help in procuring a boat across the loch, but all the buildings were shuttered and dark and he felt a growing frustration at the delay.

"What do we do now?" Valina whispered.

"Wait until morning I guess," Brick answered. He was tired, and sullen, and he took great pains to keep his horse within earshot of Valina and Matt, not trusting what the girl would say.

"We cannot wait that long," Matt said irritably. He was cold and wet from his recent swim. The temporary ferry replacing the destroyed bridge was moored on the town side of the river and he had been forced to swim across to retrieve it. "Come. We'll ride to the shore, some fishermen may still be up."

They rode across the town square, and passed between the boat builder's and the timber yard, following the same road they had taken into town days before. Matt pulled his horse to a stop and massaged his shoulder.

"What is it?" Valina asked.

"Just remembering last time we were here," he said.

Valina steered her horse closer. "Does it still hurt?"

"I'm fine," he said, "thanks to you." Then turned his mount onto the right fork, following the road down to the loch shore.

"You reckon we could catch one of those?" Brick said, pointing to the sleeping ducks and geese that lay in the long grass.

"Have you two not eaten?" Matt asked.

"The salmon a couple of days back was our last meal." Valina answered, nudging her horse closer to Matt. "If we find someone we desperately need to buy food."

Matt nodded and rode on in silence, feeling guilty for the meal he had enjoyed that evening.

Behind them a pair of swans raised their necks to watch them pass. They hissed when Mia stopped to sniff the air, and the dog quickly limped after the horses.

The road they followed wound its way along the edge of the town, and soon ended at a stone quay where fishing nets, crates and tackle lay piled against a large wooden building.

Plenty of boats sat on the beach, most of them one-man corrals, while larger boats bobbed in the harbor, rocking in the gentle swells that ran before a growing wind. For a moment Matt thought of stealing one but realized how futile that was.

Loch Fyne was wide, and in the growing wind it would be treacherous. He had no boat handling skills, and attempting to cross over six miles of open water in the dark would be foolhardy. He would have to wait until daybreak or enlist help.

"Listen," Matt said, "voices."

All three of them heard the burst of raucous laughter.

"A temporary inn?" Valina said, nodding in the direction of the wooden building.

Matt shrugged. "I'll check it out."

He loosened his sword and slipped around the corner of the building, keeping to the shadows. Without warning two men rose from behind an assortment of barrels and before he could yell Matt felt himself pinned against a wall, a knife that stank of fish pressed against his throat.

"State your business, boy!" one of his assailants growled, and Matt swiveled his eyes toward the voice. Despite the darkness he recognized the innkeeper and Matt felt a surge of hope.

"It's Matt," he mumbled. "I stayed at your inn a few days back, myself, a girl and another boy. Do you remember?"

There was a clatter to his right, and he blinked in the burst of candle light, as the shutters were pulled back on a lantern.

"Well, I'll be!" the innkeeper growled. "It is you!" Then turning to his companion he whispered hoarsely. "Let him go."

The man who held the knife was clearly a fisherman, his face worn and weathered from long hours on the water, and his deep blue eyes fixed in a permanent squint. Matt relaxed as the man slipped the thin blade into his belt.

The innkeeper leaned close and whispered conspiratorially, "Do you have any idea what trouble your last visit caused, lad? What are you doing here?"

Matt thought back to the charred remains of the inn. "The fire? They did that because of me? I'm truly sorry. I would not have come back, but my friends and I need passage across the loch. I can pay. I have gold and horses."

"And if we help, what stops our homes and businesses meeting the same fate as his?" The fisherman said.

Matt had no answer and just hung his head, praying they would help. Aldivon had told him Morgause would reach Arthur in three or four days.

"How much gold?" the fisherman's hand rested on the hilt of his knife and Matt reached slowly into his tunic for his bag of coins.

"We need food too." Both the innkeeper and the fisherman watched as Matt withdrew the little leather pouch, and they gasped as the Pendragon medallion fell free, shining with a dull glimmer in the candlelight.

Matt fumbled with the draw cord but firm fingers closed about his. "Where did you get that?" the innkeeper asked, indicating the Pendragon.

"A gift." Matt answered carefully, not sure why both men would have been so taken aback by it.

The fisherman's hand flew to his knife. "Stole it more like..."

Matt pressed against the wooden building, eying the knife that hovered inches from his chest. "It was a gift from the one I serve," he said quickly, wondering if they recognized the Pendragon for what it was.

"You lie!" hissed the fisherman, "The brotherhood is destroyed, and he who led them is but a memory."

The innkeeper shushed him. "Matt, answer me truthfully, who do you serve? We were once bound to a great lord of men, one of the brotherhood—I would know the truth of how you came by this."

Matt licked his lips and looked from one to the other. He had nothing to lose, so taking a deep breath he clutched the medallion with his right hand and answered clearly, his voice stronger and more commanding than he intended.

"I serve Arthur, rightful lord and king of these lands."

Both men gasped and the fisherman lowered his knife, his mouth dropping.

"I am the son of a Pendragon and my mission is of the utmost importance. Unless you serve the witch of the north you will not hinder me."

Chapter 24
Love and Betrayal

Loch Fyne, Scotland
597AD

The boat was one of the larger fishing vessels, and the smell of fish permeated everything on board. The ropes, the tackle, the boxes and crates were all littered with fish scales, and like the planking of the hull they were stained with fish guts and blood.

Brick sat hunched on a box toward the stern, his feet resting on a thick coil of rope. He eyed with trepidation the water that sloshed in the bottom of the boat, and he shuddered.

"You should wrap yerselves up. You'll feel a real nip in the air when we clear the peninsular." The fisherman sat at the tiller guiding his boat, while two burly men operated the oars.

"Thanks," said Brick pulling his woolen tunic closer around his shoulders. He indicated the bottom of the boat. "It leaks."

"All boats leak. Shouldn't have to bail on this trip though."

"Bail?"

"Aye. There's a pail next to you."

From the front of the boat Matt ignored the exchange and finished securing their packs. They had been stored high in the prow, and covered with animal hide to help protect them from the occasional burst of spray that whipped across the bows. "We are grateful for the supplies, we were out of food."

The fisherman nodded, watching as Matt stumbled back to his seat next to Valina. The girl was tired and as Matt sat down she leaned in close, resting her head on his shoulder. He took a last look at the receding shoreline and waved to the former innkeeper who stood on the dock, holding their horses.

"They were fine horses," said the fisherman.

"They served us well."

"The Garrons will serve you better once across the loch."

"What's so special about the Garrons?" Matt asked.

"They're highland ponies, but don't be mistaken by their small and stocky appearance. You'll not find a more hardy mount. They have the endurance of an ox, and the feet of a deer. They will cross terrain that war horses like those would find impassable." He slapped the hard wood of the ships planks and grinned. "Now me, I'm a creature of the water. Give me the sea and a sturdy keel over a horse's ass any day!"

Matt laughed and settled down for the journey. It would take at least two hours to cross the loch and he tried to get more comfortable. He looked with wonder at the long red hair that fell across his chest, and watched the slow rise and fall of Valina's breathing.

He couldn't believe she had come with them. He had asked the innkeeper if someone could escort her to Tayinloan the next day, but the girl had declined.

"Matt, I know a time will come when we have to part, but please, don't let it be now. I have nothing in this world, nothing but you. Take me with you."

Brick's objections had been most vehement, and Matt too had wondered at the change in plan, but he had quickly dismissed his suspicions. There was a growing connection between them and he was pleased she'd changed her mind.

Since his last conversation with Aldivon he no longer felt any confidence in his ability to complete the quest. He would try of course, but if he were to fail and the world were to end, he couldn't think of anyone he'd rather end it with. He let himself relax, realizing this was the first time in days he had had nothing to do.

The boat moved deeper into the loch and once beyond the shelter of the surrounding hills the wind whipped at the waters, sending a sticky salt spray over those that sat huddled in the boat. Mia lay in abject misery near the bow, periodically standing to shake water from her coat before lying down again, burying her head in her paws.

The increased motion of the boat caused Valina to stir and she opened her eyes looking up into Matt's face. She knew she was falling in love with him. The innocence of his years was long gone, stolen by the atrocities he had seen, and the things he had done, but it wasn't his youthful face that attracted her. It was his eyes. A gray, almost steel blue that looked not at her, but into her very soul. She found in him a captivating blend of strength, determination, and something else, tempered only by too much hurt and a deep driving pain of loss and loneliness.

Matt saw her smile and felt himself drawn toward her. The slap of the water on the boat, the rush of the wind, and the muffled breathing of the oarsmen slipped away as if part of another dimension, a world of which he was no longer part. All that remained in his existence was encapsulated before him in the softness of her hair, the brightness of her eyes, and the allure of her smile.

When their lips finally met, time stood still. He had never known such a sensation. He could hear the blood racing in his head like a thousand horses, and feel a swelling tightness in his chest that all but consumed him. His eyes closed, and he lost himself in the softness of her lips, surrendering his soul to the depth and sweetness of the kiss.

A rough hand shook his shoulder.

"Matt." The fisherman tried to look stern, and apologetic all at the same time. "Matt—look!"

Matt blinked, pulling himself back from Valina. With a major effort of will he pulled his gaze from hers and turned, dazed, to face the fisherman. The blood still raced in his ears and then with a sudden clarity he became aware of his surroundings, noting the grins on the rowers' faces and the amused glint in the fisherman's eye. He felt himself blush. His voice was choked and husky when he questioned the man. "What is it?"

"Look." The fisherman pointed north across the water to the shore they had left an hour before. Matt followed the fisherman's outstretched arm and then he too saw the long column of torches winding its way across the low lying hills.

"Aldivon's cavalry."

"Aye, laddie. So it would appear."

"How long until we reach the other side?"

"Another hour before we reach Ballimore."

"Thank you," Matt said.

"The honor is mine, young man. Just take care of yourself and," he added with a grin, "watch over that young lady, too."

Matt blushed and resumed his position next to Valina, but the girl was sleeping. He kissed the top of her head and felt his chest swell with feelings for her.

"I love you," he whispered quietly to himself, enjoying the sound of the words, and wondering when or if he would ever have the courage to say them aloud to her. So thinking, he fell asleep, lulled by the gentle rocking of the boat and the steady lap of water against the hull.

Argyle, East of Fyne, Scotland
597AD

"How much further?" Brick adjusted himself in the saddle for what seemed the hundredth time.

"We'll stop soon."

"Matt! Seriously? We haven't stopped since we left Ballimore. The horses need water, and we need rest."

"He's right, Matt." Valina's voice was weak.

Matt twisted in the saddle. The girl's face was pale, and her brow drawn as if in pain.

"Are you okay?" he asked, his voice full of concern.

"I have a headache, nothing a rest won't cure," she said, but in truth her head was pounding. A constant pressure threatened to crush her skull like a vice. She knew the reason, knew the cause, and she pushed back against it with all her strength, but that strength was fading. Soon the pain would be too much to resist. She focused on Matt, drawing strength from the feelings she had finally surrendered to.

"Mia's tired too."

Matt looked from Valina to the dog. The animal was clearly exhausted, walking with a pronounced limp in her right rear leg, and her tongue hung from her mouth like a sticky pink sock.

"There's a stream just ahead," he said. "We'll stop there, water the horses, and eat. We should have stopped before, I'm sorry."

"Bloody right we should!"

Valina ignored Brick's comments, "I forgive you," she said and Matt felt his spirits rise at her smile, the first since the day's ride had begun.

Guiding their mounts down a gentle incline, they pulled them to a stop beside a gurgling stream, its crystal clear waters tripping over rocks and gathering in little pools. Lush grass grew in the rich peat soil, providing a soft and welcoming bed. The companions fell stiffly from their ponies and lay back gazing at the pale blue skies above. The horses tore at the grass, munching in quiet contentment.

Valina's sobs broke the tranquil silence and Matt rolled toward her.

"Valina—"

The girl lay clutching at her head, pressing on her temples with the heels of her hands. "Valina?"

"My head! Oh gods it hurts!"

She shook her head, grinding her teeth together while tears streamed down her pale cheeks. "Make it stop! Please..."

Matt grasped the Pendragon, pulling the pewter medallion from his tunic and pressing it to her forehead. Almost immediately he felt a searing pain in his hand and a blinding pressure in his own head.

Fighting the pain, he sought the calm pulsating presence within the medallion's stone. The Pendragon began to glow, but the pain was unbearable, he felt himself slipping into darkness.

"Matt, help me, please..."

But it was too late. Matt was abruptly consumed by images that seared across his brain. With horror he realized he was witnessing his own death, and he screamed out as he watched the scene unfold. Valina was there—reaching for him, calling his name, but someone was pulling her away. He wanted to call out but he could not speak; he could not move. There was a spear in his side and there was blood; oh god so much blood, his blood. The man he'd come to know as Merlin came striding toward him but Aldivon blocked his path, Excalibur in hand. Bodies lay strewn on a cavern floor and then Matt felt himself slipping away, the faces revolving around him, spinning faster and faster. Merlin, Aldivon, Morgause, Valina, and then he was falling. From the darkness something tumbled toward him, glowing, pulsating. It was the Pendragon, and even as darkness took him he grabbed it, feeling the swelling warmth in his hands.

Struggling against the pain Matt clutched the medallion, pushing the images from his mind. "Valina, hold on." His voice sounded distant, faint, and he called again, "Valina!" and then a shimmering golden light emanated from the Pendragon, bathing them both in its warmth and protection.

The pressure in his head eased, and the pain receded. Matt rolled backward, eyes watering. He felt totally drained. Half blind, he crawled to Valina.

"Are you okay?" he asked, breathing hard, "Can you hear me?"

The girl opened her eyes, and then a look of horror crossed her face and she screamed.

Matt felt the growing shadow descending on them and rolled, gasping at the rush of wind across his face. Black wings beat the air and wicked talons missed his head by inches. The raven climbed back into the sky, its coarse screech echoing in the hills.

"What the hell was that?" Brick was running from the river, his face flushed.

"I have no idea." Matt's breathing was ragged and he struggled to rise.

"Stay with me. Please—" Valina's hand grasped his forearm. "don't go."

Falling back to the grass Matt called out, his voice slurred and thick with fatigue, "Brick, fetch my pack, we'll stay here awhile."

"Sure." The larger boy stood for a moment, a confused look on his face, and then turned to the ponies and unstrung their packs from the saddles.

Matt looked again to Valina, "Shh," he soothed, "I'm here."

"I'm sorry, Matt, I'm so sorry..." but Matt didn't hear her. Exhaustion overcame him and he slumped to the grass beside her.

Brick called across his shoulder, "You want some food?" but neither Matt nor Valina answered; they had both fallen asleep, their foreheads pressed together, each holding the other's hand.

They had been riding now for several hours and still the raven circled above. Twice more Valina had cried out at the pain in her head, and each time Matt had used the Pendragon to help ease her suffering.

He was convinced the attacks on Valina were Morgause's doing, and now more than ever he was convinced that Brick was not to be trusted. Clearly Morgause could not reach him past the protection of the Pendragon, and so lashed out at his companion. It only stood to reason she wouldn't attack her own servant.

"It's so cold." Valina pulled her woolen cloak tight.

"We're deep in central Argyle now," Matt responded, looking around at the dramatic landscape. Some of the higher mountains to the north still wore a mantle of winter snow.

He stroked the neck of his pony. Their surefooted mounts had been able to move at surprising speed, weaving through the valleys and glens, fording streams and rivers, but eventually their path had taken them away from the valley floor, winding higher into the mountains of central Scotland.

"There," Matt pointed to a rounded hill about a mile distant. "We'll rest for the night. We need to take turns to keep watch now. We're at least a day ahead of the cavalry but we can't take chances. Besides," he said, looking at the raven above, "we're not alone."

It took them another two hours to reach the hill and even their ponies struggled to reach the top. They were forced to dismount, leading their tired horses the last two hundred feet to the crest of the hill.

"Wow!" Brick said, looking back the way they had come. The land behind them stretched out like a rumpled blanket, the tops of the hills touched by the setting sun, while the valleys and folds between the mountains were already sunk in shadow.

"It's like being on an island," Valina breathed. All around them was water, marking the convergence of two of Scotland's famous lochs and the firth of Clyde. The ground before them fell steeply toward the water and to their right the Clyde stretched to the horizon.

"We can't cross that," Brick said, pointing to the loch before them. He looked to the north. "It'll take forever to walk around it too—it stretches as far as the eye can see, and look at the mountains. They practically fall straight into the water!"

"There's a fishing village."

Matt pointed to a dark fold in the land where the loch cut into the surrounding mountains. "You can't see it from here but according to the innkeeper they operate a ferry across the loch."

"A ferry?"

"Yeah. It's the only way to trade goods between east and west without using the main roads. It's forty miles to get around the lochs and mountains by road, and it's those roads Aldivon's cavalry is using. He can move faster than us, but we're taking a more direct route."

"What about the rest of his army?" Valina asked, stretching out on the rabbit-cropped grass between the boulders of the hill top and massaging her temples.

"They are coming by ship. We're probably still a little ahead of them too."

"Ur—those ships?" Brick asked. He had climbed to the top of a rocky outcrop and was now pointing to the south.

Matt and Valina exchanged startled looks and quickly climbed up beside Brick. The boats were barely visible, little more than dark smudges on the horizon.

"There's hundreds of 'em," Brick said quietly.

"Matt, what happened with Aldivon?" Valina held his arm, her face intent. "How do you know so much about what he planned?"

"Yeah..." Brick asked, "and you still haven't told us how you got away."

Matt was about to answer when the raven, still circling above, curved sharply to the south. With powerful beats of its wings it sped south toward the approaching ships.

"It belongs to Aldivon?" Brick asked.

"I don't think so," Valina answered and then quickly added, "I mean, I've never heard of him owning a raven."

Brick fixed the girl with a suspicious look and glanced at Matt, but he had already dropped from the rocks and was rummaging in the packs for food, the exchange unheard.

Justin Orton

Chapter 25
First Blood

Banks of the Clyde, Scotland
597AD

The sun had been slow to rise, and thin tendrils of mist still curled from the water to be blown inland by a gentle breeze that rocked the waiting boats. Ropes and rigging creaked, and the shrill cry of wheeling gulls punctuated the morning air. Aldivon regarded the camp and smiled in satisfaction. Earthworks had been quickly erected to provide a defensive perimeter around the beachhead, and wagons were already being loaded with supplies in preparation for the march.

Rough-cut boards and planks, along with animal skins, had been thrown across the mud flats, making it easier for those who struggled to haul additional supplies from the flotilla of boats that ferried men and equipment ashore.

A small row boat pulled alongside their ship and Aldivon greeted the man who clambered awkwardly aboard.

"Welcome. Any word from the cavalry?"

"They were sighted an hour ago, my lord. They should reach the encampment by noon."

"Excellent! They will have the rest of the day and night to rest. At dawn we march."

"To Din Eidyn, my lord?"

"Aye. To Din Eidyn."

"What of Ithius?"

"He died in his sleep."

The man followed Aldivon as he strode to the rear of the ship, a look of concern on his face.

"My lord. Our scouts report Morgause is moving."

Aldivon stopped. "So Ithius told her everything? It is well we hid from him our true destination. I had not expected her to move quite so fast. What are her numbers?"

"The vanguard of her army is already approaching Camelon. We estimate a little over a thousand men, mostly afoot. More are to follow."

Aldivon cursed. "How large a force in total?"

"We do not know, but if she believes Arthur rests at Camelon she will bring all she can to defend it. If she strips the garrisons between her castle and here she may raise five times that number."

"Our strength is almost twice that."

"Aye, my lord. But she has other means at her disposal, does she not?"

"Aye, that she does, but their strength has limits, and she must have used them to have traveled this fast. She will save the Cùra Dubh for Merlin, I have no doubt. Still we must be wary. I had hoped to avoid a major engagement. Once Scotland is mine, I will need all the men we can muster to march on the angles to the south. Stonehenge is a very long way from here my friend."

"What orders then, my lord?"

"Return to the army and issue instructions for the morrow. You are to take two thirds of the force to Camelon and bottle up Morgause. Don't waste the men, but ensure she takes us seriously, and whatever you do, keep her from Din Eidyn. The rest will march with me."

"Aye. And what of the cavalry?"

"You will need them. Reserve one squadron for me. Once we have retrieved the rod of Dardanos we will join with you and crush Morgause."

"I shall see to it at once, my lord!" And with that the man returned to the waiting row boat.

River Carron, Scotland
597AD

Lancelot had deployed his forces well.

The great west road, a broad dirt track that wound its way between the hills from coast to coast, crossed almost 200 miles of forest, moorland and marsh, skirting lochs, crossing rivers, and taking travelers through some of the most fertile farmland and beautiful landscapes of central Scotland. Morgause had staged her army in the shelter of the great forest and now she must take the last section of this road east to reach Camelon.

Of the three hundred men at Lancelot's command, fully two thirds of them stood at the bridge under the command of Marcus McNaughton. The remainder waited with Lancelot on a small hill two miles upstream, which rose from the river and gave a commanding view of the only other crossing point for twenty miles—a small ford that linked the coarse grass meadows bordering the river to the west and the boulder strewn, heather-cloaked hillside to the east. Drawn up on the reverse side of this hill Lancelot had deployed his small force, comprising mainly archers.

The men sat patiently, talking quietly while Lancelot crouched amid the boulders of the hilltop, ignoring the coarse prickle of the heather against his legs.

They were still unsure what Morgause knew, so Lancelot's plan was simple. Deny her the crossing for as long as he could before falling back to the crags at Din Eidyn. The river offered the best line of defense before Arthur's resting place, and may also lead her to believe Arthur was still in the vicinity of Camelon or Invalone. With two armies in the field against him, each outnumbering him by thousands, his best strategy lay in weakening one before falling back to his strong point, hopefully buying Matt enough time to win through.

If he still lives.

Merlin stood beside Lancelot and looked beyond the bridge, to the dirty smudge of dust on the horizon that marked the vanguard of Morgause's army.

"And so they come," said Lancelot.

"Aye," the wizard answered. "Is all prepared at the bridge?"

"They had but to cover the lines when I left this morning. They should have finished that now and taken up positions."

Merlin looked down the hillside to the little stand of willow trees and the river they overhung. Twenty of Lancelot's best bowmen occupied the forward slope of this hill. Impossible to spot from the river, they lay wrapped in blankets, nestled behind rocks waiting, watching for the signal.

Lancelot stood and jabbed his arm in the air three times. Three hours. The men continued to wait, each dwelling on what the coming battle would bring, and if they would survive it.

"So now we wait," said Merlin quietly.

"Aye. Now we wait."

Many of the men at the bridge were old by soldiers' standards. They had seen too many battles and should be sitting with their grandchildren, or tending crops and livestock, not standing shoulder to shoulder behind a row of sharpened stakes, defending a bridge against more than ten times their number. But these men were proud. Proud and free. They remembered what it meant to serve a man they loved and a creed they believed. They fingered the worn and faded cloth of the blue cloaks that had marked them as men of Arthur's personal legion. They waited silently, faces expressionless, ready to die for a legend.

The river banks were treacherous. Jagged rocks and loose stones plunged steeply to the river some fifteen feet below. Both banks were lined with gorse and broom, the evergreen bushes already showing the bright gold blooms they were noted for.

Across the bridge another row of fire-hardened stakes blocked the opposing side, and beyond that the road cut through thick grass meadows that in summer would explode with flowers and fragrance. From behind one of the many bushes a figure rose and raced to the bridge.

"They come!"

The defenders checked their weapons, changed their stance and took a firmer grip on swords and spears. The sound of tramping feet could be clearly heard as the spotter raced past their position and leaped a low stone wall to join a small company of archers that lay waiting. The wall hemmed in the garden of the lonely tavern that stood by the bridge. The small building had been a popular stop for those entering the wilds of northern Scotland.

The spotter, Marcus McNaughton, was Lancelot's commander at the bridge and he plunged through the tavern door to take his position on the upper floor. Everything was as ready as it could be.

Across the river the advance force of Morgause's army deployed for the assault.

Twelve hundred men made up the advance guard of the attacking army, and only a fraction of them were mounted, no more than a hundred and fifty cavalry in all. The officer in charge was a brute of a man, his bare head and muscled torso a tapestry of tattoos. Beside him a Cùra Dubh sat uneasily on his horse.

"Servius," the magician said. "How long to take this bridge?"

"Not long. They number too few, and they are old. They may slow us for an hour, that is all."

The magician grinned. "The fools should have destroyed the bridge. They could have slowed us down and saved their skins."

"Aye, that is true. But mark their cloaks. See how many wear the blue of Arturius? These are men who still believe in their glorious past. They are not fools, but desperate men. Men loyal to the memory of a fallen hero. For them to be here lends credence to your belief he rests at Camelon."

"How so?"

"This is the last defensible position before Camelon. You should go, inform the queen that we have met slight resistance, but the crossing will be secure by the time she arrives."

"You think it wise for me to leave? I have talents that could aid you."

"I need you not, magician," Servius sneered. "Go to the queen. This pitiful bunch is no threat—an easy victory here will bolster the troops."

The magician wheeled his horse.

"Then good luck to you," and he galloped back along the road. The queen's column was still several hours behind, but he knew she would welcome the news that Arthur may indeed be hidden at Camelon and their search would soon be over.

Servius barked more instructions. His men, once the ferocious wild men of the north, were now well trained soldiers. Instructed by Aldivon, they moved with precision, utilizing the Roman formations they had been ruthlessly drilled in.

Shield bearers came first, advancing in a phalanx ready to give cover to those ordered to clear the stakes that blocked access to the bridge.

Behind them a column waited, eight men wide and twenty men deep. Their task was simple. To charge the bridge and clear the stakes on the far side, allowing the cavalry to sweep through and rout the defenders from the road. Servius watched carefully and eyed the sun. It was already approaching midday. He could lose several men from that first column but the bridge would be his, the crossing secure within the hour. The queen would be pleased, for by the time she reached the bridge he would be in Camelon.

From the upper tavern window Marcus signaled his archers to hold their fire. It was too soon to betray their presence and their arrows would be wasted. The men on the far bank rapidly dismantled his defenses, casting the stakes to one side. The bridge was open.

With a deep throated roar the column charged.

The defenders took a step forward, the first row kneeling behind the stakes and interlocking their own shields before them. Behind them the second row raised their shields to create a roof and readied their javelins. Each man leaned into the man in front, supporting the shield wall.

For the attackers the task was simple; break the shield wall. They ran with breakneck speed, yelling as they came, launching themselves past the stakes and beating on the defenders' shields with swords and battle axes.

The defenders struggled to maintain the line as the weight of the men against it increased. Their bare legs trembled, sweat running over straining muscles, their leather sandals starting to lose grip on the sandy surface of the road. Men grunted with exertion, every muscle and fiber straining to hold the column at bay.

"Now!" cried Marcus, and a flurry of arrows arched over the garden wall falling among those still on the bridge. The rear of the column had been targeted and the first arrows were dropping among them before they could raise their shields. Men cried out as they were struck and the pressure on the shield wall lessened immediately as those to the center and rear of the column raised their shields against a second then a third flight of arrows.

This was the moment the defenders had waited for, and in perfect unison the front rank angled their shields allowing those behind to thrust past with their javelins. The front rank of the attacking column simply dissolved, sixteen men dying instantly and the defenders pushed forward driving them back onto the bridge. Rank after rank fell to the relentless thrust of the spears, unable to retreat for the press of their own men behind.

Servius swore. "Bring up the ballista and archers—suppress the fire from that wall!"

The column had taken brutal losses but they finally rallied and Lancelot's men halted their advance, backing up slowly, careful to retain the shield wall as they returned to their original position behind the stakes, stepping over the dead and the dying. They looked at the mass of bodies scattered on the bridge. Only a handful of their own number had fallen, but many now carried wounds. They could not resist many more such attacks.

Twice more the column charged, and both times they were repulsed, but now several of the stakes had been removed and the defenders were exhausted. Too many blue cloaks lay amid the fallen on the bridge.

Men coughed and tried to spit the dust from their parched mouths. Their faces and arms were caked in dirt that adhered to their sweat, and their clothes were torn and splattered with blood; theirs and that of the men they had killed. Muscles ached and the welcome lull in the fighting brought with it a lessening of the combat-induced adrenaline. Men groaned as they felt the first pain from the wounds they had received.

Across the river the enemy formations suddenly parted and the defenders paled, many looking to the tavern, anxious for the signal to withdraw.

Before them, drawn up side by side, were four horse-drawn ballista. Resembling massive crossbows, these weapons were more commonly seen on ships. Here they were loaded with projectiles tipped with barbed steel and capable of punching a hole through solid oak.

"Loose!"

The giant weapons lurched forward and the crack of the torsion springs—animal sinew twisted around layered strips of yew—made an explosive sound like cannon fire. The defenders at the bridge were already running. They had seen the heavy chains strung between each weapon and knew their purpose.

Servius grinned. This was more like it. "Archers, loose! Cavalry, advance!"

A swarm of arrows hissed into the sky and fell with an angry buzz toward the fleeing defenders.

"Loose!" Another storm of arrows arched toward the garden wall. Those behind the wall dropped to the ground and pressed themselves against the rough stone and waited while arrows rained down amongst them. First one died, then another, then a third. Two more fell, writhing in agony, their legs pierced by black feathered shafts.

From the bridge the defenders continued their flight. Behind them the remaining stakes were ripped from the ground, shattered by the flying chains. The ground shook as the cavalry pounded onto the bridge. Still the defenders ran, leaping the bodies of the fallen, their eyes fixed on the back of the man in front, painfully aware of his own exposure, waiting for the bite of an arrow.

Then they were through the storm, and leaping for shelter behind the wall. Behind them the cavalry were on the bridge.

Another flight of arrows skipped and danced around them, clattering from the stonework and thudding into the ground. Men cringed at the distinctive sound of a hit on a comrade and struggled to help their wounded friends. Shields were raised and then at last the arrow storm ceased. The cavalry were almost across the bridge.

In the stables at the rear of the tavern a team of six shire horses waited. The huge beasts wore blinkers and their handlers constantly stroked and crooned to the terrified beasts as around them the din of battle raged.

From above came the call.

"Pull!" Marcus yelled, "Pull!"

Instantly the mighty horses were let free, their handlers urging them forward. The team was harnessed together and four thick ropes led back from the harness to the river where they were secured to the trusses of the bridge. Lancelot's men had worked the night before, removing stones and chopping through critical supports and now the horses finished their work.

With the weight of the charging cavalry, the pounding vibration of their hooves and the combined might of the shire team the bridge collapsed. Horses and men screamed as they plunged into the frigid water below. Others were crushed against the boulders and rocks by falling horses, masonry and timber.

Those that survived the fall struggled to the river bank and here men were pounded to death beneath the hooves of fallen horses struggling to pull themselves from the water. Many more were carried downstream, and all around bodies floated, spinning lazily in the eddies and whirls of the river whose waters quickly darkened with the blood of the dead.

Marcus McNaughton looked on, face grim. He had denied Morgause the bridge. Now it was up to Lancelot. He raced down the stairs and joined his remaining men who were even now falling back along the road toward Din Eidyn. Their faces were tired and filthy, but each wore a triumphant grin.

Lancelot watched the men below. As he'd guessed, it had taken almost three hours for Morgause's men to reform and follow the river, seeking a place to cross. Now they had found it and he watched the man across the river deploy his men for the crossing.

"That man's a total fool!" he observed. "He doesn't believe this crossing defended."

Merlin nodded. The enemy should have swarmed across the river en mass with a shield wall raised. The crossing was a perfect site for an ambush, but the man across the river was in a hurry, and clearly enraged. He knew Morgause would be most displeased with the loss of the bridge and he was anxious to secure a crossing before she arrived. He had pushed his men hard, force marching them up the river to the crossing, and now he urged them on again.

Lancelot slid back across the hill and signaled to the row of waiting archers, their arrows already nocked.

"Loose!"

Fifty arrows arched into the evening sky, their trajectory perfect. Below, men screamed as they floundered in the water, desperately struggling to retain their balance on the uneven river bed while resisting the relentless drag of the river. To run was impossible and they stumbled and fell trying to raise their shields against the unexpected arrows. Lancelot signaled to the marksmen waiting on the slope facing the river.

Each man acknowledged and then rose from the heather. One by one they began picking off targets with carefully aimed direct fire. It was devastating, and those lucky enough to survive lost all thoughts of battle as they threw aside shields and weapons and raced for the cover of the river bank where they struggled to take shelter from the murderous rain of arrows, and direct bow fire.

Clinging to rocks and the roots of willow trees they cowered, too scared to retreat, and unwilling to advance.

Servius screamed in rage. His advance was again halted. The bulk of his force was on his side of the river while those who had made it across were pinned down cowering from the enemy and unable to move.

He considered his options. The hill above was too steep for cavalry to charge. The crossing had to be won on foot. He watched the hill and grunted with satisfaction as two of Lancelot's marksmen fell as his own archers gathered on the river bank and began to return fire.

He turned to the man beside him.

"Form the rest of the men on the river bank and charge that hill. They can't have many arrows left. As soon as I give the word, run, and don't stop running until that hill is ours."

"Yes, sir!"

Camelon was out of reach now but he would, by all the gods, secure a crossing for the queen before nightfall. He looked to the rear where the blood red orb of the sun slid toward the horizon, and shuddered with fear.

I'll lead the charge. I'd sooner die here than at her hand!

"Here they come again."

Lancelot's face was grim. Over half his marksmen lay dead on the hill and he signaled the others to retreat. He counted them as they crested the hill, willing each to safety. Two more fell to enemy arrows, only feet from the top, then the others were clear.

True to his word, Servius led the charge. He came roaring like a bull, his eyes scanning the crest of the hill. He saw Lancelot standing silhouetted against the darkening sky.

"Onward!" he cried, "Kill him!"

His own archers sent clouds of arrows over the river, sweeping the hilltop clear. Free of missile fire his men ran, swarming up the hill, each yelling furiously, shields discarded to give them more speed. Swords drawn, they would not stop. Servius knew the archers that had fired on the river were either waiting for them or fleeing, which he did not care. Whoever commanded this hill would command the ford and he needed that crossing.

Merlin sat astride his horse alongside Lancelot. Before them stood only fifty men, archers all.

In a charging mass of steel and flesh, Servius's men crested the hill and swept onto the reverse side. Their legs were tired and trembled from the frenzied climb. Breathless and uncoordinated they were totally unprepared for what met them. The front ranks tried to stop, many tripping and stumbling, but they were drawn on by gravity, and pushed forward by those behind.

Wooden stakes and spears were driven into the reverse side of the slope only feet from the crest, and behind that several small trenches had been dug, making the ground even more uneven and treacherous. The attackers cried out as they were driven into the hedge of steel, unable to halt their advance.

Many were impaled, dying horribly, and still others slipped and lost their footing falling among their allies, twisting ankles and breaking arms and legs as they fell into the trenches or lost their footing on the loose rocks that had been piled around the spears.

Lancelot was sickened at the carnage he had visited on the enemy, but steeling himself he signaled his men to fire and they loosed the last of their arrows, sweeping the hill clean of their foes.

Servius died slowly. He had fallen on a spear, puncturing a lung and then an arrow had taken him in the throat. He knelt awkwardly, surrounded by his fallen warriors while the survivors of his force fled behind him. He looked below in amazement at an army of thousands drawn up in tight formation across the meadows, their flanks anchored with glittering rows of knights, all clad in the blue and silver of Arturius.

Beside him one of his men, both legs broken, grasped a nearby spear and pulled himself into a sitting position. "My gods, there are thousands of them." His face was ashen and drawn in pain. "How can this be?"

Servius could not speak, the arrow prevented it. He gasped for air, trying desperately to spit the blood from his mouth.

"Why do they not attack? Why do they not finish us?"

A final flight of arrows arched into the evening sky and the man beside Servius stiffened as an arrow pierced his chest.

Servius coughed, blood spraying from his shattered throat. He closed his eyes against the pain, and opened them one last time. Before him the plain was empty, save for Lancelot, and the archers who calmly mounted their horses and rode away. The army was gone, having been nothing more than an illusion conjured up by Merlin. Servius felt his body getting cold. A numbness was spreading through him but his mind burned with the agony and humiliation of defeat. Through glazed eyes he saw his failure all around him in the form of the crumpled and broken bodies of his warriors. He did not feel the tears that trickled from his eyes, and at last darkness took him.

Lancelot had pushed his men to march for two grueling hours. They now lay encamped in the dense woodland twenty miles to the northeast of Din Eidyn. Fires were strictly forbidden, but the men were too tired to complain. Most slept.

"Is it passing?" Lancelot asked. He regarded the wizard with some concern. There had been little time to talk on the hard ride east, but now Merlin lay on a blanket between the trees, his face pale in the darkness.

"Just tired, old friend. Fashioning such an illusion drained me completely."

"Word will have reached Morgause by now. News of such an army will be sure to give her pause."

"She will not believe we were able to marshal such a force. She will know I had something to do with it, but following your masterful defense she will at least move with caution."

Lancelot grinned. "There is another possibility."

Merlin raised himself up, groaning as he did so. "And that is?"

"Perhaps Matt has recovered the crown fragments, and she knows it. Perhaps she may believe Arthur has been awoken and raised an army to challenge her."

Merlin fell back and watched the stars through the canopy of leaves.

"Pray that is so, for she will wait then to link up with Aldivon. That at least will give us time to establish some defensive perimeter at Arthur's Seat."

"Aye. And we must hope still that Matt is on his way."

Justin Orton

Falkirk plain, Scotland
597AD

The weight of the dog across his legs was growing more painful by the minute. They had been riding for days and for the hundredth time Matt silently thanked the villagers who had provided them with the sturdy Garron ponies. The three companions were exhausted and travel sore, but their hardy mounts continued on, picking their way seemingly with ease across the heather hills, and finally onto the rolling grasslands of the Falkirk plain.

We need sleep!

Matt pulled his pony to a stop as they crested a small hillock. It had been dark for several hours.

"We'll stop here for the remainder of the night. Brick—help me with Mia."

Brick silently slid from his mount and hobbled over to Matt. His thighs and back ached terribly from the brutal journey east, but none had taken it as hard as Mia. She was beyond exhaustion, her paws were almost raw from the hours of walking across rugged terrain, her muscles stiff and her fur matted and choked with mud and burrs.

Valina sat slumped in her saddle, watching through bloodshot eyes as Brick took Mia and laid her in a hollow between the twisted roots of a giant oak that crowned their hill. The headaches that had plagued her had been absent for two days now, but the pain of those attacks, lack of sleep, and the constant riding had left her weak and tired beyond anything she had ever known.

"Here..." Matt stood beside her. "Let me help you down."

She smiled weakly and half slid half fell into his waiting arms. She let him hold her awhile, drawing warmth and strength from the feel of him against her, and the comfort of his arms around her. She let her head fall against his chest.

"How much further, Matt?"

"One day, no more." He led her to where Mia lay, and helped her down on to the grass, kneeling beside her. Withdrawing his medallion he felt for the pulsing presence deep inside but his own fatigue was too great. He would have to try and help his companions in the morning.

"I'll tend to the horses."

"I'll get the water then." Brick said, and gathered the water skins from each of their saddles.

Matt watched as Brick limped away in search of the stream they could hear trickling somewhere nearby. He stooped to kiss Valina's hair, blind to its dirty, matted appearance, and caressed her cheek. "I'll be back in a minute."

"I'll be right here." She took his hand. "Thank you, Matt."

"You're welcome."

He walked awkwardly to the horses and removed their bridles, then pulled a rope from his saddle and led them to the oak. He secured the horses to it, making sure he left enough rope for them to graze. The sturdy animals had consumed the last of the grain the day before, and despite their stamina the horses looked travel worn and hungry.

He rummaged in his pack and brought out several lengths of twine cut from their fishing line, along with several sticks sharpened at one end. Valina was asleep, so he made his way quietly down the hill, noting the sandy earth and the holes dug in it. Signs of rabbit were everywhere and he placed his snares carefully, hoping to catch at least two good-sized ones by morning. They desperately needed to eat something more substantial than dried fish and molding bread.

Returning to Valina, he noted Brick had yet to return with the water skins. Quietly he lay down beside the girl and draped his blanket over them. Beside him Valina tossed fitfully and he worried about a return of the headaches. Since becoming convinced that Brick was not to be trusted he had kept a careful eye on him, and now cursed himself for allowing the other boy to go off alone to fill the water skins.

He thought briefly of getting up and following him to the stream, but he could not bring himself to move and quickly fell into an exhausted sleep. Beside him Valina continued to toss and turn, her breathing becoming more ragged and uneven. Beads of sweat broke out on her brow, and her lips moved as if she argued in silence with some unknown intruder. Suddenly she stiffened and her eyes opened wide in terror.

Chapter 26
To Kill a King

The river Forth, Scotland
597AD

They had risen before sunrise.

The flood plain of the river Forth stretched for miles and the land here was fertile and predominantly flat. They rode at a mile-eating canter.

"Lancelot!"

Lancelot and Merlin reined their horses as a rider galloped to the head of the column.

"What is it?"

The man who had called pointed to the south where a rider could be seen pushing his horse to the limit. "A scout, my lord."

Lancelot raised his hand signaling the men to halt.

Several minutes passed before the scout caught up to them. The man was caked in dirt and his horse was lathered and blowing hard.

"Get this man water, and tend to his horse!"

Two men ran quickly to take the tired animal, while another passed the grateful messenger a bulging water skin. Lancelot vaguely recognized the face before him.

"Murdoch?"

"Aye, my lord."

"What news?"

"Morgause. She has crossed the river and advances on Camelon." Murdoch was excited, his words tumbling out between gasps for breath. "Sir—Aldivon is deploying to oppose her."

"What?"

"Aldivon. His forces have marched from the Clyde and they stage at Camelon, denying access to the remains of the fort. They also command the approaches to Invalone. His units are massed in battle formation, and troops are preparing defensive positions."

Lancelot's horse pranced nervously and he pulled it around gruffly to face Merlin.

"What make you of this?"

"It's clear they believe Arthur is either at Invalone or Camelon, but why would Aldivon stand against the queen?" The old man's brow furrowed in concentration, a worried expression on his face. "Long he's been in her council. Maybe our troublesome general feels a king would be better placed to open the portal than a queen? But the man's no fool. He knows her powers. Only a madman would stand against her unless he had an advantage."

Lancelot smiled, "Having stood against her at the bridge I'll take that as a compliment."

Merlin ignored the quip. "I need to see this. Bring me a bowl and water. Have your men stand down. I will need some time."

Lancelot nodded and signaled his men to fetch the items Merlin had requested, then rode back along the column instructing the men to dismount and rest. Returning to the head of the troop he watched as Merlin sat hunched over the water bowl. He was struck by the same feeling he'd felt days ago when first encountering the old man in the chamber deep beneath the crags of Arthur's Seat. Then, like now, there was something about his mannerisms that was different; he lacked the mirth and gentleness of the friend Lancelot had once known. He was somehow colder. Was it simply the ravages of time? Stress over Matt? Or was there something more?

He shook off the odd feeling and led his horse up the gentle slopes of a nearby hill. To the east the towering crags of Arthur's Seat could be clearly seen. They were close, perhaps little more than three hours away.

Matt startled awake. He knew he had slept too long. Valina was not beside him and he threw the blanket aside, sitting up and rubbing at his eyes. A painful kick in the back sent him sprawling across the grass and he rolled defensively, ignoring the burst of pain in his injured shoulder.

Four men stood around him, swords leveled at his throat.

"Don't move, boy!"

"Don't hurt him!" It was Valina. A quick glance around their camp site revealed Valina held by two men while two others held their packs and equipment. Brick was nowhere to be seen.

Matt struggled to rise.

"I said don't move!"

Matt cried out as a boot slammed into his side. The blow caused him to cough and pain racked his chest as he gasped for air. Instinctively he curled himself into a ball and groaned.

"Please!" Valina was sobbing. Matt forced his eyes open. Dirt and tears clung to the lashes, making it difficult to focus, but he could see her struggling against her captors, her cheeks streaked with tears. His mind raced to figure out what had happened and his fingers fumbled for the Pendragon about his neck.

Brick must have betrayed them. He cursed himself for allowing the other boy to leave the camp alone. The pain lessened a little as he clasped the medallion in his hand.

Where was Mia?

He reached out with his mind. He felt nothing. A cold feeling of dread settled in the pit of his stomach. She had been so tired, too exhausted to offer any resistance. He pushed himself to his knees, this time calling aloud, his voice cracking with fear, shrill with desperation. He stood, the Pendragon in one hand, the other pressed to his throbbing side.

"Mia!"

One of the men reversed his sword and struck Matt a crushing blow to the base of the neck. His vision swam and his knees buckled, but he managed to hang on to consciousness and somehow stagger forward. He let the momentum of the blow carry him and he fell hard against one of the men holding Valina. Grabbing a fist full of the man's cloak he drove his knee hard into the man's unprotected groin.

"Where is she?" he yelled. "Where's my fucking dog!" The man fell back, gasping from the unexpected assault. Matt was screaming now and beat at the man's face as the pair fell to the ground rolling in the dirt. "What have you done with her you bastard! What have you done!"

Two pairs of hands grabbed Matt, and he felt himself pulled roughly upright, his arms wrenched painfully behind.

"Bind him!"

Matt continued to struggle even as they tied him but it was to no avail and he soon found himself stumbling beside Valina as they were dragged from the hill.

"I'm so sorry, Matt. I'm so sorry."

Matt coughed, spitting grass, dirt and blood from his mouth. His entire body throbbed and he coughed again. "It's not your fault…"

Valina shook her head, and fresh tears ran down her cheeks. "You don't understand. It is my fault!" She was sobbing now. "I'm so sorry. Oh god, Matt, I'm so sorry!"

Matt was startled by the anguish in her voice. He wanted to comfort her but did not know what to say. "Valina—" he began but she cut him off.

"Matt...please believe me...I love you...I—"

He felt his emotions soar but the pair were jerked roughly apart.

"Valina—"

A rope swung into view and Matt received a painful lash across the cheek. His head snapped back from the blow and fresh pain erupted in his face. The coppery taste of blood filled his mouth.

"The next one to speak will be responsible for the other's death. Now enough!"

They were then dragged in silence for almost half a mile to a small encampment at the base of the hill. It was set amid a stand of willow trees adjacent to the stream they had heard the night before. Two soldiers stood guard over several horses, and Matt noted their Garrons among them.

"We have them! Let's not keep Her Majesty waiting!"

Matt was helped into the saddle and ropes were passed through the stirrups, securing him to the horse. He slumped against the neck of the animal as they bound him to it. He had failed. The queen would awaken Arthur now—she would locate the rod and open the gateway to Mars. The world would be destroyed. Weak with pain and fatigue he could no longer hold back the despair.

He thought of his mother and felt a deep sadness that he would never know her touch, never hear that soothing lilting voice from his dreams.

I was going to come for you Mum.

A tiny spark of anger burned inside and he clung to it, feeding it, fighting the pain in his body and the utter anguish of despair that threatened to extinguish it.

Matt tried to sit a little straighter but his neck was stiff, and his vision swam. He let his chin slump forward and watched the blood that dripped from his mouth and nose darken to a dirty brown smudge on the torn, grass-stained material of his tunic. Several of the wooden toggles had been ripped away and he could see the Pendragon resting against the metal coils of his corslet. He stared hard, trying to draw strength from the medallion but he felt nothing. Blood now dripped onto the oily rings of his mail shirt. He watched, mesmerized, as it collected on one ring, and then ran slowly to another. Fascinated, he followed the little trail of crimson until his eyes were drawn to a pocket on the inside of his tunic and there, disturbed by the recent fight, was a tuft of soft white fur.

It was the tuft he had cut from Mia the day he had tried to say goodbye. He felt the well of tears in his eyes but he swallowed them back. He would not cry, not yet. Instead he allowed her loss to feed his anger. Within him the tiny spark of defiance flickered into flame.

Matt fought back the pain and fatigue and looked around the camp. Alone, he would have tried to run, tried anything, even welcoming a quick death rather than the torture he knew would be visited on him by the queen. He started to shake, recalling the terror of that night in the stone circle, the knife poised above his heart, the cold gleam of steel in moonlight.

But he was not alone. He had Valina.

Valina.

Even the sound of her name. She had said she loved him. The warmth of that feeling tempered the anger but with it he felt a new strength inside. He looked across to the girl but a rider blocked his view. He gave his horse a gentle nudge but his attention was instead drawn to the trees. There, by the willows, was Brick.

Din Eidyn, Scotland
597AD

The sun beat warmly on Lancelot's face, and a gentle breeze ruffled the dark waves of his hair. He looked at the glistening clear waters of the river, and the delicate buds of flowers that seemed to await some unspoken command before opening their petals and filling the meadow with color. He could almost sense Guenevere beside him and he pictured her long blond hair alight with the morning sun, her skin soft and pale, her lips warm and inviting. It was a beautiful morning, a day promising peace, a day promising life, a day for love.

"I miss you still." He breathed the words softly, and imagined her reply whispered on the wind. They would have ridden to a place such as this. Strolled among the flowers, sat together dreaming dreams and drinking honey wine cooled by the crystal river water, while eating salmon, and bread baked fresh that morning.

"Lancelot!"

Lancelot sat, pulling himself from the day dream. Merlin waved to him from atop the hill, beckoning his return to the column. With a final look at the river and the budding flowers, he swung into the saddle and urged his horse to where the wizard waited.

"Well? What news?"

"Grave. I fear Matt may be lost to us. Aldivon knows all. Even now he makes for the crags while his army is positioned to delay, or distract, Morgause—which I do not know."

Lancelot's face grew stern. "Matt is lost? How can you know this?"

"I first sent my sight to Camelon and Invalone, to confirm the disposition of Aldivon's forces. Your scout was right. Camelon and Invalone are both defended, and a large reserve force comprising cavalry and light foot remains in the center. He can move them quickly to crush the flank of an attack against either location."

"And Morgause?"

"She has not men enough to engage both forces, and must decide where best to use her strength. For now she waits. Her mind was closed to me. No doubt she has taken measures to guard against scrying."

"And Matt?"

"I was unable to locate Aldivon with his army. I widened my search and finally found him. He travels east at a great pace, with a force numbering close to two hundred, all light cavalry."

"East? To the crags?"

"Aye, to the crags. They were riding hard and this made my contact tenuous at best. That he has been in contact with the boy is beyond question. He knows of the crown fragments and their purpose."

"And the boy?"

"The boy was not with him. I searched everywhere. I fear he may have succeeded in recovering the crown, only to fall foul of Aldivon on his return to us. We must assume the worst."

"You believe Aldivon has the crown?"

"Why else would he ride to Din Eidyn? Morgause controls the magic users. He has no way to read Arthur's mind and divine from him the location of the rod. He must therefore awaken him—and the crown is the only way to do that. Arthur will be weak when he wakes, and vulnerable. Aldivon can easily gain the location of the rod."

"Arthur would never betray such a secret. Even under torture. And if he did, with the rod in Aldivon's hands and the crystals in hers the gate still cannot be opened."

Lancelot paused and regarded the wizard quizzically. "How can Aldivon use the crown? The spells that suspend time around Arthur would need to be removed first—"

"It's possible he does not know of the suspension of time. He may simply believe that joining the crown will awaken him. But—there is more. Aldivon is not fully without power. I felt it. It rides with him. A great and menacing power. I fear this presence could be used against Arthur and the location of the rod will be revealed. Aldivon will then use him as bait against the queen."

"Bait? To what end?"

"Morgause is driven by very powerful emotions. Hatred and love. Her hatred for me and for Arthur drives her lust for revenge. She would stop at nothing to see us dead but you must also remember it was her love for Dardanos that caused her to attempt to turn back time in the first place. The world beyond moves on, Lancelot. Centuries have passed. She may believe the power of the key can be used to break the rift and turn time back to before the death of Dardanos."

"Is such a thing possible?"

"All things are possible, and should such an act be successful it would destroy the world beyond our own. The thousands of years of progress that have been made, the billions of lives that now inhabit this world—all would be snuffed out in an instant. Then with Dardanos once more among us he will open the gate and destroy this world utterly."

"So what does Aldivon stand to gain by directly confronting Morgause?"

"He has already bottled up her forces. Once Arthur is woken he will play on Morgause's desire to see Arthur dead, enticing her to the cavern to destroy Arthur."

"It would be suicide. The man must know he cannot defeat her."

"He doesn't plan to. He already knows I will be there. Morgause and I have yet to fully test our strength against each other. Should we do so we would be completely vulnerable to mundane attack. Aldivon knows he could easily defeat us both then. He would take the crystals, the rod and the throne, all in one move."

"So how do we stop him?"

"I must leave you. I alone can reach Arthur before Aldivon. You must ride with all haste and do all in your power to keep him and the crown from Arthur's hall."

"And what will you do?"

"We are here today by my folly and mine alone. Had Arthur died as he himself requested, the secret of the rod would have gone to the grave with him. By living Arthur serves none but the enemy."

Tears glistened in the old man's eyes.

"I fear 'tis time, my friend."

"Kill him?" Lancelot was incredulous. "Did you yourself not council against that years ago, citing then that none would know the location of the rod, and if it should be found by chance along with the crystals, what then? By living he has remained a focal point for the rod's location, by living we've had one place to guard, one thing to protect!" Lancelot tried to keep his anger in check. "This cannot be!"

"There is no other way!"

The wizard turned his back, focusing his will as he prepared to translocate himself to Arthur's hall, deep beneath the rocky crags of Arthur's Seat.

"Merlin, no! You cannot do this!"

But it was too late. All that remained of the wizard's presence were the crushed stems of meadow flowers and the bent and broken blades of grass where he had stood.

Tears of anger stung Lancelot's eyes as in a fury he swung up into the saddle and jabbed cruelly at his horse. The startled animal leaped forward, clods of grass and dirt flying as Lancelot descended the hill toward his resting men.

Matt's shoulders had finally gone numb. All that remained now was the incessant thirst.

They had arrived in the queen's encampment about an hour before. Valina had been taken away and Matt had been hung by the wrists from a branch of an ancient oak, with a gag thrust into his mouth. Despite the burning in his throat and the numbing ache in his arms and shoulders, he could think of little but what may be befalling Valina.

"You thirsty, boy?" Two guards had been left to watch him and had spent the past hour tormenting him.

"Here!"

They threw a cup of water at him and he probed desperately at the cloth in his mouth but the rag remained dry and his swollen tongue stuck to it, causing him to retch. He felt the precious water run from his cheeks and drip from his chin.

His captors laughed, slapping each other on the back as they walked away.

Matt closed his eyes, seeking comfort in the mind exercises Merlin had taught him, but the moment he did so he was haunted by the sight of Brick's body laying beneath the stand of willow trees. The boy's lifeless eyes had stared directly at him, one arm flung out as if imploring Matt to somehow help him. Brick had evidently been cut down without warning the night before as he returned from the river with the heavy water skins. The lamb's wool jerkin he had worn was stained a dark red from the single slash across the back. Matt felt again the crushing weight of guilt for his earlier mistrust of the boy.

It was clear now that neither of his companions could have been the traitor Aldivon had warned him of. He just hoped Brick had died quickly and not suffered too much.

A shadow passed across his eyes and he opened them to see one of the guards standing before him. Rough hands pulled the rag from his mouth and held a wooden bowl of water to his dry and bleeding lips.

"Drink."

Matt gulped the water down sobbing at each spilled mouthful. He coughed and fell heavily to the ground as the knots about his wrists were cut. The rush of blood into his arms and hands brought the nerves alive and he cried out at the sudden onset of fresh pain.

"Get up! The queen wishes to speak with you."

He swayed unsteadily on his legs and allowed the men to turn him to face the woman who now stood beneath the tree. Behind her Valina stood, her hands bound in front of her and her face flushed. Matt breathed a sigh of relief. She had not been beaten, at least not yet. He tried to smile but it was a grimace. He could almost see his pain reflected in her gaze. She lowered her eyes, and he looked to the queen.

"You have been busy since last we met." The queen's voice was cold, her anger barely held in check.

"It would have been far better had Merlin allowed me to kill you at our last meeting."

Matt remained silent. He knew what was coming and it was all he could do to keep control of himself.

"Where is he, Matt? Where is Arthur?"

Matt looked at the ground, and clenched his jaw. He pictured Mia in his mind's eye and clung to the memory of her, determined to resist Morgause for as long as he could, hoping that somehow he could die before she hurt him enough to drag the truth from him.

The nearest guard grabbed a handful of hair and pulled his head back sharply. "You will look at the queen when she speaks."

The man's breath stank.

The queen held out Matt's bag containing the precious crown fragments. "Where were you taking this Matt? Was it Invalone? Camelon?"

He felt a surge of hope.

Lie!

She would keep him alive until she knew the truth.

"It is useless to lie to me."

He could feel the pressure of her mind probing his own and knew she spoke the truth. While the medallion about his neck might have offered protection from her power, preventing her plucking the location from his thoughts, she would clearly know if he lied.

The queen raised a slender hand and clenched her fist. There was a tightening in his chest, and he gasped for breath. The pain became intense and his knees buckled.

"I can take the pain away, Matt. It can all end now. Just tell me what I want to know." Her voice was somehow soothing, a counterpoint to the pain, offering release, and comfort. It could all end now if he just told her what she wanted to know.

He raised his head and felt the pressure ease in his chest. A glowing red nimbus had formed in the queen's hands, and there beating in her fist was the image of a heart. With horror he realized it was his own.

"Well?"

Her fingers slowly tightened and then his vision became a white fire and agony burned in his chest. His body jerked spasmodically and he experienced the crushing pain of a heart attack.

"A cavern!" He was gasping, his body convulsing as the blood stopped pumping and his muscles became starved of oxygen.

"The crags—please—oh god let it stop!"

Mercifully the pressure eased and he sucked in mouthfuls of air, not remembering when anything had tasted so sweet.

"A cavern? Crags? Where, Matt? Where?" Her voice was desperate, a hungry urgency in her words.

He rolled in the grass and tried to regain his knees. He opened his eyes and through streaming tears could see Valina struggling to break free and run to him. Her mouth was moving but he couldn't make out the words. He felt dirty. What had he done? What had he said? He had betrayed everyone! He had told her where Arthur was!

No. You have not, not yet—

But I will!

With a terrifying clarity he knew he would tell all. He could never endure that pain again.

Matt held his chest with one hand, and struggled to push himself up with the other.

"Get down!" a guard pushed him down with a heavy boot and he collapsed again to the grass.

"What crags, Matt?" She took a step forward. "Where is he?"

The queen's hand reached out once more and her fingers hooked like claws into the pounding image of his heart.

Matt gave a blood-curdling scream and clenched his hands so tightly the jagged and broken nails of his fingers dug painfully into his palms. He managed to gasp a shallow breath, arching his back as he fought for air. Just a few more minutes and it would be over. He could feel the onset of death. Just a few more seconds to resist and Morgause would have gone too far. Matt's vision was darkening, the searing white light now a spinning tunnel along which his tortured mind sought to escape. He wanted to die. He prayed for death, begged for this nightmare to end.

A roaring sound filled Matt's ears, punctuated with the pounding beat of his faltering heart.

Oh god, let it stop!

He tried to will the growing darkness to swallow him, and then above the throbbing roar in his ears came another sound. A voice he would recognize anywhere, a voice he had come to love. He could hear Valina, her voice coming from a great distance as she cried out, finally breaking free of the men who held her.

"Mother, no!"

For a moment the pain eased. The tunnel of light blinked out and the darkness became a red haze through which he could make out the ghostly shape of figures. Valina was on her knees tugging on Morgause's dress, her eyes awash with tears, imploring her.

"Din Eidyn. He was taking them to a cavern beneath the crags at Din Eidyn."

Mother?

Matt struggled to make sense of the words.

"Mother, please. Don't hurt him. No more. Please." The girl was sobbing uncontrollably and the queen slapped her away, her expression a mixture of disgust and triumph.

Chapter 27
Revelations

Arthur's Sear, Scotland.
597AD

A rthur's Seat is a dramatic upthrust of land rising above the Firth-of-Forth and the city of Edinburgh. On three sides it falls away to almost sheer and jagged cliffs, while the fourth side is a more gentle slope leading to the grassy plateau beneath the summit. For the two forces converging on it there was simply no time to deploy.

Coming from the southwest Aldivon had an almost direct approach to the gentle slope at the rear of the escarpment and already his men were urging their mounts up the grassy incline.

Lancelot had ridden like a man possessed. He led his small force on lathered horses beneath the towering crags, pulling their straining mounts up the steep grassy banks that led onto the saddle of land behind.

Both sides were surprised by the appearance of the other and what ensued was a disorganized clash of mounted men. Lancelot's smaller force crashed into the unsuspecting flank of the other. Few of the men even had time to draw weapons, but those that did dealt swift and deadly blows. Several riders slumped in their saddles and a handful of horses ran riderless as the two groups of horsemen swept apart, pulling their tired mounts around in a desperate bid to do battle with the other.

With little room to maneuver and no time for formations, the next several minutes saw a chaotic running battle between isolated groups of combatants. Yelled warnings, savage curses, and unheeded instructions were punctuated by the wild neighs and screams of horses and the relentless ring of steel on steel. Swords gleamed in the midday sun and each rider was caught up in a fierce fight for survival as he sought to keep his horse away from the sheer drop of the escarpment while struggling to overthrow his enemy.

"Disengage!" Lancelot barked instructions but his men were scattered and they either failed to heed his order or were unable to follow it.

"To the cavern!" A small detachment remained close to Lancelot and they tried desperately to drive a wedge toward the escarpment. Lancelot led with reckless abandon, dealing blows left and right as he fought to clear a path.

"To me!" Lancelot's sword was red with blood and his cloak was torn, rent where glancing blows had cut the cloth only to be turned aside by the chain mail beneath.

Eight of his men joined him at the escarpment edge and they leaped from their horses, turning the terrified mounts loose to add confusion to the frantic battle.

One of Aldivon's men rode too close and Lancelot swept the man from his saddle. He hit the ground hard and lay there stunned. Without pause Lancelot plunged his sword into the shocked man's chest. "To me! To me!"

Aldivon surveyed the hill top. He noticed the gathering of men at the escarpment edge and yelled commands to his personal guard. He had the advantage, but only in the open. If Lancelot reached the caverns any narrow space would lead to a bloody battle of attrition, a fight he knew he could win, but one he wanted to avoid.

More men were gathering around Lancelot now, and those with bows used them with devastating effect, picking off the milling riders as they sought for targets.

Aldivon cursed. He was losing the initiative. Quickly he began rallying his men, bellowing instructions left and right.

The lull in the fight allowed Lancelot time to urge his men to fall back toward the narrow ledge that led to the cavern entrance. There was less than a hundred yards of rocky ground to cover. Would they make it? He looked around, his face grim and spattered with blood, his hair matted with sweat. Of the fifty riders that had accompanied him onto the plateau, less than half remained.

They all heard the bellowed command to charge and the glinting of the sun's rays on the forest of drawn swords was like a fire from the heavens. Lancelot's men took a hesitant step backward.

"Stand!" Lancelot's voice was steady and masked the fear he felt at the oncoming rush of death and destruction.

"They cannot charge the cliff! Two volleys then we run."

The thunder of hooves made the ground shake and the clatter of falling rocks behind reminded the men how perilously close they were to the drop.

"Loose!"

The first volley arched high into the sky before falling on the approaching riders. Most of the arrows fell long, but enough riders went down to cause mayhem in the formation as horses crashed headlong into those before them.

"Loose!"

The second volley was more direct, but Aldivon had wheeled his formation right, taking them parallel to Lancelot's position. Several horses screamed and their riders were thrown, to be trampled by those behind. A horse, free of its rider, swerved from the formation, seeking escape from the madness of battle. It galloped directly at Lancelot's men and too late saw the escarpment. Lancelot threw himself to the ground as a shower of stones sprayed across him and then his sword went tumbling over the cliff, knocked from his hand as a hoof clipped his shoulder with stunning force. Cursing, he struggled upright in time to see two of his men swept over the edge along with the crazed animal.

Further up the hill Aldivon's men were dismounting. Some drew bows of their own.

Lancelot struggled to his feet and pulled a knife from his belt. "To the cave!"

The drop to his left seemed to suck at him as he ran, making him giddy with vertigo. He ignored it, leaping the bodies of his fallen men and exhorting those around him to greater efforts.

Aldivon's men were all on foot now. Leaving their horses, they cut across the escarpment in a desperate bid to cut off the path to the cave. Once more it became a running battle, men stopping to hack at their pursuers, breaking free and then straining on, ever upwards, lungs burning, pulse racing, legs rubbery with fatigue.

From his mount Aldivon watched. Lancelot would reach the cavern first—of that he was sure. He looked around. Was there no other way? A flash of green to the east caught his attention and he stood in the stirrups to get a better view. There it was again. Something fluttered in the stunted shrubs that clung to the edge of the crags on the far side of the plateau. He pulled his mount around and rode at breakneck speed across the escarpment.

The grayness around him ripped apart and with an ear-splitting crack Matt found himself stumbling forward into the light. Weak from the recent abuse and disoriented from the translocation he was powerless to act and found himself quickly dragged to his feet by the soldier who had held him. Twice more the air split apart like ripping fabric and Morgause, Valina and two soldiers stumbled onto the plateau.

"My queen!" the man that held Matt shouted urgently. "Look! There below!"

Matt looked in the direction of the man's outflung arm and saw the large body of horsemen that raced for the plateau on which they stood.

"It's Aldivon!"

The queen turned to Matt. "Time grows short, boy. Where is the entrance?"

Matt sneered at Valina. "Ask your daughter—she seems to know everything."

The slap made his ears rings.

"Where is it?"

"Matt. Please—" Valina tried to reach out for him but one of the soldiers restrained her.

"You, shut up!" The queen's voice was shrill, her face drawn from the effort of the translocation she had just performed. Her fingers clenched and Matt felt again the stirrings of pain in his chest.

He looked at Valina. "All along you were using me." Tears welled in his eyes now as he looked once more to the queen. "You killed my mother, you killed my dog. Do you think I give a shit if you kill me?" He pressed forward, straining against the grip of the man that held him. "Come on bitch, do it! Kill me!"

The horsemen were out of sight now but the thunder of hooves could be heard as they swept around the escarpment.

Valina finally broke free of her guard and ducked quickly beneath his arm. Her thick woolen cloak snagged on the gorse bushes as she lunged toward Matt. She tugged at the clasp about her neck and tore free of the cloak, leaving it whipping in the wind as she dove to the ground before Matt.

"She did not kill your mother Matt, nor did I betray you!" She clutched at his legs even as her guard stooped to drag her away from the boy. "I aided your mother's escape. For that I was to die unless I agreed to spy on you!" The man had her now but she flipped to her back and lashed out. Her kick broke his grip and she pulled herself up turning again to Matt. "I fell in love with you, Matt. I wanted us to run away, but you would not forsake your quest. Remember the headaches? Remember the pain I suffered? That was me resisting her!" She pointed to the queen. "She broke into my mind the night we were captured. She swore she would kill you unless I brought her to you. I did what I did to save your life!"

Valina was crying now and she turned to face Morgause standing as a shield before Matt. "You promised, Mother. You promised!"

Morgause stepped forward and lashed out hard. The slap sent Valina reeling.

Matt struggled to make sense of what he had just heard. "You freed my mother?"

Valina looked back; a trickle of blood ran from the corner of her mouth, and her beautiful green eyes brimmed with tears. She searched his face and nodded.

"Where? Where did she go? Where is she?"

She took a step toward him, "I—" then her face twisted in agony and she stumbled, clutching at her chest. She took one more drunken step and Matt caught her as she fell. Her body twitched and writhed in his arms and her feet beat at the stony soil. Matt looked up to where Morgause stood before them, a beating heart clasped in her hand, her fingers hooked into the pulsating image.

"Let her go!"

The din of battle broke out on the plateau behind them and the soldiers closed ranks, drawing swords to protect their queen. Morgause could not hide the urgency in her voice.

"Tell me, Matt. Refuse and I kill her. Tell me and I'll let you go, both of you."

"Stop!" Matt's cry was desperate.

"The cave!" Morgause clenched her fingers tighter. "Now!"

Valina's face was purple and her hands tore at her throat as she struggled to breathe. Her back arched and her neck stretched as she convulsed, throwing her head back into Matt's lap. He looked down into her terrified eyes. There was a desperate pleading there, a pleading for forgiveness, for understanding, and above all for release.

He suddenly saw her not as she was now, but as she had been on the boat. He felt again the softness of her kiss, the warmth of her mouth against his. He held her close, cradling her body in his arms.

"I'll tell you! Just stop! Please. You're killing her!"

The queen relaxed her grip but still the stuttering image of the heart remained in her hand. Valina collapsed to the ground, sucking in air, before coughing violently. She rolled from his arms onto her side and vomited into the dirt.

"Well...?" The queen raised the heart toward him, fingers clenching one more.

"No! Don't!" Matt stood up. "I'll lead you to it. I swear!"

Lancelot's ears rang with the clamor of battle and he yelled as he flung himself at two men who were about to overtake one of his own. Wrapping his arms around their necks he pulled them down, slashing at the throat of one with his knife. The blow went wide and the knife left a bloody furrow across the man's face barely missing an eye. The three went down in a tangle of limbs.

Several of Lancelot's men had reached the ledge that led to the cave entrance and they formed a line covering their comrades with bow fire. For a moment it looked as if they would prevail; their steady fire was taking a heavy toll and Aldivon's men were paying for each foot of ground they gained.

Arms slick with blood, Lancelot roared as he regained his feet. Another man loomed beside him and he thrust upwards taking the man in the throat.

The knife was wrenched from Lancelot's hand as the man fell, gurgling horribly as he drowned in his own blood. Unarmed, Lancelot looked around for a weapon as two more soldiers lunged at him. The first suddenly flew backward, felled by the force of the arrow that took him in the chest, and then the other was upon him.

Lancelot failed to avoid the blow and fire erupted in his thigh as the sword sliced across his leg. He struggled up, back-pedaling away from his attacker, but his injured leg failed and he fell again. Eager for the kill, his adversary lunged forward but an arrow took him in the arm, knocking him off balance.

Lancelot lashed out with his good leg, sweeping the injured man off his feet. The soldier fell back into a sitting position and before he could rise first one then a second arrow thudded into his stomach. The man remained slumped in the dirt and Lancelot crawled toward him and pulled the sword from the dead man's grip.

"My lord, come, we must flee!" Two soldiers ran to Lancelot's aid, and using the sword as a prop he forced himself to his feet and hobbled with them onto the ledge.

His shoulder throbbed from the blow from the horse and his leg burned as if hit by a blazing torch. Blood ran thick from the gaping wound.

His men had spent the last of their arrows covering his retreat and they now formed a shield wall as he passed. Slowly he and the last of his men fell back into the darkness of the cave.

When Merlin opened his eyes it looked as if the cavern was on fire. The candles previously frozen in time had simply glowed, but now, released from the spell, they flickered and danced in the currents of air that drifted through the vast underground chamber. Tendrils of smoke curved up and away and the air had become warmer and thick with the scent of burning tallow.

Merlin was tired. The days of hard riding, the battle with Morgause's army, the scrying of Aldivon, and the translocation here had left him almost drained of energy.

He had rested for over an hour in the cavern, building his strength for the task ahead, but even so this last work had weakened him further and he clutched at his staff, grateful for its support.

He looked across the bridge at the recumbent form of Arthur. The would-be king's chest was no longer frozen in time, but rose and fell with each breath and Merlin half expected him to stir into wakefulness. Part of him wished he would, for then he would not have to do what he had come to do. That Lancelot would ride after him was beyond question. He imagined the earnest soldier pushing his horse to the utmost as he raced to prevent Arthur's death. How long had it been since he had left him? Even now he could be approaching the escarpment.

The old man took a hesitant step toward the bridge that crossed the chasm in the cavern floor. He paused by the pedestal that held the single crown fragment he had placed there days before.

"You at least can remain here," he whispered, and with heavy heart he stepped carefully onto the bridge.

The bridge was stout. Built to enable four men to carry the dead weight of Arthur, it barely swayed as Merlin rushed across, but the thick ropes that suspended it still creaked ominously. The heavy thump of his staff on the stout oak planks echoed around the chamber and he closed his mind to the dizzying drop below.

Aldivon ran the soft wool through his fingers. The sound of battle still rang behind him but it no longer mattered. He had found the entrance. It had been cleverly concealed behind shrubs and a large hanging slab of rock, but now the bushes had been hacked apart and ripped to one side. He could see the tunnel angled steeply into the ground and he once more fingered the woolen cloak. Who had left it here? Who was ahead of him? Was he walking into a trap? Had Lancelot deliberately led him to the far side of the plateau in an attempt to keep the tunnel's location a secret, or were there two entrances into the cavern below? He drew his sword and steeled himself for what lay ahead. With one hand on the tunnel wall he inched his way slowly into the absolute blackness of the passage.

As soon as they had entered the tunnel, Morgause had stopped and issued curt instructions to her soldiers. Both Valina and Matt were bound and gagged, then steered through the tunnel by their captors. Morgause led the way, a faint glow emanating from the hand she held before her, while the third soldier brought up the rear. He clutched the leather bag that contained the remains of the broken crown and shuffled in the darkness, anxious not to lose sight of those ahead. Both Matt and Valina stumbled often, and their lungs ached for air. The natural confines of the tunnel were claustrophobic enough but the gags made it worse. The filthy rags cut from their own garments prevented them breathing freely and they were forced to take in what air they could through their noses.

Valina wanted to scream, but her one attempt had simply drawn the coarse material deeper into her mouth, choking her and causing her to panic for several minutes.

Matt's mind raced. He had to do something, but what? He could not deny his feelings for Valina although he still wrestled with her actions. Had she really tried to prevent this, and then only acted to save his life? He would only know the answers to that if they survived this ordeal, but more pressing was the news of his mother. What had Valina done for her? Where had she taken her? For now, Valina was the only person in the world who knew anything of his mother, and the fact she might still be alive gave him a renewed reason to live.

The mind-numbing despair he had felt before was gone. Now, despite his aching tortured body, he sought for any opportunity to escape.

Merlin pulled the knife from Arthur's belt and laid it gently on the sleeping man's chest. He had known this man since he was a babe and had loved him as a son. Now he must take the life he had labored so hard to shape and protect.

Locked in time, Arthur had not aged nor had his hair grown. He looked no different from the day he had been placed here. His hair was brushed and pulled back from his face, spilling across the crimson and gold-trimmed pillows that cradled his head. A faint line of stubble gave a steel tinge to a broad and angular jaw, and shallow lines at the corner of his eyes fanned out toward his temples. The proud nose and broad cheekbones, even in sleep, spoke of a strength and sternness that those who had seen him in life would oft times see swept away by a smile that was boyish yet roguishly handsome.

Tears ran unashamedly down Merlin's cheeks as he beheld the man on the bier before him.

"It wasn't supposed to end this way, my son."

He ran an old and callused hand across Arthur's cheek. "I have failed you, failed us all. I've doomed this world to disaster, and only you can save it. Your death will save us all." Merlin felt the weight of his years pressing upon him like the vast bulk of the mountain above. He wiped away the tears and took up the knife.

But he could not strike. His hand shook as he wrestled with indecision. Would the onset of death break the spell that bound him in slumber? Would Arthur awaken in the searing agony of the blow, and see Merlin standing there with dripping blade in hand, and never know for what or why he died?

I cannot do it! Merlin lowered the blade, just as the sound of hurried footsteps echoed in the cavern across the bridge.

Lancelot clenched his jaw against the pain as one of his men pulled the leather thong tight across his thigh. The makeshift tourniquet held and the flow of blood lessened. He cursed the wound and his inability to walk unaided. Faint from loss of blood, he had fallen back into the tunnel while his men valiantly held the entrance.

"Help me up."

He leaned against the wall, breathing hard, and waited for his head to clear.

"I have to stop him."

"My lord, you must rest. We can hold them here."

Lancelot shook his head, "You don't understand. He's going to kill him. Help me back to the cavern—the rest of you hold this passage with your lives."

"Sir –"

The man stopped talking as everyone looked to the tunnel entrance. Aldivon's men had paid dearly to gain entrance to the tunnel, and many lay dead along the tunnel floor. For several minutes no attack had come, but now renewed activity could be seen. Men had cut broom and gorse and made bundles from the spiked bushes. These they lit, and as their lead soldiers fell back from the tunnel mouth, those behind thrust the burning bundles forward, pushing them into the tunnel with spears. Others fanned at the flames with their cloaks, driving the choking smoke into the tunnel.

Lancelot's men fell back, coughing and spluttering in the acrid and pungent smoke that swirled about them. Many tore strips of cloth from their cloaks and quickly bound them across their faces. As the heat intensified so the cloaks of the dead that littered the tunnel floor started to smoke and the exposed hair and flesh of the fallen began to sizzle and burn. The air became rank with the smell of smoke and burning flesh.

A frantic rustling began above Lancelot's head.

The bats! He had forgotten the bats. They would be unable to escape the tunnel in the smoke that now rolled in oily black clouds across the ceiling.

The terrified creatures would add mayhem and confusion to his already demoralized force. They had to fall back, but in the open space of the cavern he could not hope to overcome Aldivon's men.

"Steady now!" he tried to shout but the smoke burned his throat and he coughed. His men pressed further back.

"Keep together!"

Already he was formulating a plan. His men looked to him for strength; their faces clearly showed the terror barely held in check. The black rock walls of the tunnel closed around them and the angry red light of the fire gave everything a hellish cast.

"When we reach the cavern, form two lines on either side of the entrance. They cannot be allowed to break into the cavern or we will be overcome!"

No one acknowledged his statement, for at that moment a thunderous explosion of sound pressed around them as the bats left their roost. Men flailed at their heads and beat at the little fury bodies that flapped all around them. Faces were scratched and bitten, and bats became entangled in hair. Those creatures beaten to the floor flapped feebly before they were crushed underfoot. It was too much for some of the men and the formation broke. Driven to the edge of panic, some preferred to take their chance with the fire and die like soldiers on the swords of their enemies than choke to death on smoke. They charged back through the tunnel. Others stumbled, blind and disoriented, dropping their weapons and falling against the tunnel walls or each other.

It was then Aldivon's men struck. Using spears and maces they dragged the burning bundles from the tunnel and cast them down the rocky crags. Several men received superficial burns to their hands and faces but in short order the tunnel was cleared. Even before the smoke had time to vent they charged into the confusion of the tunnel, leaping the fallen and pressing deeper into the darkness.

Those of Lancelot's men that had broken and fled never stood a chance. No mercy was shown even to those who threw down their weapons and dropped to their knees, hands raised imploringly in surrender. In moments they were overcome, and Aldivon's men pressed on.

It was the bats that saved Lancelot from an immediate massacre. With the sudden opening of the tunnel mouth they wheeled and flew over the heads of Aldivon's men, causing them to duck and pause their advance.

For Lancelot there was little time to restore order to his shattered group. The cavern was still too distant to reach. They would make a final stand.

Stand, and likely die!

"Shield wall!"

Men who had dropped their shields groped desperately for them, feeling amongst the bats that flapped in pitiful circles, their fragile wings broken.

Those who had retained their shields pushed past their comrades and dropped to their knees, locking their shields together. Behind them a second rank formed, their shields raised almost to the ceiling. Lancelot's small force was decimated. Less than a dozen men stood with him to block the tunnel.

He slumped wearily against the wall. There was no chance for him to reach Arthur now and he dimly reflected on the futility of the battle they fought. Arthur was probably already dead and he and his men stood ready to die to protect a memory. He pushed the thought aside, remembering he was without a weapon. With a crash Aldivon's men slammed into the shield wall.

Merlin was almost to the bridge when he realized that the footsteps did not belong to Lancelot.

"You! But how?"

Morgause became instantly wary, watching the old man while she took in the vast cavern, the lake, the bridge and the body on the bier. Her roving eyes caught the glint of gold on the pedestal and a triumphant grin lit her face. Behind her Matt and Valina were pushed into the cavern.

"Matt?" Merlin was shocked. The boy looked terrible. The poor light and distance across the cavern hid most of the details but even from here he could tell the boy was in bad shape. His filthy clothes were bloodstained and hung on him like rags. His face was battered and bruised and his hair was a tangled mess.

Morgause beckoned to her soldiers while keeping her eyes locked on Merlin. "Assemble the crown on the pedestal and keep those two under control."

Any hesitation Merlin had about killing Arthur was swept away as he realized what the soldier held in the bag.

So Matt had found the fragments!

Merlin lunged toward the bier, the knife raised to strike.

"No!" Matt strained against his captor, the yell muffled by the gag.

Despite his predicament he had felt a steadily building excitement as he had approached the cavern, knowing that here he would finally come face to face with his greatest champion and hero. Matt had clung to a nebulous thread of hope that some final opportunity would arise here, that somehow he and Arthur could overcome the queen.

But now the wizard's intentions were clear and Matt's already fractured faith shattered into nothing.

Every time he had put his trust in someone they failed him, or were taken from him. His parents were either dead or lost. Valina. He had come to love her, but did she love him or had she just used him to bring Morgause here? Even Brick, the person he had trusted least, had proved to be a friend only to die because of him. Images of Mia swirled before his eyes and he felt the suffocating sense of loss and self pity that threatened to choke the spark of defiance he had nurtured in the tunnel. Bitter tears stung his eyes as he looked to Merlin. He had come to believe in the wizard, looked on him almost as a surrogate grandfather until Aldivon had named him Dardanos.

And even now the old man's knife swept down in a killing blow.

"No!" Matt tried again, breaking free of the soldier that held him and stumbled across the cavern floor. Arms bound behind him he could not retain his balance and he fell. Somehow he managed to twist and break the fall with his injured shoulder, and grazed his cheek across the rough and rocky floor. Winded by the impact, he struggled to rise, gasping for breath, floundering like a recently landed fish.

The knife shattered inches above Arthur's chest and shards of steel flew in all directions. Merlin felt fire race up his arm as his fist slammed into the unexpected resistance of the protective barrier.

"You've failed, old man!"

Merlin stumbled back as Morgause strode across the stepping stones of the lake.

"Do you think I'd let you kill him after getting this close?"

She thrust her hands toward him and he felt the invisible wave of her will rise from Arthur and crush against him. Somehow he blocked it, but the force was still enough to send him crashing to the floor. He lay there panting.

Morgause could barely contain her excitement now. She was so close to achieving her goal. Beside her the soldier with the crown fragments stood in stunned fascination of what he was witnessing.

"Don't just stand there, you fool! The crown—get on with it!"

Matt had twisted himself onto his knees and struggled to get to his feet, but was slammed painfully to the ground as the soldier he had escaped shoved him down.

Merlin watched, dazed. He knew he was beaten. He reached for the staff leaning against the bier and dragged himself up, arms shaking. It took every ounce of concentration to hold a protective shield before him, and his head throbbed with the effort. Morgause stood waiting for him.

"You disappoint me, Merlin."

He would not waste the energy required to respond; instead he surveyed the cavern beyond. Matt was pinned to the ground. The soldier who held him had a sword across the back of the boy's neck. Beyond them was another soldier holding what looked to be a girl but they were too far back in the shadows. He took a hesitant step toward the bridge and stared across the cavern.

Who is she? Why a captive?

The sight of the third soldier running toward the pedestal roused him, and Merlin pulled his eyes from the girl. He had to do something, but before he could react Morgause struck again. Another crushing blow rippled through the air toward him and he rocked from the impact but this time remained standing. He felt the familiar tightening in his chest as Morgause reached for his heart.

Always she goes for the heart!

Easily he repelled her, thrusting her from him with the full weight of his mind. The effort made his ears ring and his vision became a misty red haze. The queen, however, stood unaffected by his attack.

Bright fire sprang from her hand.

Matt watched as the first ball of flame missed, but the second slammed into Merlin's chest and the overwhelmed wizard crumpled to the ground. A third and fourth leaped from the queens outstretched hands but somehow Merlin deflected them and part of the cavern was plunged into darkness as the diverted balls of energy incinerated a path through the candles that lit the giant hall, narrowly missing the pedestal and sending melted wax and tallow spluttering in all directions.

Again Matt tried to move but the cold bite of steel across his neck ceased his struggling. Then as if from some far distant place he heard the voice of Merlin in his head.

"I need your help, boy."

Matt stiffened in surprise. It was more than a voice—there was a presence in his head, something tangible and he tried to hold it with his thoughts. It was weak, fading away yet he found it and without knowing how held the tendril of thought in his mind.

"I know who you are—Dardanos!"

The name rang like a thunderclap in Merlin's mind.

"Dardanos?" The unexpected and powerful flaring of the thought in Matt's mind almost blinded him. Matt was stunned by the emotions that came from the wizard's thoughts. There was anger, confusion, but above all ran an abundance of hurt.

"*Aldivon told me the truth, old man!*" Matt fired the thoughts across the cavern. "*He told me he is Arthur's brother, he told me you are Dardanos. That you killed Merlin and used me to get the crown.*"

The tendril of thought pulled back, not in retreat, not in anger, but in absolute defeat. As the contact withered Matt felt the complete sense of hopelessness and surrender from the wizard's mind. Matt grasped the ghostly remains of the thought and tried to hold it a moment longer. This utter despair was not the response he would have expected from Dardanos, and he found himself wanting to give the man a chance to explain. The fading thoughts slipped through his mind like dye poured into a river, the strands of color spinning away, diluting and fading, yet once more he somehow held it.

"*Aldivon gave me the crown. He was to meet me here and together we were to save Arthur.*"

There was a momentary swell of understanding in the old man's thoughts and Matt felt the threads of thought surge and strengthen.

"*He lied to you, Matt. It's all a lie! He wanted you to lead him here. He wanted you to kill me, didn't he? What else did he tell you? That Arthur is your father? It's all a lie, Matt! He played you, boy. Aldivon wants the rod and crystals for himself. Now I understand! His army has already turned on Morgause, but that's not all...*"

The thoughts were flowing faster now, shooting into Matt's head like golden sparks, "*There's a third component to the key, Matt. Something I hadn't told you about. Do you remember I told you I sent you to the home to protect not just you, but your blood line...?*"

Matt's head throbbed with the mind contact, but his eyes continued to record the events in the cavern.

The soldier had reached the pedestal and the golden shards of the crown tumbled onto the rich velvet as he upended the bag. Blue sparks danced around the gold, illuminating the pedestal and casting an ethereal pallor to the soldier's face. The crown pieces seemed to pulse with an energy of their own and the man leaped back. Morgause turned, breaking her lock with the wizard.

"*Matt! You must trust me!*" The wizard's thoughts were frantic, desperate, almost pleading. "*I can't do this alone. I cannot defeat her. I'm weak, I'm hurt. I need you, boy. There is no time to explain, this is our one chance. Now!*"

And with that Matt felt the weight across his back vanish as the soldier that pinned him down was hurled across the cavern to slam into the man that held Valina. The three went down hard and Matt felt the bonds fall from his arms. He tore the gag from his mouth and swept the soldier's fallen sword from the floor.

The wizard had freed him, but whether because he was truly Merlin or for some other reason Matt did not know.

That doesn't matter now!

Blind fury and adrenaline spurred him on.

I'm done with all your games.

All he wanted in that instance was to kill Morgause.

Then take Valina and together we will find my mother!

Who Merlin truly was, who Aldivon was, whether Arthur lived or died no longer mattered. He was free and but a few desperate paces from Morgause's back.

Matt gripped the sword with two hands, the blade arching up over his shoulders as he pulled his arms back in readiness for the stroke. Every muscle strained as he raced to close the gap. Already the queen was turning, her arms coming up, orange light dancing about her fingers.

"*She cannot block us both, Matt!*"

The thought rang clear in his mind and the boy saw the pouch, in which the queen kept the crystals, peel away from her hip. It hung for a moment in the air, and then dropped to the floor pulled toward the chasm by the wizard's will.

The orange light that had almost consumed him blinked into nothingness as the queen tried to step away from the boy and turn her will to the pouch that slid inexorably closer to the gaping drop.

Merlin was up and on the bridge. His steps were faltering. The strain of his mental wrestling with the queen had cost him dear, and blood ran from his nose and ears. Where the fireball had struck, his tunic was burned away, and charred fragments of smoking cloth clung to the blackened sticky mess of his chest. He gripped his staff with gnarled and bony fingers and doggedly continued across the bridge, his attention locked on the bag.

Morgause screamed to her soldiers now and Matt could sense the two men running behind him. To his left the man at the pedestal drew his weapon and leaped to protect his queen but he was too far away—another step and Matt was there. Yelling, he swept his sword forward and saw his own reflection in the wide and terror-stricken eyes of the queen.

Blood ran thick on the rocky floor of the tunnel and still they held. Aldivon's men were desperately tired but they still outnumbered Lancelot's ragged band. The sheer weight of their numbers pressed against the shield wall drove the defenders several feet back along the tunnel. Leather sandals and boots fought for purchase on the blood-slick rock, dust, and bat droppings of the tunnel floor. Again the front rank turned their shields, but this time those behind thrust down with their swords.

Pinned against the shield wall as they were, Aldivon's front rank could not defend themselves. Shields and chain mail had prevented killing blows to the body, but this time all four lead men fell heavily as their legs were cut from beneath them.

Lancelot's men pulled their shields back but they were exhausted, weakened from wounds. The soldier to the left slipped on the twitching hand of one of the fallen, and a gap appeared in the shield wall as he tried to keep his balance and lock his wavering shield into place.

A spear thrust through the gap and took the weakened man in the armpit. His agonized scream echoed in the tunnel and he dropped his sword and shield as he pushed down with his legs trying to lift himself off the terrible shaft that was embedded in his body. The shield wall was breached.

In an instant the man found himself slammed against the tunnel wall, and a swift slash with a sword mercifully ended his agony and his body crumpled to the floor.

Lancelot was having trouble standing. His leg burned with pain. If not for the sword he had snatched from the floor he could not have stood at all. His vision was blurred with sweat and loss of blood. His mouth was parched.

"Third rank form wall!" his voice cracked at the agony of the command.

The men in the third rank knew what that order would mean for those before them, but they also knew it was their only chance to live. Less tired than those in front they locked shields and braced themselves, effectively cutting off retreat for the men of the second rank who now fought like crazed demons as the shield wall before them was overrun.

A strange thing is said to happen to a man faced with the inevitability of death. Aldivon's men fought with steady determination. Each of them could sense victory close and each wanted to live to see beyond it. Such was not the case for the seven remaining men of the front two ranks. Lancelot's command had sealed their fate, their lives were spent. Behind them they heard the wooden clatter as the stout shields locked together. All they could do now was to die honorably and buy a chance for others to live.

Almost as one they cast aside their shields and threw themselves at the enemy. Ignoring each fatal wound they spent the last of their strength shoulder to shoulder, delivering death and injury to as many as they could before death's cold embrace freed them from the agony and hell of those final moments.

The ring of steel echoed like a bell in the cavern, and the jarring shock sent fires of pain coursing through Matt's wrists and elbows. Sparks flashed before his eyes and his sword was deftly turned and driven to the rocky floor.

Aldivon emerged from the shadows and kicked the weapon from Matt's throbbing hands.

"So you would kill your mother, boy, and deny me the pleasure?"

His deep voice growled and his towering presence seemed somehow magnified by the darkness of the cavern. He spun quickly, bringing Excalibur up in a powerful block that snapped the soldier's blade clean in two. Following the stroke through, Aldivon brought Excalibur around and sent the man's head bouncing into the chasm. The body tottered drunkenly on legs that didn't know it was dead, then fell, sending spurting gouts of blood high into the air.

Aldivon did not pause, and his next step carried him to the queen. She screamed in frustration as she was forced to divert her attention from Merlin, who now stooped to recover the crystals.

Rolling drunkenly, the wizard staggered to the pedestal where the crown shards sparkled with their mysterious blue light.

An orange glow suddenly bathed the queen's arms, coating her hands as Excalibur bore down. She reached up, spreading her arms apart, leaving what looked like a shimmering orange sheet between them. The sword's downward motion stopped, but the force of the blow still drove Morgause to her knees. Sweat poured down Aldivon's face and his shoulders shook with the effort to drive the blade through the barrier the queen held above her.

Mother?

Matt looked at the queen. Her pale face drawn in effort, her thin lips twisted in a fierce grimace as she matched the strength of her will against the physical might of Aldivon.

Matt stood, rocked to his core by the big man's words.

Mother? Beside him the two remaining soldiers raced past in a desperate effort to finish Aldivon.

Gradually the blade was forced higher, and as it rose so did Morgause. Her snarl of defiance twisted into a grin of victory. Aldivon cursed and pulled the blade away from her. The ensuing lack of resistance caused Morgause to fall and she rolled on the cavern floor, panting from exertion.

Aldivon's face was a thunderous mask of fury as he felt victory slip from his grasp. With a roar he met the approaching soldiers' blades and again the cavern rang as steel met steel. Aldivon's skill with a blade was legendary; few men could match him. One stumbled back, a bloody line across his chest, and the second cried out as Excalibur painted a crimson streak across his cheek.

Both men lurched back against the furious onslaught, and Matt realized that Aldivon was driving them toward him. Behind the battling trio Morgause was up, and Matt saw her pivot toward Merlin. The magician turned to face her.

The queen was battered, her rich cloak was torn from one shoulder and her hair was disheveled, but Merlin looked far worse. He could barely stand and blood continued to leak from his nose. Matt saw the resignation on his face, and then she was on him.

Fingers hooked like claws, Morgause raked her nails across his face, seeking to gouge his eyes. Deep scratches left bloody furrows on the ancient skin and he dropped the bag and his staff as he grappled with her wrists, tottering backward, mere steps from the chasm.

Matt remained forgotten, standing numb and alone until un unexpected spray of blood splattered, hot and wet, across his face. He staggered back, horrified as Aldivon drove Excalibur through the collar bone of one of the soldiers. The blow split the man to the breast and he fell back twitching, his heels drumming on the ground as blood pooled around him.

The second soldier fared no better, and dropped his sword to grab the coiled blue mess of entrails that spilled from the gaping rent in his chain mail. Despite the disgusting spectacle Matt could not take his eyes from the man as he fell to his knees, deep racking sobs shaking his body as his life seeped away. Then Aldivon was on him and Matt found himself pinned, his back held tight to Aldivon's chest, the man's left arm crushing the air from his lungs.

"Hold!"

Aldivon's voice boomed in the hollow chamber and reverberated from the cavern walls like rolling thunder. Both the wizard and the witch turned to see Matt in Aldivon's grasp. The blood-spattered warrior gazed at them along the dripping length of his sword.

"I'll kill the boy!"

Merlin was the first to move. He pulled himself from the queen and held his hands out before him. "Wait! No!"

But the queen just laughed, the sound even more mocking amid the carnage that littered the cavern floor.

"And I should care why, traitor? Kill the whelp!" and she raised her hands to strike once more at Merlin.

"Because he is your son, Morgause! Your son!"

Matt stiffened at Aldivon's words.

"I have no son!" Morgause's voice was harsh, yet she stopped her attack. There was a bitterness to her words as she pointed to Merlin. "He saw to that and you think now to mock me with this! How dare you!"

"He robbed you twice, Morgause. Mordred was not your *only* son."

Merlin shook his head, hands reaching out imploringly.

"Aldivon! Enough!"

"Oh no, old man. She shall hear the truth of what you did that night."

The queen's voice was a cracked whisper. "What is this, Aldivon?" She took a hesitant step toward him. "You will tell me—"

"The night you birthed your second son, he was not stillborn. That very night Merlin stole into your chamber and took your babe from its crib. In its place he left the stillborn wretch of Guenevere."

Matt somehow knew it was true. With mind numbing certainty he knew Aldivon spoke the truth. He recalled the vision of so many weeks before in which he had been carried from a room, and how lightning had burned away the shadows, revealing the hulking presence of Aldivon. His knees buckled as he realized that the woman he despised above all others was his true mother; not Guenevere as he'd believed. He struggled weakly in Aldivon's grip but the man held him easily. "I went against your will to protect him, to save him. Now, would you have me kill him when you could so easily enter his mind and make him your own? Would you have me kill the true heir of Dardanos?"

"You lie! This cannot be!"

"But it is so!" Aldivon roared. His face flushed with anger and the sword in his hand trembled. "And there is more, for when you killed Naveena you doomed your own son to death. Dardanos never told you, did he? That without the blood of a Marsonian the crystals and the rod will not function." Spittle flew from Aldivon's lips as he continued to berate Morgause. Matt could feel the tension trembling in the arm that gripped him.

"He never told you because I—*I* was to be his heir! You usurped me, dammit! You think I bedded you for pleasure? You pathetic whore! You think I brought Merlin's pupil to you because I felt sorry for her? For you?"

The queens face blanched, and her eyes flickered with anger and pain.

"You thought my interest in Naveena was purely physical?" Aldivon sneered lasciviously. "Aye, I would have taken her too, but the value of her body was as nothing to the value of her blood!

"You raised her thinking she was the get of Dardanos. Well she was not! Naveena was his!" Matt was jerked to one side as Aldivon waved Excalibur at Merlin. "Vivian never lay with Dardanos. He already knew she was with child, Merlin's child. Dardanos simply used her to get to Arthur, to get to Merlin. You raised your enemy's bastard daughter and then killed her!"

Aldivon pulled the sword in close, pressing the blade to Matt's neck. "Only one child of Marsonia still lives, Morgause—your son!"

Merlin was stunned. Tears coursed down his cheeks, and the sting of them in the bloody cuts from Morgause's nails fueled his anger.

There had been a daughter! His daughter!

Merlin turned to face the queen. "I had a daughter?" And then all thoughts of magic were cast aside as he threw himself at her snarling with rage.

"You stole my son!" she screamed back. All control was lost as the adversaries slapped and clawed at each other, locked in a battle that was primal, almost animal in its brutality.

Aldivon sheathed his sword. "And so, finally they will destroy each other."

He pushed Matt forward, guiding him across the cavern until they stood by the bag containing the crystals. Stooping carefully, Aldivon kicked aside Merlin's staff and recovered the bag, slipping its neck through his belt to hold it.

"You're not Arthur's brother are you?" Matt's voice was resigned.

"No, boy, I am not."

"And Dardanos is my father?"

"He was."

Aldivon was inching closer to the pedestal and the rolling, flailing bodies of Merlin and Morgause. Once more he drew his sword.

"What did you mean about the blood? About the children of Marsonia?"

"You as the son of Dardanos, and Naveena as the daughter of Merlin were the last two of almost pure Marsonian blood. With Naveena's death, and Merlin's imminent demise, you are the last vessel of that precious substance. So relax. I have need of you boy, at least for now." He gave a cold and somewhat bitter laugh. "You will die, but not—"

Aldivon stumbled, loosening his grip on Matt, and the boy twisted free. Valina had made her way around the cavern and she now stood behind Aldivon a bloodied knife clutched in one trembling hand.

"She did not kill me, Aldivon." Valina's voice was calm, and she spoke in slow and measured tones. "I still live!" She thrust the knife again at his side, her voice rising in anger, "And you will never, never have me!"

Aldivon turned and lashed out with his leather gloved hand. The back-handed blow sent Valina lurching away and blood ran once more from her shattered lip. She dropped the knife and stumbled, hands clasped to her face. Aldivon pulled his hand from his wounded side. It was red with fresh blood.

He looked in shocked surprise at the girl.

"Naveena? But I saw you. I saw your body. You were dead."

"It was an act." She spat a mouthful of blood to one side. "The queen no longer trusted you!" She backed away from him.

"Naveena—"

Aldivon kicked the dropped knife into the still waters of the lake and glanced to where Merlin and Morgause battled. The woman now sat astride the wizard and was bringing her full strength to bear, her hands clasped about his throat. The veins in Merlin's arms stood out like knotted ropes, and his shoulders shook as he fought to pull her hands away. The queen's eyes blazed with madness and Matt could see she was gathering her will to strike.

Aldivon turned from Valina, sword raised.

"You will be my queen, Naveena, but first they must die!"

"Not yet!" Matt grabbed Merlin's fallen staff and now he swung it like a club. The heavy wood cracked against Aldivon's back and the impact jarred loose the iron shoe at the base of the wizard's prop. The wood vibrated in Matt's hands but the boy kept his balance and jabbed at Aldivon, aiming for the wound Valina had inflicted. He struck high but he still saw pain blossom in the warrior's eyes.

Aldivon swung Excalibur but the blow was not aimed, merely intended to drive the boy back. Matt ducked the shimmering steel and rolled away from Aldivon. Bringing the staff around he lashed out again, this time at Morgause. The blow slammed into her arm just above the elbow, breaking her grip on the wizard and shattering her concentration. The iron shoe finally tore free from the staff and whistled across the cavern to be lost in the darkness.

Matt swung again, and this time clipped the queen on the forehead. Morgause slumped forward, stunned, and with a herculean effort Merlin pushed her from his chest. He lay there wheezing, each ragged gasp for breath whistling in his throat.

"Matt!" Valina's cry was shrill and Matt turned, bringing the staff across his chest defensively. He was too slow and Aldivon's fierce cut clove the staff in two. The tip of the sword cut into Matt's tattered tunic and the razor sharp steel sliced the links of the boy's chain mail vest. Blood bloomed upon Matt's cotton undershirt.

The boy danced back and dropped the remains of the staff. The bottom section struck the ground first and a large wooden plug, previously concealed by the iron shoe plate, popped free and rolled across the cavern floor.

Morgause was on her hands and knees now, and Merlin too was struggling to rise.

Fire burned along Matt's chest and he could feel the trickle of blood on his skin. He didn't know how badly he was hurt and his body ached with fatigue. Valina was running toward him.

"Valina! Get away from here—save yourself -"

But the girl ignored him and threw herself at Aldivon.

Matt ducked the next sweep of the blade but his injured shoulder took the force of the blow from Aldivon's fist. He rolled with it, grabbed the heavy end of the shattered staff, and came to his feet. Raising the stump like a club he backed away from Aldivon. Then all movement in the cavern ceased.

Before Arthur had given the staff to Merlin, the end had been hollowed out. Rolled in silk, and locked in place with a wooden plug, the rod of Dardanos had been carried by Merlin for years. The iron shoe plate designed to protect the wood from wear had concealed the plug, but now the rod fell free.

As it fell the silken cloth unfurled. A dull clang rang in the cavern as the rod, almost a foot in length, wrought of pure Marsonian gold, struck the cavern floor. It bounced, and the gold glowed orange in the dancing light of the remaining candles.

Both Morgause and Merlin lunged for the fallen treasure. Merlin was faster and clutched the relic to his wounded chest.

"Matt!" The terror in Valina's voice caused him to turn, and he went weak with fatigue. His fingers relaxed and he let the remains of the shattered staff drop to the hard stone of the cavern floor. Aldivon had Valina in one arm and Excalibur held against her throat as he backed across the stepping stones toward the side tunnel he had entered by.

Merlin tottered forward, his bloodied face somehow defiant. He raised a hand toward Aldivon.

"Let her go!"

"Strike me Merlin and she dies!"

The shadows closed around Aldivon as he backed further into the cavern. His voice was hoarse and he limped heavily, the pain of the wound in his side finally taking its toll.

"Try anything and you lose your daughter. Will you chance that to have these?"

Matt could see Aldivon held the bag with the crystal pyramids.

"These are useless to me without the rod, old man. I have but two thirds of the key, you have the other." He took another heavy step back. "No one wins today, Merlin...no one..."

Beside Merlin, Morgause rose and with a desperate fury gathered her will to tear the bag from Aldivon's hand.

"No!" Merlin stepped in front of her, spreading his arms to block the flow of her will. "Not my daughter!" The clash of their wills rocked the cavern with a crushing report and Matt watched, horrified, as Merlin stumbled backward. His hair and cloak billowed out behind him as if he stood before some mighty tempest. Merlin's eyes were wide but still they blazed with some last surge of power as he battled Morgause. Gradually he stood straight and Matt could see the energy pouring from their hands to collide between them. Where it met the air shimmered and grew hot, a wall of energy like molten glass crackled and sparked, and the stones of the cavern floor began to glow.

Imperceptibly at first, the wall began to move. Slowly, it crept ever closer toward Merlin. Then the old man groaned, his eyes rolled in his head and he collapsed. The rod of Dardanos rolled from his hand. Unchecked, the shimmering wave of energy from Morgause leaped across the cavern and Matt looked to Aldivon.

But he was gone.

Matt looked back to Morgause. She was breathing hard, panting from exertion. She watched the boy as she slowly stepped to Merlin's inert form and picked up the rod of Dardanos. She struggled with the weight of it.

"Come here, boy." Her voice was cracked and strained, and Matt could see one eye was shot with blood. He took a hesitant step back and shook his head.

"It seems I'm your mother, Matt. Please...?"

Tears stung his eyes, yet he continued to shake his head.

"It's all you ever wanted, isn't it? To be loved. To have a family. I can give you that."

And then she was in his head. Like Merlin before, so now Morgause caressed his mind, numbing him with waves of love, and images of happiness.

He pulled his eyes from hers and looked to the sleeping form of Arthur.

"Yes..." The voice in his mind was lulling, coaxing, seductive. "*Help me, Matt. We can awaken him. He will make a fine king, and I his queen. You will be our son...*"

The thoughts surged through him and he took an involuntary step toward the pedestal. "*Yes...*" The honey-smooth thoughts clung to his mind, blocking his own emotions and thoughts as she suppressed in him any attempt at flight or resistance.

Then he understood.

She could talk to him this way because of who he was. Merlin had known all along that Matt was Marsonian, a descendant of Dardanos. Not just the blood of Dardanos ran in his veins but so did the power! He had no knowledge of how to use it, but could he try? Could he somehow push her from his mind just as he had held Merlin in it?

It's all a case of belief, Matt. That's all magic really is. The power comes from within, boy—it's the power of the mind.

Matt recalled the words Merlin had spoken during his training.

All men possess it, Matt—what they lack is the ability to believe that what seems impossible is in truth possible.

Matt had seen enough in the past few days to believe anything was possible, but it was getting harder to think. Already he could feel the queen taking control of his body as he took another step toward the pedestal.

"You can do it, Matt!"

This time it was not a memory—it was a faint tremor of thought from Merlin. Matt forced his eyes closed. His eyelids seemed to slide through a wall of syrup as he fought the will of Morgause. He retreated to the last pocket of his mind that remained his. He touched the probing tentacles of her will. Like sinuous tar-coated fingers he felt her presence in his head.

"She may have birthed you, Matt, but she does not love you. Guenevere loves you." Merlin's voice contested with the queen's cajoling tones in his head.

Matt took another step toward the pedestal and allowed his mind to trace the tendrils of her thoughts, seeking for a way to expel her.

She sensed him then.

"Matt!" her voice was harsh in his ears now, and a stark contrast to the whispered soothing in his head. She knew he was aware of her and she felt the stirring of power within him, and he struck.

As before, when he had followed the wisps of Merlin's thoughts and held them in his mind, so this time he grasped hers, only now he followed them back. With elation he found himself breaking free of his body as he traced the tether between her mind and his.

In an instant he was inside her, and he could feel her weakness and vulnerability. She had paid a terrible price for her victory over Merlin. He felt the naked fear inside as she struggled to pull herself from his mind.

Matt's thoughts strayed to the rod in her hands and he could feel the weight of it. He tried to control her fingers to take it from her.

"Drop it..."

"No!" Her breath came in gasps as she struggled with both the weight of the rod and her effort to overcome his mind.

"Drop it!" he spoke aloud, once more in control of his voice.

"Drop it!" He pictured his words stabbing into her brain like needles, and he could sense the pain it caused.

"I will never love you, never serve you!" he rejected her totally, and he could feel the anger as she fled his mind and returned fully to her own.

She was struggling now to retain her hold on the rod, and in desperation she expelled him.

He reeled, dizzy with vertigo as he found himself back in his own body, but he recovered quickly, much faster than Morgause who stood slumped and panting, staring at him with a mix of fear and renewed hatred. He knew he had the strength; despite the battering his body had taken his mind felt sharp and strong. He flung out a hand and pushed at her, willing her to smash against the hard rock walls of the cavern.

"Matt, no! Not that way!" Merlin's voice echoed into the cavern, but it was too late.

The queen flew through the air—but so did Matt. The laws of physics apply to any force applied be it strength of muscle or the power of the mind, and with almost equal velocity Matt found himself sailing away from Morgause. He crashed hard to the floor, face first, and cried out as his wounded chest slid across the jagged stones of the cavern.

"Merlin!" Matt yelled as his legs slid into nothingness and he found himself on the very edge of the chasm with death sucking at his heels.

Chapter 28
To Raise a King

Mia was spent. She had run, then limped, for miles before finally crawling up the grassy slope of the escarpment. Her paws were bloodied and her once thick and lustrous coat was little more than a tangled mess of mud and twigs that hung upon her gaunt frame like an over-sized blanket. Her tail no longer arched above her back but hung limp behind her, and the once bright and excited eyes were dull with weariness and pain.

Yet still she struggled on, pushing herself beyond the limits of endurance to reach the cavern. Matt had "told" her where they were headed when he had carried her across his lap two days before. Too tired to fight that night when the soldiers had come, she had slunk away, and then trailed Matt to the queen's encampment.

ABut the strength to rescue him, she had started the lonely trek east toward Arthur's Seat. That she had made it this far was a miracle, and now she surveyed the wreckage of battle that littered the plateau. Carrion crows and ravens scavenged among the dead and the dying. Injured horses whinnied, thrusting their heads to the sky in a desperate attempt to rise.

The smell of death hung heavy in the air.

A black horse thundered across the grass and Mia shrank low, cowering, her eyes wide with fear. Aldivon sat astride the beast and before him perched Valina, her hands bound and her face bruised and bloody.

Mia whimpered at the sight of the girl but she could not follow. Instead she traced the scent of the horse to the tunnel entrance. There she found Matt's scent and hope spurred the exhausted dog on.

Wearily she limped through the tunnel, following each twist and turn deeper into the rocky hillside.

"Merlin! Help me!" Matt's voice was desperate and the husky redoubled her efforts to reach him. The sharp scent of blood filled her nose as she crawled into the cavern, skirting the bodies of the dead.

"Merlin!"

The voice came from beneath a wooden bridge and ignoring her pain, Mia limped three legged toward the chasm, passing the old man who crawled slowly across the floor toward the bridge.

"I'm coming, my boy. I'm coming," he chanted, his feeble voice too faint for Matt to hear.

For Matt the last few minutes seemed like hours. He had managed to grab one of the ropes that secured the bridge to the cavern floor but he could not hold on much longer. His neck, shoulders and upper arms throbbed.

He had watched in stunned surprise as Morgause had stopped herself from being smashed to pulp on the rock wall of the cavern, and then with a loud curse of frustration she had used the last of her strength to flee the cavern, transporting herself to safety, taking with her the rod of Dardanos.

Matt had considered using his newly discovered talents to do the same to move himself back to the cavern floor, but he lacked the skill and the knowledge. His own brush with death had terrified him and he was not prepared to try again in case he made matters even worse.

"I can't hold much longer! My hands, they're slipping!" Matt's voice became shrill.

He was crying now, fear, frustration, and exhaustion catching up with him as he dangled above the chasm. Matt had closed his eyes, trying to will the pain away, when stones rattled above him and showered down into his already filthy hair.

Merlin!

He looked up with relief and found himself staring into the piercing blue eyes of his dog.

"Mia?"

She barked. Her front paws hung over the lip of the chasm and her hind quarters were thrust into the air. For the moment all sense of exhaustion had left her.

"Mia! Oh god, Mia!"

Merlin's face appeared beside Mia's and he gazed down at the boy.

"I cannot pull you up Matt."

"Magic me up then!"

"I can't. I'm spent." Merlin looked terrible. His lined and weathered face was drained of color, resembling more a lifeless canvas upon which dirt, grime, and blood had been painted in wild abandon. Blood still trickled from his nose and dripped from one ear, further staining his beard. "I have nothing left boy. You must do this."

"I can't. I don't know how!"

"Listen to me! Look up. Look at the bridge."

Matt turned his head.

"Stare at it Matt. Feel the image of the bridge burn into your mind. Close your eyes, can you still see it? Can you frame it clearly in your mind's eye?"

"No. Yes. Shit! I don't know! I can imagine it—sort of."

"Good. That's good. Now, translocating yourself is nothing like what you did to Morgause. You don't have to worry about balancing out the forces you are going to use. Simply hold the image of the bridge clearly in your mind, and then put yourself in the picture. See yourself standing there, laying there, sitting—whatever is the easiest. Picture it, then feel yourself flow into it."

"I...how do I know I've got the picture right? There's no detail—it's kinda fuzzy, almost black and white."

"Concentrate, boy!"

"I'm trying, dammit!"

Merlin made no reply and Matt took a deep breath. "Merlin, I'm scared!"

"Focus, Matt. Burn that image of the bridge into your mind. See the ropes, the wooden planks, focus, focus. Now push yourself into that picture, flow into it—"

Matt felt a sickening disorientation and then he was there.

Fatigue, stress and the pain of the past several hours hit him and he dropped to his knees on the bridge. Tears of joy and relief streamed from his eyes as Mia limped to meet him and he flung his arms about her neck and sobbed.

In the tunnel Lancelot sat against the wall, his sword held loosely in his hands. His strength was gone and it was only a matter of time before the last of his men fell around him. That they had held this long was beyond belief, and he felt a pang of disappointment that he would not get to tell them how proud he was, or how well they had fought.

The constant pressure against the shield wall slackened and Aldivon's men finally backed up. Most were bloodied and all were breathing hard.

"Throw down your weapons!" One of Aldivon's men called. "You die needlessly!"

Lancelot wished he could find the strength to talk. The enemy soldier was right, they died for nothing. By now Arthur would be dead. Strange Merlin had not come to their aid. Surely the sounds of battle had carried to the cavern? Lancelot's mind wandered and then fresh shouts and the ring of weapons pulled him back to the present.

There was fighting in the rear ranks of Aldivon's men.

Marcus?

Lancelot pushed the fatigue from his mind. Foot soldiers under the command of Marcus McNaughton had arrived! The battle-scarred veterans of Arthur's old guard must have marched without rest. Pride swelled in Lancelot's chest.

"For Arthur!" he croaked. "For Arthur!"

The men around him took up the call, but looking down at their half-dead commander they changed the chant. "Lancelot!" they yelled, and as one they pushed the shield wall forward. "For Lancelot!" and they took the fight to the enemy.

The unexpected assault to their rear caused panic in the enemy's ranks and there was no time for them to take a defensive stand. Those that tried to fight were quickly overcome; those that threw down their weapons hoped they would be shown more mercy than they themselves had given. In minutes the fighting was over and tired bloody hands reached down for Lancelot.

"My lord. The day is ours!"

He looked at each of the faces he could mark in the dim light of the tunnel and grinned. "You've brought much honor to your names, to your families." He paused, taking a deep breath of the fetid air. "I am proud of you all! Proud to have fought with you, proud to have bled beside you." He coughed, then continued, "I would have been honored to have died amongst you."

"Lancelot!" the voices rang in the tunnel.

He raised a hand. "My friends. Carry our dead from this rat hole. Tonight we must honor our fallen and see their spirits home." He grasped the arms of the two men nearest him. "You two help me to the cavern. We must see what has befallen our prince."

Merlin pulled Matt to his feet and helped the boy from the bridge. Mia danced around them and the cavern echoed with her barks.

"So what now?" Matt sighed. "Aldivon has Valina and the crystals."

"Aye, he does." Pain reflected in the wizard's eyes. "And Morgause has the rod of Dardanos."

"Will they join forces?"

"I don't know. Aldivon has a powerful army already poised to crush Morgause. He may strike now while she herself is weak, but he may instead march here. Remember, when he left I had the rod."

"We can't defeat an army!"

Merlin slipped his arm from the boy's shoulder and patted the back of one of his hands.

"No we cannot. For that we need an army of our own." He inclined his head toward the bridge. "Come lad. To raise an army, we must first raise a king."

Here ends "To Raise a King"—book one of The Broken Crown.

In book two Matt will find himself thrown into the bitter fight to protect the portal of Marsonia, while he struggles to come to terms with his newfound power and the conflicting wills of those who would use him as their pawn. Will loyalty to his childhood hero overcome his desire to free the girl he loves, or will he embark on a personal quest to save her and his mother?

Justin Orton

Author's Notes

Surprising Facts hidden in Fiction

It is often said that truth is stranger than fiction, so I thought it would be fun to share some of the facts hidden within this story. Most have heard of Arthur and the Knights of the Round Table. Books, movies and plays abound and I struggled long and hard over the value of bringing yet one more story to what many may consider an already tired tale in a crowded genre. It was the discovery that my childhood hero actually existed - not in England as most stories proclaim but in Scotland that kept my fingers on the keyboard.

I would encourage you to read "Arturius - A Quest for Camelot" by David F. Carroll if you are interested in the research behind Scotland's King Arthur. It makes the case beautifully, and clearly shows that only in 6th-century Scotland can you find many of the key characters and places of legend, located in the same geographical region and historical period.

Scotland

Scotland was founded from the old realm Dalriada. By the 6th Century the realm had spread far and wide and there were many skirmishes and battles with the neighboring Picts and Angles. In the 6th-century the ruler of the Scots was King Aidan MacGabran who also had interests in Northern Ireland. That he ruled from Dunadd is without question but who governed for him in the East? In the 6th-century it would have been tremendously difficult to rule effectively a Kingdom divided by mountains, numerous lochs, and the vastness of the Caledonian forests. King Aidan would have sent a trusted person to rule in his stead, and we find in record that his son Arturius did indeed lead the vassal kings of this region as "Dux Bellorum" or war leader.

Camelot

At the sound of the word we imagine grand castles more akin to Disney, or the mighty fortifications of the Norman period that came many hundreds of years AFTER Arthur. Many cities over the years have been tagged as the home of Arthur, built on the bones of Camelot - but there has been no historical record of such a fortress-city. However, in Scotland- there is documented evidence of a known to the Romans as Ad Vallum, but to the Britons of the time as Camelon - later corrupted to Camelot. This fortress was an impressive structure and guarded not only the central region of Scotland but also the strategic crossing point of the River Carron. What's even more interesting to note is that a warrior prince used this fortress - and his name was Arturius. The town of Camelon remains to this day, 1.5 miles west of Falkirk.

The Round Table

Conditioned by movies, novels and epic poems we all think of a gigantic round table within the halls of Camelot, around which Arthur and his knights held council. Of course no true table has been discovered, and were a round table to be unearthed it would be incredibly difficult to prove it was that of legend - unless perhaps it were found at Camelon. Interestingly enough there is, not far from Camelon, beneath the towering castle of Stirling, a mound known as the King's Knot. It is known that this mound has existed for centuries and there is a poem that actually names this mound the "Round Tabill." The poem admittedly was written in 1370 and tells of the flight of King Edward after his defeat at Bannockburn by King Robert the Bruce. *"An besouth the Castill went they thone, Rychte by the Round Tabill away..."*

It is conceivable this place was a neutral meeting place for "Arthur" and the vassal kings of the North.

Camallan

North of Camelot is the river Allan - or the crooked Allan. In legend King Arthur died fighting the Picts at Camallan. Recorded in the Annals of Ulster in the year 582AD is the battle of Mannan fought at the Crooked Allan. Crooked in Gaelic translates to "Cam," thus the river was known as Camallan. The historical figure Arturius, war leader of the North, is reported to have died at this battle - fighting none other than the Picts.

Avalon

In the legend of Arthur, the king, mortally wounded, is taken to the island of Avalon by his sister Morgan. No historical record exists for a place named Avalon. However records do show the land immediately adjacent to the battlefield of Camallan was originally swamp. In fact an island existed formed by the river Allan to the east, the river Forth to the south, the river Teith to the west with the intervening land water-filled swamps. Being on the banks of the Allan this land would have probably been known as Av Allan - on Allan. That sounds very much like Avalon. Furthermore a settlement, Invalone, existed in this area which also sounds remarkably similar to Avalon.

Morgan

One could argue that the above historical records are mere coincidence, but it becomes harder to ignore the facts when you consider that King Aidan MacGabran - the father of Arturius - also had a daughter named Mergein, meaning sea birth.

Guenevere

There is no record of Guenever (Gwenevere) until Geoffrey of Monmouth's fanciful history. By the time of its writing (600 years after the death of Arturius) the language had changed, and spellings had changed. However, it is interesting to discover that the wife of Arturius - who was probably taken by the Picts - was named Anora. In the time of Geoffrey of Monmouth it was not uncommon to prefix a name with Guan (literally meaning white, often representing fair or pure), later written as Gwen. Arthur's queen would thus have been recorded as Fair Anora, or Guan-anora or phonetically as Gwenanora. It is feasible that this later corrupted into Gwenevere. While this is not conclusive, it does add yet another link to Arturius of the North.

Merlin

It's hard not to get just a little excited when you hear the name Merlin. What you may not know is that a true figure of history existed with the name Merlin or Myrddin. Documentation shows he was allied with a pagan prince who was defeated in battle in 573AD at the Battle of Arderydd - just north of Carlisle. Known as a druid, or bard, he fled this battle and lived in the wooded areas of Celyddon between the two Roman walls - the Antonine and Hadrians - the same place where Camelon is located! Merlin later came under the protection of one of the kings of the north - King Ryderrch - and as we know,

Arturius was war leader of these northern kings, vassals to his father Aidan. It is extremely likely that Arturius and Merlin were known to each other.

Dunadd

As mentioned before, Dunadd is the home of Scotland. While nothing but fallen stones remain of Dunadd Castle, the history is well documented and you are able to follow Matt's path from the standing stones in Kilmartin Glen, to Dunadd, and south into Kintyre. If you have the good fortune to visit Scotland, the glen of Kilmartin is well worth a visit. While lacking the majestic beauty of Scotland's "Great Glens," Kilmartin holds its own special magic and mystery. The whole vale seems to exude history and you can feel the weight of the ages as you follow the footsteps of Scotland's earliest kings.

Mars

While the Marsonians are a complete fabrication, there are some interesting theories about a lost civilization on Mars. If you are interested to learn more about the "pyramids" and "face" of Cydonia I would encourage you to read "The Mars Mystery" by Graham Hancock, Robert Bauval and John Grigsby. As NASA continues to send probes to our planetary neighbor, and evidence that life once existed on the red planet continues to grow, one has to wonder if this book's findings carry more truth than we know.

The Pyramids

An excellent book for anyone interested in the history of Egypt and the pyramids is Robert Bauval's "The Orion Mystery." This book is an easy read and provides overwhelming evidence that the pyramids of Giza are in fact older than most historians will acknowledge, and are deliberately aligned with the stars of Orion's belt. I find this work both conclusive and fascinating.

Combined with the ancient Egyptian tales of "Sky Gods" and "Travelers" one wonders - are the Marsonians a figment of my imagination?

A Final word -

Time these days is a most precious commodity. That you chose to spend some of yours reading this work is truly appreciated. I hope you enjoyed the book and I would value any feedback - good or bad. You can contact me at justin@jaortonwriter.com and while I can't promise a timely response to every email, I will read them!

Book Two is now underway and if you would like advance notice of its release, please join my mailing list by following the sign-up link below. I will not spam you with marketing material or use your address for any purpose other than letting you know Book Two is on its way!

For an author reviews on Amazon are critical! So if you enjoyed the story I would really appreciate a review to help spread the word.

Thanks again - until next time...

Justin

Mailing List: http://eepurl.com/ctZaDH

Made in the USA
Lexington, KY
05 January 2018